CW01207446

For my wife and sons for their love and continued support.

CONTENTS

SIKES: MISCONSTRUED

(Growing Up part 1)

William S Allin

JOKApress

Cover design by: William S Allin
Cover photography by Clive Stanley Williams

WHEN HE WAS YOUNG

"I hope I ain't got nits again." The shorter of the two boys worked his dirty fingers through his blond hair.

"Nits? What's nits?" His taller friend was puzzled.

"They're sort of like... er... bugs that get into your 'air and lay eggs. When the eggs 'atch, they eat your scalp and make your 'ead itch."

His friend giggled. "Get lost. There's ain't no such thing."

"There is too, and once you got them, you've got a bugger of a job to get rid of them. That's what my nanna says. She used to work in an 'ospital up in London, and there was this man there, really dirty he was, and he had a bed full of nits. My nanna said they was like a blanket on his bed."

"Urghh, a blanket of bugs, that's horrible. What do they look like?"

"Well, they're really small, and my nanna only saw mine by looking over the top of her glasses. She grabs them in her fingernails and pops them dead. She said they're like little specs of dirt, but she can see them moving and grabs them quick. She's also got this special comb thing that she puts in my hair to get any she can't see. Nanna says she doesn't want anyone to know that her grandson has got nits. Mam said it was normal to have them and called my nanna a panoid snob."

"Panoid? What's tha' mean?"

"I dunno, but it must have been a naughty word because my nanna went bonkers with her. She was shouting and everything. Mam took me home then."

The taller boy inspected the street.

"So, how do you know if you got these nits?"

"Nanna said that you scratch your head all the time."

"Well, I ain't got them 'cause I don't scratch my head all the time."

"That's because you got a skinhead 'aircut. Nanna said you used to have nits, and I caught them off you. She said you used to have them, but then your mam started giving you skinheads, so the nits haven't got hair to live in."

"No, no tha... that's not true. My mam can't afford to take me and Chris to the barbers, so she bought an electric shaver off the catalogue. She can only do one style. That's why my hair is always short."

The shorter boy sensed an opportunity for mischief. "Nah, she cuts it short because you got nits."

"I haven't."

"Yes, you have. You're nits boy you are." The younger boy gently pushed his friend and then backed away.

"No, you're nits boy," the other laughed as he pushed his friend in retaliation.

"Nits boy, nits boy, nits boy." The shorter boy giggled as he ran away.

"I'll catch you, nits boy." His friend chased after him.

The two scruffy but happy young boys made their way through the walled passageway. Still laughing, they playfully pushed each other into the tall, grey, concrete block wall that lined the path from the part of their housing estate in which they played to the area where they lived.

The moon, clearly visible in the cloudless early autumn sky, provided the only light in the high-walled alleyway. They made slow progress through the short dark passageway by giggling, jostling and wrestling harmlessly.

Their laughter stopped suddenly. Not defeated by any action of either boy or the absence of light, but sounds arising from the communal garage area down the path to their right.

Intrigued but more than a little fearful, the pair crept down the grassy path toward the source of the interruption. Instinctively sticking close to the left side of the trail, the friends tiptoed along the garden fences. The metal chain link fences were overgrown with the last of the season's foliage from the bushes bordering the gardens. They both took great care not to rustle any branches or leaves. By chance, they found themselves in a spot that offered them good visibility but was dark enough to hide them from those they were watching.

They saw two teenage boys. One smoked a cigarette as his accomplice effortlessly moved an aerosol across the recently repainted garage doors. The smoking boy laughed as more spray splattered onto the metal doors.

Neither of the watchers dared to move. The actions of the older boys transfixed them. The two stood wide-eyed but motionless, breathing quietly, not daring to utter a sound. The younger one wanted to scratch his head but silently grabbed the other's arm.

Eventually, the teenagers grew bored with their antics and turned away from the garages. The young boys watched as they walked down the lane to the main street, stopping only to toss the spray paint into a garden, before heading off into the night.

The smaller of the two boys released his friend's sleeve.

"Come on, let's go." He turned to head back to the path home.

"Hang on," said his friend. "I wanna see what they was doing."

"Okay... but we better be quick. They might come back," said the shorter boy, feeling very nervous.

They moved to the front of the garages. It was a lot lighter here, and they could read the graffiti left on the garage door.

The taller boy formed the words slowly.

"Paul-a lov-es Ani-mal. True love," he read aloud. His eyes moved to the adjoining garage. "Please sh-ag, shag me ag-a-in...again Animal Luv from Paula." A third message lay on the door of the fourth of the eight garages. "Animal, I want to give you an-oth-er another blow job Luv Paula," said the taller boy before turning to his friend. "What's a blow job?"

"I dunno," answered the other, looking around anxiously. "Come on! Let's get back up to my house. My mam will be off if I don't get in soon."

The taller boy studied the garages again, but there were no other messages.

"Aye, come on 'en. Let's go. Race you to the top, nits boy."

"You're too slow, nits boy, " the other shouted as the race began.

Playtime was more routine the following evening. The pair had tired of aimlessly throwing a threadbare tennis ball back and forth over the roof of the local bus stop and turned for home. Once again, they played as they progressed through the alleyway.

Neither spoke of head lice or the distractions from the garages. Not a thought of the previous evening's events entered their minds.

A police car outside the shorter boy's house brought them to an abrupt halt.

"What's that doing there?" asked the taller boy stopping at the steps at the end of the alleyway. They were looking up at his friend's house.

"I dunno. Better go in and check, I s'pose. Come in with me?"

"Aye, alright. As long as I don't get into trouble." He followed his companion up two flights of concrete steps and through an already open gate. The smaller boy nervously opened his front door and stepped inside. His friend followed quickly.

"Hello, young lad. Been out playing, have you?" The policeman saw the youngster was not alone. "Oh, hello, I didn't see you there. Come on in."

Both boys nodded at the uniformed policeman, holding his helmet in his right arm.

The policeman spoke again.

"Well, come on in then. I've been waiting for you. It's alright for them to sit down, isn't it, Mum?"

"Of course." The mother smiled warmly but did not

move from in front of the unlit gas fire. Her fingers fiddled with the collar of her baggy, faded, blue denim shirt.

The boys glanced at her and then at each other before sitting on the sofa. Both sat uneasily, fidgeting on the cushions.

The policeman maintained eye contact with the shorter boy as he spoke.

"Now then, lads. A little bird told me you spotted two boys writing things on the garage doors last night. Is that true?"

Still shuffling on the settee, the taller boy glanced at his friend and gave a look that suggested they could not tell the truth.

The shorter one spoke.

"Well, we heard something and could see someone, but we don't really know what they were doing. Do we?" He looked at his taller friend for support.

"No," said his friend shakily.

The policeman was now looking at the second boy. "So you didn't see who it was?"

"No," said the shorter one.

"No," repeated the taller one a little louder.

The policeman placed his helmet on the grey-flecked carpet and crouched down. His head was now at the same height as the children's. He stroked his chin and spoke softly once again.

"Right, I see, but my bird told me that in school today, you told your friends that you saw two boys spraying paint on the garages. Is that true?"

It was the shorter one who spoke again.

"Well, I did say we saw something, but we didn't really. I sort of made it up. Everyone was talking about the garages and how Paula Jenkins' mother had called the police. Her brother Richard, Richard Jenkins, is in my class in school but I don't bother with him. Mam says he's cheeky." He glanced at his mother, who smiled and nodded reassuringly.

"So why don't you tell me what happened?" said the policeman.

The shorter boy looked at his friend, who nodded at him to speak. The boy fidgeted again before continuing.

"We was coming back from the bus stop, we was only playing lob the ball, and we wasn't making no trouble. We heard a noise as we got to the gap that leads to the garages."

It was the policeman's turn to nod.

"Go on."

"When we looked down at the garages, we saw someone, but we didn't know who it was. They was laughing an' that, pointing at the garages. When they were gone, we went down to look at what was so funny. That's when we saw the garages and the writing on them. In school, we just told everyone that we saw people writing on the garages, but we didn't really."

"I see," said the policeman collecting his helmet and standing upright. "That's very interesting. Thanks for explaining that to me. You've been a great help."

The shorter lad looked at his friend and smiled.

"One last thing..."

The boys looked up at the tall policeman.

"My little bird also told me you knew one of the boys. Someone called Animal."

Fear again. The taller boy nudged his friend's elbow encouraging him to speak. The younger boy took a breath, and the words spilt out again.

"Well... er... we didn't really see them up close...in school, everyone was going on about Animal going out with Paula, Paula Jenkins, and we'd seen the name on the garage door. So we just told everyone we'd seen Animal do it,"

"'ats right," added his friend.

"I see," said the policeman. "But did you see Animal by the garages?"

Both boys shook their heads.

"Do you know Animal?"

"No," said the shorter boy, "But I think I've seen him

around here before."

"Me too," said his friend.

"Well, you probably know he is a very nasty boy who has caused a lot of trouble. If he's been doing bad things, he should be punished, don't you think?"

Both boys nodded.

"And punished he will be." The policeman winked at the mother. "We only need one brave person to speak up and tell us what Animal has done, and he will not be around here for a long time."

He looked at the boys who were both rooted to their seats, mouths clamped shut and eyes wide open.

"Never mind. You can't help if you didn't see anything, but I had to ask. You know you should always tell the truth, don't you?"

Both boys nodded again.

"And you also know you should never lie to a policeman. You could get into serious trouble."

More nods.

"Right, Mum. I think these boys deserve a treat for being so helpful to the police."

"I think so too," said Mam. "They can have a drink and a biscuit in a minute. I'll see you out first. Say goodnight, boys."

"Goodnight," they said as the policeman moved toward the door.

Mam followed the policeman onto the garden path and walked him to the gate.

"Sorry about that, Ted. Wasted your time."

"Not really love. It doesn't take a genius to know that they are hiding something. It's not surprising. All the kids around here know Animal only too well. Practically everyone in town knows of him or his family. The lad fancies himself as a bit of a hard man. He's been giving young Paula Jenkins a hell of a time. Her little brother told us that your boy and his mate saw something. They're probably terrified of him. It's a shame. Lowlife like that could do with a spell behind bars." He walked through and closed the gate behind him almost in one movement. “Never mind, we’ll get him for something. I hope it’s before he can do any real damage.”

The mother shivered slightly.

“I hope so too. This place is like the Wild West as it is. We can do without more idiots about.”

The policeman tried to change the subject. “How is that husband of yours doing?”

“Not too badly, thanks. He’s gained some good contacts, so business has picked up a bit.” She rubbed her expanded stomach. “Need it too, with another little one on the way.” She leaned on the gate and glanced up the empty street.

The policeman smiled.

“Well, look after yourself and give him my best. Also, give my regards to your brother. I haven’t seen him for a while.”

“We hardly see him either since that new job, but I’ll pass your message on when we do. Goodnight, Ted.”

“Yes, goodnight, love. Sleep tight.”

“Fat chance. It’ll be darling daddy snoring in my ear if it's not junior making me uncomfortable.” She smiled as Ted laughed. “It’s presentation night, and he has a late one. I don’t know why he’s gone to a presentation night. He never does anything worthy of a trophy. There again, perhaps they’re giving a prize for the loudest snore!”

The policeman let out a deep cackle before walking down the steps and into his car. Glancing back, he saw two eager pairs of eyes staring at him through the Venetian blinds. Ted said, “Good night,” as he closed the door and drove off.

Peace at last, she thought. Settling back into her pillows, she picked up her book and then glanced at the clock. It would be at least another hour before her husband rolled home. She smiled at the thought and found her page.

She was pleased that her son had taken the policeman’s visit in his stride but shared Ted’s view that he and his friend had not told the whole truth. Her son was hiding something, but she had not pressed him further. She let him follow his regular bedtime rituals, and he was fast asleep in the room next door. She would speak to him again in the morning but try to be easy on him. He had enough on his plate already. He already had to adjust to the prospect of moving to a new area, a new school and making new friends. If that weren't enough, he would have to adapt to life with a new brother or sister.

She rubbed her stomach, hoping for a reaction. She wanted the baby to kick again. The doctor assured her that there was probably nothing to worry about, but the longer the baby remained motionless, the more concerned she became. She tried hard to relax.

Reaching a state of comfort was never easy in her current condition, but her attempts were made all the more difficult by a tapping noise from the landing. Rising from her bed, she ignored her slippers but slipped on her dressing gown, which was hanging on the back of her bedroom door. She left the bedroom, turned right, and walked toward the landing window. The noise was louder here. It sounded like something was hitting the window. Every hit on the window was accompanied by three or four taps on the outside wall.

She stood with her back to the wall, in line with the window, and looked out into the street. She could not see a lot and stepped closer to the window. Her heart missed a beat as she heard voices in her garden. She guessed that whoever was causing this noise was directly underneath the window. The taps were getting heavier and louder.

Resisting the temptation to switch on the light and working hard to control her breathing, she put her face closer to the glass. Looking down into the shadows, she saw two male figures. One had an arm in the air facing her as the other reached for something in her rockery that she had painstakingly erected a few summers past.

That was all she saw. Glass exploded from the window and fell about her as something hard struck the side of her head.

Her body fell sideways.

As she toppled down the stairwell, she looked, but nobody was there to see her.

She screamed, but nobody was there to hear her.

She stretched out her arms, but nobody was there to grab her.

There was nobody there.

THE MORNING AFTER...

The weary head tried to persuade its long, lean body to get out of the warm, comfortable bed.

One eye opened and glanced at the red liquid crystal display that served as a clock face on the radio alarm on the pine bedside cabinet. The three digits were a four, a five and an eight. 4:58

"Five o'clock? Is that all it is?" The half-awake brain sent a sandpaper tongue over parched red lips. "I've got to get a drink."

The right arm moved into action and, after flicking on the small bedside lamp, the body brought the fingers up to the right eye and rubbed. The eye burned.

"Jesus. What's on my hands?"

The face scrutinised the hand. The nose smelt the fingers, and the stomach threatened to expel whatever contents it had left.

Nausea brought back memories.

Peering over the side of the bed, the eyes saw a plastic bowl half full of dark, cloudy liquid with all manner of unmentionable things floating on top.

Nausea grew worse.

Wiping its right hand on the duvet cover while the left rubbed its left eye, the body shook as the stomach sent excess wind up the internal pipework to the mouth. The body stifled the belch, but it didn't taste very nice.

The body could feel something behind it and stretched the arm back. The hand grabbed a pillow which it brought to the face. The body looked at this pillow with only one eye open. The body could not think why the cushion would be there. The right hand tossed the pillow toward the middle of the room.

The body tried to roll onto its back but found its path

blocked. The long arm reached behind again and extracted another pillow, followed by two smaller cushions. The body stared at the mountain of pillows that had snowballed in the middle of the room. As hard as it gaped, the body got no nearer an explanation.

The taste in the mouth brought the brain back to more pressing demands.

"What a night," said the body to itself. "I need a drink."

The long legs slowly swung around until the feet touched the floor. Successfully avoiding the bowl, the body manoeuvred the head upwards until the essentially naked figure sat uneasily on the edge of the wooden frame single bed.

As the right hand scratched the partially covered area between the legs, the head perused the scene of chaos in the bedroom.

Not much of the green short pile carpet remained uncovered. In addition to the pillow mountain, someone had used crumpled and soiled clothing to hide large areas of the floor

Slowly lifting itself to its six-foot vertical height, the body belched again. The taste was even more revolting. The tongue was bone dry, and the back of the teeth felt very coarse. The remedy lay downstairs. The difficulty lay in getting there.

The arms reached for a pair of black tracksuit bottoms hanging from the back of a black leather swivel chair. The body braced itself for what it had to do next, putting on the trousers.

The body could not move quickly. Balance was not easy to achieve. The inside of the head started spinning. The chair transformed itself from a wardrobe to a resting post. The body was relieved that the chair did not revolve too far.

Regaining composure, the body struggled to get tracksuit bottoms to cover the long legs and then worked hard to put on a dark green t-shirt.

Looking downwards, the brain manipulated the reluctant long feet into a pair of moccasin slippers. This action proved less of a problem than anticipated. The body felt more confident about making the next manoeuvre –walking down the stairs without waking the rest of the family.

A dog's bark from outside the partially opened window, the only one in the room, caused the body to pull back the thick, dark curtain to look at the outside world. The face creased, and the eyes hurt at the sudden influx of natural light.

"Shit, it's bright at this time of the morning." The eyes squinted. "What's old man Doveden doing? Why is he walking his dog this early?" The arm waved as the older man looked up at the window.

The older man's face broke into a broad grin before he started to laugh as he waved back.

The brain grew more confused. "Why is he laughing? Strange old twat!"

Allowing the curtain to fall back into place, the body switched off the bedside lamp, opened the bedroom door and ventured out onto the landing.

Stopping briefly in the upstairs toilet to rinse its eyes and wash its hands, the body crept slowly but quietly down the stairs.

The feet arrived in the hall. The head faced the door that led into the lounge. The door was open, and voices from the television appeared to summarise sporting results.

Reality bit hard.

"Oh shit! It's five in the afternoon. The morning has long gone."

It was teatime on Saturday. The body had slept all day. The family was up and about. A deep breath was required.

The father's voice boomed from the lounge.

"Good afternoon Simon. I hope you're feeling terrible. You were in a bloody mess last night. You can look out when your mother catches you."

He'd seen enough mess. He was unsure what other damage he could have done but was not curious enough to enter the lounge to ask.

"Sorry, Dad. I'll... er...I'll sort it later. I need a drink."

He turned towards the kitchen in the hope of sanctuary, but the presence of his mother in the kitchen doorway removed any hope of finding peace. He was not in the mood for a lecture but knew he had no chance of avoiding one.

"Oh, you're finally up, are you? Well, I hope you're suffering?" His mother stood in the doorway, glaring at him. She had her arms folded.

"Never in all my days have I seen anyone as drunk as you were last night. My God, what a state. You could hardly walk up the bloody street. But that didn't stop you did it? You kept shouting nonsense at anyone who just happened to be passing. Poor Mr Doveden was only coming from the club, and he has to contend with you. I'm not sure he knew what to say. You hardly ever speak to him, but suddenly he's your best friend. 'I love living by you, you old fart. You are great you are.' You'll have to apologise to him."

At least he knew why the older man had laughed. "Sorry, Mam."

His mother had not finished.

"Then you fell over onto next door's garden. Your father and I were worried that you had hurt yourself, but you didn't care. You just screamed with laughter. God knows what you found so funny. We couldn't lift you at first, but you eventually managed to get yourself up so we could help point you toward the door. When you stood up, you realised you had your hands covered in dog shit. You thought this was hilarious. Did you wait to wash them indoors? No chance! You decided to wipe your hands on the car. What fun you had smearing dog shit like that. My God! The smell! The mess! Dad has spent all afternoon cleaning it."

That explained the smell and the stinging eyes.

"Yes Mam. Sorry Mam."

"I'm relieved there weren't many people around to see you. People around here are not used to it, Simon. They don't expect drunks. I feared we would never be able to show our faces in the street again. You have never been as drunk as that before." She shivered at the thought. "When we eventually got you inside and upstairs, you wouldn't let us wash your hands properly. We did our best, but then you started throwing up everywhere. We put you in the bathroom where you fell asleep leaning on the toilet bowl." She shook her head at the memory. "From there, your father and I dragged you into your bedroom, and he got you into bed while I stuffed pillows behind you to stop you from rolling onto your back. We left you a bowl and went to bed ourselves."

She paused for a second, apparently deep in recollection. "I didn't sleep a wink all night worrying about whether you would be alright. I heard you use the bowl during the night, so I guessed you were okay. You'll have to clean up your mess today. It's taken me ages to tidy everything up down here, and I'm not doing your room. God knows what mess you made up there. I'm scared to go in there. I just hope you kept it in the bowl. What a state you were in. You must have drunk everybody else's share. I bet Gareth and Mark are nowhere near as bad as you. Why can't you be more like them?" She shook her head again. "I'm very disappointed Simon, and it had better not happen again. I'm telling you something now, Simon Ikes, I never put up with it from your father, and I'm not putting up with it from you. Don't think you can start making a habit of this behaviour."

His mother's finger was prodding into his arm. It was time to move away."Yes, Mam. Sorry, Mam. Can I get a drink?"

"Beer or lager?" asked his mother, leaning against the kitchen door frame.

"No...er...pop, I think."

His mother moved to the fridge. She reached inside and removed a can of lemonade which she then passed to her weary son. Simon had settled on a stool at the breakfast bar.

"Can I have one too, Mam?" asked a young voice charging into the kitchen and climbing up onto the stool next to Simon.

"Course you can love. Lemon or cola?"

"Lemonade, please. Just like Simon."

She collected a second can, opened it and placed it on the breakfast bar.

"What's the matter Si?" asked his younger brother as Simon took a long sip from the can.

Simon did not want to answer the question. He was focusing on finishing his can. The sugar seemed to kick in immediately. His body seemed a little more alive. It would take long before he had everything under control. He said nothing but smiled meekly at the little one.

"Simon's just a bit delicate, Philip," said his mother. "He had a heavy night."

The younger brother raised his eyebrows as he sipped his can and smacked his lips. "Pissed, was you Si?"

"Philip Ikes!" shouted his mother. Her attention had left Simon. "What did you just say?"

Philip stared at his mother. His big round blue eyes opened as wide as they could. His fair-skinned cheeks turned the brightest red. His mother's face told him he was for it. He looked to his big brother for support, but Simon had become transfixed by something on the breakfast bar. His big brother clearly had troubles of his own. Philip had to face this one alone.

"What have I told you about using bad language?" His mother had covered the ground between them at record speed. "I've warned you before that if I ever hear you swearing, I'll wash your mouth with soapy water. I'm very disappointed in you. I will not tolerate bad language. I never put up with it from Simon, and I'm not putting up with it from you. Wherever did you hear such a word? She lifted him roughly from the stool and placed him on the floor. Now go see your father and tell him what you've done."

Philip started to cry. He cried along the hall and into the lounge, where he dutifully told his father what had made his mother so angry.

Mrs Ikes saw Philip enter the lounge and returned her attention to the saucepans.

"It's curry for dinner," she said. Her voice was back to its regular volume,

Simon Ikes winced again. "Lovely Mam, but I'll have mine later if that's okay?"

"We all will," his mother replied. "I've only just started cooking it. I'm running a bit late. Uncle John called down today."

"Didn't know he was home," Simon squeezed the empty can. "How is he?"

"He's fine. He's come down to see Nanna." She kept her back to her son as she busied herself with the contents of the saucepan. "He's been offered a job in Cardiff and has come for a meeting. He thinks he's going to accept. It's more money than the one he is in now and nearer home." She used her shoulder to satisfy an itch on her chin. "He looked a bit down if I'm honest. I think your grandfather's death has hit him harder than I realised." She thought about her words. "I suppose it's really hit all of us hard, being so sudden." A tear began to well in her clear blue eyes. She reached for a piece of kitchen towel from the dispenser and dabbed her eyes.

"Where's Clare?" Simon asked, changing the subject.

"Er...umm... she's gone up Nanna's with Uncle John. Philip didn't want to go. He's been waiting for you to get up. You promised to take him swimming this morning, if you remember?" She had regained her composure.

"Aye. Sorry. We'll go tomorrow. I'll go and have a word with him."

"Do you want some tea and toast?" She anticipated his answer and dropped three pieces of bread into the toaster. "Your father always swears by it when he's feeling fragile."

"Aye, please, Mam. That would be great."

Simon left the crumpled can on the breakfast bar as he rose from his stool and walked towards the lounge.

In the hall, he scrutinised the family portraits which had accumulated on the wall over the years. There were pictures of Simon at varying ages, images of Simon and his parents, photos of Simon and the twins, who arrived much to Simon's surprise some twelve years after him, and pictures of various family groups. Simon savoured the memories behind the photographs of the three children with their grandparents.

One picture, in particular, held his attention.

Simon smiled at the grey-haired gentleman, with his trousers rolled up to his knees, holding up his walking stick as if in salute. He recalled the day out in Tenby with his maternal grandparents. He could remember the exact moment the photo got taken. Gransha was laughing and joking with the children as they walked back towards the car. He had left his trousers rolled up despite his daughter's constant requests that he return them to normal.

He thought about the family cricket match that had taken place on the beach that day. Simon, his Gransha Dilwyn, mother and brother were on one side, while his Nanna, father and sister formed the opposition. The match had taken place on North Beach and had lasted ages. It only ended when Nanna reminded her son-in-law that she needed to get home to take her medication.

Simon grinned at the older man again as he remembered how he and the twins, accompanied by his father and grandfather, travelled in his father's car while his mother and Nanna set off in his mother's car. The men stopped off for a sneaky pint on the way home. Simon had shandy, the twins had cola, and the adults had a beer. His mother had nothing until she got home and had to make do with a cup of tea while her mother devoured her tablets. He cherished the memory. It had been a fabulous outing.

He entered the lounge to see his brother sitting on his father's lap, watching a cartoon. His father absently stroked his brother's blond hair. He smiled at the sight and thought of the times he had been in the same position.

His brother's tears had long dispersed as Philip giggled at the antics on the television.

"Sorry Phil, I'm not up to swimming today. Shall we go

tomorrow morning?"

His brother's eyes never left the screen.

"There's no rugby tomorrow, is there, Dad?"

"No, the rugby season's over."

"Right, we'll go tomorrow then. Is Clare coming?" He did not wait for Simon to answer. "And will Dicey, GarGar and Anthony be there?"

"Clare can come if she likes. I'll ring the boys later and ask them if they want to come along."

"That'll be good. Me and Clare can push them in the pool again." He looked at his father. "When is Clare coming home, Dad?"

"She won't be long."

"Good. I want to beat her at the new game. I'm getting better at it now, Si. Do you fancy a game later?"

"Probably," said Simon sitting at the far end of the sofa. He watched the animation on the screen while trying to remember the events of the previous evening.

"Mark rang and wondered if you were going out tonight. He said he was going up to Gareth's," said his mother as she delivered his tea and toast. "I sometimes wonder why you can't be more like Mark. He is such a polite, quiet boy. I bet he never gave anybody any trouble last night."

Simon tried to hide a smile as he pictured Mark Dice vomiting profusely as the staff frantically tried to get him out of the bar. His memory was interrupted by his mother.

"He wants you to give him a ring."

"Will do, Mam. Just eat this first?"

"Anymore toast there, Mam?" asked Philip.

"Course there is love. I'll bring you some in."

Showered, dressed and refreshed from a large dinner, Simon hastily tidied his bedroom. He put his dirty clothes into the laundry basket, stuffed the pillows back into their storage box and gingerly emptied the bucket. He took great care not to spill the contents of the bowl as it entered the pan of the upstairs toilet. He disinfected the bowl before washing it under the tap on the rear porch.

A short time later, Simon left the house for the twenty-minute walk that would bring him to the home of his best mates GarGar and Dicey.

Gareth Hughes earned the nickname 'GarGar' because his ginger hair had prompted suggestions that he looked like Garfield, the ginger cartoon cat. Gareth Garfield or Garfield Gareth got shortened to GarGar. Almost as tall as Ikes but leaner, GarGar was always chatty and the source of much gossip. GarGar believed himself to be the ladies' man of the three.

He and Mark Dice, Dicey or Diceman as he was known, had been friends since junior school, having grown up together in the same village. Simon Ikes joined the friendship when he entered secondary school years later.

At five foot seven, Dicey was shorter than his friends and this, coupled with his youthful complexion, meant he frequently had difficulty proving his age. Having a birthday in September, he was the oldest of the three, but his face suggested otherwise. He was grateful his father had pushed him into driving lessons.

Dicey's infectious humour made him very popular with the local girls. He had lost his mother while a teenager and had taken the loss badly. Had she lived, Mrs Dice would have been concerned about how much her son regularly drank.

Simon had three options for getting to his friends. He could ask his father for a lift, but not much chance in the circumstances. He could catch a bus, but public transport could be erratic on Saturday nights. His third option was to walk. Walking had the added advantage of giving his head more time to sort itself out.

Driving should have been a further option, as Simon passed his test twelve months earlier, but Mr Ikes steadfastly refused to let his son drive until at least 48 hours after drinking. Simon never argued the point as his father's employee had lost an arm following a car crash involving a drunk driver.

Simon lived in a bespoke house on the southern tip of the town. His friends were some three miles away. Dicey lived in a larger-than-average terraced house on the edge of an estate, GarGar, in a semi-detached right in the heart of things. It was there that Simon headed.

Cutting through the back streets of the town, Simon was surprised by the quiet. He felt sure that when he was younger, there would have been many children out and about, playing stupid games in their streets. Tonight there were very few. While he thought he understood why kids no longer played outside, he was disappointed that children were not out enjoying the warm, early summer air. He recalled his childhood and the long hours spent outdoors.

The rows of terraced stone houses led him to the top end of the town centre. Ikes checked his watch. It was quarter past seven, and standing for a moment outside the derelict hotel, he looked down the square towards the covered bus stop outside the "Fried Chicken" shop. There was no queue, so Simon guessed the bus had gone. Walking became the only option.

Moving steadily alongside the long glass frontage of the central library, he turned left just before the old town hall buildings and walked across an empty car ark to the concrete façade of the Jobcentre Plus. Simon looked at the graffiti that covered the entrance doors and smiled at some of the comments.

Climbing the short incline, he reached the overflow car park that had once been the site of a local pit. Here Simon cut across to the front of the houses rather than relying on the back lanes. Ikes knew from experience that several of the yards contained dogs. Dogs barked when anyone passed the back gates. The barks were usually followed by abuse from the owners, telling the dog to be quiet and the intruder to leave the area. The instructions would not be very polite. He did not want any hassle, so he moved as stealthily as possible.

Arriving on the main road, Simon stood in front of his mother's old school, which she had attended as a pupil and teacher, although her working life had a much shorter duration than her time as a pupil.

Simon turned left, passing the Chapel of Rest. The town park was now very close. He had completed over half his journey. Someone called his name as he strode up the road parallel to the park. He recognised the voice and, looking back, saw the tall, slim, shapely frame of Robyn Howells waving as she jogged to catch him.

Simon stood quietly, admiring how her shoulder-length fair hair flowed behind her. He liked how her breasts bounced up and down under her lemon polo shirt. When she stood beside him, he noticed that the open collar buttons had exposed a hint of cleavage. He tried not to stare.

"Hiya Rob. Where you off?" he asked.

"I'm meeting Dave up at Chockie's house" She fussed with her hair. "We're going for a drive down to the coast with Helen and Keith. What about you?"

"I'm...er...just off to meet Dicey and GarGar.

"Are you going anywhere nice?"

Robyn was always optimistic.

"No, we'll have a wander around, I expect. Possibly go for a pint. You know, the usual boring stuff."

"I thought you would have had enough last night." Robyn was now at his side and had placed her arm through his. "You were well gone."

He had forgotten she was at the party. He felt his face flush.

"Aye, you're right. I'd better take it easy." He stared ahead, avoiding eye contact.

Robyn laughed aloud and continued.

"Mind you. You were not as bad as Dicey. I managed to talk Dave into giving him a lift home, but Dicey threw up all over the backseat. Dave was not at all happy. He got me a taxi home, dropped Dicey off and then tried to clean his car. He rang me this morning from that new valeting place on the estate. You can tell Dicey that he can expect a hefty bill." She laughed again.

"Will do," said a smiling Simon. He was not smiling at the thought of Dicey's car cleaning bills. He was pleased that his mate had caused Dave Farley to miss out on a night of passion with Robyn, who currently occupied one of the top spots on Sikes' lust list.

Ikes hated Farley. He loathed him far more than he fancied Robyn, which was a lot. Robyn had no idea how Simon felt about her. Sikes would never tell her. His friends frequently teased him about his feelings for Robyn, but Sikes maintained the lie that it was better if he and Robyn remained friends. Their parents were very close, and any relationship between them might affect that friendship, especially if they broke up. In reality, Sikes doubted he had any choice or chance. Robyn's current boyfriend, local hard man David Farley, kept a close eye on his beautiful girlfriend, and she thought a lot of the thug. Dicey spoiling Farley's night made Simon feel very happy.

"Are your parents looking forward to the holiday?" Robyn asked.

"Aye, very much," replied Simon. "The twins are looking forward to it. Philip will not shut up about Paella after your father told him about it. I think he'll have a shock when he tries it."

Robyn smiled but said nothing.

"Are you going anywhere?" Simon asked.

"Not this year. Dave is busy at work, so we can't get away. He's off to Italy for a week, lucky devil, but that's with work, and he won't have much fun."

"No, I don't suppose he will," Sikes said, not believing even Robyn could be that naive.

"You'll have to pop down when the folks are away. We'll be company for each other. You could bring a few beers."

Simon thought he might enjoy an evening with Robyn

on her own and thought about what he would like to do with her, but then remembered he was not on Fantasy Island.

"Aye, sure, sounds great," he said, knowing he would not.

Further polite conversation ensued until they reached Chockie's house, a detached bungalow at the bottom end of Gargar's estate, alongside the secondary school at which Robyn had studied.

Chockie's father and grandfather had been known as Chockie, so it was a name Keith Edmunds inherited in his earliest years. He and Dave Farley were best mates but were several years older than Robyn and Sikes. Chockie was married to Helen and had used compensation from a work-related accident to buy their bungalow. He was more feared than Farley and was someone that hard men from far and wide tried to avoid.

Approaching the front of the bungalow, Robyn spotted her boyfriend, let go of Sikes' arm, moved slightly ahead, and announced her arrival.

"Hi, Dave."

Farley smiled as he reached out a hand for her to take. He was standing in the driveway of the bungalow next to his bright red Golf GTI, which stood behind Chockie's blue BMW 525.

"Alright, Sikes?" Farley asked before he kissed Robyn.

"Aye, good ta. You?" Sikes did not look at them as he spoke. His attention had been taken by Chockie and Mrs Chockie inside the bungalow. He stood in the bedroom window waving at him while she sat in front of a mirror, brushing her long dark hair.

"Cracking." Farley placed his arm around Robyn's shoulder. "Shame about the Diceman last night. It took the valet boys ages to clean up his mess. Tell him he owes me big time. I'll call up to see him in the week."

"Aye, Robyn told me. I'll be sure to tell him." Sikes could not wait to get away.

"Right, I've got to be going. See you, Robyn, 'bye Dave. Have a good night."

"We will," said Farley, tucking his spare hand into the pocket of his jeans. Sikes saw a plaster on Farley's left arm.

"See you, Si," said Robyn

"What does she see in that twat?" Sikes asked himself as he walked up the hill.

Sikes arrived at GarGar's house to be greeted on the drive by Gareth's large black Labrador dog. The dog barked and ambled to him.

"Hi-ya Tiny." He stroked the dog's head and neck. "Where's GarGar, eh? Go fetch GarGar."

Tiny barked loudly at the mention of his master's name and trotted around to the back of the house. Sikes followed the ageing dog.

Gareth and Dicey were talking on the patio. The large patio door that led into Hughes's dining room was partially open.

"Yo Sikes," said GarGar.

"Hell-o," Simon replied softly.

"Hi, Si. How's the head man?" asked the Diceman.

"Okay now, ta. How are you feeling?"

"Pretty good. Me and Gar have been down the White Lion this afternoon. The hair of the dog and all that."

Simon shook his head in disbelief.

"You should have joined us, Sikesy," said GarGar.

"No chance. I was fast asleep, and anyway, I couldn't face it after last night." The dog was back at his side, and Sikes stroked its head. "Hey, Dicey, is it right that you threw up in Farley's car last night?"

"What's all this?" asked GarGar, surprised. "You kept that quiet little man. Tell us more."

Dicey laughed loudly. "I did indeed. You should have heard him. He went ballistic. He was threatening to kill me. He was going to rub my face in it and then do all manner of evil things to me and my father. I think he was also threatening to come around to my house." Dicey shrugged. "Lot of good that's going do as there's never anyone in."

"Fucking superb," said Sikes as Tiny wandered away again.

GarGar slid the patio door across, fearful of what those inside the house might hear. "You know Farley hasn't shagged her yet," he said quietly.

Tiny dropped a stick at Sikes' feet.

"Aye, as if you'd know," replied Sikes, casually tossing the piece of wood for Tiny to retrieve.

"No, Chockie's missus is big mates with Anne in our shop. She told Anne, and she told me."

"Could be right," added Dicey, "GarGar's normally pretty reliable with the news."

Sikes had to admit that his friend was rarely wrong regarding local gossip.

"But they've been going out for ages," he said. "There must be something wrong if he hasn't shagged her yet."

"Maybe she's frigid," suggested GarGar.

Sikes cast him a look as if is to say he shouldn't talk about Robyn in such terms.

"Perhaps she's waiting for you, Sikesy," said Dicey.

"Fuck off," mouthed Sikes as Tiny's paw reminded him it was time to throw the stick again.

"Well, she's certainly waiting for something. She's been going out with him for what? Eight months. If she's not careful, it'll seize up," said GarGar.

Dicey laughed aloud, Sikes smirked, and Tiny barked. Sikes looked at the stick.

Dicey was still grinning as he said, "Anyway, Sikes, how did you find out about me puking in his car?"

"I just walked up with Robyn." Simon threw the stick as far as he could down the long garden. Tiny raced off after it. "She told me."

"Oh right," said Dicey watching the dog.

"Aye, Farley was waiting for her at Chockie's. He gave me a message for you." Simon saw the dog trying to collect the stick, which had become entangled in a bush. "He told me he'll call in the week to get what you owe him."

Dicey looked at his friend with a mildly concerned expression.

"Oh shit. I suppose I will have to cough up for a valet." He looked at the ginger boy. "It's a shame your old man sold the car cleaning place, Gar."

"Yeah, but he would have charged you double for puke," said GarGar.

Dicey shrugged his shoulders. "Typical. Anyway, Farley can't have what I haven't got, and I sure as hell won't have anything left after tonight." He checked his pockets. He had a couple of notes, and some coins, which he calculated were just enough for a few pints. "Where are we going? The White Lion?"

"Why not?" asked GarGar.

"Just a couple, eh?" said Sikes. "Are you two up for swimming tomorrow?"

"Are you paying?" asked Dicey.

"I'm sure I can sub the man who upset Farley," said Simon. "But watch your language, the twins will be there, and Philip had a bollocking tonight for asking if I was pissed last night." He pointed at his ginger-headed friend. "He picked that up off you last week."

"Sorry," said GarGar, laughing.

"My mother didn't find it funny," said Sikes, who then thought about something Philip had said. "Are you going to bring Tony swimming?"

"Nah, not this time. He'll be okay where he is," said GarGar.

Sikes and Dicey exchanged glances and shrugged.

"Now, where's the beer?" GarGar leaned through the patio door and shouted. "Mam, I'm just off out. I've got my keys."

Mrs Hughes shouted back. "Righto love, have a nice night."

"Bye, Gareth," added his younger brother Anthony. He made it sound like Garuff.

"Bye," said GarGar.

"Ah, that's a lovely send-off," said Dice as the three stepped off the patio onto the path leading to the drive. "What do I get off my old man? Don't come home pissed again."

"Hmm." GarGar's mind was elsewhere.

"All I get is "why can't you be a nice boy like Mark?" said Sikes, placing his arm around his shorter friend's neck and tightening the grip.

"Shit! Your mother doesn't know me at all, does she?" Dicey winced and tapped Sikes's side showing that he wanted to be released. Sikes obliged.

As they walked out of the front gate, Sikes quickly looked back at GarGar's house. His attention focused on the upstairs rooms.

"Is Emily home?"

GarGar shook his head at the mention of his older sister. "No, she's away on her course."

"Oh right," said Sikes, disappointed.

The three walked out onto the main road through the estate. A car screamed past them with horn and music blaring. They saw Farley and Chockie in the front of the Golf with Robyn and Helen in the back. The girls smiled as they passed.

"Pity you didn't spew up in his engine," said Simon. "He would have been off the road a lot longer."

"I'll try that next time." Dicey laughed.

GarGar's eyes were following the Golf.

"Chockie's missus is a bit of alright though, isn't she?" He scratched his groin. "I reckon she fancies me."

"As if," said Sikes.

Dicey shook his head in disbelief.

"You've got no chance Ginge."

"Well, I wouldn't be so sure if I was you," said GarGar

smugly. "She comes into the shop often enough and always gives me a massive smile. Rumour has it that she's played away before. You know the saying if she does it once, she'll do it again. I hope I'm around when it happens. I could do with a slice of an older woman."

"She's not that much older," said Dicey. "What is she? 23...24?"

"That's still older than us, and she's far more experienced, not to mention as sexy as fuck to boot." He rubbed his crutch through his jeans. "She could teach me a thing or two. I think she'd be a right-goer, and I'd be a keen learner. I'm getting hard thinking about it."

"Fuck off," said Dicey. "You've been out with Pam too long."

"Says who?"

"Says your hand. Pam is well blistered," said Dicey.

GarGar looked at his right hand.

"That's from hard work. You ought to try it sometime, short arse."

Sikes laughed.

"Anyway, once Mrs Chockie has tried some GarGarlove," He pronounced the word love as lurve. "She won't be looking for anyone else, and I'll probably never need to go out with Pam again." GarGar strode ahead of his friends.

Dicey was doubled over, his shoulders shaking uncontrollably. He turned to look at Sikes and tried to repeat GarGarlove, but his efforts came to nothing, lost in hysterical sniggering.

"I know. He's on his own, isn't he?" said Sikes quietly, also giggling like a buffoon. He struggled to get his words out. "But...the sad part is...he believes it too."

Dicey let out a very loud cackle which caused GarGar to stop and look back.

"Fuck off, the pair of you," he said, marching further away from his friends.

A NEW BEGINNING

Lunchtime. Cardiff.

A cool, dry spring day in the Welsh capital and the lounge bar at the Royal Albert pub in St Mary Street was filling nicely, much to the delight of Steven Moores, the licensee.

Moores liked the pub to be busy. It reassured him that his efforts, in the previous six months, had been worth it. The Royal Albert was getting a good reputation, and Moores felt that was down to his actions since getting the licence half a year before.

Another reason why Moores liked to be busy was that it stopped him from getting bored. Boredom caused him to drink. Drink added weight. More weight meant more complaints from his wife. Moores often said he needed more grief from that woman, like he needed a second hole in his arse.

The tall barman knew that his wife had a point. When they had first met, he had been a bronzed athlete. He used to be addicted to physical fitness and staying in shape. His physique had always been his trademark. Everyone commented on it, especially the ladies.

No one commented anymore, and Moores knew why. His stomach had started to sag. He frequently pledged to reduce his drinking and spend more time at the gym. All he needed was the time. Sadly for him, there was never enough of that. It was hard work running a business, and he could not rely on extra help from his wife.

"It's your bloody pub, so why should I do all the bloody work?" He shivered as he recalled the words of his other half.

Stretching to his six-foot-four inch frame, Moores' mind returned to the job at hand. He quickly pulled two pints of Stainthorpe's Special and placed them on the counter. He was confident that the beer was perfect with just the right amount of head.

Moores knew he was a "natural puller". He had a gift for it. The Stainthorpe's training manager had said as much on his training course. She repeated the compliment as they lay in her hotel bed the morning after the social event.

He had been grateful that Sue had opted out of the course, not that she had opted in, to begin with, "You're the one who wants to play bloody landlord. Why do I have to go?"

As he studied the now full pint glasses standing proudly on the drip trays he had strategically arranged, Moores reviewed the two gentlemen waiting for their beer. They were busy in conversation and were paying him no heed.

Moores thought himself to be a people person. He had always found it easy to converse with and engage with his customers, even if he thought many of them were grumpy bastards who could not be arsed to give him the time of day.

He often said that this talent for people, coupled with his easy-going but confident style, had earned him the right to run this pub, which was once the jewel in the crown of Stainthorpe's Brewery. Moores knew that Stainthorpe's had given him the job of returning the pub to its former glory because they were confident he had the skills required to do it.

Others were less certain. They suggested, but never to his face that it had more to do with the twenty-three caps he earned as a star player in a not-very-successful national rugby team. They thought his minor celebrity status and contacts within the game had influenced the brewery more than anything else.

Moores smiled at his two newest customers as he wiped his hands on the white towel hanging from his apron.

The one on the left, the taller one with the steel-framed glasses, round chubby face and receding hairline, was a businessman. That was evident from his dress. The man wore what Moores perceived to be a quality, blue pinstripe suit. He thought it had been tailor-made to fit around the bulges on the man's waistline. The man's white shirt looked pristine. Moores guessed it was a light cotton shirt and wondered if the burgundy and black diagonally striped tie was silk. He did not see an emblem, so he could not be sure if it represented a club of any sort.

The other one was harder to fathom. He was shorter than his companion, only about five foot nine, but had the stature of someone who had served in the armed forces. Lean but solid-looking, tanned face with a black moustache speckled with grey and short greying hair.

As he listened to the polite, meaningless conversation between the two, Moores sensed that while both spoke very well, the shorter one was the less stuffy. He was dressed casually in trousers, a blazer and open neck shirt. The barman knew the shorter man was Welsh, unlike his English companion.

Having wiped his hands, Moores took the crisp twenty-pound note offered by the suit.

"Are you still serving food?" asked the fatter man.

"Serving food?" thought Moores. "Most people ask if I'm doing it."

"Yes, certainly," he replied. "Food *served* until 3 pm. The regular menu is on the table, and there's a range of specials on the blackboard. I can particularly recommend the cod. I caught it myself in the Taff this morning. It's guaranteed fresh, only one head, and it will not glow in the dark, ha! ha!"

"Yes, very good," said the suit. "Shall we order here, or will you come to the table?"

I'm a bloody waiter now, am I? thought Moores. "No problem," he said. "You sit down, and I'll be over in a minute. I need to get some ten-pound notes anyway. I'll bring your change over at the same time."

"Good man," said the suit. "Shall we sit by the window, Jack?"

The slimmer man muttered something that Moores could not catch and followed the suit to a table below a large window. The bottom half of the window had frosted glass.

The suit glanced at the framed photographs of old Cardiff that hung on the wall.

"Cardiff is changing beyond recognition," he said. "It is developing into a lovely little city. I think I'll enjoy working down here. I think I made the right choice."

Jack had eased himself onto a stool. "I'm glad to hear it, Geoffrey, considering I've already signed the bloody contract."

The suit smiled. "And I'm very pleased to hear it. It's just a shame that it took such bad news to make you change your mind."

"Bad news? That's an understatement," thought Jack. He paused for a moment as he thought about the recent events which had utterly changed his life.

If his father's death had been unexpected, Shirley's had hit him like a lightning bolt on a snowy day. She was only forty-three, a year younger than him. She was fit. What was she doing having a brain haemorrhage at her age? The fact that she had been involved in the car crash was difficult to comprehend. She was a brilliant driver with a spotless record. How did she lose control on a dry surface in a good light? Then she suffered a brain haemorrhage. Where had that come from? The doctors told him she had suffered only minor injuries in the accident, but they buried her two weeks later. Why? How? No one offered any solutions. He hated that. He hated the doctors for missing the bleeding and not providing an explanation. He hated the other driver involved in the crash, although the police absolved her of any blame. He hated the police, even though he had worked with them for years, but most of all, he resented Shirley for leaving him. He missed her terribly.

"Yes...well, life must go on," he replied.

"Indeed, indeed," said Geoffrey, oblivious to his companion's grief. "We need someone like you, Jack. Someone who can help us ensure that DoMO gets its fresh start. We've gotten rid of the old regime, and now it is time for the

Department to show what it can do." He took a deep drink, smacked his lips and continued. "The new DoMO could be this minister's final throw of the dice. The PM came into power promising his idea would help improve standards across the NHS, but he has so far failed to find a minister to make it work. This current chap has one last chance. The Government remains committed to modernising the NHS without privatisation, and some say that DoMO could be the deciding factor in the PM's plan to secure another term in office."

He looked directly at Jack.

"You know that DoMO failed in London because the staff didn't want it to work. The information given out was not clear enough. There was no proper audit function; workers were slapdash, lazy and unconnected from what DoMO was trying to achieve. We have a greater level of independence than any other department has ever had. We need the right people, people we can trust, and we want you to help us recruit them and to look after them when they are in place."

Jack nodded in appreciation of what he thought was a decent enough speech.

"Your change, gentlemen," said Moores interrupting their discussion. "Have you decided what you'd like to eat?"

"Oh yes. Food. I'll go with your recommendation. Cod for me, please. Jack?"

"Cod for me too. Thanks."

"That's two cod. Thank you."

The suit took two more notes from his wallet. "Please. Keep the change, but I would like a receipt,"

"Thanks very much. I'll bring it over in a second. It's all freshly cooked, so I hope you don't mind a short wait?"

"No. Not at all, provided there is plenty of it," replied the suit, reaching for the beer.

Moores took the hint.

"Thanks again, gentlemen."

Snotty twat, thought Moores as he walked back to the

bar."I don't know who he thinks he is. Plenty of it, indeed.

"So, how are you settling back into Wales? All good, is it?" The fat man laughed at his own failed attempt at a Welsh accent.

Jack smiled politely. Up until Shirley's death, he had no strong desire to return home to Wales. He no longer felt very Welsh. Having lived in Manchester for so long, he did not share the anti-English beliefs of many of his fellow Welshmen. He thought their attitude was too parochial and disliked what he considered insincere patriotism of the Welsh. He questioned what the Welsh people had to be proud of.

He frequently asked Shirley what the Welsh had ever done as a race. She never attempted to provide him with an answer. She simply reminded him that, in her view, the Welsh were a race of a few million people, many of whom had an inferiority complex. Not that she thought they had any reason to feel inferior, she told him everything she admired about Wales and the Welsh. She loved Wales. She loved the Welsh people. She loved him. He loved her for that. He loved her for many reasons.

There were some positives about coming home. His mother, his sister and her family would all be close by. He loved them too. His nephews and niece were progressing well. That little girl was a natural diamond. He supposed her confidence came from growing up with two brothers. It also came from being influenced by her mother, his sister. She was indeed a gem. His thoughts broke off when he sensed his companion was waiting for a response.

"Yes, I've found a house on the outskirts of Newport, and I can move there in a few weeks. In the meantime, I have rented a flat close to the office."

Geoffrey looked surprised. "You're not staying with your family then?"

"No, I had a couple of nights at my mother's, and that's enough." He laughed at a memory of his mother and him arguing about what to watch on the television.

"I thought you had a sister down here too?"

"I do, but she has enough on her plate." He knew this to be true. Sure, there had been times in the last three months when he knew he would never have managed without her, but he could not burden her further. His sister's life had not always been easy. She had encountered more than her fair share of pain, yet she remained solid and available for others, especially her big brother. He thought it was funny that she had been there for him. Shouldn't it have been the other way around? Shouldn't he have been there for her? No, he knew that she was happier providing support. It had always been the same.

Geoffrey spoke again.

"So you are all set to start as agreed?"

"Yes, I'd probably like to spend a few days in the office next week, just to get used to the place and read some of the background papers. If that's okay with you?"

"No problem. Excellent. Good man." Geoffrey took out a business card. "Here's my new details, ring my secretary, and she'll organise it. The place isn't fully operational yet, but she'll find you a desk and a computer. The sooner you get involved, the better."

Jack tucked the card into his shirt pocket.

"The office is in a great location, quite a nice block from what I remember. But probably needs a bit of refurbishment work now, I guess."

"Too true." The larger man took a sip from his beer before placing the glass on the octagonal Stainthorpe's beer mat. "It needed work to bring it up to modern standards, but that's almost complete."

"Expensive?"

"Very."

"So where is the money coming from? I thought it was all about budget cuts these days?"

"Ah, thereby hangs a tale. It just so happens that a certain Middle Eastern business wanted our London HQ at a time when the government is committed to getting civil servants out of London. As such, it's a real win, win situation. We've agreed with Treasury that we get to keep the lion's share of the proceeds from the sale of the London site and will use that to pay relocation costs and for a full refurbishment. The Treasury objected initially, but the PM put his foot down."

"I see," said Jack, nodding. His expression changed. "But how did this overseas government happen to know that the DoMO office might be available?"

His friend chuckled as he tapped the side of his nose. "I couldn't say, but it certainly helped that Charles' brother-in-law is a diplomat and has connections. As far as HM Treasury is concerned, it's an agent of the Arabs that recommended the site and subsequently made the approach."

"So it's not what you know..."

"It never is, Jack," the fat man raised his glass, "It never is."

"It was ever thus," laughed the smaller man. He picked up his glass, joined the toast and drank what remained of his beer. "Same again?"

"Hmmm, please," Geoffrey replied. "And tell him to get a move on with the food. I've another meeting at three."

Moores cleared away their empty plates and fussed around.

"Was everything okay, gentlemen? The food was good, I hope?"

"Yes, fine, thanks," replied the thinner man. His friend nodded in agreement.

"Would you like to see the sweet menu?"

"No. Thank you," said the fatter man firmly.

His friend shook his head.

"Right. I'll leave you in peace."

"We'll have two more pints, though," said the larger man.

Bloody table service again, thought Moores. "Certainly, sir, I'll bring them over."

"Nice bit of cod," said Jack breaking the short silence. "You did well to clear the plate, Geoffrey. That was a lot of fish, and he gave you a mountain of chips."

"Hmmm, I might be regretting it soon. I'm a bit stuffed," Geoffrey said, rubbing his extended stomach. He belched into his hand. "Excuse me. I'm not sure I should have another pint, but I'll drink it as it's been ordered."

"You'll be okay." The thinner man eased back into the seat. "What's your next meeting about?"

"It's with the barrister."

"Serious stuff."

"Yes. I mentioned that we had to rid ourselves of a few wasters?" He saw Jack nod. "Well, we have to go back to the Court. I'm just checking that we are squeaky clean, legally."

"I see. That reminds me, have the background checks been completed on the new staff, those already offered employment?"

"Yes, nothing has turned up so far, but we had a tip-off that the troublemakers were trying to get their friends and family to apply for jobs, so we will have to wait and see. I imagine the real test will come when we start the large-scale recruitment. You haven't forgotten we have the open day in a few weeks?"

"No, that will be interesting. I am looking forward to it." He saw Moores approaching and fell quiet.

"More beer, thank you, you serve a lovely drop of ale." Geoffrey grinned as he leaned back in his seat.

"Thank you very much. I am pleased you like the beer," said a smiling Moores. "Stainthorpe's pride themselves on the quality of their ales. We are lucky here as we're almost on the brewery's doorstep. The beer does not have far to travel." He pointed out through the window where just across the river could be seen a tall chimney bearing the brewery's name in different coloured bricks down one side.

"I see. Fascinating," said the larger man showing little apparent interest. The thinner man smiled politely.

Moores felt embarrassed but managed a smile. He took the smaller man's money and thanked him for the offer to keep the change. He returned to his bar.

As he put the money into the til, Moores cursed ignorant customers who couldn't be bothered to give him the time of day.

"Steve. Have we got any more lime juice?" It was the voice of Anne, his pint-sized, part-time barmaid.

"I'll get some now. Give me a minute," said Moores.

"Okay, okay, keep your wig on. I only asked," replied the barmaid.

"I don't wear a wig," said Moores, slamming the till shut and storming off to his cellar and storeroom, his retreat, at the rear of the building.

"About that open day," said Jack.

Geoffrey was all ears.

"If it's okay with you, I might invite my nephew along. He's a bright lad and is looking for work during the summer."

"Not a problem. Get him to complete a form, and we'll fix him up with something."

"Thanks," said Jack sipping his beer. "I have a feeling he might prove very useful."

"Even better," said Geoffrey, smiling widely again. "I can see that you are already settling into the green, green grass of home." His Welsh accent had not improved.

"Don't you bloody believe it!" said Jack, a trace of a smile on his lips. "And no, I don't much care for bloody Tom Jones either."

WORKING LIFE

"Mr Sikes? Mr Harvey will see you now."

Simon rose from the vinyl-covered chair and followed the short, forty-something-year-old secretary into the inner office, the workplace of Christopher Harvey - the owner of "*Harvey's Bakery - Bread the natural way*".

He looked at his watch and thought, "Half-seven. Shit, I should still be in bed."

The secretary knocked lightly and then opened the door. Sikes thought she straightened up as she entered the room as if she was preparing for inspection. Her rounded bosom seemed to raise a few inches. The rim of her dress appeared to move further away from her knees.

"Simon Ikes, Mr Harvey."

"Thank you, Mary. Come on in, Simon. Sit down."

Simon did as instructed, taking up position in a green leather chair which swivelled as he sat. Sikes was grateful the leather did not fart as he settled.

Across the walnut, double-pedestal desk with green leather inlay sat Christopher Harvey. He, too, had a green leather chair but a much higher back.

The bakery owner sat smiling at Ikes with his elbows supported by the arms of the chair and his hands joined, almost in prayer, just below his chin. Sikes noticed that Harvey wore a white shirt and navy tie under his white overall. Simon was pleased that he had followed his father's advice and also worn a shirt and tie, even though he initially thought it was a bit over the top.

I'm only doing a summer job in a bakery. What's the point of dressing up? No one will see me.

But it's your first day. Create a good impression. Christopher always wears a shirt and tie.

Dad! You're so old-fashioned. People don't dress like that these days.

Do it for me, Simon. Please.

Simon forgot the conversation with his father and listened as Mr Harvey spoke, with great pride, about what he and his father had achieved in business. From humble beginnings, the bakery now supplied numerous national chains and eleven Harvey's bread shops across south Wales.

Many of Harvey's bread shops had expanded into cafes, and there were also plans for Harvey's to take over the franchise for the refreshment areas in a major supermarket chain. That would increase turnover by twenty-eight per cent. As an accountant's son, Sikes knew to nod appreciatively at the mention of percentages.

Christopher Harvey spoke warmly about Simon's father referring to him as Thomas or Tom, depending on whether he referred to him as his accountant or friend. He also appeared to know Mrs Ikes, Carolyn, who was in school with his wife and had taught his youngest sister.

Sikes learned he was to work as a delivery boy helping Timothy Martin. Martin was a trustworthy employee with the company for twenty years. Mr Harvey warned Sikes that Martin was a practical joker who liked to tease his workmates but was very hard-working and meant no harm. Martin served as a delivery co-ordinator but also had the role of taking cakes and delicacies to Harvey's Bread shops and fulfilling any late, missed or short orders.

Mr Harvey gave Simon a brief lecture about hygiene requirements and health and safety regulations and outlined the domestic arrangements, including tea and lunch breaks. He also reminded Simon that work usually started at five thirty a.m., so he could forget about having a lie-in for a while. On the positive side, work was typically finished by three o'clock unless problems occurred, so he could look forward to an afternoon nap if he wanted. Simon laughed politely.

Handing Simon a white overall and matching trilby hat, Mr Harvey led him through the outer office, where they received a warm smile from Mary, and down the stairs to the bakery floor.

Trailing his new employer down the stairs, Simon looked to see between thirty and forty people, mostly women, busying themselves with the work of the bakery. As they reached ground level and walked across the floor towards the loading bays at the back, Simon remained silent as the employees turned to face their boss.

"Morning, Mr Harvey."

"Morning, Jane."

"Hi, Mr Harvey."

"Morning Emma."

"Morning, Mr Harvey."

"Morning, Fred."

And so it went on, the smile to the owner not hiding the fact that there was great interest in the young lad. Sikes thought he knew what they were thinking. *Who's this geek? What's he doing here?*

Simon and Harvey eventually stopped behind a white van with "*Another delivery from Harvey's bakery – Bread the natural way*" on the sides.

Sikes saw somebody in the back of the van counting items of stock on the pile of wooden trays neatly slotted into steel frames.

"Tim, come here a minute," said the bakery owner.

"Coming, Mr Harvey."

Simon watched as a tall, thin man with a long hook nose emerged from the wagon's rear. He wore a trademark white overall, which had lost some of its whiteness, and an equally greying trilby hat broadly covered his greying hair. He carried a metal clipboard and a cheap pen.

"Timothy Martin, this is Simon Ikes. Simon will be helping you for the next couple of weeks."

"Hello, Simon. Nice to meet you."

Martin extended his long thin right hand, and Simon shook it politely.

"Oi Timmytits, have you got a new apprentice?" asked one of two girls emerging from a refrigerated area. Sikes saw that they had their hair covered in thick hairnets.

Timothy winked at Mr Harvey as he responded.

"Shove off. Ain't you got any work to do?"

"Oh, bit touchy are we?" joked one of the girls.

Mr Harvey appeared oblivious to the discussion. He simply waited until he had regained Mr Martin's attention and continued.

"Have you had your delivery sheets, Tim?"

"Yes, thanks, Mr Harvey. It looks like a quick trip down and around the valley, then onto Cardiff and Barry. We should be back by lunchtime."

"I hope so but go steady," said Mr Harvey.

"Always do, Mr Harvey, you know me."

Christopher Harvey smiled.

"Right then, Simon, I'll leave you in Timothy's safe hands."

"I wouldn't trust anything in his hands, Mr Harvey."

Simon looked to see the younger of the two girls from the fridge, passing Timothy a tray of cream cakes.

"Watch it, you," said Martin taking the tray. "Young Simon here will get the wrong impression."

"Simon, is it? Well, I'm Karen and that there is Carla. We are the best two workers in this bakery. Isn't that right, Mr Harvey?"

Mr Harvey smiled at Simon.

"Best two skivers, you mean," said Timmytits, climbing into the back of his van.

Bella shrieked.

"Hark who's talking! At least we don't take three hours to drive ten miles and back."

Tim gave his response as he placed the tray in the frame.

"I told you there was a nasty accident, and I was a

witness."

"So how come nobody else saw this accident? I think he's having a laugh, Mr Harvey."

"Ain't you got any work to do?" said Martin.

The girls laughed as they walked away. The bakery owner wished Simon good luck and left the scene. As Simon watched him climb the stairs to his office, he wondered what else the day had in store.

"Thing is see, Si, can I call you Si, Si or do you prefer Simon?" asked Martin as the van made its way down the link road.

"Any," replied Sikes. He studied Martin's driving technique. Both hands were securely on the steering wheel, eyes focused on the road and mirrors.

"Thing is see, me and the girls enjoy a good laugh, but the secret is not to let it go too far. That Karen, she's a hell of a tease, and I wouldn't mind having a bit of it if you know what I mean..."

Sikes did. While he did not consider Karen a beauty, something about her attracted him.

"...but it doesn't pay to shit on your own doorstep. Take last year. I could have easily got off with Karen's friend Tina at the barbecue in the club. She's a cracker she is. Nice big tits. Thing is, though, if I had done the business there, every bugger would have heard about it. That's not good. As tempting as it gets, I always avoid shagging any girls I work with and their friends. Timmytits lesson one that."

Simon smiled.

"Why do they call you Timmytits?"

"Oh, that's that bloody Carla's fault. She reckons I choose my women by the size of their tits. That's not true. Not true at all. Granted, I like big boobs, but she's got to have a reasonable face an' all. Everyone knows that nobody likes snogging a dog

"No, I suppose not," said Simon, his face showing that he had never previously heard the saying.

"And before you say anything, it works the other way, too. Women don't go with ugly men." He pursed his lips. "Well, some do, but I think they might do it for a joke."

The rest of the outward journey to Barry, via numerous Harvey's Bread Shops, was an education for Sikes.

He learned that his new workmate was forty-five, single and lived with his mother in a council house. Tim had never married, though that was not for the lack of looking, and had a long-standing relationship with a single lady from a neighbouring village, whom he saw every other night. Tim kept it to every other night as more than that could be seen as a commitment. He was unsure if she was ready for a serious relationship with him.

Timothy John Martin told Simon how he had a spotlessly clean driving licence and took great pride in his job with Harvey's, for whom he had worked for nineteen years and seven months. He had started the month after his father had died, so he would never forget the date.

His father had worked in the National Coal Board's smokeless fuels plant in the valley. Timothy commented that he found it funny that a factory producing smokeless fuels could deposit so much shit and mess in the environment. That said, he lamented the plant's closure as it meant the end of some of the best-paid jobs in the area.

Simon discovered that Tim's father had died of lung cancer caused by smoking fifty cigarettes a day, not the side effects of working with smokeless fuels.

Mrs Martin, Tim's mother, was a martyr to ill health, without any real symptoms until she suffered her first heart attack six years previous. Two more episodes followed until she reached the stage where she could not do much. She now relied upon Timothy for all her shopping, cooking, carrying and cleaning.

Cleanliness was another thing in which Tim took great pride. Simon could tell this from the cab of the van. Nothing out of place, no wrappers on the floor, no drink stains and, most predictably, no cigarette butts anywhere in the cab. Simon learned that the pleasure Timothy once gained from smoking ceased when his father became ill.

Sikes learnt that Timothy had a younger brother, Barry, who was doing very well for himself in Brighton. He had moved to Brighton after he left university.

"Hard years they were, what with Dad's illness and everything, but we muddled through. Thing is, we had to support Barry. I worked in the pit then and worked all the overtime I could get. Still, it was worth it to see the look on Mam's face when we saw him get his cap and gown. It was a real picture. He hasn't always been successful. When he first went to Brighton, he worked for a small electrical installation business but started his firm afterwards. Me and Mam got shares in it too. Barry made me take them because my redundancy money got him started. He always looks after us, does Barry."

Although his brother sent regular birthday and Christmas cards, Barry couldn't get back home very often because his electrical business kept him fully occupied. He'd been busy for the last fifteen years solid. Still, if Timothy wanted anything, he only had to ask. Barry would always provide. He had sent a lovely bunch of flowers the last time his mother had a heart attack, and his mother and brother received regular company cheques from him.

"Thing is Mam puts the cheque into an account which I think she is saving for the grandchildren. We don't really need it. We're doing okay as we are. Barry is good to us even though he has a lot on his plate."

When it came to Simon's turn to speak, Martin listened intently as Sikes told him about his life, his family, his schooling and, surprisingly, as Simon had not intended to say anything, his dreams. Timothy was very interested to hear about Robyn and thought he knew the Farley family but could not think why.

Sikes discovered Timothy had something in common with his mother. They both idolised Doris Day.

Mrs Ikes liked Doris Day because she loved to hear her sing, and Mr Martin loved Doris Day because his mother always made him sit through any Doris Day film that happened to be on their rented television.

At the Culverhouse Cross interchange, several miles from the centre of Cardiff, Martin pointed to one of the office blocks.

"See that place there? Barry did all their electrics, a massive contract for him, that was. Thing is, he didn't do the wiring himself. He got workers to do that, but he sent in the tender and everything. Him, his wife and three kids went on holiday to the Caribbean out of the profits. They are lovely kids. Well, they look like they are. I've never met them because they go to private school down in London and don't get much time off. Mam rings now and again but mostly keeps in touch by writing and sending them presents. The oldest is thirteen now. Pretty little thing she is, looks just like her mother. She came from Worthing, you know."

Sikes did not know. He suggested it was funny how life gave one brother so much when the other had so little. Timothy did not take it as an insult.

"Que Sera Sera. Whatever will be will be."

"What's that then?" asked Sikes, feigning ignorance. "Kay Sarah Sarah? That's a funny name for a girl?"

"Well, I'm not sure why she used those names, but that's what Doris sang in that film."

"What film is that?"

"Not sure what it was called, but the words went 'Que Sera Sera, whatever will be will be'" Tim sang the rest of the verse. His voice was good, and Sikes was tempted to join in for the chorus, but he stayed quiet, aware that he did not possess the best singing voice.

By the time the van returned to the bakery at eleven

thirty, Simon had warmed to his new friend.

Mr Harvey met them on arrival.

"I've just had a 'phone call from the Mount Street shop. Janice has gone home ill, and Jane is there on her own. She needs some help. Lunchtime is always busy, what with the local factory staff. Simon, do you think you could help us out for a couple of hours? Tim will drop you down there and pick you up after he finishes his next delivery. He'll explain a few things to you on the way."

"I suppose so," said Sikes. "But I've never worked in a shop."

"No problem. Jane is good as gold. She'll show you what's what, but Tim needs to fill you in on a few things you must be aware of." He turned to his driver. "Are you okay with that?"

"No problem," said Tim solemnly.

Within minutes, Simon found himself back in the van and on his way to another new experience. He agreed with Tim that Janice had not looked particularly ill when they called in earlier that morning.

"Be careful of that Jane mind. Listen to what Mr Harvey told you. Thing is, she is a lovely, kind girl, but she'll show you what's what and in more ways than one, if you get my drift?"

"What do you mean?" Simon asked.

Tim's face was solemn as he spoke.

"Thing is, Si, and I'm only telling you this because I like you and, anyway, Mr Harvey told me to fill you in, so it's not like I'm telling tales out of school or anything," said Timmytits.

"What are you going to tell me?" Simon was slightly anxious.

"Well, the thing is that Jane is a bit of a man-eater. Back last month, when Janice was away, the Mount Street shop had three different lads start work on three different days, and not one lasted more than half a day. Rumour has it she had them all. She wore them all out. Mr Harvey tried to find out why they left so quickly, but they told him nothing. After this morning, I think she's after you, and I wouldn't be the least surprised if Jane persuaded Janice to go sick knowing that Mr Harvey would send you down there. Not that Janice would need an excuse to leave early because she's got big problems at home. Thing is, I'm surprised Mr Harvey ain't wise to Jane by now. He's had words with her in the past."

"You are joking?" said Sikes nervously.

"No, I'm being honest. Forewarned is forearmed, as my Mam always says. I wouldn't appreciate being left there without warning. I'm only telling you for your own good. Watch your step. I thought something was up this morning when she started asking those questions about you."

Sikes recalled the earlier delivery; now that Tim mentioned it, Jane and he had been talking for a long time. At the time, Sikes had resented having to do all the carrying.

"My advice to you is not to go to the staff room. I reckon that's where she will make her move. You can't see the staff room from the shop so stay out the front. Unless that is you fancy a bit of it. I wouldn't go near her mind. Thing is, she has got a cracking pair of tits and a sexy arse, but you don't know where she's been."

Sikes did not fancy any of it.

They arrived at the shop to find Jane waiting for them on the doorstep.

"Ah, Tim, thank goodness you are here."

"No problem Jane. I'm not staying because I've got a delivery to make down Swansea, but young Simon here has agreed to help. Look after him, won't you? It's his first day, and he's very raw, but Mr Harvey told him you can teach him a thing or two."

"I certainly can," said Jane smiling at Simon. "I'll look after him. Thank you for bringing him Tim, and thank you for helping Simon. I'm very grateful."

"Right, I'll see you later then. Pick you up at about three, Simon. I'll sort it with Mr Harvey so I can take you straight home. You'll probably need a rest by then."

"You're right there, Tim, but I'll try not to wear him out too much," said Jane, smiling.

"Cheers," said Sikes, glaring at Timmytits. The driver had a smirk on his face as he walked away.

The first hour and a half of his life as a shop assistant went very well, and time passed quickly despite the saucy comments from the shop's regular female customers.

"You've got a new toy boy then, Jane?"

"Good job Janice isn't here luv, or you'll have the pair of them fighting over you."

"I'll have him in a baguette, please, Jane."

When the factory trade quietened, Simon found himself alone with Jane for increasing periods. She made him cups of tea and kept inviting him to go into the back room. She appeared bemused that he did not want to watch the television. Simon insisted that he was happy standing in the shop, watching as the world went by.

"Well, I'm going to put my feet up. Come and join me if you want. Close the shop door, and the bell will tell us if anyone comes in. Not that many people do on a Monday afternoon. The next person we see will probably be Timothy, and he'll be at least another hour yet."

Sikes watched as she opened the door behind the counter and walked through to the staff room. He saw her sit in the armchair, kicking off her shoes and placing her feet on the small table covered in magazines. Simon saw her legs were bare, taut and tanned.

He sought distraction outside the window but became compelled to look again. Jane was not bad looking. He thought she was pretty with her mousy-coloured hair and brown eyes. She did not wear a lot of make-up and very little jewellery.

What was that Tim had said about her having a cracking pair of tits? Simon looked and quietly agreed with Tim's assessment.

"Come on in here, Simon. No need to stand out there. I won't bite!"

Unsure what to do, Sikes simply said, "No, I'm fine here, thanks."

"Suit yourself," said Jane. "I'm not going to force you."

Sikes finished what remained of his latest cup of tea and tried to concentrate on the shop price list that hung on the wall. He checked his watch, quarter past two; Tim would be at least another three-quarters of an hour.

He walked to the drink refrigerator on the other side of the counter and opted for a can of cola.

"I'm just going to have a can. I'll put the money in the till."

"Don't worry about that. I'll pay for your drink," said Jane. "Get me one as well, please. I'll have an orange. It's hot in here. I think I'll open a window."

Simon wished he had not bothered with the drink but taking another can in his spare hand, he closed the fridge door with his foot and prepared himself for what lay ahead.

Entering the restroom, he faced Jane's tanned legs as she stood on her toes, trying to open the window. As she stretched higher, her skirt rose, exposing her tanned thighs.

"Er... here you are," said Sikes holding out a can. "That's a nice tan you have. Have you been abroad?"

"Yes, I've been to France," said Jane, standing at her regular height but angling her leg to admire her tan. "I got back about a fortnight ago. I expect the colour will start fading soon. Still, it was nice while it lasted. It did me a world of good to have a break. Things get on top of me now and again. I get where I just can't help myself. I thank God that Mr Harvey is a very understanding man. Do us another favour Simon and open that window. You're taller than me. I can't quite reach it. Janice normally does it."

Simon placed the cans on the table and, stretching his arm, grabbed the window's handle and pushed it upwards. The window opened outwards, taking Sikes forward with it.

"Whoa, careful, we don't want you falling out there," said Jane gripping him around the waist before easing him backwards. “I can’t have you getting injured on your first day.”

Sikes stepped backwards and could feel Jane’s breast rub against his back. He could smell her perfume; it was light but pleasant enough. Her one hand moved from his waist to his shoulder.

“Oh shit,” thought Sikes. He was unsure whether to feel relieved or disappointed when Jane tapped him on the shoulder, released his waist and returned to her chair, pausing only to pick up her can.

“Ah, that’s better. You get a nice breeze when the window’s open,” said Jane.

“That’s good,” said Simon, returning to the shop area.

At ten minutes to three, Simon was comforted to see Timmytits arrive.

“Alright, Si? Jane’s looked after you, has she?” Timothy winked at Simon.

“Er...aye...great, thanks,” Simon said as Jane emerged from the staff room.

“Hi, Tim. Good journey?” she asked.

“Yes, not bad. They are running that special offer at the Mumbles shop this week, three loaves of uncut for the price of two. Going like hot cakes, they are, or should that be hot bread? Ha ha.” Timothy John Martin laughed as his colleagues showed no emotion.

“Well, my boy, have you opened your account in Harvey’s?” Timothy Martin barely took his eyes off the road as he spoke.

“What do you mean?” asked a surprised Sikes, realising that they had been in the van for less than two minutes, and Tim was already expecting a blow-by-blow account.

“You know. Did you give her one? She seemed happy enough when she came out of the staff room.”

“No, I did not,” said Sikes indignantly. “I never laid a hand on her...mind you...”

Sikes recounted the events of the previous three hours,

culminating in an exaggerated account of the window-opening incident.

"She patted me on the arse, so I went back out into the shop."

Martin shook his head as if to appreciate Sikes had a lucky escape.

"Never mind, it'll soon be time to go home. By the way, I've got to take you back to the bakery. Mr Harvey wants you to sign some form or something to do with insurance."

Timmytits parked the van, and the pair entered the bakery.

"Hello, Simon. Was everything alright in Mount Street?" Mr Harvey was walking down the stairs.

Sikes looked at Tim. He had bowed his head to hide his sniggering

"Fine thanks, Mr Harvey." Simon glanced around. There were about a dozen people in the loading area, but Sikes did not recall seeing any of these faces earlier.

"Jane was okay, was she? Didn't try to persuade you in any way?"

Simon feigned ignorance. "Sorry, Mr Harvey. I don't know what you mean."

Mr Harvey looked around the bakery, but Tim was already hanging up his overalls.

"I am sorry. I asked Tim to tell you."

"Tell me what, Mr Harvey?" Simon asked, believing dishonesty to be the best policy.

"Well, you see, Jane had some personal problems that caused her to have a breakdown a couple of years ago. While recovering, she found solace in the arms of the Church. Nothing wrong with that, I am a firm believer myself, but I think it is each to his own. Jane's problem is she does not know when to stop. She preaches the gospel to anyone and everyone who comes into the shop. I had a word with her and things improved as far as the customers are concerned. I thought that was that until Janice went on holiday, and we needed to get some temporary cover."

Mr Harvey folded his arms and then continued his tale.

"We went through three young lads in as many days. I couldn't understand it, none of them lasted more than half a day, and none would tell me why they left. Anyway, on the fourth day, because it was Thursday and half-day closing, I didn't bother getting anyone in and instead, I asked Karen and Carla to help. Karen was on the 'phone within half an hour, laughing her head off at the fact that Jane was pressing Carla to join her faith. Knowing her view of religion, I'm not surprised Karen found it hilarious." The baker smiled at the image.

"I had to have a word with Jane, and I also spoke to her family and priest to ask them if they could do anything. I told them Jane had to leave her beliefs at the shop door or I would have to review her employment. I didn't want to sack Jane because she's a lovely girl, very smart and highly intelligent even though she has had more than her share of bad luck." Mr Harvey allowed himself a pause as he recalled the incident. "Everyone knows her in that area and, thankfully, we do not appear to have lost much trade because of her actions. Most people are very tolerant. As it happened, her Church arranged for her to have a holiday at one of their foreign retreats. They were also able to give her counselling which I think has helped. I still speak to Janice regularly to ensure things are okay, and she tells me they are. If you've had no trouble, I can assume everything is alright for a while. Thanks for that, Simon, and I am sorry you didn't know. I thought Tim would have told you. He probably did not want to worry you."

Mr Harvey stood beside Simon. He unfolded his arms and used the left one to pat Simon gently on the back.

"Anyway, off you go home now. I'll see you bright and early tomorrow morning."

"Thanks, Mr Harvey," Sikes remembered something. "Tim said something about a form?"

Harvey looked at him blankly.

"A form for insurance purposes?" Simon suggested.

"I think he might be winding you up, Simon. Tim is very good at that." Harvey walked off laughing.

Simon could hear Timmytits singing 'Que Sera Sera' at the top of his voice as he left to go home.

TIME TO PARTY

A long, tired arm emerged from the soapy water and stretched over the side of the cast iron bath. Circling, apparently aimlessly, inches above the tiled floor, fingers glancing across the floor, the hand eventually found its target. It picked up the towel and brought it to the face.

"Good evening. You're listening to the authentic sound of happy summer radio. Welcome to your weekend." said the mid-Atlantic voice from the battery-powered radio resting on the chair in the corner of the bathroom.

"Piss off," said a Welsh voice from the bath. "Does it never rain in your world?"

Simon rubbed the towel over his eyes. It removed the sweat that had run into his eyes from his forehead. Glancing around the bathroom, he saw that steam filled the air. Its vapour had covered the reflective surface of the long bathroom mirror that his father had meticulously secured to the bathroom wall earlier that year. The smaller mirror above the hand basin was also obscured.

Sikes liked his baths hot, and this one was no exception. He eased his shoulders under the water as he thought about his working day.

It had been a busy day. Busy but enjoyable. Timmytits had been on good form, and Sikes had loved helping his new friend wind up the female contingent at the bakery. He had particularly enjoyed being grabbed by Karen as he teasingly made off with her hat on their return from a tea break. Was it his imagination, or had she held onto him longer than necessary? Hadn't she also squeezed his arm tighter than usual?

Karen had risen in Sikes' estimation in the few weeks he had known her. Moving his hand down between his legs, Sikes felt something else rise at the thought of Karen.

"Still alive in there, are you, Simon? You haven't drowned?"

"No, Mam. Just coming," said Simon, quickly sitting up in the bath water. Water splashed over the side.

"Gareth just rang. He'll meet you in the pub at seven. It's quarter past six now. You want to get a move on. By the way, your dinner is nearly ready."

"Okay, Mam. I'll be there now." Simon eased himself back into the water. Five more minutes would do it.

Fifteen minutes later, Simon entered the living room wearing jeans, a shirt, dark socks and black shoes to see his father enjoying his regular cup of tea while watching the early evening Welsh news.

"Anything exciting happening in the world, Dad?"

"Not much apart from that place John mentioned. It is having an open day in a couple of weeks."

"That statistics place? Why is that news?"

"They reckon they'll have over a thousand working there by the end of the year, and people are invited to go along to see what the office does and apply for jobs."

"What is it they do again?"

"They compile statistics about the Health Service and then publish them."

"What for?"

Thomas Ikes swung around in his chair and faced his son. He was careful not to spill any of the contents of his large tea mug. 'Best Dad in the World', a father's day gift from the twins.

"Good God, Simon, Uncle John told you, not me. Don't you ever listen? Do you have any clue about what's going on around you? There's been enough fuss about it."

"Sorry, Dad, I've been so tired lately." He was not lying. These early mornings would be the death of him. He was glad he could walk to work, even though it took a long time, as it allowed him to wake up.

"Welcome to working life. Uncle John said that every hospital in Britain sends returns to that office. They compile statistics and release them so people who need treatment can check which hospital provides the best treatment for their illness. People can then add their names to the list of their chosen hospitals. The government uses statistics to indicate the most successful hospitals and puts more resources into them. The greater the demand, the more cash the hospitals get. The poorer hospitals must either improve by using better staff or merging with other, possibly, better hospitals. In this way, the government hopes the NHS will improve services for everyone."

"And Uncle John said all this? No wonder I switched off," said Simon.

His father settled back into his usual position on the leather chair, but a more comfortable seating position did not silence his father.

"No, smart arse. Uncle John told you about the job opportunities and that they would be looking for trainee accountants. He thought you might want to apply so that they can pay for your higher education."

"That's charming. You don't even want to pay for your son to attend university. Your own flesh and blood. Does Mam know about this?" laughed Simon.

"Does Mam know about what?" asked his mother entering the room. She carried a portion of lasagne and salad and placed it on the table at the spot usually occupied by her elder son.

"I was just reminding Simon about the opportunities at that Health Services Records Office that John was telling us about," said Thomas Ikes.

"Records office?" She stopped to study the television, "Oh yes, that's where they sacked those workers for no reason, then forced the others to leave their homes and families to move to Cardiff. There's democracy for you. That sounds like a great place to work. Simon, your food's out. Get a move on, or you'll be late for Gareth."

Simon took the few steps necessary to reach the table. He sat at the table and picked up his knife and fork while his mother made to return to the kitchen. His father's voice stopped her movement. Simon realised that this was one of the few occasions where his father disagreed with his mother's view that the conversation had come to a close. He decided to listen.

His father had changed his sitting position, so he faced his wife.

"They must have had a good reason to get rid of those people, or the Courts and Tribunals would have clobbered them. John said those that got sacked had fiddled with the figures. Others were not very good at timekeeping. There was only a fuss because it was jobs in London. If it had been Welsh workers who gotten the push, nobody would have said anything. As John made clear, those who got sacked deserved it, and nobody was forced to move. Anyway, if I know government, those that have moved probably got a fortune for their trouble. Furthermore, house prices are much lower here compared to London, so they probably all made a mint before they got their compensation. Not that I begrudge them that. I think it is about time they moved jobs out of London. Why should all the jobs be there? Cardiff is just as accessible. I still think Simon could do much worse than going to the open day to see what is on offer."

"Great. Move from one overcrowded and expensive metropolis to a smaller overcrowded and slightly less expensive metropolis. It makes perfect sense. Now, do you want Parmesan on your lasagne?"

"Yes, please," said her husband. It was time to let go.

Simon was ten minutes late for GarGar. Not that his friend was surprised. Punctuality was not Simon's strong point.

GarGar sat at the bar, emptying what remained of his pint of lager. He placed the glass on the drip tray and was pleased to be spoken to by the barmaid.

"Same again?" The bar was quiet, and she was happy to be kept busy.

"Yes, please, and a pint of lager for my mate" GarGar smiled warmly at the barmaid. He knew her from her visits to the shop. She reciprocated.

He turned to his friend. "Got any clocks in your house, have you?"

"Aye...sorry, Gar. I'm knackered. It's been a hard day. Where's Dicey?"

"He's giving it a miss. He's meeting that girl from down the valley. You know the one. He met her in the club last Friday."

"Aye, and shagged her last Saturday. Or at least reckons he did. Fuck me! Dicey seeing a girl after he's done the deed? Is he in love?"

"Not really sure, Si. He could be. He's been feeling a bit down lately, so that could have something to do with it, as could the fact that he's got an empty house because his father is away in London watching the cricket."

"Randy little bastard. A whole night of it! Shall we miss Chubber's party and go up Dicey's house to spoil his fun?"

"Spoil his fun or ask him if we can watch?"

"Fuck off." mouthed Sikes smiling. He handed money to the barmaid.

Two pints later, with the time approaching a quarter past eight, the two friends left the pub and turned right into the town's main shopping area. They passed the now quiet shops, the last shoppers having departed the scene hours earlier.

GarGar checked out his hair in the reflection in the window of the Chemist shop, then toyed with the idea of getting chips. He decided not to and crossed the road in front of the fish bar. They said little as they continued their stroll

Simon opened the door of the pub selected as the gathering point for the evening. The pair entered the lounge to be greeted by many friends and acquaintances. Simon bought the beers as Gareth teased a mutual friend about him still being a virgin.

Two more pints and the enlarged crowd, a round dozen, made their way down the street towards the local rugby club. Someone questioned whether the rugby team had won their league. Nobody knew the answer, but the discussion resulted in GarGar snatching a bag from one of the girls and passing it to Sikes as if it were a rugby ball.

Simon passed the bag onto another mate, Nobbo, who quickly got smothered by the girl's boyfriend.

"Fucking hell! It's only a bit of fun," squealed Nobbo.

The boyfriend did not see the funny side.

"Giz that back, you fucking mong."

He snatched the bag back and gave it to its rightful owner. As he did so, GarGar smacked the boyfriend's head before turning him and pushing him into four other friends.

GarGar shouted. "Hold this twat for me."

The four did as instructed. They held the boy's arms and stopped his legs from kicking out.

GarGar unbuttoned the boy's shirt and removed it. He had no difficulty getting the boy's arms out of the sleeves. Holding the shirt in his left hand, GarGar slapped the boy's face with his right.

"You want to loosen up, you do, Mikey. You're too tense. You can't go around calling people names like that. Do you hear me?"

The boy's plump white torso was visible to the world, but he tried to pretend he was still in control. "Fuck off, you twat. Give me my shirt back. That's a genuine Le Shark, that is. It cost a bomb, and you'd better not damage it."

"Genuine be fucked," said GarGar, nose-to-nose with the boy. "Your sister told me that your auntie brought a stack back from Greece. It's a fucking fake. It's more fake than your girlfriend's tan."

The girl looked at her legs in embarrassment.

The other lads laughed and let the boyfriend go. He stepped nearer the ginger boy, but neither he nor GarGar gave way. They just stared at each other, standing toe-to-toe.

A non-Welsh voice broke the standoff.

"Alright, lads, move along now. You've had your fun. We don't want any trouble, do we?"

Sikes looked to see two police officers, one nearing retirement age, the other a more recent recruit. His friends, including GarGar, stared at the men in blue.

Simon knew the older policeman and held his hand up in greeting. The police officer winked back in a nonchalant way that would not have been seen as anything special by Simon's friends.

Sikes walked over and took the shirt out of GarGar's hands. He shook it and handed it to the shirtless boy.

"Here you are, Mikey but do us a favour, eh? Give the party a miss." Sikes then put his arm on GarGar's shoulders and led his friend away. "Come on, Gar, let's party."

GarGar walked with Sikes, but his eyes glared at Mikey.

"Fucking twat, I'll kill him if he uses that word again."

"Okay, okay," said Sikes. "But not today, eh?" Let's get some beers in."

The police officers formed a barrier between GarGar and Mikey and walked with Sikes and his mates for a few yards.

"Where are you lot off to now?" asked the older policeman. "Rugby club, is it? We heard there would be a bit of a party tonight, although you look like you've had a party of your own already. I don't know why you bother wasting all your money in the pubs in town. You won't find anywhere cheaper than the Rugby Club." They stopped a few strides away from the door. "Anyway, have a good night and keep out of trouble."

Simon smiled, nodded then heard someone call his name. He checked behind, saw another friend approaching and then checked the rest of the crowd. Mikey and his girlfriend were talking on the opposite side of the road. Simon took his arm from GarGar's shoulders and pushed him up the stairs.

Steve Edwards caught up with Sikes.

"He's alright for a copper, isn't he, old Jim Grimshaw? Bit of an old woman and that, but my Dad reckons he's helped him a lot over the years."

"And mine," said Sikes. He looked for GarGar as they entered the function room.

"He's staying 'round here when he retires. Dad thought he'd return to Yorkshire, where he came from, but Grimshaw told him he'd be happier staying down here. Harvey's Bakery has promised him a job in security or something. You're working in Harvey's, aren't you, Sikesy? That'll be nice for you, working with Grimshaw."

"It's only a summer job. It's not permanent or anything." Sikes looked around and saw GarGar by the bar.

"Oi Sikes. Get a move on. Whose round is it?"

Sikes pointed to himself, told Steve he would see him later and stood beside GarGar. They were soon joined by Chubber's sister, Kelly, and her cousin Samantha.

Kelly was a popular figure around the town and was in the corresponding year at the Girls' School. GarGar had been out with Kelly a couple of times. Simon had seen Samantha before, but only casually while walking around town. They exchanged nods as they passed. Chubber had mentioned to him that Sammie liked the look of Simon Ikes.

It occurred to Sikes that he might have roped into a double date. He did not mind. Sammi was a pretty girl with a happy round face, short brown hair and smooth skin. Her legs were lightly tanned with a small tattoo of a Welsh dragon above her right ankle.

From early conversation exchanges, Simon learned that he and Samantha were roughly the same age. He was grateful for this. It made a change for the dates arranged by GarGar.

Simon usually ended up with younger girls. Sammie seemed easy to talk to, and he did not flinch as she touched him as they spoke.

Having bought the drinks and put them on the table, which the four stood around, GarGar dragged Kelly off to dance. Simon and Samantha gathered their drinks and retreated to the corner to talk.

Sammie was from Pembroke and was staying with Kelly for a week. She had just completed her first year at Bristol University, where she studied for a degree in Business Administration. She enjoyed university and would recommend it. Her social life was superb, which made a pleasant change from her home town where very little happened.

Simon found her easy to talk to and learned she was quite self-conscious. He reassured her that, by no stretch of the imagination, could she be described as fat. Simon told her she had a lovely figure and reassured her that he did not feel like she had been dumped on him.

Sammie told of Kelly's fondness for GarGar and, although the relationship had gone nowhere, Kelly hoped they would get it together soon. Simon joked whether Kelly knew what she was letting herself in for, to which Sammie replied that Gareth should be the more concerned.

The night passed swiftly. More drinks and a series of dances saw Simon and Sammie kiss on the dance floor. Sikes was enjoying the sensation and was disappointed when GarGar tapped him on the shoulder.

"Come on, you two, we're off to Dicey's."

"What?" asked Simon, easing away from Sammie but taking her hand. "How?"

"This place will be shutting soon. I've just 'phoned him, and he said we could continue the party up there. He's got plenty of booze in, apparently."

"What about his girl? Won't she mind?"

"Nah, you know Dicey, he can be a boring bastard

sometimes. She'll probably be glad of the company."

Sikes did not relish the long walk up to Dicey's and used his mobile to book a taxi for himself, Sammie, GarGar and Kelly.

Fifteen minutes later, he and Sammie were sat on Dicey's sofa, glasses of Bacardi and Coke on the table in front of them, continuing where they left off on the dance floor. They quickly became oblivious to the crowd that grew around them.

When they paused for a drink, Simon could not see GarGar or Kelly, so he guessed they had gone somewhere quieter. He also noticed that another couple had occupied the remaining space on the large sofa. He wondered if anywhere quiet remained for Sammie and him.

Making an excuse about going to the toilet, he ran up the stairs. The first door, which he knew was Dicey's room, was shut, and he could hear Dicey talking inside.

Dicey's father's room was to the left, but that door was also closed. The padlock on the outside suggested that while it was unoccupied, it was intended to remain that way. The third bedroom door was also closed, but Sikes knocked on it anyway.

"Go away. We're busy," said GarGar. Sikes could hear Kelly giggling softly.

He returned downstairs. The kitchen was filling up fast, as was the main living room. Many guests from Chubber's party had invited themselves to Dicey's.

Simon was desperate to find some privacy. He was sure he was onto a good thing. Re-entering the main room, he remembered the partition folded against the wall at one end. He knew Dicey used this when his friends came around, but his father was at home. It split the room into two unequal portions. The end nearest to the entrance hall was the larger area. Once the partition was extended, the smaller portion of the room only housed a sofa and television. Dicey's father often watched the tv behind the false wall while Dicey and his mates utilised the other end of the room.

Glancing at the other couple on the sofa, Sikes walked to

the partition. He unhooked it and said,

"Hey, you two, move up that end of the room. Dicey wants me to pull this across so his father's stuff is safe."

Sammie went to move, but Simon held up his hand, telling her to stay where she was.

The other pair looked confused.

"You heard. Come on. I've got to pull this across. There's plenty of room up that end."

Sikes was happy that the pair did as he said without argument. He quickly extended the wooden partition and secured the hook on the wall. Small glass squares had been inserted into the panel to allow light to filter through. Additional lighting was not required. Sikes switched off the lamp.

"Now then, where were we?" he asked, sitting next to Sammie.

"Sneaky." Sammie smiled before kissing him.

The necking intensified, and Simon's mouth moved from Sammie's lips to her neck, moving down from her ears to the collar of her T-shirt. Sikes was wearing an open-necked shirt and sighed as Sammie undid another shirt button and placed her lips on his neck.

Sikes' hand eased Sammie's shirt from her skirt, and his right hand slipped underneath, moving from her waist to her right breast.

Sammie jumped sharply. Sikes thought that he had gone too far and quickly removed his hand.

"I hope nobody can see you." Sammie kicked off her shoes and swung her feet up onto the sofa.

Simon was relieved that Sammie was simply getting more comfortable. She lay down on her back. He, too, kicked off his shoes, ignoring his father's advice that he should always undo the laces, and lay beside her on the sofa.

"Peace at last," he said.

Sammie whispered in agreement and put her arms around Simon's head, easing his lips to her mouth.

Simon's hand remade the journey towards Sammie's breast. He gently massaged the breast through her bra. Sammie's kissing became even more intense, and Simon eased his thumb inside the bra and stroked the nipple. Her mouth moved to his neck, and she began squeezing his flesh with her teeth. As her mouth moved slowly across his exposed shoulder, Simon could feel her undoing more shirt buttons.

Simon's fingers pulled back the bra cup and grasped the whole of Sammie's right breast in the palm of his large right hand. He closed his fingers around it.

"Ow! Easy."

Sammie removed her mouth from Simon's neck and her hands around his head. She reached up inside her top and unhooked the bra.

"I hope nobody can see us," she whispered as she replaced her hands around Simon and her mouth on his.

Simon did not care whether he could be seen or not and muttered, "We're okay here."

He returned the kiss and placed his hand on her waist again. This time he lifted her shirt until the bottom edge of it lay just below her neck. He had fully uncovered Sammie's top half exposing her breasts which still had the opened bra dangling on either side. He pulled away from her mouth to admire the view in the low light.

"If anyone comes in here, you are dead meat," said Sammie, grinning.

He returned his lips to hers while his free hand moved from one breast to the other, gently gliding over the skin but pausing momentarily on each nipple.

Sammie's tongue briefly met with his before retreating to the sanctuary of her mouth. She moved her lips to his neck again, and Simon placed his mouth on her breasts. Taking the left breast in his right hand, he kissed the flesh, licked the nipple and then gently put his lips around the nipple and suckled, not knowing why.

His hand moved down the front of Sammie's skirt and

rested on her bare thigh, just above the knee. Simon squeezed the muscular thigh as Sammie tensed her leg.

Sammie's left hand moved Simon's face back to hers, and she kissed him even more deeply. This time her tongue circled his mouth with no reservations.

Sikes's right hand continued exploring. It slid smoothly up her right thigh until Simon could feel her knickers against his thumb. Softly lifting her skirt out of its path, Simon's hand touched the top of her knickers before returning on a downward journey outside her underwear. He rested his hand where his fingers could caress her leg while the back of his thumb pressed against the area between Sammie's legs. He increased the pressure slightly. Her tongue tangled with his.

Sammie's mouth pulled away. Sikes moved his hand, concerned that he was rushing things. Sammie's left hand picked up his right hand and placed it on her knickers.

"I hope no one is watching."

"We're okay," he replied.

"I know that, but we'd better not get seen."

Simon kissed her again and then moved his mouth to her neck. He flexed his fingers, and Sammie groaned. He caressed her, and she moaned again.

Feeling braver, Simon slipped his fingers inside her knickers and sighed as they came into contact with a narrow path of soft pubic hair. He slid his fingers down between her legs, stroking gently, just as his first "conquest" had shown him some six months earlier.

Simon had been with five other girls since then. One was memorable, unexpected and loving, the others quick, uncomfortable and regrettable. The prospect of adding to his experiences excited him. He shivered nervously.

Sammie's hands left his head and cupped his crutch through his jeans. Simon exhaled as she ran her hand along the path of his erect penis. Sammie deftly, partially, opened Simon's button fly and placed her hand inside his trousers.

Simon's fingers entered Sammie, and he enjoyed the

experience of her underwear pressing against the back of his hand while Sammie's hand stroked his penis. They had found a rhythm as easily as they had found each other's mouths. Her hands undid the rest of his trouser buttons. She pushed his trousers down to below his backside, rubbing against him as she did so.

Simon's journey into ecstasy was cut short by a brief explosion between his legs.

"Oh fuck I've come in my pants!" He thought as he quickly pulled his groin away from Sammie and removed his hand from her knickers.

Sensing the sudden loss of interest, Sammie whispered, "What's wrong?"

"Er...I thought I heard something," he lied. Sikes stood with his back to the sofa as he pulled up his jeans.

"There's nobody there. Come back here."

"Umm...hang on. I haven't...er...got a condom."

"Don't worry, I trust you. Anyway, I am on the pill."

"Aye ...but you shouldn't trust me. I know where I can get one. Stay there a sec."

"You must be joking. Wait! What's wrong? I was enjoying that"

"I just thought I'd better get a condom. It is not as if you know me, is it?" Simon felt uncomfortable; the front of his boxer shorts felt soaking wet and sticking to his body.

Sammie took a drink. "Are you sure that's all it is?" She looked him full in the eye. "You haven't gone off the idea, have you?"

"Of course not." Simon reached down and kissed her. I'll be back right away. I've just got to go to the toilet." He rose and did up the rest of his buttons. He was about to walk out of the door when Sammie spoke.

"Hurry back."

Sikes smiled and watched as Sammie entirely removed her bra and tucked it into her handbag. Until that moment, he hadn't even noticed she had been carrying a bag.

He opened the partition, stepped through and closed it behind him before sprinting through the kitchen to the stairs. He was desperate to get out of his damp, sticky underwear.

He was thankful that the upstairs toilet was empty. He slammed the door behind him and locked it. Ripping off his jeans, he threw them to one side before removing his boxer shorts. He did not believe he could have made such a mess but put it down to the fact that it had been a while since he had been so excited. After removing his shorts, he crunched them up and used them to wipe his private parts before replacing his jeans.

Taking the opportunity to release the alcohol that had built up in his bladder, Simon wiped his penis with the undies again before doing up his buttons.

"Hurry up in there! There are others here too, you know."

It was GarGar, knocking at the toilet door.

"Fuck off," said Sikes. Not that Gareth would have recognised the grunt.

"Come out here. I'll give you fuck off." GarGar had not realised to whom he was speaking.

"Leave it, Gar. Come back here. You can get rid of them later. We've got unfinished business."

"Them? Randy fucker" thought Sikes as he heard GarGar stamp across the landing back to Kelly.

Sikes couldn't decide what to do with the soiled underwear. He couldn't flush them for fear that they would block the system. There was no bin.

Looking for somewhere to dispose of his undies, Simon spotted the narrow frosted glass window in the corner behind the cistern. He unhooked the top section and pushed the window. The aperture was very tight, and Simon could not get his hand through the window from the floor. He stepped up onto the side of the toilet pan to gain extra height, grateful he had left his shoes downstairs.

Reaching his arm through the window, Simon tossed the underwear away from the house. He closed the window and eased backwards, ready to dismount the toilet pan. Sikes placed his left foot onto the linoleum floor. The shift in body weight caused his sock-covered foot to slide along the edge of the pan before slipping off the rim into the water in the bowl.

"Oh shit. I haven't even fucking flush that." He was grateful for big feet. Only his toes were wet. He removed his sock and went to wring it until he remembered where it had been.

Simon removed the other sock, partially rolled the wet one into the dry one and stood once again on the pan, this time flushing the pan before he did so.

Opening the window, Sikes threw the socks in what he thought was the same direction as his underwear. He hoped he would be able to find his clothing when he came back later to retrieve it. Closing the window, he climbed down from the pan, unlocked the door and moved swiftly downstairs.

"Where have you been?" asked Sammie as Sikes walked through the door with two more Bacardi's and Coke. "What happened to your socks?"

"I ...er...had a slight accident in the kitchen. Someone tipped something over them, so I had to rinse them and put them to dry." He handed her a drink and sat beside her.

"Nice feet. I like big feet. You know what they say about men with big feet?" Sammie placed the fresh drink alongside the other she still had not finished and turned towards Sikes, placing her right arm around his neck.

"What? That they wear big socks?" Sikes put his lips to hers. He was not really in the mood to continue but did not want to let Sammie down too roughly.

The door opened, and Dicey walked through, followed by his girlfriend.

"Who closed this partition?"

Sikes and Sammie sat upright and stared at Dicey.

"Oh, Sikesy, it's you. I should have guessed. Sorry to bother you. I had a bit of a shock coming down to find all these people here, and the partition pulled across. See you in a bit."

Dicey and his friend went to walk away.

"Dicey. Hang on!" Sikes stood up. "Sorry about the partition, but we wanted some privacy. Have you met Sammie?"

Sammie looked surprised but smiled at Dicey and nodded in greeting.

Dicey looked strangely at Sikes, said hello, and then introduced Amy.

"Great party," said Sikes. "I've really enjoyed it" He smiled at Sammie.

"Er...good. I'm pleased. Perhaps you can give me a hand to clean up in the morning?" replied a confused Mark Dice.

"Tomorrow morning? It's Saturday tomorrow. Shit, I've got to be up early in the morning to take the twins swimming. Sorry, Sammie, I'd better take you home."

"Oh, right." The smile had wholly left her face.

Chubber lived a ten-minute walk from Dicey's house, provided they could cut through the park. The walk seemed much longer as Samantha was silent, confused at the change in events and unhappy at having to climb a small fence to get into the park, which was locked for the night. Simon was quiet, embarrassed at his actions.

The moon shone down, casting long shadows from the Oak trees around the park's perimeter. Simon and Samantha walked silently until they were halfway through Aberdare Park. They stopped just beyond the children's play area.

"Sammie, I'm so sorry. I don't know what came over me. I think it was the drink." Simon's hands dug deeper into his pocket.

"So if you had not been drunk, you wouldn't have gone with me? Is that it?" She glared at Sikes.

"No! No. I'm not saying that. I was happy to be with you...I am happy to be with you. Shit, this is so embarrassing."

"So I'm embarrassing now, am I? Thanks a lot."

"No! You're not embarrassing. You're...you're great. This

is embarrassing. Oh shit...I'd better tell you the truth."

"Please! I'm all ears."

Sikes took a deep breath, blew it out loudly and said, "When we were on the sofa, I was getting really...er...you know, excited ..."

"I thought that was the intention," said Sammie walking a few yards ahead.

"It was. It is. Hang on, let me explain." Simon quickened his pace until he stood beside her.

"Well, get on with it. I don't understand what went on back there. One minute you're all over me with your hand in my knickers. The next, you can't wait to get away from me. Am I so bad that I let you get me off? I have a right to enjoy it too, you know. I didn't hear you complaining."

"No. You did nothing wrong. It's just that I got worked up and..."

"As I said, I thought that was the intention."

"It is, but I didn't mean to come in my pants..."

She stopped dead. "What? You came in your pants?"

"Aye, I did but don't say it so loudly. I don't want everyone to know."

"Fucking hell Simon, it's twenty past two in the morning. We're in the middle of nowhere. Who the fuck is listening?"

"I suppose you're right, but it's still not funny to me." Simon walked toward a nearby bench and sat down. Sammie followed and stood in front of him.

"You mean to tell me you couldn't wait to get away from me just because you shot too soon?"

"Aye. Sad isn't it? Premature ejaculation at my age, I am so embarrassed."

"But why didn't you say something? I wouldn't have been upset. I might even have been quite pleased that a bloke can get off just by getting me off."

"Would you?" said Simon, hopefully.

"Unlikely, but you never know. I just said that to make

you feel better." She shook her head. "So your performance back there was simply to cover your embarrassment?"

"Aye, but you don't know the whole story."

Tears rolled down Sammie's cheeks as Simon explained what had happened to his underpants and the socks.

"You really are an arsehole!"

"Thanks," said Simon, smiling meekly.

"But quite an attractive arsehole." Sammie grabbed Simon's arms and pulled him up. She took his face in her hands and moved his head until she could kiss him.

Simon put his hands around her.

"Come in your pants indeed. Well, we'd better make sure that doesn't happen again."

She glanced around the park and then took Simon's arm. She led him around the back of the bench onto the grass, stopping between three giant Oak trees. The moonlight only reached parts of the grass, and Sammie selected one of the brightest areas. She placed her hands on his shoulders, forcing him down onto the floor.

"What? Here?"

Simon sat on the floor.

"Why not? There's nobody around. It's a private spot, and we've nowhere else to go. We can hardly go back to your mate's house."

"But what if someone comes..."

"That's the intention," said Sammie, putting her hands under her skirt and pulling down her knickers. She lifted one foot out of them.

"You know what I mean," said Simon as Sammie casually kicked her knickers off her other foot. They landed to the right of Simon's arm.

"You worry too much."

Simon sat motionless as Sammie kneeled, undid his trousers and pulled them down below his knees.

"I was right about men with big feet," she said as she sat on Simon before placing her mouth on his.

BOASTING BY THE POOL

The town council erected the swimming pool in the late 1960s. The dark brick and glass façade looked in excellent condition, apart from the odd graffiti message.

The top floor of the building houses the upper viewing gallery, function room, bar, snooker tables, sauna and beauty treatment facility. Three pools, a lower gallery and changing rooms occupy the ground floor.

The first pool, nearest the lower gallery, is a learning pool with a maximum depth of one metre. The walls around the beginners' pool are decorated with images of children's cartoon characters.

The second pool is the main swimming pool. This pool is of competition length, and the depth is one metre at each end and two metres in the middle. At peak times, one end gets cordoned off to provide space for a sizeable inflatable hippopotamus that children play upon.

The third pool is for the exclusive use of those wanting to dive.

Saturday is traditionally a busy day at the pool, whatever the season or weather. Visitors need to arrive early to get the best out of the facilities. By the time Sikes and company arrived, many serious swimmers had already been and gone, happy to get out and dried by the time the rush came. It's not the numbers they seek to avoid but the noise. The shouting and screaming probably exceeded recommended Health and Safety levels. Many of the attendants loathed Saturdays.

After their exploits the previous evening, neither Simon nor GarGar were in any mood to do anything, least of all swim, until late morning. Simon was awoken at eight by Clare shaking him while Philip tried to remove his duvet. Sikes could not allow that. He was completely naked under it.

Four and a half hours of sleep was not enough, and Simon had to resort to bribery to persuade the twins to allow him to stay in bed longer. He was amazed that the promise of gravy and chips from Joe's chip bar still did the trick. He'd even have thrown in a can of cola if necessary.

Eventually getting out of bed at ten-fifteen, Simon took a light breakfast, toast and coffee and rang GarGar. He was out but returned the call on his mobile. They arranged to meet at eleven.

They arrived at the pool at 11.30 am, peak time, much to the delight of Philip and Clare. They loved it when it was busy, but Simon and GarGar thought it was too noisy.

After a quick swim to shake away the cobwebs, Simon and Gareth headed to the middle of the pool, where they sat on the edge with their back to the changing rooms. They dangled their feet in the water at its deepest point.

Sikes watched as the twins jumped off the inflatable, swam around a little and then scrambled back on board the bright orange hippo. He knew the twins would be okay. His mother had put them both through swimming classes, and regular practice had made them proficient swimmers. Simon was grateful for this as he was in no mood for heroics. He kept a watchful eye in case of any trouble.

He looked on in amazement as Philip the brave climbed up to the highest point, the hippo's head, pinched his nose and jumped into the pool. He came close to landing on someone's head, and Simon stood up momentarily to ensure everything was alright. He could only see Philip's shoulders and face. His little brother was looking studiously at the person he almost hit, an older boy. Simon saw that the older boy was talking to Philip and braced himself for trouble, but he relaxed and sat back down when Philip grinned from ear to ear and swam off.

"So where did you disappear to last night?" GarGar asked.

"Oh...um...nowhere, really. We stayed up at Dicey's until about two-ish. I walked Sammie home and then went home to bed myself." He saw no need to go into detail. He kicked his feet in the water. "What about you? You didn't stay around long. One minute you were with the rest of us in the room, next thing, you were gone."

Someone next to them jumped into the air, hitting the pool with an almighty splash. Much of the displaced water landed on Simon and GarGar.

"Bastards," GarGar mumbled.

Simon snorted.

"Come on, tell me then. Where did you get to?"

"Upstairs. Dicey's spare room. That Kelly. Fuck me. What a girl! Do you know what she said to me when we got to Dicey's?

"How would I know?" Simon asked. "You'd better tell me."

"She said she had a three-pack in her pocket and wanted to use them all." Gareth put his lips together and blew through them. "Phew! What could I say? I grabbed a bottle of vodka, a carton of orange juice and two glasses then we nipped upstairs. It took me no time to get her kit off, and we're away. We didn't get to drink much, thank God. I'm not that fussy about vodka." GarGar placed his hand inside his shorts and adjusted himself. "What a night. I never expected that. I thought I might have a chance, but she offered it to me on a plate mun. You should have heard her. 'Gar, I've always fancied you. I've waited a long time for this. Can't wait to get you inside me'. Wherever did she learn things like that? She was exceptional mind, fair play." He shook his head at the memory. "Did you get anywhere with Sammie?"

Simon shook his head. "Fat chance. Where could we go? From what I heard, all the best spots were taken." He scratched under his arm and looked at the inflatable again.

"Come off it. You had your chance. Dicey told me you'd pulled the partition across. Wasn't that private enough for you?"

"Oh aye, that was great! I forgot the fucking thing was

there. As soon as I remembered and pulled it shut, Dicey and whatshername Amy came storming in. I felt a bit awkward." He paddled his feet again. "Anyway, I am not sure Sammie was up for it, first date and all that."

"Well, she's fancied you long enough. That's why Kelly brought her along."

Sikes had guessed as much. "The room was packed," was all he said.

"Are you seeing her again?"

"Aye, tonight. She's coming around my house. I'm looking after the twins while Mam and Dad go to the cinema."

"That sounds promising."

"Hardly, the twins won't leave us alone, and she's off back to Pembroke tomorrow."

"Why don't you take her out this afternoon?"

"She's going to Cardiff with Kelly. Didn't Kelly tell you?"

"We were too busy to talk, mate."

"Aye, aye. What's that smell? Bullshit, I think!" Simon rubbed his hand over his chest and shoulders. "Anyway, when did you see Dicey?"

"This morning at breakfast. Kelly and me stayed up at his house overnight but don't tell anyone. Her mother thinks she stayed with Tommo's sister."

"You lucky bastard. I'm surprised you've got the energy to swim this morning."

Gareth was looking hard at his chest.

"Well, I think I shot my bolt too soon. We'd used up the rubbers before two, and Kelly wouldn't let me go bare back, so we were stuffed. Plenty of touchy, feely and the odd bit of oral, but that only lasts so long. I thought about asking Dicey if he had a few spares, but when I listened at the door, he was obviously in need of them himself. Tell you what though, for a little bloke, he ain't half a randy twat."

Simon laughed.

"So we had no option really but to get some sleep."

"My heart bleeds," said Simon, running his hand

through his wet hair.

"Oh, Sikes! I almost forgot. I've got something to tell you." GarGar excitedly placed his hand on his friend's shoulder, ensuring he had Sikes' full attention. "Some dirty bastard threw his soiled niks onto the fir trees in Dicey's garden last night."

"What? You're joking. How did that happen?" Sikes feigned surprise. He understood why he had failed to find his boxers when he returned to the scene after taking Sammie home.

"Don't know, but we found them this morning. It must have taken ages to get them up there. Right at the top of the trees, they were. Dicey reckons it was Stevie Edwards and his mate; they always get their kit off. Wait until Dicey sees him. We found his socks on top of the carport by the back lane. They were soaking too. We think he probably pissed himself."

"Something like that," thought Sikes.

"Tell you what, pissed or not, they must have worked hard to get them up so high. I know it took us a long time to get them back down. I was a bit pissed off about it, but you know what Dicey is like. He wouldn't stop until he had them. He was on a mission. I suppose his old man would go spare if he had found them. Know how fussy he is about his garden."

"So what happened to the pants and socks?" Sikes wiped an invisible water drop off his shoulder. "Did Dicey keep them as evidence?"

"Nah, they were minging. They went straight in the bin."

"They weren't that bad," thought Sikes before releasing a smile of relief.

"That Stevie is off his head," he said as the twins arrived to push Gareth and him into the pool.

MOTORBIKING

The following Saturday, Simon returned to the park, accompanied by GarGar, Kelly, Dicey, and Amy, to watch the annual motorbike races.

The ordinarily sedate park transforms into the Welsh Motor Cycle Grand Prix venue for two days annually. Motorcycle enthusiasts congregate from across Wales and beyond to see the races featuring motorbikes of various sizes.

Simon felt awkward at being a stool pigeon and wished his mates had told him they were bringing their girls. Kelly's comments about him coming again and shooting off too soon did not help him much. He sensed that Sammie had confided in Kelly, and Sikes was unhappy about it. He could not be sure that GarGar didn't know his secret too.

When he and Sammie had got it together again the previous Saturday evening, after the twins had gone to bed, too full of Chinese food and lemonade to argue, he thought they had made a pact. They would keep the incident at Dicey's to themselves. It was not as though it would happen again, and he believed he had made up for it since. It might have been easier to take had Sammie not shared this secret with a blabbermouth like Kelly. He resolved to split from the group as soon as the opportunity presented itself. That opportunity was not long coming.

Having paid their entrance fees, and as the gang of five made their way through the main gates, Sikes was relieved to see a familiar face.

"See you later. I'm just off to see a mate over there."

The others looked on as Sikes walked to meet the tall thin man with the hooknose. The man seemed a little out of place, wearing light blue trousers, a white open-neck shirt and brown sandals.

Simon waved as he walked from them and saw Amy grab Dicey's arm and drag him away, quickly pacing ahead of Gareth and Kelly. Simon guessed that Amy also wanted privacy. He saw Dicey remove his arm from Amy's grip and place it around her waist. He rested the palm of his hand firmly on her buttock. She put her hand in the back pocket of his jeans.

"Well, Simon, you couldn't wait to shoot off, could you?" said Kelly sneering.

"You don't want me hanging around you like wet lettuce, do you? Have fun." Sikes knew his repost had been feeble and that he would have to speak to Sammie about saying too much.

"We will," said GarGar. Kelly wrapped her arms around his and nestled into his shoulder as they followed their friends up the hill.

Sikes walked over to his workmate.

"Tim, what are you doing here?"

"Hiya Si. Didn't see you there, mun." Timmy was resting against a wall, nursing a full shopping bag. "Nice day innit? Thing is, I bring my lady up here every year. She loves the bikes an' all the doings. What about you?"

"We've come to the races for the last few years." He stood beside Tim and put the sole of his right foot on the wall. "I thought we were having a boys' afternoon, but they brought their girls."

Tim nodded knowingly. "Wasn't that young Amy Tomkins with your friend?"

"I don't know her surname, but her first name is Amy. Do you know her?"

"I do. That's Janice's daughter. You know, Janice from the Mount Street shop."

On visits to the shop, Sikes had heard Janice moaning about her wayward fourteen-year-old daughter and how she had taken up with some older lad. Janice and her husband were unhappy that she often stayed out all night. Sikes was sure Timmytits had made a mistake. He doubted this could be the same Amy.

"Nah. That can't be Janice's daughter. That Amy is my mate's girlfriend. She's studying for her "A" levels in the college at Pontypridd."

"Well, I am sure that is Janice's daughter. I should know because when Janice lived in town, I was big mates with her old man, Cliff. He worked for Harvey's when I first started. Then Janice's mother fell ill, and they moved. He wasn't happy at having to travel to Harvey's, so he left to work in a furniture factory. But we keep in touch, and I've watched young Amy grow up. That's definitely her. You're right about her studying in Ponty, but it's for her GCSEs at the Welsh school, not the college. That mate of yours? He's a bit old for her, isn't he?"

"He thinks that she's seventeen," said Simon.

"Shit. Well, you better tell him the truth and warn him he's playing with dynamite. That's jailbait. She is two years underage. Cliff and Janice will not be best pleased if they find out." Tim heard a door closing, turned his attention away from Simon and broke into a smile. "Here's the light of my life."

Simon saw a petite, well-dressed emerge from the portable toilet. She wore a light flowery dress with a white cardigan over her shoulders and white sandals. She looked older than Sikes would have imagined, but her face, with just a hint of make-up, exuded warmth.

"Dot, I'd like you to meet a good friend of mine, Simon Ikes, also known as my partner in crime at work."

"Hello, Simon. I am pleased to meet you at long last. Tim has told me a lot about you and the tricks you play on the girls in the bakery." She shook Simon's hand.

"It is nice to meet you too. I hope Tim hasn't been saying too many bad things about me?" Simon smiled weakly.

"No, not at all. Tim only says nice things about you. He's very complimentary about his new young mate. He's got high hopes for you, you know."

Simon had not known. He smiled when Timmytits winked at him from behind Dot's back.

"Thing is, I'd better go an' all. Look after the stuff a minute, love."

Simon jumped at an opportunity to move on.

"I must dash as well. I'd better catch up with my mates, or they'll wonder where I've gone. It's been nice to meet you, Dot. See you on Monday, Tim."

Tim and Dot bade farewells, and Simon walked up the main path towards the race circuit. At the top of the slight incline, where the bandstand lies to the left and the lake and shop are to the right, Simon stopped to take stock. He could see his friends settling amongst the crowds on the embankment in front of him, so he decided to avoid that area for the time being.

The racing circuit passed by where he stood, and Simon thought this might be an ideal vantage point for spectating. However, crowds quickly formed around him, and e gave up on that plan, deciding he had earned a drink.

Looking to his right, just behind the point where the circuit passed by the shop, Simon could see a sign for "Stainthorpe's beer". He headed towards it. Moving slowly through the crowds, Sikes reached a small wall of hay bales strategically placed around the track's perimeter. Sikes ran across the road following the Stainthorpe's sign, squeezing through a narrow gap. A steward shouted at him.

"Hey, Sikesy, get your arse off that track!"

He knew the voice instantly and turned toward it. Miko still had the same dark complexion and curly jet-black hair he had as a child. Mrs Ikes had often commented that people would die for hair like that. Miko's bib partially covered a black T-shirt that had risen out of black cargo trousers.

"Miko!" Simon walked toward him. "Why are you dressed like that?"

"Impressive, eh?" Miko stretched the luminous top. "It's a favour to Chris. He's helped to arrange things this year, and I agreed to give him a hand."

"You get in everywhere! Has Chris still got his bike

shop?"

"Yup, but it's not just bikes now. He deals in cars too. I'm working for him as a trainee mechanic. I take my finals next year. We're pretty busy fair play. What about you?"

"Just waiting for my A-level results. Working at Harvey's bakery at the moment, I cannot plan anything until my results come through."

"How's your family doing? Are your parents and the twins ok?" Miko glanced around to ensure the others were still placing bales. They were.

"Fine, thanks. How is your mother?"

"Yes, she's fine, ta. No problems. We are still living in the same place. It's got a bit rougher lately. We want Mam to move, but she won't hear of it. Too many memories, I think. Funnily enough, she was only asking about you last week. She pulled out some old photos to show my girlfriend, and you are in almost all of them."

"Girlfriend, eh? Who is that, then? Anyone I'd know?"

"Unlikely, her name is Donna...Donna Thomas. She's from the top estate but has only lived there for about two years. I've been with her about three months now."

"How did you meet her?"

"She kept coming into the garage with problems with the car. It was all just an excuse to see me, really."

"As if..."

"Michael, are you working here or what?" shouted a voice behind them. "Oh, sorry, Simon didn't know it was you."

Simon recognised Chris immediately. He was an older version of Miko but without curly hair. Since Simon had last seen him, Chris had put on a bit of weight.

Chris looked like a typical biker with leather trousers, black leather boots and a black T-shirt. He carried a heavy-duty black leather jacket covered in sponsors' logos. Chris held his free hand out towards Sikes.

"God. I haven't seen you in years, mun. The last time must have been when I brought Mam up to see your mother and father just after they had the twins. When was that? Six years ago?"

"Aye about that."

"Are they all okay?"

"Aye, not bad, thanks."

They exchanged small talk. Chris explained that he had married Paula Jenkins a couple of years earlier. They lived in the new estate on the edge of the village with their two small children. Dan was three, and Ben was eighteen months. His business was growing, and he had often thought about asking Sikes' father to become his accountant. Chris told him that his mother thought the world of the Ikes family and still went on about the antics that Michael and Simon got up to when they were younger.

"She always lets us know if she meets your mother in town and takes any excuse to get the photo albums out."

"She's a lovely lady. She helped Dad and me a lot when Mam was ill." Sikes did not want to think sad thoughts. "We used to have a good old time, didn't we, Miko?"

Miko grinned as he nodded in agreement. Chris spotted that his brother was genuinely pleased to see his friend again.

"Tell you what, Mike. Give us back that bib, and we'll call it a day as far as you are concerned. Those bales are in place. The safety steward has already given us the green light, so it's only the extra finishing touches. The lads can handle that. You speak to Simon. He looks like he could do with the company."

"Thanks, Chris. Is that okay, Si?"

"Aye, great. You can buy me a pint with all this overtime money you're earning."

"Overtime? Who said anything about overtime?" Chris laughed. "He said he'd do me a favour. I pay him enough as it is." He reached into his jacket pocket and removed a card. "Tell you what, though, take this pass. It'll get you in the sponsors' section of the beer tent. I've got a spare, so you can have this one." Miko took the plastic card from his brother. "Good to see you, Simon." They shook hands again. "Don't leave it so long next time. Call over to see us. Mike will give you my address." He looked up the track. One of his team was waving at him and pointing toward the starting point. He held up a hand to show that he had received the message. "Right, I've got to fly, lads. Enjoy the races, and I'll catch you later."

Miko and Sikes sauntered to the Stainthorpe's tent, reminiscing about their younger days. The public tent was packed to capacity with queues at every service point. Crowds of people had gathered in the surrounding grass area, and most held a drink.

A couple of oversized men stood at the entrance to the beer tent. Both wore Stainthorpe's T-shirts. One had his eyes covered with dark glasses. They stared at Simon and Michael as they approached. Miko held up the pass, but the sunglasses man held up a hand to stop them.

"You need to go through the gate to my right." He said in a voice that suggested he gargled glass.

Sikes and Mike did as directed. They followed a corded path, around the back of the tent, to a gap in the wooden fence blocked by what looked like a nine-foot, twenty-stone gorilla wearing a suit and tie. Miko waved the pass again, and the giant stood aside to allow them in. No words got spoken, but Simon still felt intimidated.

"Shit. I wouldn't want to tangle with him," Sikes whispered once they were safely inside.

"He's probably gay," said Miko.

"What? Serious?" Simon looked back at the bouncer.

"Doubt it," said Miko. "Anyway, no need to worry about him. Do you want beer or lager?"

"I'll have a beer, please."

"It's free, you know, this bar. It's for sponsors and reps only. You grab a bench, and I'll get the beers in."

"I'm in Heaven," said Sikes as Miko disappeared into the large tent.

The large fenced area contained several wooden benches and parasols. The smell of freshly cooked meat filled the air.

Simon saw a barbecue smoking away close to one end of the enclosure. Surrounding tables were filled with people eating food off paper plates.

Taking a table nearest to the tent, Simon sat with his elbows resting on the wooden surface. He surveyed the area. It was less than half full, and Sikes smiled smugly at the thought of the long queues at the other end of the tent, just a short distance away.

Looking back at the food eaters, he became transfixed on a girl sitting at the bench nearest the barbecue. Another fair-haired girl and a dark-haired man accompanied her. He looked like a motorcyclist with long hair and a scruffy T-shirt. Simon saw that he was also wearing cut-down denim.

"Who wears shorts on a day like this?" thought Sikes. "It's not exactly boiling."

He returned his attention to the girl. Her navy vest blew freely in the light breeze, and Simon thought he saw a navy bra beneath the vest. Her blonde shoulder-length hair was gathered into a short ponytail at the back, revealing the true beauty of her face and the smoothness of her neck. Simon hoped he was not beginning to drool as he observed her bringing a bread roll up to her mouth and biting into it with shiny white teeth. He shifted in his seat.

Replacing the roll on her paper plate, the girl picked up a napkin to cover her elegant middle finger and remove any crumbs from her mouth. She took care not to rub too hard in case she smudged her lipstick. Simon's head tilted to one side as she stretched her mouth to wipe it before placing the napkin back on the table and reaching, instead, for her drink. Sikes swallowed with her as she took a sip from the glass. Holding the drink away from her lips, she allowed her tongue to emerge slowly and travel gracefully over her nigh-perfect lips. She covered both lips in one motion.

Sikes suddenly felt uncomfortable as he realised that the watcher had become the watched. Looking from the girl to her companions, his eyes met those of the male companion, grinning widely. The man said something to the girls, and all three looked at Sikes. He flushed as the lush blonde, and the other female laughed. He turned his head away quickly to inspect the tabletop. He heard their laughter and lowered his head further.

Miko returned with the drinks and was stunned at the speed with which Simon finished his pint.

"Christ, Sikes. You got a drink problem?"

"Don't think so. I'm just thirsty. Same again?"

"Yeah, okay. Could you get me a fresh one? I got us the Special. Okay?"

"Aye. I won't be long."

Simon was a bit taken aback by the low light inside the tent. His eyes took a moment to adjust. Around him were more tables, occupied by stiffs in suits, while other men stood by the bar in bibs or overalls. He did not see a female face. A large table to the side of the bar was occupied by a small, suited, moustached man with cropped hair, reading from a clipboard, and four other suited men, apparently hanging on the man's every word. Simon ignored them and made his way to the bar.

"Two pints of Special, please."

The barman reached for two fresh glasses and walked to the next available pump.

"Didn't your mother ever tell you it was rude to stare?"

Simon looked to his right to see the longhaired biker who had caught him looking at the girl.

Shit, what if it is his girlfriend? He thought before he said, "Aye, sorry. I didn't mean to, but…"

"You couldn't help yourself. Is that what you're trying to say?"

The man's accent, while Welsh, was not local. It reminded Sikes of GarGar's uncle from Swansea.

"Aye, sorry," were his words. Here it comes. Be ready, were his thoughts.

"Don't worry about it, pal. She gets it all the time. She's stunning, isn't she?" The man leaned on the bar.

Where is this going? Sikes thought, wishing the barman would hurry up. "Yes, she is indeed," he said.

"Her sister's even prettier. I should know. I've been going out with her long enough."

Pennies dropped into place, but Sikes was still unsure what the man wanted.

"Ah right. You're a lucky man," he said weakly.

"I think I am. Jamie's the name. Jamie Johnson." He reached out a hand.

"Simon. Simon Ikes." His hand trembled a little as they shook.

"Don't be afraid. I'm not here to hit you. I'm sorry we were laughing. It's just that Laura spotted you earlier, and we just found it funny that you were looking at her too. It's odd, you know. She gets looked at all the time, but lads seem scared to talk to her. I hope I didn't embarrass you or anything."

"Nah, not really. I get embarrassed about anything me."

The barman placed Sikes' beer on the counter.

"Will there be anything else?"

"Would you like a drink...er...Jamie is it?"

"Aye, that's right. Go on, then. I'll have a pint and two halves of lager, please. Thanks, pal. Thanks a lot."

"Don't worry about it," said Sikes. "It's not as though I'm paying, is it?" He picked up his pint and sipped from it.

Jamie laughed aloud.

"Nice one, pal. I didn't think of that. Would I like a drink!"

Sikes smiled as he picked up the other beer. He turned and headed out of the tent to re-join Miko. As he walked into the sunlight, he saw the girl looking directly at him. He flushed again, smiled and lowered his head.

A good afternoon's motor bike racing followed more beers. The sun shone brightly, making Sikes wish he had worn his shorts. The conversation never stopped as Sikes and Miko caught up on each other's activities in the time since they had last met and relived past glories. Simon was thoroughly enjoying himself.

With the final race over, the pair made their way through the crowds back to the sponsor's tent. It was much busier, and Simon had to fight his way to the bar. Collecting two pints, he joined Miko, who had established base camp on a small table.

"I'm just off for a piss," said Miko as Simon returned. "I won't pee long!"

"Aye, hilarious. First time I heard that, I fell out of my pram."

Simon took a mouthful of beer and stared out through the gaps in the wood-panelled fence. He saw masses of people making their way to the exits, having enjoyed a good afternoon's entertainment. He saw the children's playground was awash with children and recalled his own visits to the park. His grandparents and his mother had usually accompanied him; his father would have been at work. Beyond the playground, Simon saw the large Oak trees that had been so many things to him over the years. While playing football with his Granddad, they had served as goalposts, hide-outs when his family tried to find him, and more recently, had provided a love nest for his activity with Sammie. He wondered what she was doing at this moment

"Hi there, my name is Justin, and I was wondering whether I could ask you a few questions?" asked a small, suited, moustached man with cropped hair carrying a clipboard.

Sikes sometimes had a problem with the Welsh accent, notably a broad south Wales accent as possessed by Justin. He thought it sometimes sounded too camp, almost effeminate. Simon knew he and his friends had been guilty of calling other lads gay simply because of how they spoke. Sikes had no such problems with the north Wales accent which, in contrast, he thought to be very coarse, rough sounding, as though the owner spoke from the back of their throat. This man's south Wales accent was very smooth, perhaps too much. Sikes thought Justin sounded very effeminate.

He wondered what the man wanted.

"Aye, go on then."

"Have you had a good day?"

"Great, thanks."

"Me too. Oh, wasn't it exciting? My God, those bikes can move, can't they? However do they manage to stay on them? I don't know, the riders are so brave."

Gay, thought Sikes. "Suppose so," he said.

"Right then, let's get down to it. My name's Justin. As I've said, just in case you weren't paying attention, hee hee hee. That's just my little joke."

Definitely gay," thought Simon as he faked a smile.

"I work for Stainthorpe's brewery in Cardiff. Now Stainthorpe's are expanding into the Valleys, and to help them with that process, I'd like to ask you a few questions. It's part of our market research. If you're a good boy and give me the right answers, there'll be a little prize for you. Would you like that? Course you would Hee hee hee."

Absolutely no doubt, thought Simon. "Aye, great," he said without enthusiasm.

"Can I ask you your name, address and age? Don't worry. You can tell me the truth. I won't tell anyone. Hee hee hee."

Aw fuck it, thought Simon. "Simon Ikes, that's I-K-E-S." He gave his address and then added. "I'll be 19 in November."

"Course you will hee hee hee. You live in Ty Bach. Small house, bet it's no such thing. Bet you live in a mansion, don't you, eh?" Justin moved his elbow and gave Simon a slight dig in the ribs.

Sikes offered a pathetic excuse for a grin as he thought, why did I ever agree to this?

Justin took an age to ask Sikes questions and record his answers on the paper on his clipboard. The conversation was constantly punctuated by Justin's little jokes, innuendos and curious body movements. The area around them was becoming more crowded, and Sikes was sure people were listening to them and, he feared, mocking them. To make matters worse, Justin appeared to get louder the more people looked at him. And they were looking at him.

"Thank you for that, Simon, or can I call you Si?"

No, you fucking can't, was what he wanted to say. "Aye, whatever," was all he said.

"Thanks, Si. Now please read this list. You can read, I hope. Hee hee hee."

You're going to have one off me in a minute, thought Sikes, nodding meekly.

"Oh, I'm so glad hee hee hee. Which of these brands are known to you?"

Simon scanned the list and picked a couple of names at random.

"That's lovely. Not much longer now. The end is nigh, Si. Hee hee hee. Do you get it? Nigh Si. I always was a bit of a poet. Hee hee hee. I could have been the next Dylan Thomas."

One more. Just one more, and you are dead. Again, Sikes nodded, smiled lamely, but said nothing.

I see you've picked Stainthorpe's, which I am happy about, as it means you get your prize. Are you excited?"

"Ecstatic."

"Good, good. Now, if you wouldn't mind looking at this list and telling me which Stainthorpe's brands you have tried and which you would try again? Sorry to ask you to work so hard, but I promise it'll be worth it."

Sikes looked at the list and picked off a few. Most were selected randomly, except Stainthorpe's Special, for which he was developing a taste.

"Excellent. You like your Special, do you? I had you down as a special fella myself. Hee hee hee."

Sikes winced as Justin nudged him in the ribs with his elbow again.

"Now, what is a big strapping lad like you doing next weekend?"

This bloke is going too far, thought Sikes taking a deep breath. "Why?" he asked.

"Because I've got a special offer for you that I'm only giving to people I like. You get a date with a few of my special friends and me."

"Eh? What do you mean? What are you trying to say? I ain't like that," said Simon, raising his voice. More people were looking. They were looking at him.

Justin looked horrified. He had not anticipated such a reaction. It had never happened before. He was embarrassed and decided to finish this one quickly.

"No...no...I never meant to say you were... it was just my little joke." He quickly rattled off the end of his speech. "Now, as a reward for answering my questions, I'd like to offer you a free meal for two, the food is free, but you pay for any drinks at the re-opening of the Red Lion next Saturday. Do you know where the Red Lion is?"

Sikes nodded. His head bowed.

"Good. Stainthorpe's have spent a lot of money doing up the place and are throwing a celebratory party on opening night. Hope to see you there." He handed Simon two vouchers.

Simon took them and thanked him.

"No problem. Bye Si."

"Clearly a nutcase. He's probably a drug user." Justin said to himself as he hurried through the crowd. "He seemed such a nice boy at first. We were having a laugh. Whatever got into him? It was just a little harmless innuendo. Mind you, Avril warned me to be wary of these Valley lads. She was right, but then she is usually right. The sooner I get home to her and the kids, the better. It's not safe up here." Reaching the sanctuary of the tent, he composed himself and looked for his next victim.

Simon was pleased to see Miko return.

"Sorry Sikes. Saw a mate of my brother round the back there. Got talking, you know how it is. Much happened?"

"Nah. You ain't missed much" Simon slipped the

vouchers into his back pocket and drank his beer.

Sikes and Miko recounted more tales of their youth as they consumed more beer. The evening air was warm, and Simon quickly forgot about his incident with Justin.

When it was Simon's turn to replenish the drink, he pushed his way through the crowd. Nearing the entrance to the tent, he found his route blocked, so he cut back sharply to try a different path. He cut back a little too sharply and walked straight into the back of another guest.

"Oh! Watch it, pal," said the man trying not to drop his drink.

"Sorry, I was just..."

The man straightened up and looked at Sikes. "Ah, Simon, I didn't know it was you."

Sikes found himself next to Jamie Johnston. He stood with his arm around his girlfriend. Laura sat on the edge of a bench opposite.

"Sorry, Jamie, but I couldn't get through over there."

"No worries, pal." Jamie turned his upper body away from Simon toward the two girls. "Hey Laura, this is Simon I was telling you about." He faced Sikes. "Simon, this is the beautiful Laura we were talking about, and this is her gorgeous sister Caitlin."

"Stop it, Jamie," said Caitlin. "You're making him blush."

"And me," said Laura.

After only hearing two words, Sikes thought he could fall in love with that voice.

"Hello," he said.

"That was a great afternoon. Does this happen every year?" asked Jamie, his once smooth face punctured by emerging stubble.

"Aye, pretty much. You haven't been before then?" Simon was not quite confident enough to look at Laura, so he focused on Jamie.

"No, we've only just moved up here. Well, these two have, and I will move up shortly as soon as I can find a flat."

Jamie turned towards the ladies again. "Their father has just bought a pub in town. Ain't that right, Laura?"

"Yes, the Bird in Hand. Do you know it?"

Sikes felt he had no choice but to look at her. He looked into blue eyes. Laura was still smiling at him, and Sikes felt as if he was glowing. He remembered the question.

"Yes, aye. I don't go there much, though. It's a bit of a … not my cup of tea, if you know what I mean."

"Go on, say it. It's a bit of a dump. Don't be afraid to say what you think. We agree with you, don't we, Cait?"

Caitlin nodded in agreement as Laura continued.

"But Mum and Dad have high hopes for it, and it's not as though we'll be there much."

Simon noticed the way she called her mother Mum, not Mam.

"Why? Where are you going then?"

"I hope to go to university, and Cait will move in with Jamie."

Simon had no interest in Caitlin and Jamie's plans.

"Which university?" He hoped he hadn't sounded too eager.

"I've been accepted in Cardiff, but it depends on my results. Why do you ask?"

Simon noticed how her hands gripped the bench on either side of her body as she rocked back and forth gently. He swallowed hard before replying. "I'm going to university myself if my results are good enough, so I was just curious."

Simon and Laura discussed their planned courses and what grades they hoped to achieve. The conversation continued, and Simon had forgotten about Miko and beer.

It was Jamie who broke the exchange.

"Hey, Cait. We'd better be off," he said. "I'm due to start at half nine, and I haven't showered yet. You'll be okay here, won't you, Law? Simon will look after you, won't you, Si?"

"Er… yes, aye, sure …no problem. If you want to stay, that is."

"Of course she does," said Caitlin winking at her sister. "She wanted to get to meet some locals. In any case, it's only a short walk home."

Laura knew when she had been duped.

"That's fine. I'll stay here with Simon. You two have a good night. Hey Jamie! Break a leg, you bastard." She hugged her sister. "I'll see you later."

Jamie smiled, patted Simon on the back and blew Laura a kiss as he and Caitlin walked towards the exit.

Simon collected two more pints and, in a change from the previous rounds, a half of lager. He carried all three glasses at once, hoping he did not get bumped on his return journey. Laura waited for him by the table, and Simon was pleased to find her alone on his return. He held out the glasses, and she took her lager. She was surprised that Simon was carrying two more pints.

"Thirsty are we?"

"Eh? He saw her look at the pints of beer. "No, sorry. I've just got to take a pint to my mate. He's up at the end there. I'll be back in a second if you want to wait here."

"I'll come with you if that's okay?"

"Aye…sure." Sikes led the way. He was uncertain what Miko would make of this development.

The chat was easy and flowing, but Miko noticed how Simon's questions were no longer targeted at him. Sikes's attention was on Laura. Miko volunteered to get more drinks even though Simon's consumption had slowed markedly. He was not halfway through his pint while Miko and Laura nursed empty glasses. He returned with a pint and a half.

"Sorry, Sikes, I've got to go. Donna's picking me up at eight, and it's ten to now. It's been good to see you again. I had a great time. Give us a ring. My number hasn't changed." He turned to face the newcomer. "It's been lovely to meet you too, Laura. All the best with the pub and your results."

Laura smiled.

"Yes, thanks. It was nice to meet you too. Hope to see you again sometime."

Sikes grabbed Miko and hugged him.

"Cheers, Miko. Look after yourself. I'll give you a ring. Maybe if you're free, we'll go out next weekend?"

"Yeah, great. See you both. Have fun." Miko made his way through the crowd.

"He's a nice boy. Have you known him long?"

"All my life," said Sikes without hesitation. "He was my first and is my longest-lasting mate."

Even if he is a lousy liar, thought Simon. "Meeting Donna my arse. He had already told me he was not seeing her tonight, and his mobile was in a different pocket. He's obviously 'phoned her to come and pick him up. Nice one, Miko."

"What did he call you? Psyched?"

He laughed. "No Sikes. Simon Ikes, Sikes see? Everyone calls me it. Have done for as long as I can remember."

"Thank God for that. I was a bit worried then."

The pair continued talking, oblivious that the crowd around them had thinned out markedly. By the time Laura noticed, only four others were in the area, and the bartenders were packing up.

"I suppose we'd better make a move," she said.

They left the park and strolled towards town, still chatting away eagerly. The church clock struck ten. Time had flown. Sikes did not want the evening to end and hoped he had found a way to make it last longer. He saw the Indian restaurant on the corner of the high street. He checked his pocket. His money was intact.

"Do you like Indian food?"

"Yes. Is that a good one?"

"It's not bad." Sikes nodded towards the restaurant. "If we get in there now, we'll get a table. They're normally quite empty until the pubs turn out. Do you fancy it?"

"I do, but I haven't much money. She reached into the pocket of her shorts and pulled out a note and some change.

Sikes had forgotten she was wearing shorts.

"Are you warm enough?"

"Yes, I'm fine, thanks. It's not cold even at this time of night."

Sikes had not noticed until now.

"Don't worry about the money. It'll be my treat. I haven't spent a penny all day, and I'm starving."

"Okay, then I'll pay next time."

"Great," said Sikes letting Laura take his hand as they crossed the road.

The restaurant was empty apart from a crowd of eight at the table nearest to the bar. To his disappointment, Simon saw the party comprised Robyn, Farley, Chockie, Mrs Chockie and two other couples that Simon did not know.

A waiter met them at the door and led them to a corner table. Simon sat with his back to the other customers. That did not stop him from having to hear Farley's gang making pathetic jokes and stereotypical, racist comments.

Hey, Shuna, two more fire waters over here.

That was chicken I just ate, wasn't it? It wasn't dog?

"Nice people," said Laura. "I see every town has its share of dickheads."

Simon did not admit to knowing them.

When the waiter called to take their order, he made a few suggestions based on what he had enjoyed on previous visits. They kept their head down as they chatted.

Eventually, the other group called for the bill, and Sikes shivered nervously when Farley's voice filled the restaurant.

"Hey, Robyn! Look who it is. It's Sikesy, sexy Sikesy. He's with a lady." He pronounced lady as lay-dee.

Sikes sensed people approaching and readied himself.

Two hands came down heavily on his shoulders.

"Who's the lady Sikesy? You've picked a cracker there, mate." Farley was oblivious to the awkward silence. "If I may say, it makes a nice change to see you out without your boyfriends. I thought you three were joined at the hip."

Sikes did not turn around. He knew Farley's party would be laughing at the comments.

"Sorry," Sikes mouthed to Laura.

Laura smiled, showing she understood.

"Aren't you going to introduce us then?"

Simon faced Farley and noticed the customary plaster half way up Farley's left arm.

"Laura, this is Dave Farley..." as Robyn arrived at his side. "...and Robyn, his girlfriend."

Robyn closely examined Laura before she said, "And your friend Si. I knew you before I met Dave remember?"

How could he forget?

"Sorry, Rob." He looked back at Laura. "Robyn and I have known each other since we were tiny. Our parents are big friends. Is that better, Rob?" He looked up at her.

"It'll do." Robyn's eyes met his, and she smiled.

"Law-ra is it?" asked Farley.

"Yes, Laura," said Laura. She met his stare and maintained eye contact.

"It's nice to meet you, Law-ra."

"The feeling's mutual."

Simon thought he ought to say something.

"Where are you off to now?"

Farley took his eyes off Laura to look at Sikes.

"Back up Chockie's," said Farley. "We're having a bit of a party. The syndicate had a big win on the horses today, so we're celebrating. Do you want to come with us?"

"No... not tonight, thanks," said Simon firmly, well as firmly as he could manage. While Dave had diverted his gaze, he spotted that Robyn was still studying Laura.

Farley spoke again.

"What about you, Law-ra? Do you fancy coming to a party? It'll be more fun than being stuck with boring old Sikes here. He'll be lost without his buddies."

Simon grew more embarrassed but said nothing.

"Don't be horrible to Simon, Dave," said Robyn. "Leave him alone. Simon's alright. You've said so yourself."

Simon was pleased that Robyn had spoken up for him but was unsure what to make of Farley's endorsement.

Farley giggled and said, "He knows I'm only joking. Seriously though, Sikes, you are both welcome to join us."

Laura spoke before Sikes had a chance to open his mouth.

"We're fine here, thanks. We've had a lovely day, and I'm enjoying getting to know Sikes."

Hmm, I'm Sikes now. He thought. That's progress.

"Well, suit yourself. I hope you have a lovely evening. Don't take offence. I was only teasing, honest." He looked at Laura while pointing at Simon. "He's a good lad, is Sikes. We're old mates, and he knows I'm kidding. Don't you, Si?" He playfully thumped Simon's shoulder.

"Aye. You're a hell of a boy you are, Dave." Simon was a poor liar.

"That's right. We like a laugh, don't we, Sikes." Farley turned to face his crew. "Are we ready then? Come on, let's get this party started. Ricko. Have you booked the taxis?"

"They should be outside anytime now."

The rest of the gang walked to the door.

"We'd better be off, said Robyn. "Hope you have a nice night."

"You too," said Sikes.

"Bye," said Laura.

Farley held Robyn's hand as they cut between two tables to join their friends.

"Good man. See you Shuna," he said. "Keep the curry hot, and the lager chilled. We'll be back soon." He looked back. "See you, Sikesy and you Law-ra. Don't do anything I wouldn't do. That gives you plenty of choices, eh Rob?"

Robyn smiled but said nothing.

"Aye, see you," said Simon waving.

Sikes sighed as the restaurant door closed behind the

parting gang.

"Sorry about that."

"Don't worry about it."

Her smile reassured Sikes, but her next question surprised him.

"Is Robyn an old girlfriend or something?"

"Robyn? No. We're just good friends."

He realised how pathetic his response was. He saw Laura smirking as she tried to hide her mouth behind her napkin.

"No, we've grown up together, but there never was anything between us."

"Oh right. Then why did she check me out so much? She made me feel much more uncomfortable than that dickhead boyfriend of hers."

"Not sure...perhaps she's just very protective of me. We've known each other a long time."

"I'll believe you. Thousands wouldn't." She looked into his eyes. "I thought I had competition then."

"No chance," said Simon, laughing. He wondered if she was teasing.

"That food was great," confessed Laura as they strolled toward her family pub. "I enjoy a good curry. Thank you."

"I enjoyed it too. We even had free entertainment. Did you know we had clowns in this town?"

Laura laughed.

They walked beyond the entrance to the pub and took the next turning. Simon stopped and rested against a whitewashed wall. Laura stood a short distance in front of him.

"I've had a brilliant afternoon," she said. "It's been a great day. I thoroughly enjoyed it."

"Me too," said Simon.

"The company was great too." Laura stepped in closer. "I'm pleased I met you. Thank you for taking such good care of me."

"It was my pleasure," Simon said. "I'm glad I met you too."

"Where shall we go next time? That is if you want a next time?"

"Yes, of course, I do." He could not wait.

Laura leaned forward and pecked him on the lips.

"Good" was all she said. Her face hovered in front of his, waiting. She did not have to wait long.

Simon placed his arms around her waist and pulled her to him. His mouth met hers. He could smell her perfume and taste her breath. Both were to his liking. Laura was not slow to respond when he kissed her more passionately. She placed her hands first on his shoulders, then around the back of his head, as the intensity increased.

AFTER BEFORE

The corridor was long and felt cold despite the heating system being at full blast. There was an old-fashioned feel about the place, which was hardly surprising as the refurbishment programme had not yet reached this section. It would not do so for another three months. In the meantime, they were stuck with it.

Fluorescent strips, placed at regular intervals along the corridor, provided light. Not all of them worked properly. The one in the middle, a little distance from where they sat, was beginning to irritate. On-off. On. Off. On-off. The intermittent and irregular flashing was getting on his nerves. It did not take much for things to get on his nerves. He looked the other way. The clock at the end of the corridor read two-forty. No change.

"Dad, when can I see Mam?" The eight-year-old boy shifted uneasily on the uncomfortable wooden bench in the waiting area for the intensive care ward.

"When the doctors tell us that we can see her." The father squeezed his son's hand tightly, fighting to hold back his tears. Why had he gone out? The event was nothing to do with him. He had only gone for a pint and a laugh. Some laugh it had turned out to be. He had gone to have a bit of a break, some break.

"Go on. We'll be okay. Nothing's going to happen tonight." She had assured him before he left. "It'll be alright."

It wasn't alright. Something did happen. This had happened. Why had he drunk? If he had stayed sober, he could have brought her here. He wouldn't have had to wait for the ambulance. Why had that taken so long to arrive? They lost precious minutes. They had wasted valuable time.

That voice again. That sweet, innocent voice. That sweet, innocent, angelic voice. That sweet, innocent, angelic voice was starting to hurt him.

"What did the doctor say to you just now, Dad?"

"Oh...er...nothing really. He just wanted to tell me that Mam was being looked after and was in good hands." He saw no reason to tell the little one the truth at this stage. That could come later. Much later.

"But Dad, why can't we see her now? We've been here ages."

"I know that, but we have to be patient. Mam has had a severe accident, and the doctors want to ensure she's okay before we can go in. We want her to be fit to see us don't we?"

"Yes, Dad."

Silence for a moment. Peace. Would he ever be at ease in this dreadful place? If only he had stayed at home. Everything would have been fine. This monstrous event wouldn't have happened. What did happen? The ambulance man said something about calling the police. Why would he want to do that? Why did the police have to be involved? He remembered seeing glass. There was glass on the stairs. He spotted it as he ran to make sure his son was okay. The glass was close to the landing window. He visualised the scene. The landing window was smashed. How had that happened? Was it deliberate? He pictured a stone. Was there a stone on the landing? Was it a stone, or was it a brick? Why was there a brick on the landing? What was it doing there?

The angelic voice spoke again.

"Mam will be okay, won't she, Dad? She will won't she? And the baby? Is the baby going to be okay, Dad? When can we take Mam and the baby home, Dad? When?"

"I don't know, son." He wiped a tear from his eye. "We'll know more when the doctors come out after seeing your mother. I'm sure they'll tell us more when they are ready." For the moment, he had heard enough. He had heard things he had not wanted to hear. Things no husband on earth would like to hear. Certainly, things no father should have to hear. He let go of his son's hand and hugged the boy tightly, squeezing the little boy's slight shoulders. He placed his forehead on his son's head and let his tears flow.

SUNDAY LOVELY SUNDAY

Simon Ikes hated Sundays. Nothing ever happened on Sunday. It was the most boring day of the week. He could not recall the last time anything exciting happened on a Sunday. Sundays were horrible. Sundays were a waste of a day. Usually.

This Sunday was different. This Sunday, he had something to look forward to. This Sunday, he would be seeing Laura again. Laura, Law-ra, Laura. The name slipped easily off his tongue. Thank God for Sundays.

Lying in bed with his arms behind his head, Sikes looked forward to the evening ahead.

He and Laura had arranged to go to The Venue where Jamie would perform. Sikes should have known Jamie was a musician. He was so confident, so extrovert. Who else would have taken such steps to bring Laura and him together? So what if he had embarrassed Simon in the opening exchanges? He had helped Simon meet the girl with blonde hair, Laura. He would never have had the confidence to speak to her otherwise.

Had Jamie spoken the truth when he said Laura had noticed Sikes before the incident in the sponsors' beer garden? Had he really commented about him to her sister and Jamie? Was that the reason why they found Sikes's stare so funny? He hoped Jamie was telling the truth. He wanted it to be the truth. Why else should he say it?

Sikes was so pleased he had spoken to Jamie. Jamie was totally unlike anyone that Simon had met previously. But then, Laura was different from any girl Sikes had met before, so there must be something about them. He thought he knew what made them different, confidence. Simon felt his new friends were much more confident than the people he usually encountered. How confident was Jamie to approach him at the bar? Extremely confident. Equally, Laura must be supremely confident in agreeing to stay with a stranger. How did they acquire such self-assurance? Where did it come from?

Sikes guessed it had something to do with them being from out of town. Local people didn't seem so assured. He could not imagine a local girl he had just met agreeing to stay with him and Miko. Sikes found it strange that he had met three outsiders recently, and they all possessed confidence. Jamie. Laura and Sammie had shown far greater confidence than any local girls he had ever met, except for Kelly, but then Kelly was a one-off.

A thought brought him back to reality.

"Sammie! Shit. What should I do about Sammie? I am supposed to be seeing her next weekend. She is coming up especially. How can I put her off?"

He told himself to relax. He would think of something. Friday was another five days away. Today was Sunday. Sunday, lovely Sunday.

"Let's make the most of this wonderful day," said Simon to nobody in particular. Rising from his bed, Simon put on a T-shirt and shorts.

Opening his curtains, he saw that the back lane was deserted. He whistled as he linked the tie-backs to the hooks on the wall and then made his way downstairs.

He ignored the sarcastic opening comments from his father, who was carrying a bottle of car wash liquid out of the front door.

"Good God, Simon. It's not even ten o'clock yet. Feeling okay, are we?

"Morning Dad. Yes, I am fine, thank you. How are you?"

His father did not answer. He laughed as he exited the house.

His mother shouted from the living room.

"Good morning Simon."

Simon poked his head around the door to see her sitting on the sofa eating a piece of toast while reading the Sunday paper. The paper was spread out on the couch in front of her, and she was leaning over it, examining every word. Mrs Ikes was taking her regular, mid-morning, five-minute break for breakfast and a cup of tea. A radio played softly in the background.

"Morning Mam. You okay?"

"I am but are you?"

"Yes, fine, thanks. Why?"

"Well, your father is correct. It is unusual for you to be up so early on a Sunday."

Simon shrugged. "It's a nice day, and I thought I make the most of it. Do you fancy a cuppa?"

"No thanks, just got one." She held up her cup to prove it. "There should be one in the pot if you want it."

"Cheers." Simon walked into the kitchen and grabbed a mug from the green monkey mug tree that Clare had brought back from a visit to Bristol Zoo. The mug tree was obviously out of place in this plush kitchen, but Mam insisted they use it. Reaching the fridge door, he saw the "Happy Mother's Day" pictures the twins had prepared the previous March. They were looking a little faded now, but the fridge magnets, one a giraffe and the other a monkey, held them firmly. The magnets had constituted Philip's present from the zoo.

Gathering the milk from the top shelf, Simon poured some into the mug and then put the container back on the shelf before closing the door. The teapot was covered in a furry rabbit tea cosy. He had always hated the tea cosy and had no idea who had bought it.

The Sunday joint was slowly roasting in the oven, and the smell made Simon hungry. He reached to a shelf and brought down a biscuit barrel. It was in the shape of a giant teddy bear. He removed the bear's head and extracted two chocolate digestive biscuits.

Philip ran into the kitchen wearing shorts and wellington boots.

"I'll have a biscuit Si."

A voice from the lounge.

"Don't have too many. You won't eat your lunch."

"Right Mam. I will only have one," said Simon as Philip giggled.

"You know who I was talking to, thank you."

"Yes Mam. Sorry Mam". Simon pulled a face that made Philip giggle some more. He slipped his brother two chocolate biscuits. Simon winked, and Philip put his index finger to his lips. Secrets.

"I'm helping Dad wash the car."

"Oh, you are, are you? Then what are you doing in here? The car is outside."

"I know that, silly. Dad said I was a great help but was making more work than the worth of it. He told me to take a break because he could see I was thirsty." Philip had already devoured one biscuit and was starting the second. "Can you get me a glass of squash, please, Si?"

Simon left his mug and biscuits and took a glass from the dishwasher. It was clean and cool. He rinsed it under the cold water and then returned to the fridge to get the bottle of lemon barley water. Emptying a little into the glass, he went to the sink unit and flicked the tap. Letting the water run for a few seconds, he topped the glass up with water.

"Do you want ice?"

"Yes, please. Four."

"You'll have two." Sikes returned to the fridge, opened the freezer section and retrieved two ice cubes from the container. He dropped them into the glass and handed it to Philip. His brother emptied the contents almost in one swallow. Only the ice cubes remained. They had not even begun to melt.

"Thanks, Si." Philip placed the glass on the worktop next to Simon's cup and munched on his second biscuit.

"Needed that, did you?"

Philip giggled again. His whole body shook as he did so.

Simon took a sip of his tea and bit into his biscuit.

Philip had rested enough.

"Right. I'd better get back to help Dad. It's hard work, you know?"

"I can imagine. Where's Clare?"

"She's out there too, but she don't like getting wet, so she's just playing with her dolls. See you, Si."

"Aye ta-ra." said Simon. He doubted Clare could ever play with anything. Simon smiled at the thought of his little sister fussing over her dolls as she fussed over everything.

He picked up his tea and walked through to the lounge. He sat in his father's chair and swung it round to face his mother.

"Anything interesting, Mam?"

"Not really. You can have it yourself in a minute. I don't know why your father buys this trash. It's full of rubbish about soap stars and football players. No real news in it."

Every Sunday, his mother would complain about the newspaper but still read it from cover to cover, stopping only to tut-tut at the so-called exploits of some celebrity or other.

"Good night last night, Si? You were home early. Well, early for you lately. What was it about half past eleven?"

"Aye, about that. It was an amazing night, a great day, actually. I bumped into Miko up the park. Chris was there too. I was talking to Miko for ages. They were asking about you."

"How is their mother? I keep meaning to call down."

"She's fine by all accounts. Miko wants her to move. He reckons the estate is getting a bit too rough nowadays."

"Well, it was never the quietest of places." His mother seemed to lose herself for a moment. "It might be for the best if she did move. Is it only her and Michael now? Christopher is married, isn't he?"

"Yeah, he married Paula Jenkins." He knew she would remember the name. It was best not to let her dwell. "Has two kids too, Dan and Ben".

"Dan, after his Dad, and Ben, after his mother's father. That's nice. Chris was always close to his grandparents, especially after his father became ill."

Although Sikes was very young at the time, he could remember conversations about Miko's father. He had always had breathing problems, something to do with working down the pit for so long. Miko's dad seemed to be old. Simon later discovered that Miko's father was twenty years older than his wife. That explained why some children thought he was Miko's grandfather on the rare occasion he collected his son from school.

"Are you naming your sons after your father and grandfather?"

"Well, Thomas isn't bad, but Dilwyn is slightly off!"

"What do you mean?" His mother chuckled. "Dilwyn is a lovely name."

"Thomas Dilwyn Ikes! The poor little bugger would never forgive me!"

His mother placed her cup on the wooden floor for fear of tipping her tea as she laughed.

After lunch, Simon performed his weekly sort-out of his bedroom. Sifting through his wardrobe, he debated which clothes needed a wash and which could survive a few more days. If his mother had her way, it would be one wear and in the wash, but Simon found his clothes were not so much getting worn out as washed out. He became much more selective about what went into the dirty basket. He inspected his jeans particularly closely, having been too afraid to put them in the wash the previous week. He did not want questions about the grass stain. They smelled the same as his other clothes, so he dropped them into the washing basket, only to retrieve them and remove the slip of paper from the back pocket.

He opened the paper and read Sammie's telephone numbers, then folded it again and put it in his wallet, which lay on his bedside cabinet. He breathed out heavily.

"You're going to have to sort that, Sikesy."

Just before three o'clock, the phone rang. It was Dicey.

"Sikesy man. Fancy a game of footie? There's a gang of us going down. Are you up for it?"

Simon was and subsequently found himself on the losing side in an improvised seven versus six football match on the local playing fields. Coats and jumpers shaped the goals.

It was another glorious summer afternoon, too hot to play football. Before very long, what the gang had perceived as skilful inter-passing play at the start of the game, deteriorated into a pushing and pulling contest, resembling rugby more than soccer. Simon had the ball and was knocked off it by GarGar, who hit Sikes on the hip with his shoulder to bring him down. The ball ran free to Dicey, who, in an attempt to score from over thirty yards, completely misjudged the strength of his shot. He fell on his back, laughing as his shoe shot towards the goal while the ball headed over the fence and into the river beyond.

"Well, that's that. Nice one, Dicey," said GarGar, as his friend retrieved his shoe.

"Come on. We can get that. The river narrows at the bend, and we can get the ball back." Chubber was always an optimist.

"Carry on Chubb. We'll be right there," said Sikes. He started to raise himself off the grass, saw Chubber and the others run to the river, and then dropped to his knees again.

Sikes, GarGar and Dicey sat alone on the grass.

"Did you have a good day yesterday?"

"Pretty good," said Gareth. "It was a laugh, wasn't it, Dicey?"

"Aye, it was good," said Dicey. "Where did you fuck off to, Sikesy?"

"Well, you didn't want me hanging around like a spare prick at a wedding, did you? I met up with Miko. I spent most of the day in the sponsor's tent."

GarGar was checking the sole of his trainer."What were the prices like in there?"

"Free bar," said Sikes.

"How did you manage that?" GarGar was most impressed.

Sikes smiled and tapped the side of his nose. "Contacts."

"Contacts my arse," said Mark Dice. "Never mind fucking contacts, what about looking after your mates? The beer prices were horrendous, and it tasted like shit. That's if you could get served. The place was rammed. You should have come and fetched us."

"I bet it was an expensive day for you, Dicey," said GarGar. "That Amy can drink a bit, can't she?"

"Don't talk," said Dicey taking the bait. "She drinks like a fish all afternoon, gets all lovey-dovey down the park. She was even trying to get my dick out. I take her back to my house, which is only up the road, as you know, and she's a completely different person. She got irate, told me she was feeling rough and then started puking up all over the place. I had to put her in the spare bed with a bowl. I was awake all night watching her throw her guts up. Her father gave her some serious grief on the 'phone this morning. He told her he wanted to meet me. I'm glad she offered to walk down to meet him alone. I think he would have killed me." He rubbed his face. "And the worst part was I didn't even get a shag!"

GarGar shook his head, trying hard to hide that he found this hilarious. "Shame that."

Sikes winked at GarGar and said, "Her father's probably just concerned about his fourteen-year-old daughter."

GarGar's wide eyes revealed his surprise.

"Aye, I suppose," said Dicey before hearing his friend's words again. He stared at Sikes. "What? Fourteen?"

He saw Sikes nod.

"Fourteen be fucked! She's not fourteen? Amy is seventeen. She's in college. She told me that the first night I met her."

"Sorry Dicey. She's been having you on, mate. She's fourteen and her mother, Janice, works for Harvey's. She's always going on about her daughter Amy, but I never sussed it was the same Amy until yesterday."

Dicey motioned for Sikes to tell him more.

"You know that bloke I went to speak to at the races?"

"The tall twat with the big nose?"

"Aye, but he's no twat. He's okay. He's a good bloke. That was Timmy from the bakery. He knows Janice and her husband Cliff well. As soon as he saw you yesterday, he recognised Amy. He told me all about her. She goes to the Welsh school in Ponty, not the college."

"Well, I'll be buggered. No wonder she's never keen to go out down her neck of the woods," said Dicey before a more worrying thought hit him. "Shit. What am I going to do? She's really clingy. If I dump her, she will be pissed off and might tell her parents what we've done. They'll probably go to the cops. Fuck! I'll be done because she's underage. I'll be on the fucking sex offenders register." He placed his hands on his cheeks and then pulled down his mouth. "Bollocks! What do I do? If I keep seeing her, her father will meet me sooner or later, and he'll do me anyway. I can't stay with her, and I can't dump her..."

Dicey looked across the grass and saw Simon and Gareth rolling on the floor, laughing.

"Thanks, lads. Thanks for fuck all." Dicey stood up, ran across the grass and jumped on Gareth.

All three were laughing when GarGar turned and threw him onto the grass.

Seven-thirty on the dot, Simon walked into the Bird in Hand. His hopes of a quiet entrance got dashed as soon as Jamie spotted him.

"Simon, over here, pal. Come and have a pint."

Simon walked towards his new friend.

"Mike, this is Simon. He's why Laura is taking so long in the bathroom."

The balding bar man, of average height, wore a white shirt and dark tie with a ship emblem. He walked down the bar and held out his hand.

"Take no notice of him. Laura doesn't need an excuse to spend a long time in the bathroom. She is like her mother, but woe betides me if I try to sneak in for a read. All hell breaks loose." He stopped to smile. "Still, I suppose that's what comes of having three women in the house. I'm pleased to meet you, Simon. You can probably tell that I'm Mike, Laura's father. What do you want to drink?"

Simon shook his hand. He recalled Laura telling him her father was English, born in Liverpool. He had met Laura's mother while she was on holiday in Plymouth, where Mike was serving in the Navy. The Scouse accent broke through on certain vowels.

"Nice to meet you too. I'll have a pint of Special, please."

"Careful, Si. He charges double for family."

"Shut up you. This one is on the house, Simon."

"Can I get you one, Jame?"

"I'm okay, Si. I'm driving. I've got a lot of stuff to carry, so I need to take the car."

"I'm glad to see a young man drinking a real drink rather than that bloody lager. Look at Cinderella there. Long hair and lager, it's like having a fourth woman around the place. He poured the beer and headed back to join the boys.

"He loves me really, Simon. We get on like a house on fire! He's only showing off because you are here."

Mike laughed. It was a deep raucous laugh.

Simon thanked Mike for his pint and stood beside the others at the bar. Their conversation was interrupted when Mike saw some other customers come into the pub. He went through to the lounge bar to serve them.

"So what type of music do you play?"

"Covers mostly. I'll do anything from the sixties to the present day." Jamie checked his pony tail. "I'd love to record my stuff, but I'll concentrate on the popular stuff for the time being. It's what the punters like." He scratched the back of his neck. "I'm in a band back home, but we're still a bit raw and not ready for gigs yet. I'll keep on with this for a few more months and see what happens. The money is not bad, and it's helping me learn the trade." He sipped his lager. "Do you play anything?"

"An instrument, you mean?" Sikes saw Jamie nod. "No, I have never been interested. The only music I listen to tends to be the stuff in the charts."

"As long as you listen to something," said Jamie. "Have you been to the Venue before? What's it like?"

"Aye, it's not bad. It's a friendly place. I know a lot of the lads down there. It's a bit of a gathering place for the cricketers in the area. It's normally packed on a Sunday. What time are you on?"

"Half eight until quarter past nine, then ten until eleven or until they chuck them out, I imagine."

Sikes hoped they would chuck them out quickly and on time. He had to be up at five to get to work.

Laura and Caitlin walked into the bar just as Simon finished his pint. He beamed as Laura smiled at him. She wore a sleeveless red dress that stopped just above her knee and black shoes. He thought she looked stunning and felt like he had hit the jackpot.

Caitlin kissed Jamie on the cheek and said, "Right. Are we off?"

Jamie nodded and shouted, "See you, Mike. Don't worry, Simon, and I will take good care of your princesses!"

"You make sure you do. Have a good night…and Jamie! Break a leg. Please break a bloody leg."

Simon heard that deep raucous laugh again.

Simon took Laura's hand.

"You look great."

"Thanks. You don't look too bad yourself."

Simon was pleased he had taken his mother's advice and dressed more smartly but had ignored his father's advice to wear a tie.

I wore a tie on my first date with your mother

Yes, Dad, but everyone wore them then. Nobody wears a tie out these days.

Well, I do.

You would.

His mother spoke. You smell nice too? What aftershave is that?

Not sure. I pinched it off, Dad.

Cor Simon. You smell funny, said Clare.

Philip added his two penneth worth. Yes funny.

And there's me thinking Claire would like it," said Simon.

Well, I do, but...

Don't worry, love, Simon's only teasing you. I like it too, that's why I bought it for your father, but he never wears it.

I would wear it, but where do I get to go?

"Well, I've told you I'd look after these two, said Simon.

His mother seized the opportunity. If you're offering Simon, you can look after the twins on Tuesday. Your father and I will go out. He could wear the aftershave then. What do you say?

Hooked.

Aye, alright then, how can I refuse? You've got a deal providing Dad gives me a lift up to town. I don't want to be late.

Bloody hell, Simon wants to be on time for something. This one must be important.

Jamie played well and was warmly received. Simon recognised many songs from his parents' regular music sessions. These occurred when his father, usually fuelled by a couple of glasses of Australian red wine, would insist on playing his classic CDs and singing along. Simon and the twins would roar with laughter as their parents danced and tried to sing the old hits. In a nation of three million singers, the older Ikes, Simon included, were not blessed with excellent singing voices. The twins, however, sang well and frequently moved their parents to tears singing the songs they learned in school.

Simon felt a little jealous of Jamie's ability. He played his guitar well and sang effortlessly. He had a way with the audience and was blessed with quick wits. This was evident when a couple of the locals made sarcastic comments, and Jamie could silence them using very few words. As Jamie performed, Simon and the two girls talked, drank and frequently sang along, although Sikes opted to mime rather than show himself up.

When it was time for Jamie's break, Caitlin went to join him at the bar, and Simon took her seat next to Laura. She took his right hand in hers.

"Are you okay?"

They kissed lightly.

"Aye, great, thanks. He's good, isn't he?"

"Yes, fair play. He's better in the band, though. Wait 'til you see them. They're awesome even though they haven't been together long."

"How do you meet them?"

"When we lived in Swansea. They all live there. I went out with the bass player for a while."

Simon felt a little different. Jealously was not usually an emotion from which he suffered, but tonight he had experienced it twice.

"What happened?"

"When Mum and Dad bought the Bird, there was not much point in carrying on. We're miles apart, and he can't drive. There's no way I'm fetching and carrying him from Swansea."

This was not the answer he wanted to hear. "So, if you still lived down there, you two would still be together?"

"Possibly. Who knows? You're not getting jealous, are you?"

"Hardly. I've only known you for two minutes. How can I be jealous?"

"That's okay then."

Simon placed his arm around her shoulder and kissed her. Laura stared into his eyes. Simon wondered if her big blue eyes could read what he was thinking.

Eleven thirty-five, with Jamie's gear packed up, the foursome returned to the family pub. There was no good night kiss against the outside wall of the pub for Simon. After helping Jamie take his stuff inside, Sikes went inside for a drink. Jamie and Caitlin joined her parents and a few regulars for a lock-in downstairs while Simon and Laura took off to the upstairs living quarters.

"It's quite big, isn't it?" Simon settled on the sofa while Laura busied herself in the small kitchen.

"Yes, not bad. Dad will extend the pub into the house at the back, meaning larger living quarters. Pity he won't be able to stop the noise. You wait, any minute now, Jamie will knock out a few tunes."

"Doesn't anyone complain?"

"No. There's nobody next door or behind, and he only plays acoustic; it's only us up here who can hear it. The locals seem to like it, and it is not as if we do it every night."

She handed Simon a mug of coffee, and he immediately placed it on the small table by the sofa.

"Thanks."

Laura placed her coffee next to his and walked over to the television. She switched it on, picked up the remote control and walked back to Simon.

Simon saw that she had kicked off her shoes and was now bare foot. He admired her feet.

As Laura sat down, Simon grabbed her hips, one hand on each side, and lifted her, so she sat on his lap.

"Oh, you're pushy."

"I am." Sikes put his arms around her and pulled her into him. They kissed deeply. Laura dropped the remote control onto the sofa.

Jamie's voice, accompanied by his guitar, drifted into the room.

Simon allowed himself to fall backwards along the length of the sofa. He kept his right leg on the floor while his left foot strayed over the arm of the couch, narrowly missing the coffee cups.

Laura fell with him, slightly altering her body position so that she lay on top of him. Her blond locks tumbled around her face.

They kissed more deeply, their mouths finding common movement. Simon gently rubbed Laura's back. His fingers moved from fabric to flesh as they found parts of her body not covered by dress or straps.

Simon transferred his hands to Laura's buttocks. With a soft flick, he lifted the skirt, exposing her knickers to the room.

"It's not unusual," came from the floor below. Neither Simon nor Laura sang along.

He cupped both buttocks in his hands as Laura's tongue entered his mouth. Simon continued squeezing and pressing her flesh. The necking grew more frantic.

Sikes' thumbs touched the waistband on Laura's knickers and waited for a reaction. Laura did not seem to mind, so he lifted the elastic and inserted his right hand. His fingers touched the bare flesh of Laura's backside. It felt firm, smooth and soft. His left hand joined the right, and Simon's tongue chased hers.

The bar door slammed. Footsteps were coming up the stairs.

Laura lifted herself off Simon, but his hands did not want to leave the warmth of her lingerie.

"Let go, quick. Someone's coming."

Aye me, thought Sikes. He removed his hands from her underwear and accepted her assistance in helping him upright. He grabbed his coffee. Laura picked up the remote, pressed button one, collected her mug of coffee and flopped down next to Simon just as the lounge door opened.

Caitlin entered the room carrying a pint of bitter and a glass of white wine.

"Are you two okay?"

"It's you! You almost gave me a heart attack," said Laura.

"Why? What have you been up to?" Caitlin smirked.

"Nothing. We were just talking."

"Oh right...well, I just thought you'd like a drink. I know it can be thirsty work...just talking." She looked at Simon. His hair was messy, and his shirt had risen from the front of his trousers.

"Thank you," said Simon, taking the pint.

"Yes, thanks very much," said Laura, looking daggers at her sister.

Caitlin laughed and then turned to leave the room. She told them to be good as she closed the door and made her way down the stairs.

Simon placed the coffee on the table and slumped back on the sofa. Laura laughed loudly and put her head on his shoulder.

AS ONE DOOR OPENS...

"Ladies and gentlemen, the train is now approaching Cathays. Cathays is the next station stop." The voice from the train's communication system said no more.

Simon smiled at Laura. He was pleased that she had offered to come with him to the open day at the "Department of Health Medicinal and Surgical Records Office", known by employees and government ministers as DoMO - Department of Medical Options.

Sikes had no idea what to expect. He had never attended such an event before and had no real intention of doing so this day. He had wanted to give it a miss. However, pressure from his father and uncle, the latter of whom had been accepted for a job in DoMO, coupled with the suggestion that he and Laura could spend the afternoon in Cardiff, had persuaded him he had nothing to lose.

"Right, this is where we get off." He rose from his seat and stepped into the aisle between the seats. Laura stood, collected her bag and did likewise. Simon took a step back, allowing her to go first.

Laura had known Simon for under a week and was impressed by his politeness and kindness. Many other things about him impressed her. She had thought about Simon a lot in the previous six days and had spent numerous hours analysing what he meant to her. He was proving to be a severe distraction, but she did not know what to call him.

Boyfriend! Laura thought that was an accurate but boring description. But how else could she describe him?

Lover? She did not believe that was not appropriate. They had not progressed that far, although Laura doubted that would remain the case for much longer.

Friend? Laura already knew that Simon was more than a

friend.

Date? That term seemed more suitable for a one-off, not when you see someone five times in six days; she had not seen Sikes on Thursday because she had been flat hunting with Caitlin. That is more than a date.

Partner? They were not planning to go into business together.

Her steady? Not yet, although Laura did not know what might happen.

Did she need to give him a title? Why didn't she go with the flow and see what happened? They had a good laugh and got on brilliantly, so she would enjoy it while it lasted. They had only just gotten together. It was better to take things slowly.

When Simon called in the pub the other night, her father shouted to tell her her young man had arrived.

Fathers! Who needed them?"

Laura did. She loved her father very much. She loved her mother too, they got on extremely well, but her relationship with her Dad was different. He had always been there for her and was easier to talk to than Mum. Mum would always offer advice, but Dad would listen. Dad would always hold a special place in her heart.

Laura wondered if Simon was making a place in her heart too, but her common sense head told her she was talking nonsense. It was too soon. They were too young, and, in any case, Simon was too new.

She liked the fact that Simon was so polite. He always opened doors for her and answered invitations with an effortless please and thank you. Simon, who, although she had known him just six days, had already proved to be so kind and generous. Simon was easygoing and made her laugh, even if he had not intended to. Simon touched her so gently on their first proper date and made her feel so relaxed that he came closer than he realised to getting something no other boy had had from Laura on a first date, something that not many boys had at all. Good old Caitlin, always there in the nick of time.

Laura had never let anyone get so close so quickly before, not even David, her boyfriend - that word again - in Swansea. He still called her at least twice a week and would probably call that evening. Her father knew what to say. She would end David's calls if she and Simon stuck together. During their last conversation, she had almost told David about Simon, but her common sense head told her there was no need. It was too soon. Why end it? David was okay where he was, twenty-odd miles away in Swansea, with no means of getting to Aberdare unless Jamie brought him. She knew Jamie would not do that because Jamie could not abide David. She also knew that Jamie already liked Simon.

He's a lovely lad, Law. He's a bit shy but seems like a good laugh. Caitlin and her father shared this view.

Jamie never said anything nice about David, partly because he did not trust him but mainly because Jamie thought David was a pretentious knob-head for refusing to be called Dai. By Jamie's standards, David was also rubbish at playing the bass guitar. Caitlin had recently told Laura that Jamie only kept David in the band because he knew that Laura would be upset if he threw him out. Jamie would do anything for Caitlin and her family and believed that Laura and David were very close. Until recently, Laura had thought so too, but now she had second thoughts. Were they that close? Did she really like him? Did she like him as much as she thought when she saw him almost daily? Her feelings had changed.

David was a good-looking bloke with a very muscular body, much more so than Simon. David spent much more time in the gym, and always turned out perfectly. At twenty-three, he was a few years older than her, and his well-paid job in the council meant he could afford to take her for meals. He also spoiled her with gifts, although the clothes he bought were rarely to her taste.

Laura used to feel so happy as she held David's hand on long romantic walks. Did that mean she liked him? Or was she just grateful for his attention? He was undoubtedly a significant attraction as far as the Swansea girls were concerned. Many had told Laura that she was a lucky girl, and others had warned her that they would take him off her hands if she were not careful. At the time, she had been pleased that so many thought David was lush, but having the biggest fan club in Swansea did not guarantee he was what she wanted. It did not make him perfect. They had their rows. They had more than their share of arguments. David was opinionated and selfish. They disagreed over many things, including his refusal to learn to drive a car. He gave no reason for this decision apart from the fact that he did not want to.

She recalled the last Sunday they shared before her family moved to Aberdare. She and David had walked down the Mumbles. It was a warm May afternoon that cooled as evening approached. Then, not for the first time, she had wished he could drive. As the heavens opened and they both got soaked, she wished he had a car. His efforts at making jokes about their situation became grating. Laura realised that she did not share his sense of humour. He did not make her laugh. Could she continue to be an item with someone who she did not find funny?

Item, that was another terrible description. If she and Simon became an item, then Laura would have to tell David they were no longer an item. She thought that might upset him, although probably it would only be his ego that got dented. She wondered whether Jamie kicking him out of the band would be harder for David to accept than Laura ending their relationship. Caitlin had confided to Laura that Jamie's mate, Beko, was ready to replace David. He had already been tried and tested. Jamie said that the best rehearsals were those when David was working late or away and Beko had taken over. Most of the other band members thought the same.

Laura was not sure what she should do. Should she finish with David or leave things as they were? She liked Simon and believed he felt the same way about her. He had not said as much, but Laura sort of knew. There again, they had only been together for six days. Maybe it was lust. Perhaps he was only after one thing. She would have to tread carefully. Take her time. It was not as though there was any rush, but his effect on her was undeniable.

That morning as Laura had waited for Simon to collect her from the pub, she had butterflies in her stomach. That had not happened before with David or any other boy. She could not wait for him to arrive. She had wanted to see Simon the previous evening, but he was working late at the bakery, and Caitlin had arranged for the sisters to see a few flats in the area. They visited a couple that had potential, but Laura had not been interested. Her mind had been elsewhere. She was wondering what her new friend was doing.

Simon had been with GarGar and Dicey. They met for a pint and a chat. Dicey had finished with his underage girlfriend. At least that was his version. In truth, she had dumped him in favour of a twenty-year-old, unmarried father of two from further down the valley. Life was full of surprises. Amy's announcement shocked Dicey, who was still unsure whether to feel relieved or hurt. He tried to appear relaxed and presented a brave, uncaring face to his friends.

"I had to tell her, look, you're under-age. I'm not doing time for shagging you. We're finished. Of course, there were tears, but..."

Simon listened, although his mind was elsewhere. He was more interested in thinking about a certain pretty blond.

After Dicey had completed his update, GarGar filled them in about his plans for that weekend. Kelly's parents would be away in their caravan, leaving Chubber and her to mind the house and the dog. Chubber would stay in a mate's house, which meant that Kelly, GarGar, Sammie and Sikes would have the place to themselves. He asked Simon if he was ready for it. When Simon failed to answer, GarGar asked again, this time more loudly.

The question snapped Simon out of his daze long enough to remember he had not told his friends about Laura and that he had changed his mind about the weekend. Looking at the expression on GarGar's face, Sikes knew he had no option but to tell all. He told his friends of recent developments in his life and was not surprised when GarGar became agitated.

"But, Sikes, you've got to be there. You said you would. Come on, mun. We're both on fucking major promises here. Two nights shagging, and now you tell me you don't want any of it. Fucking 'ell, some mate you are."

"Sorry Gar, but... shit... I meant to tell you. Honest, I did. I meant to ring Sammie and cancel, but I forgot all about it. I've been so busy this week. I'm off to Cardiff tomorrow to see about a job. Mr Harvey has been good enough to give me a paid day off, but I have to make the hours up this week. By the time I get home, it's gone seven, and all I've had is time for food, a quick change, and then it's off to meet Laura."

"Who is this Laura who causes you to ignore your mates?" GarGar was incensed. "Four times I've rung you since Sunday. Four fucking times! Did you ring me back? No chance." GarGar reached for his lager.

"I rang you tonight, didn't I?"

"It's a bit fucking late now."

Simon could see a few of the regulars beginning to stare at the three boys in the corner.

"Okay, I've said I'm sorry. Calm down before we get kicked out."

"Who gives a fuck? Why should I calm down? You've known about this weekend long enough. You even told me you were looking forward to it. I know Sammie is because she told Kelly."

That's not all she's told Kelly, thought Sikes.

"And now you're going to spoil it for all of us just because of some new bird who none of us knew about, let alone met. She must be pretty special."

"I think she is," confessed Simon.

"Have you shagged her yet?" asked Dicey.

Simon almost choked on his beer.

"Shit, Dicey! Don't beat about the bush, will you? If you've got something to ask, just ask it why don't you?"

"Don't know why you're so touchy. You'd ask me quick enough."

"I would not." Simon realised the regulars were now looking only at him. He calmed himself and lowered his voice. "I think it's GarGar who's more interested in your shags."

"I don't fucking believe this. What are you trying to say? Now I'm some kind of pervert who gets off on Dicey's exploits?" He glared at Simon. "Thanks a fucking bunch, mate."

Sikes opened, closed his mouth, took a deep breath, and then said, "This is getting stupid. Look, GarGar, I'm sorry if I've screwed things up for Kelly and you. I'll ring Sammie and tell her not to come up this weekend. That will leave it free for you and Kelly. Okay?"

"What classic excuse will you use this time? Bubonic Plague? The whole area has been shut off." GarGar was livid.

"I'll think of something."

"You'd fuckin' better."

They spoke about other things, but Simon was only marginally interested. His mind had wandered off again.

With GarGar at the bar, Sikes headed outside to use his mobile. He avoided the small group of smokers in the garden and went to the corner of the street. Taking out the folded piece of paper from his wallet, he dialled carefully. Samantha's father answered on the fourth ring and passed the handset to his middle daughter.

"Hello."

"Hiya, it's me… Simon."

"I know it's you. I recognise the voice. Is everything okay?"

"Aye, I'm not bad. How are you?"

"I'm great, ta." Sammie updated Simon on recent events in her life. He listened without hearing.

"What about you? Are you looking forward to tomorrow? I've got a surprise for you."

Oh shit, this is not how it is supposed to happen, thought Simon. "Hmmm" was all he could manage in reply.

Sammie continued talking.

"I should be there by about 5 pm. What time do you finish work on Fridays?

"I...er...I'm not working tomorrow."

"Brilliant. Shall I come up earlier and come to yours as soon as I arrive? We can see the others later. I'd like to spend some time alone with you first."

Shit" This was proving to be much more challenging than he had imagined.

"I am sorry, Sam. That's why I'm ringing. My uncle is... umm... moving down from Manchester this weekend and I've been roped in to help his fetch his stuff. So I've...umm...got to change the plans for this weekend."

"You're joking!" She was not happy.

"No, I'm serious. Sorry. We're...er...travelling up to Manchester in the morning, setting off about eight o'clock, and I won't be back until about ten, maybe eleven tomorrow night. Then, on Saturday, Dad and I will be helping him move into his new place in Newport, so I'll be busy all day. I can't see you this weekend. I'm really sorry. Can you come up next weekend instead?" Sikes had rehearsed the lines and was confident they would sound genuine.

Silence. Sikes became a little anxious. "Sam?"

"So when was all this sorted out? Couldn't you have told me before?"

He had expected this. It was good that he planned what to say. Improvisation was not his strongest point. Simon once again uttered his quickly rehearsed lines. He had convinced himself the words would be easy to say and sound plausible.

"Oh...er... his solicitor rang him this morning to tell him

he can move into his house on Saturday, so he's been ringing around all day getting a van for tomorrow. I only found out an hour ago. I can't let him down, can I? He's my uncle and has always been good to us."

"But it's alright to let me down, is it? I've been looking forward to this weekend for the past fortnight. Me and Kel have been talking about it for hours on the 'phone."

"Aye, that's not all you've talked about." Sikes had not rehearsed that line.

Sammie picked up on it immediately. "What is that supposed to mean?"

"Er...nothing really..."

"What are you trying to say, Simon?"

He used his free hand to punch the wall. There was no going back.

"It's just that Kelly keeps making jokes about...you know...me shooting too quickly. I think she's told GarGar. It's embarrassing."

"I'm sure it is. And you think I told her?"

Simon's silence confirmed her suspicions.

"Well, thank you for trusting me, Simon. As it happens, I haven't told her. So is this really what this call is all about? You are off with me because your pride is hurt?"

Sikes looked up and down the terraced street, seeking inspiration. All he saw was a car slowly moving towards him. He wished his father had not put his 'phone onto a contract. He could not even claim he was about to run out of talk time.

"It's just that when you said you'd been talking..."

"You put two and two together and made five, did you? Again, thanks for trusting me, Simon. I said I wouldn't say anything, and I didn't. If you must know, and Kelly told me not to tell you this, but it wasn't me who told her. It was some girl, Angela."

Simon recognised the name, his first "conquest" the previous Christmas. He knew she had been lying when she said he'd been great.

Sammie had not finished.

"All I told Kel is I had no complaints, which I haven't. If anything, I've been sticking up for you. Saying how happy I am, how nice you are, and how lovely your family is." Her voice lowered, "Can't tell you what else I've told her just in case my father hears me. Anyway, you shouldn't worry about Kelly. Ignore her. She's just a tease, that's all."

Simon knew that already.

"Sorry, Sam, I shouldn't have thought it was you."

"No, you shouldn't have. Now am I coming up this weekend or not?"

Simon had not expected this to be so difficult.

"I'm sorry, Sam, but I am helping my uncle. I'm not making excuses...honestly." Easy words, but he found them difficult to say.

"Oh, alright then." Sam sounded disappointed. "Can I see you next weekend?"

"Aye, of course, next weekend, no problem." Sikes was relieved to have a few more days to work on his story.

"Right, I'll give Kelly a ring and tell her I'll see her next week. You'll have to work hard to make this up to me."

"I'll try my best," Sikes said, cringing as he did so.

"I'll bring the DVD back then too. I watched it. It's a bit tame by modern standards but tell your father I enjoyed it. Will he mind waiting another week, or shall I post it?"

Simon had forgotten Sammie had borrowed one of his father's classic horror films. Whatever happened, he needed to get that back. He knew what he wanted to say, but guilt stopped him.

"No, don't bother posting it. Next week will be fine. That's no problem. I'll see you then."

"I can hardly wait."

"Nor me."

More easy words, but the kisses being blown down the line were tougher to reciprocate.

Simon returned to the bar and quickly summarised his

telephone conversation. GarGar was much calmer and agreed Simon had done well by sorting it.

"So where are you taking this Laura?"

"Tomorrow, we're off to Cardiff in the day, and hopefully, we'll be staying in all night. I'm babysitting. Saturday, we're going out for a meal."

"Very posh," suggested GarGar, "And when will we get to meet her?"

"Soon." He saw both friends were not content with his response. "It's just a bit awkward, what with you going out with Kelly, but I'll see what happens this weekend. If it looks promising, I'll dump Sammie, and there'll be no problem."

"So you like her a lot?"

"Aye, very much. I can't stop thinking about her. Tell you what, I've seen her every night since Saturday, and I can't wait to see her again." Sikes took a big sip from his glass and almost spat it straight out, nearly choking on the directness of Dicey's question.

"So, have you shagged her then?"

Simon dragged his mind back to the present as he and Laura stepped off the train. They crossed the metal bridge over the railway line and walked down the lane, nipping through the busy road traffic, before taking the path between two large university buildings. This brought them to the front of the office block, undergoing refurbishment on behalf of the Department of Health Medicinal and Surgical Records.

Wherever they looked, they saw workers going about their duties. Grass cutters, painters, bricklayers, and carpenters were all busily working around the perimeter of the building.

"Looks like they haven't finished yet," said Simon, as they stopped at a red and white wooden barrier.

A tall, plump security guard dressed in a black uniform with a peaked cap approached them.

"Open day?"

Simon nodded.

"Thank you. Please go through the revolving doors, and my colleague will show you where to register. The last time I looked, it was at the table on the left, but there's so much going on. Don't be surprised if they've moved it somewhere else."

Simon and Laura smiled at him and carried on walking.

The pair entered, through different revolving doors, into a waiting area. There were long armless sofas along two of the walls. It was darker here than outside, where the sun was shining brightly. The place was also full of workers.

Another security guard, dressed as the first but older, pointed them through an open door to his left.

Simon spotted a sign saying "Registration". It was above a desk just to the left of the most enormous and grandiose staircase Simon had ever encountered.

"This looks like a film set," suggested Laura.

Sikes agreed.

"It must have cost a fortune."

Behind the registration desk sat a man and woman. Simon handed a plain brown envelope to the man.

"Won't be a minute," said the man before disappearing into a side room.

The lady explained that her colleague had gone to check the applications list. Simon shrugged his shoulders and waited. Laura squeezed his hand gently, but he resisted the temptation to kiss her. This was neither the time nor the place.

The man reappeared.

"Mr Ikes. If you'd like to follow me, Mr Millington wishes to have a word with you."

Laura let go of his hand.

"You go on. I'll wait here for you."

"Will you be alright?"

"Course I will. I'll wait over there by the television."

Simon followed the man down a corridor and into a large office. They met a tall, round-faced, chubby man wearing steel-framed glasses, a blue pinstripe suit, a pristine white cotton shirt, and a yellow tie. His dark hair was receding. The man held out his hand. Simon shook it.

"Good morning Simon. Glad you could make it. Your uncle told me you might be calling in. He's told me a lot about you." The man checked his watch. "You're bang on time too. That's a good start. Please sit down."

Simon smiled uneasily and did as he was told. He wondered why his uncle had been talking about him.

"Would you like a drink? Coffee or tea? Perhaps something cooler?"

Englishman thought Sikes. "No thanks. I'm fine."

"Your uncle tells me you want to become an accountant?"

"Yes, that's right."

"Well, we need accountants. Much of what we do involves analysing figures and financial records."

"Right. Great," said Sikes, not sure what else to say.

"I see from your application form that you have tried four A- levels."

"That is right. Mathematics, Economics, English and History." Sikes had been one of only five pupils allowed to attempt four rather than the usual three.

"Are you confident of passing them all?"

"Hopefully. The exams went pretty well. I didn't feel flummoxed by any of the questions."

"What grades do you need for your first choice university?"

"I think two A's and a B would do it."

"And is that for Oxford or Cambridge?"

You must be fucking joking, said Simon to himself. "I don't think I'm that bright," said Simon to the fat man.

The man said nothing leaving Simon to fill the void.

"I struggled with English and History. My parents paid for a tutor to help me through." Simon recalled the long nights in January and February when he had to endure extra hours on the two subjects he liked least.

It will be worth it in the long run. His mother had insisted. You need to keep your options open.

But Mam, I want to be an accountant. Why do I need English?

Even accountants have to read and write Simon.

The man spoke again.

"You know that if you were successful in an application for a permanent job here, then we could probably contribute towards your higher education?"

"Yes, my uncle mentioned that. How does that work exactly?"

"It's quite simple. You would go away to university, as you would normally, but we would pay your fees, and you would get paid for your efforts. You would then work here during your holidays and would be expected to work for us for five years after you qualify. We would arrange any post-graduate development you require to get your letters, etc."

Simon had already gone through this with his uncle but thought it best to make the right noises if they were the right ones.

"That sounds good but don't mention it to my father. He'll be begging you to take me on. He'll probably bug you until you do."

Geoffrey Millington laughed heartily. A little too cheerfully, perhaps for what Simon considered a weak joke. Simon was not sure what to do or say. He gave a small smile and looked suitably humble.

Millington took Simon on a whistle-stop tour of the office and expanded on the department's work. He told him that the main DoMO building had five floors, including the ground floor, currently accommodating over 250 employees. A further two hundred staff worked at various regional offices around the country, but these offices were gradually closing, and the work transferred to Cardiff. The London headquarters had already closed, and around ninety staff transferred to

Wales. Eventually, a thousand people would be employed on site, with a further two hundred at another office block in Cardiff.

The work at the main office involved collecting information on patients, treatments, operations, average waiting times and success rates from every hospital in Britain. While only NHS-funded hospitals were obliged to submit returns, many private hospitals also provided comparable information so their performance could be included in the statistical returns that were published monthly. The statistics were much more than league tables as the press perceived them. They had accurate data on many different aspects of performance. The data was made available, at cost price, to GPs and the public. This meant that an individual requiring treatment could consider all the available options for that treatment and apply to their preferred hospital for treatment. The hospital could then decide whether they could take the patient and, if so, when. Millington explained that DoMO staff would also visit the hospitals to undertake audits.

The other Cardiff office focused on offering help to hospitals perceived as failing. DoMO had a team of trained advisors who could cascade lessons learned from the best hospitals to others not performing as well. They could also appoint consultants to provide direct support to the poorer hospitals. These services came at a cost. The staff at the other office also marketed a wide range of services to health service professionals within the UK and further afield. The marketing and consultancy side of the operation was highly profitable.

Sikes was taken into the "Oasis" coffee shop and could hardly believe his eyes. A counter stood to his left with tables and seats scattered around active fountains that shot water into the air. The water landed in a small lagoon. Long chains stretched from the lagoon to a glass roof at the top of the building. Climbing plants clung to the chains as they headed towards the sun. The people in the offices overlooking Oasis went about their business oblivious to the activities in the coffee bar.

Simon declined the offer of coffee and followed Millington back to the main corridor. The pair passed a sign that read "Management Suite" and turned towards an office on the right. The door was open, but Sikes caught sight of the nameplate - Jack Phillips, Director of Human Resources. Phillips rose from behind his desk to greet them. He was five foot nine inches tall, with a pale complexion and black moustache speckled with grey. The moustache provided a natural accompaniment to his predominantly short grey hair

"Ah, Jack. There is someone here I would like you to meet."

"Would never have pictured him as a Jack," thought Simon.

"This is Simon Ikes. We are hoping to persuade Simon to join us. He wants to be an accountant."

Jack smiled warmly and held out his hand.

"Hi, Si. Looking after you, is he?"

"Yes, fine thank you." Simon shook Phillips' hand. He was not sure why this introduction was necessary.

Phillips continued.

"Has Geoffrey told you that we are on the lookout for trainee accountants?"

"Yes."

"And has he mentioned that we pay all costs and give you a job during the holidays?"

"Yes."

"When can you start?" Millington asked.

Both men laughed. Simon smiled.

A lady's voice came from inside Phillips' room.

"Mr Phillips, there is a call for you. It's your sister."

"Families, eh?" Phillips winked at Simon. "You just cannot get away from them. Well, good luck Si. I'll see you soon."

"Yes, thanks," said a bemused Sikes.

"So what did they say?" Laura was anxious to find out what had happened in the hour or so she had waited in reception.

"They told me I can start the week after next on a temporary contract and then apply for a permanent post when I get my results. We'll see how it goes, but if I get a permanent post, they will consider me for a bursary scheme, which means they will pay my uni fees." He looked around. "Shit, Law, I can't believe it. I'm starting work here a week Monday."

Laura hugged his arm.

"Well done."

A practical thought hit him. "What will I wear? I can hardly wear my normal clothes."

"They look okay to me. Anyway, there are stacks of clothes shops in Cardiff. How much money have you got?"

"Quite a bit, and I've got that credit card my father gave me for emergencies."

"So what are you worrying about? We've got all afternoon. Come on. You can buy me lunch and then we'll hit the shops. Let's pick up something to drink too. We've got some celebrating to do."

AFTER BEFORE AGAIN

Laughter is the best medicine. That is what his father had said, and he believed his father. For once, he could think of nothing to laugh about.

He always believed his father. If his father told him everything would be okay, it usually was, but it would not be okay this time. This time things had gone wrong. Not even his father could fix things this time.

At least they were all home together. Not that the new house felt like home, it was not like their old home. Some walls smelt funny, and he did not understand why there were not carpets on all the floors. The old house was full of carpets. Carpets felt nice under your feet when you walked on them without shoes and socks. His bedroom had carpets. He was happy about that. It felt warm. He felt safe with carpets. He did not feel safe everywhere in this massive, new house.

He did not feel safe in the big room downstairs. The floor in the big room was wooden. It was long strips of shiny painted wood. What had his father called it? Varnish? Varnish must be very expensive because his father had been angry at the cost of the floor.

The stairs were bare wood too. The wood was smooth but not as lovely as a carpet. At least the stairs did not creak when he walked down them late at night. The stairs in his Nanna's house creaked, and Gransha always knew when somebody was sneaking downstairs. Gransha said the stairs creaked because they were old. In this house, the stairs were new and did not creak.

He was happy his mother was home. For a long time, he hoped she would bring the baby home but she did not. The baby was dead. His father said not to mention the baby because his mother would be upset. He did not want to upset his mother anymore. She had been upset enough and was still getting better. She appeared to be a lot better earlier that day when the nurse called around, but as soon as she left, mam cried again. She would not tell him why she was crying. She just kept hugging him, repeating his name. He had asked his father why his mother cried so much, but his father wouldn't say.

Nobody told him things anymore. That's why he had started to listen. He listened at the door when his father took his Nanna and Gransha into the room at the hospital. He was supposed to go and get a drink, but he had waited. He had listened. He heard his father talk of complications, and the death had nothing to do with the accident. The death probably occurred in the womb. He did not know what a womb was. He guessed that it was part of the hospital. His father told his Nanna and Gransha that mam would not be able to have another baby, but that would be alright so long as she was okay. The important thing was that she was okay. He heard his father cry and his Nanna trying to stop his Dad's tears.

His father said he had not yet broken the news to the little one. He knew they were talking about him. He was always the little one. His Nanna said there was no rush. Little one was upset enough and was still not sleeping properly. Gransha said he had heard little one sneaking downstairs in the night. He wanted to go home. Those stairs always gave him away.

That was all weeks ago, while Mam was in the hospital, but he had kept listening. He listened in the new house. Nobody knew when he crept down the stairs. They were new and did not creak. He would sneak down the bare stairs and listen by the door. He could hear everything. He heard his father or mother get up from their chair and walk toward the door. That was one thing he liked about wood. When anyone walked across the floor, it made a sound. Carpets made no sound. Wood was good for listening.

He had listened earlier that evening. His mother had been crying again, saying she was sorry for what had happened. His father had told her that it was not her fault. His mother was so sorry the baby had died. His father said she had no reason to be sorry. It was not her fault. It was nobody's fault.

Little one knew whose fault it was.

His mother said she was sorry because they could not have another baby. His father said that was not her fault either.

He had heard the policeman arrive and listened to his father talking to him. He had listened to the policeman telling his father about what had happened that night and whom they thought threw the stone.

Little one now knew who was to blame.

After the policeman left, he heard his mother and father talking about the little one and how he would not be able to have a brother or a sister. He would like a brother or sister. He had no friends since they moved into this new house.

He had heard his father saying there were other things they could do. There was always adoption. That would get the little one a brother or sister. Little one knew about adoption because a girl at his old school had been adopted. Some boys got told off because they had teased her about it. When you are adopted, you don't live with your parents. You live with someone else.

He had heard his mother asking how the little one would cope with adoption. His father said there was no need to worry about that now; the first thing they had to do was get her better. Then, when she was ready, they would consider adoption. The process could take years. There were a lot of stages to go through. His father was sure the little one would understand. There was no need to tell him anything just yet. There was plenty of time. His parents said they needed to talk to Social Services, whoever they were. Dad said they were in the council offices. That probably meant they were not nice people. His father did not like anyone in the council. He was always saying that the council was full of crooks. He had heard his father say that many times.

He heard his mother agree that adoption would be

good. Adoption would give her something to look forward to. Mam said adoption would be good for the little one once he understood why they had to do it.

Nobody had heard him sneak back up the stairs and walk into his huge bedroom. He had kept his crying very quiet and stayed silent when his mother opened his door to do her nightly check that he was okay. He had stuck his lips together to ensure his mouth did not speak when she said, "Good night, sweetheart."

While his mother was in the hospital, he missed her calling him sweetheart and kissing him good night. He missed a lot of things. He missed the old house. He missed his old school and his old friends. He really missed Miko. The tears started to well in his eyes again. He would miss his new bedroom. He would miss the stairs and the wooden floor in the big room. He would miss his Gran and Gransha and his Uncle John but his mother and father most of all. The tears rolled faster and faster. He would miss a lot of things when he was adopted.

MESSAGE RECEIVED

Thomas Ikes poured himself another glass of his favourite Australian red wine, Shiraz. The bottle stood conveniently on the small table, one of a nest of three, so he did not have to move far to replenish his drink. He swung his seat around to see if his wife wanted a top-up.

Caroline Ikes lay stretched on the leather sofa, her head supported by two burgundy cushions. Her eyes had closed. Her husband smiled as he studied her. He believed she was still a beautiful woman. Her blonde hair had become darker over the years, but regular trips to her hairdresser meant that nobody needed to know. The colour she applied looked natural until the roots started showing, but Caroline Ikes never let it get that far.

He admired her figure. She had always kept herself fit, a habit that had started when she was a young girl. She was always on the move. Her parents repeatedly told him that she was a live wire. Her mother would probably continue to tell him.

Thomas Ikes liked the way his wife dressed. She didn't go for anything flashy, preferring stylish but casual. Caroline chose the classic look and avoided getting too involved with current fashion. He wondered why everything in the classic line was so expensive. Was it always necessary to pay for quality as his wife claimed? He often teased her about the price of her clothes, not that she took any notice. He threatened to take away the credit card, but he did not. He would not deny her anything and did not begrudge her regular shopping trips. Some of his friends' wives let themselves go after years of marriage but not Caroline. She kept herself looking smart. Thomas was very proud of her.

He toyed with the idea of joining her on the sofa but

thought better of it. Caroline only rested when she needed to, and, in any case, having rested, she might be more awake at bedtime. He glanced at the clock. It was five to ten, and the bed was still an hour away. There was ample time for another glass of wine. He turned his chair back to face the television and reached for the remote control. Flicking through the channels, he was disappointed he could not find a decent horror film. Thomas Ikes liked horror films but could never find a decent horror film on the television when he wanted one. He considered watching a DVD.

Ding dong ding dong ding dong ding dong.

"That bloody doorbell!"

He wondered why he had agreed to install that bell. He knew the answer. It was because the twins had heard Gran's doorbell and wanted one. Seventeen tunes. A microchip inside the plastic box randomly selected one of seventeen poorly synthesised tunes. Thomas Ikes considered putting a knife through the thing or knocking the box off the wall. There would be no more pathetic tunes then, but Caroline had been right. The twins would only want another one. Better to leave the novelty to wear off. She was confident it would, soon enough. He could not wait for that moment to come.

He supposed he ought to be grateful that the microchip had not selected the Mexican tune. That sounded horrible.

"Better get to the door before whoever is there presses the bell again," thought Thomas.

He scratched his blossoming stomach as he walked to the hall. He decided it was time to get that exercise bike out again.

Stopping by the mirror in the hall, he looked at his reflection.

"You could do with a shave." He looked closer. "Still, it'll be okay 'til tomorrow."

He studied himself as he ran his fingers through his hair. In the reflection, he could see the family portraits. He saw a photograph of his father-in-law, Dilwyn, playing the fool in Tenby. Dilwyn always played the fool when the kids were around. They all missed him terribly. Everyone missed Dilwyn and his stupid jokes and funny little sayings. He had been a brilliant father-in-law. Thomas often wished he could be more like him, more of an extrovert, less inhibited.

He smoothed his hair again.

Ding dong ding dong ding dong ding dong

"Okay, okay, I'm coming." He muttered to the person outside. "That's funny. I thought that bell was supposed to play a different tune every time?"

He opened the front door. The outside light was already on. A young girl stood on his doorstep. He recognised her but could not think of her name. He knew she had been to the house with Simon a couple of weeks before. The pair had baby sat for Caroline and him to go to the cinema. What was her name? It was not Laura, the one who baby-sat with Simon the previous evening when he and Caroline went for a meal. Laura was always around the house these days.

He greeted the girl with a smile and hello.

"Hi, Mr Ikes. I'm Sammie. I've been here before with Simon."

"Sammie, yes... of course I remember you."

"I'm sorry to bother you so late, but is Simon in?"

"No, sorry. He's out with his..." better not say, girlfriend. "He's out somewhere...gone for a pint, I expect."

"Probably thirsty after working so hard today."

Working hard? Simon? What is she on about? Simon hasn't been working. He and Laura took the twins swimming and then returned for lunch before taking them to the cinema. Tonight they've gone to the opening of a new pub, thought Thomas Ikes. All he could think of was, "I suppose so."

"Did the move go okay?"

"Sorry, what move?"

"Simon's uncle's move? Didn't he come down from Manchester yesterday? You and Simon helped him move into his new house?"

"That move. That was last week, but Simon did not help. He was watching the racing in the park. The move went very well, thanks."

She seemed a bit confused.

"So Simon has been here yesterday and today?"

"Well, he was in Cardiff yesterday, and he's been out and about today, but yes, I suppose he's been here. Why? Was he supposed to meet you?"

She turned her head and looked down the street. She was muttering something under her breath, but he could not catch what she was saying. Her face turned towards him again. Were those tears forming?

"Sammie, is everything okay?"

"Yes. Simon was supposed to see me yesterday, but..." Her words faded off. She lifted the sleeve of her baggy jumper to her face.

"Are you sure you're okay?"

"Yeah. I'll be fine. Tell him I popped up to see him on the off chance... but I was clearly a bit slow in getting the message. Oh, and here's your DVD back, by the way."

"Thanks." He did not know it had gone anywhere. "Did you enjoy it?"

"Yeah, it was...um... good while it lasted."

With that, the girl turned and walked down the street. Thomas Ikes watched her for a moment before returning to his glass of wine. He stopped en route to replace the DVD in his treasured collection.

"Who was that?" Caroline Ikes was now sitting up on the sofa stretching.

"Sammie. She was here a couple of weeks back with Simon."

Caroline stretched her arms.

"What did she want?"

"To see Simon I think. She brought a DVD back."

"DVD? Which one?"

"Just one of my horrors. I didn't even know she had

borrowed it. It's strange that Simon never said anything."

"You know Simon. His head is everywhere but where it should be."

"I suppose you are right."

"Any more wine in that bottle?"

"Yes, plenty, thanks."

"Very funny. Here's my glass."

Simon Ikes arrived at his doorstep twenty minutes past midnight.

It had been a brilliant day. It had been a superb forty-eight hours. He had got a new job and had made his father happy because it looked like someone else was going to pay for Simon to go to university.

He had strengthened his relationship with Laura. The previous evening had proved very successful. They had not done the deed yet, but there were signs that it was not too far away. He might have made more progress had the twins gone to bed when he asked them.

The twins liked Laura. His parents liked Laura. Simon liked Laura. Simon liked Laura very much and was not just after sex. While it would be nice, and he thoroughly enjoyed all the touchy-feely bits that had taken place, he was prepared to wait. He liked spending time with her. This was new territory for Simon. He thought he might be falling in love.

They had spent the whole day together. Swimming, he thought she looked gorgeous in her bikini. Cinema, okay, so what if it was a cartoon? He had enjoyed it. He wished the twins had not insisted on sitting between him and Laura. Simon had taken Laura and the twins to see his Gran. Nanna had been pleased to see them but equally pleased to see them go. *Saturday night is bingo night, and I have to get ready.*

What did Laura say about Italy? Something about the fact that if Italian men take a girlfriend to meet their Grandmother, it's a sign that they are about to get married. He knew she was teasing, really.

To finish it all off, they had enjoyed a meal at the Red Lion, courtesy of the camp brewery guy he had met at the bike races. After that, it was back to hers for another drink, and a chat with Jamie and Caitlin, followed by long, slow, good-night kisses and a quick walk home. He felt good. Life was great. It had been a brilliant day.

He entered the hallway, locking the door behind him. He only stayed in the lounge long enough to switch off the lights and close the door. Reaching the top of the stairs, he visited the loo before entering his bedroom. His hand was on the handle of his bedroom door when he heard his father's voice. Thomas Ikes spoke in a loud whisper.

"Simon."

"What?" His son whispered back.

"You had a visitor."

Simon was intrigued.

"Who?"

"Sammie."

Simon froze.

"What did she want?"

"To see you. She thought you were helping Uncle John today. Why was that?"

"Er...no idea. She was...umm... probably just a bit confused. Did she want anything else?"

"She brought my DVD back. Thanks for lending my stuff without telling me."

"Sorry, Dad."

"She said that she had popped up on the off chance you might be in and something about being a bit slow getting the message. She didn't say anything else but didn't seem very happy."

"Well, that sorts that one out then."

"What?"

"Nothing...um...I'll...er...give her a ring. Goodnight, Dad."

"Yeah 'night Si."

OFFICE LIFE

"So when are your results out?"

"Tomorrow, I collect them from the school at about ten-ish."

"Have you booked the day off?"

"Yes, and I've warned Steve that I'll be in late on Friday too. We'll be doing a bit of celebrating on Thursday night."

"Celebrating or commiserating?"

"We'll have to see."

Simon sipped coffee from the cardboard cup.

His uncle adjusted his collar.

"How are you getting on with Steve?"

"Okay, aye. He's alright. Marty doesn't like him much, but I think he's okay."

"You be careful of Marty. I fear he's a troublemaker."

"Is he? He's always been alright with me. We get on well. Marty's a good laugh. A gang of us are off out on Friday. He said I could stay at his flat if I miss the bus."

"I thought you were going steady now."

"Going steady? How old are you?"

Phillips laughed.

"What I mean is what does Laura think of you out and about in Cardiff on your own? In any case, I'd have thought you'd want to celebrate with your girlfriend."

"She's cool about it. As it happens, she's off to Swansea to celebrate with her friends. She won't be back until Sunday. We'll go out then."

"You be careful on Friday. Cardiff is a bit different from home."

"I know that, Unc. Anyway, I'll have to get back. Mam wants to make sure I'm home safely before they go on holiday."

His uncle glanced around the coffee bar, scanning those

that had arrived for their tea break.

"What time is their flight?"

"Half two. They want to be down there by twelve, so the taxi picks them up at eleven. I'd better catch the last bus home on Friday night. We are starting at four, so I'll probably have had enough by ten o'clock anyway."

"You watch yourself. Take it easy."

"I will. Don't worry." Simon finished the last of his coffee. "I'd better get back, I suppose."

"You carry on; I want to speak to someone else. I'll see you later."

Leaving the coffee bar, Simon made a left, then a right, followed by another right until he had reached "Cardiac Care branch 3 – Wales and the West".

The branch was responsible for collecting and collating data on cardiac care treatment from every hospital in Wales and the west of England. When fully staffed, the unit would consist of fourteen people. Until then, there were seven working to acting team leader Steve McKenzie, a Scot who had transferred from London when DoMO moved down earlier that year. McKenzie was twenty-five, unmarried, short, fat, bespectacled, balding, but ambitious. He had been made temporary team leader and hoped that his branch head, Anna Emery, would keep her promise to consider him for the job on a substantive basis.

Anna Emery, a twenty-eight-year-old English graduate from Newport, had joined DoMO two years earlier. She had jumped at the chance to return nearer home. Working in London had not suited her. It had made her bitter. It had made her doubt herself. Anna had always considered herself brighter than average and had every confidence in her ability, but she quickly discovered she was average. The other thing she learned was that London never stopped. Anna struggled to keep up with the pace. Unbeknown to her superiors and colleagues, she started using other means to sustain herself through the long working days and equally long social evenings she shared with her like-minded equals. Too many drugs, drinking and not enough rest had seen her weight plummet by two stone in as many months and her bank balance fell equally rapidly into the red.

Fortunately, the compensation awarded as part of the relocation package helped to reduce her debt. The move into a flat just a quarter of an hour from her mother and younger sister had started to heal the scars left by her old lifestyle. Anna was grateful for a return to a more normal life. Slowly but surely, she regained her self-confidence and almost natural superiority complex. Anna was happy to keep McKenzie near her because she knew he was inferior. She also knew she could bully him, which she frequently did, confident McKenzie would never respond. He would not bite back. He was too afraid that he would lose his temporary promotion.

Simon sat at his desk reading a message placed on his telephone. It was in Maggie's handwriting telling him to ring Mr C Lyonns at Bristol Gardens. He did not know such a hospital existed.

He turned to Maggie.

"Bristol Gardens?"

She held up her hands.

"That's what he said."

"Fair enough." Simon picked up the phone and carefully dialled the number on the bottom of the pink post-it.

"Good morning, Bristol Zoological Gardens, Michelle speaking. How may I help you?"

Simon was scanning through the half-opened files on his desk, looking for one relating to Bristol Gardens. He was not giving the call his undivided attention.

"Hello, may I speak to Mr C Lyonns, please?"

"Who is this?"

"My name is Ikes. I'm calling from the Department of Medical Options in Cardiff." Sikes had given up looking for a file. He rested his elbow on his desk and looked across at the mountain of papers that covered McKenzie's desk.

"Yes, very funny. I haven't heard that one before."

What was she on about? Simon moved his head forward until he was studying the note again.

"Sorry? Can you put me through to Mr C Lyonns, please?"

"No, I cannot. We do not allow our animals to take calls. If you want to speak to them, you'd better get Dr Doolittle to make a house call." With that, the line went dead.

Sikes was baffled, wondering what had just happened. He stared at the receiver as he mentally replayed the conversation.

"Zoological Gardens? Did she say Bristol Zoological Gardens? Have I just tried to call Mr C Lyonns at Bristol Zoo?" Simon heard sniggering.

He lifted his head and glanced around the unit. Seven pairs of eyes were looking at him. Seven mouths were smiling at him, but he knew who had set him up. Again.

"Marty! You..."

"Had ewe. Sheep shagger!" Marty Freeman leaned back in his chair, tossed his head over the backrest until his long dark hair flowed backwards, and roared. "God, you Valleys boys are so easy." He spun in his chair to face the large whiteboard on the wall behind him. Taking a red marker pen, he scribbled a single stroke under the column marked 'Simon' and then mentally totalled the number of strokes under each name. "Four one now, It looks like you're buying the beer on Friday."

"Just you wait. I'll get my own back."

"Bring it on, woolly back!"

"Children, please. Haven't you any work to do?"

"You can talk, Maggie. You wrote the note for him. You're as bad as him"

Looking older than twenty-one but acting younger, Maggie Hendrickson smiled as she said, "I didn't want to get involved in your games, but Marty made me."

"I bet. It must have been murder for you."

"Well, not really. I thought it was quite a good laugh, if

I'm honest. You'd better get a move on, though, Simon. He's leaving you behind."

"I'll think of something." Sikes returned to one of his files, trying to remember why he needed to contact the Llandudno General Hospital. He was unaware that Maggie Hendrickson was still watching him, smiling at him as he turned the pages of the latest report from Llandudno.

Maggie Hendrickson, full name Magdalena Anna-Victoria Hendrickson, was born and raised in the Rhondda Valley to a Spanish mother and Swedish father. Her parents met during a cultural exchange visit to what was once one of the roughest housing estates in Europe. They met, fell in love and decided to stay in the area. She became a teacher. He lectured at the local university.

Maggie was born three years into the marriage when her parents were still enthused about life in the Rhondda. By the time Maggie reached puberty, her father had tired of the area, and her mother had missed the heat of her native Catalonia. They started planning a move to Barcelona, which took them another five years to achieve.

Maggie had been brought up to be independent and refused to move to a strange country. She moved into her friend's house further down the valley. Within eighteen months, Maggie had a flat of her own, gained two A-levels and a place at the same university where her father had been a lecturer.

Her parents left her a large lump sum, which had to remain in trust until she was eighteen, and made significant monthly credits to her bank account. She had used the trust money as the deposit on her two-bedroom flat and the monthly payments to buy furniture and food.

Three weeks before her nineteenth birthday, Maggie found a part-time job in the local sports centre, which allowed her to earn money doing what she enjoyed – fitness training. She thought she was set for life. That was, however, B.C. – the time before she met Colin.

A year later, Maggie had lost her flat, owed thousands of pounds on credit cards and had to withdraw from her college course to get a job to repay her debts. Her flat and belongings got sold for a pittance. Maggie took several temporary positions until she found herself at DoMO. She was grateful that her parents continued to send her monthly money without asking why she had moved three times in less than two years.

Maggie was unusual for a Welsh girl because she was short, had long auburn hair, dark Mediterranean skin and a large chest. The clash of cultures had given her an almost unique look. She shared her father's blue eyes but also had her mother's features, smooth skin and attractive face. Her breasts were undoubtedly larger than they should have been, considering her lack of height. Had it not been for the regular visits to the gym, an adherence to a healthy diet and a cash shortage that restricted her ability to drink, Maggie would also have had her mother's shape. She did not want a weight problem.

Maggie had joined DoMO when it first moved to Cardiff earlier that spring. It was her first full-time, permanent job, and she loved every minute. She enjoyed it all the more now that younger people were working there. There were many more boys, and two, in particular, had made work all the more pleasurable.

The first was Marty Freeman. The one she called Wild Marty. To Marty, life was one long joke. He had only worked there a month but had already received a verbal warning about his antics. Marty's real love was music; he dreamed of singing in a successful rock group. Freeman also fancied himself as a lady's man. He frequently made suggestive comments to Maggie, for which she had severely rebuked him in front of their colleagues, but Marty was not put off. He felt sure that if he played his cards right, he would get what he wanted from Maggie.

Freeman was twenty-two, Cardiffian through and

through, currently unattached and living alone. He had a child from a short-term relationship when he was eighteen and paid for the child's maintenance even though he had never set eyes on his daughter. Marty was five foot ten inches tall, of average build, with long dark hair, frequently worn in a ponytail. He was obsessed with the suggestion that the management of DoMO was corrupt. Maggie did not much like this aspect of Marty's behaviour.

The other recent addition to DoMO, who had impacted Maggie, was Simon Ikes. Shy and naïve, Simon took all the insults about his accent and the fact he lived in the Valleys in his stride. Maggie found it strange that Simon seemed unaware that he was attractive to the opposite sex.

Simon was young and willing. No job was too menial for Simon. If he could help you, he would. He was always happy to chat and enjoyed a laugh. Maggie also thought Simon was smart, both in appearance and intelligence. He knew much for one so young. Maggie believed Simon was going places.

There was another side to Simon that intrigued Maggie. Why was he so close to the bosses? Millington and Phillips regularly spoke to Simon, whereas they barely acknowledged the existence of the rest of the teams. Why wouldn't Simon tell her how he knew them? Why was he so reluctant to talk about his home life and family? Was it just shyness, or was there something he wanted to hide? She was also concerned about his health. Why had he gone to the hospital twice in the last week? Was he ill? Did he have a disease? Maggie thought that unlikely, but she wanted more information. Simon would tell her things if she asked, but why would he never volunteer information? There was a lot about Simon that Maggie wanted to know, but she was careful not to press him too hard too soon. He had only worked here three weeks. She did not want to scare him off.

The other two members of the team were on a training course. They were Adam Sluman, a twenty-three-year-old Cambridge University, Economics student from the north of the city working during his summer holiday, and Sue Smith, a twenty-eight-year-old divorced mother of two. It was Sue's first job since her younger son was born, and she was finding it hard to cope.

Maggie was pleased that Simon and Marty had joined her on the unit. Before them, things were very quiet. Adam rarely spoke, and Maggie thought he was highly snobbish. Sue was always in a rush, never having time to chat, hardly ever in on time in the morning and frequently having to take days off. That situation should change now that Anna had arranged to alter Sue's hours.

Simon looked up from his file. Steve was in Anna's room, and Maggie was on the telephone. He rose from his seat.

"Hey Marty, I've just got to pop around to records. There's something weird about this one." Marty laughed as Simon picked up his pocket recorder.

"Nobody is going to pinch it, you know. You Valleys boys don't trust city folk, do you?"

"I can't be too careful. I borrowed this from my dad. Be back in a tick. Just going to get this checked."

"Another one? I told you, Simon. There is something strange going on in this place. The records don't always add up."

Simon shook his head.

"That's as maybe, but I've told you that you need proof."

"That union bloke that I met when I had my warning, he was one of those that got sacked up in London. He reckons they were all set up and that the bosses here are corrupt."

"So you said, but you still need proof. I'll see you in a bit." Simon disappeared around the corner. Marty returned to his file.

To the rest of the office, Marty was reading papers and making notes. He wasn't. He was too busy scribbling down words for the new tune that had filled his head that morning. His mind was full of guitar and bass lines, and Marty was not happy about being interrupted by Simon's 'phone.

"Maggie, be a love and get that will you?"

Maggie did not answer. Marty saw she was engrossed in her own telephone conversation. Marty watched as Maggie twirled her hair between her fingers as she listened to her telephone call.

He picked up his phone, hit the hash button then typed in Simon's number.

"Hello, Cardiac Care 3. Marty Freeman speaking. How can I help?" He read his script efficiently but without enthusiasm, only using those words because he had to. He thought it sounded crass.

"Hello, is Bill Smith there, please?"

Not another fucking call for Bill Smith. That's the third one this week, thought Freeman before speaking. "Sorry, there is no Bill Smith in this section. Are you sure you've got the right number?"

"Yes. You said you work on Cardiac Care 3."

"I do, but..."

"You deal with Wales, and the West, don't you?"

"We do, but there is no Bill Smith here. Sorry"

"Well, can you take a message for him?"

"There's no point. He doesn't work here, and I don't know anybody of that name."

"But can you take a message?"

"I can, but there's no point. He doesn't work here, and I don't know anyone of that name."

"Whether you know him or not is not the issue. I've been given this number, and I want Bill Smith to ring me back as soon as possible, please."

"But he doesn't work here! Which part of that sentence don't you understand?"

"I beg your pardon. What did you say your name was? Freeman, wasn't it? I'm not too fond of your attitude. Put me through to your supervisor."

The last thing Marty needed was more grief.

"I'm errr...sorry, I over reacted. Of course, I'll take your number," Marty could not sound more insincere.

"Don't bother if it's too much trouble. I'll ring back later." The line went dead.

Marty was still reflecting on his latest call when Simon returned a few minutes later.

"Si, do you get any calls for a Bill Smith?"

Simon looked puzzled. "No. Why? Should I?"

"Nah, it's probably nothing. It's just that people keep ringing this section and asking to speak to some Bill Smith. It's starting to get on my fucking nerves."

"No, I can't say I've heard of him. And I haven't had any calls for him either. Have you, Maggie?"

"Have I what?"

"Had any calls for Bill Smith?"

"Bill, who?"

"Never mind," said Freeman. "It's not important."

Sikes looked at Maggie and shrugged his shoulders. Maggie looked bemused.

Thursday morning at ten o'clock, Simon, GarGar and Dicey walked through the school gates to collect their A-level results.

GarGar had two B's and a C, which suited him; he was not interested in attending university and had only taken his exams to keep his mother happy. GarGar was content working in the family newsagents.

Dicey had one A and two B's, enough to get him into university to study Aeronautical Engineering.

Simon had four straight A's. The results were just what he wanted but had never expected.

"What the fuck happened, Sikesy?" asked GarGar as they sat in the park. GarGar popped one of the cans of lager they bought from the local shop.

Dicey was on his mobile calling the office for Simon.

"No idea. I don't understand it," Simon scratched his crotch through his jeans. "Maths was always my best subject, but I can't believe I've got A's in English and History. My mother will be well-chuffed. All that tutoring paid off."

"So you'll be off to uni after the summer?"

"Aye, I suppose so, but since I've been working, I've started to wonder whether to take a year off. I might delay going to uni for a year. I'll have a word with my parents and the bosses at work. They'll pay to put me through uni if I get a permanent job."

"So you could leave without any student loans?"

"Probably."

"You are a lucky twat Sikesy."

"And I get to spend some more time with Laura." Sikes swallowed from his can and then pulled a face as beer droplets spilt onto his T-shirt.

When GarGar went to the toilet, Sikes lost himself in thoughts about recent events. His life had taken quite a turn, and he was looking forward to the future.

Dicey's voice brought him back to earth.

"Don't look now, but Farley's approaching. I still owe him money for that valet, so I'll just nip to the bog with GarGar."

Sikes turned to see Dave Farley and another man, both in overalls, walking towards him. The pair looked engrossed in conversation, and Farley took a while to spot Sikes. When he did, he studied the pile of cans on the bench.

"Yo Sikesy boy! It's a bit early in the day to be drinking isn't it?"

"I've just had my results, so I thought I'd have a bit of a party," said Sikes. Farley had rolled up his shirtsleeves, and Sikes noted that his arm bore the obligatory plaster. He even wears it to work, he thought.

"So are you celebrating or drowning your sorrows? What did you get?"

Sikes updated him on his results and said he appreciated Farley's congratulations. He asked how Robyn got on, and Farley told him she also had good grades. She had not done as well as Sikes but had done enough to get her into Cardiff University.

"I don't know all those brains and good looks. What is she doing with me?"

No accounting for taste," thought Sikes, who offered no comment.

They struggled to talk until Farley's mate told him it was time for them to get back to work. Farley repeated his congratulations. Sikes thanked him and told him to say well done to Robyn from him. After which, there followed another awkward silence before Farley bade him farewell.

Sikes' two mates returned once they were confident Farley was out of sight.

"How is Dave?" Dicey watched as Farley moved further away.

"Still a prick," said Sikes.

"What is it with you and him?" asked GarGar. "You've never liked him, have you? Is it because he's going out with Robyn? If it is, then get over it, I think Laura is ten times better than Robyn."

"You're right there Ginge," said Dicey.

Sikes shook his head.

"No, it's nothing to do with Robyn. It's a long story, but I don't want to talk about it." He grabbed the bag of cans. "I thought we were celebrating?" he said, handing out the beer.

Simon had arranged to meet Laura at the pub later that afternoon. He arrived earlier than expected. It was not a problem. Mike told him to go straight upstairs and mentioned that his wife had gone shopping. He made a joke about the likely cost. Simon laughed politely.

Laura wrapped her arms around his neck.

Simon returned her kiss and asked, "Well, how did you get on?"

"I had an A and two Bs. Not bad, eh?"

Simon smiled. "That's great, Law. Well done."

What about you? How did you get on?"

Simon told her his results; Laura was delighted.

"Well done you, so what happens now?"

"I think I will defer for a year if you can put up with me sticking around for a while longer?"

Laura beamed.

"No problem," she said, as her arms went back around Simon's neck.

They kissed again. Simon squeezed her buttocks. "I've got something for you."

Laura smirked.

"I can tell."

Simon shook his head. "Well, that and all, but first, there's this."

As Laura stepped backwards, Simon handed her a carrier bag containing a box.

Laura looked at the package.

"What is it?"

"Open it and find out."

Laura excitedly opened the bag, then the box, and held a camera in her hands.

"Si, it's lovely and the one I wanted. That's brilliant, thank you." She reached up and kissed him again.

"You're worth it. Congratulations," said Sikes. "I've got something else to tell you."

"What's that?" Laura saw Simon was smiling and sensed it would be good news.

"I've had the test results back, and I'm all clear. On all fronts."

Laura's eyes opened wide, and the outer edges of her smiling lips almost touched her ears. "It was never in doubt, but when did you find out?"

"Yesterday."

"Why didn't you say?"

"I thought I'd give you a surprise."

"You've done that alright. That's great news."

Laura placed her hands on Simon's chest and pushed him onto the sofa.

"Stay there a minute." She rushed back to shut the door that led down to the bar and flicked the lock. Retracing her steps, she unhooked the button on the waistband of her shorts and allowed herself to fall on top of Simon.

Simon wrapped his arms around her, and they kissed passionately.

"What about your parents?" Simon asked, breaking his mouth away from hers.

"My mother's gone shopping, and my dad won't leave the bar," said Laura. She worked her teeth into Simon's neck. "Cait is out with Jamie. He's got a day off."

Her hands were undoing Simon's shirt.

"Are you going to be okay here? It's not too uncomfortable, is it?"

"Stop fussing. Other times I've got to fight you off." Laura's hands were undoing Simon's button fly.

"But why here? There's a bedroom over there."

"That's right above the bar. My father might hear something. Anyway, I'm fine here."

Laura stayed still, allowing Simon to remove her top. He touched her softly.

"That feels so good."

Laura eased her shoulders downward, and their mouths locked again.

HAPPY DAYS

Simon Ikes had a spring in his step as he walked into the office the following day. His parents were delighted with his examination results and happy to go along with his decision to defer. The university confirmed they would keep his place open. His uncle told him that, provided he was successful in his application, DoMO would sponsor him, but he urged Simon to take his time. There would be no need to rush this decision. He had a year to decide.

Sikes felt like a child on Christmas morning. His father transferred money into his account as a reward for his effort. He and Laura had done the deed for the first time, and it had been more meaningful than the sex he had previously enjoyed. Afterwards, they had lain together on the sofa, stroking, touching and kissing. That was also enjoyable, and Sikes thought it was probably his best-ever experience.

The previous evening the pair had been out with GarGar and Kelly together with Dicey, and his latest girlfriend, Hannah. It had been a good night, allowing for Kelly's sarcastic comments. Simon was relieved that he had told Laura what Kelly was like and how things had turned out with Sammie. He and Laura finished their day together as they had started it, making love on her parents' settee.

He enjoyed a peaceful sleep, woken to find a sunny summer morning and his mother ironing clothes ready to go into the suitcase. She stopped long enough to make him breakfast.

The train had been on time, and the seat next to him remained empty for the whole journey. Simon disliked being bothered by strangers and having to make polite conversation.

Life was good. He felt great and thought he looked good. He was ready for a few beers, possibly a club, after work, then a bus or taxi home depending on the time of night.

Marty greeted him with his usual warmth.

"Fuckin' 'ell sheep shagger, you look like the cat which caught the cheese."

"How can a cat catch cheese, you dozy prat?" asked Maggie. "Morning Simon, you do look rather dapper today."

"Dapper! What the fuck does that mean?" laughed Marty.

"Piss off," snapped Maggie, checking that McKenzie was away from his desk.

Cardiac Care 3 was laid out the same as the rest of the building. Groups of three desks joined each other in a block. Two desks joined together lengthways, with the third attached at ninety degrees to the ends of the other two.

Maggie sat to Simon's right, and Marty sat opposite him. The other members of the team sat behind Marty. Their desks were empty. McKenzie sat behind Maggie, which allowed him to see all his staff. The section was separated from the other branches by large purple screens that matched the carpet.

Simon pulled his seat out from under his desk. Sitting on it, he was surprised when it sank to its lowest point. His bottom shuddered as the seat stopped dead against the metal support, and his back collided with the backrest.

"Had ewe!" Marty roared. He placed another line against his score. "You are too fuckin' easy, valley boy. That's five to me and only one to the sheep shagger. And it's the last day today. You've had it, sunshine. I've whipped your Valleys' ass. That'll be a tenner, please."

"Whoa, slow down, man. It's early days yet. I've still got plenty of time to get you back."

"But you'll never get me five times today, Si. Come on, pay up."

"Hold on. We continue until we go down to the pub, as you said. It's ten o'clock now, and I still have five and a half hours left if we plan to leave at half three. I'll think of something."

"You've got no chance woolly back. Us city folk are too fuckin' smart for ewe valley bumpkins."

"We'll see," said Simon winking at Maggie.

She smiled at him as she picked up her bag and walked off the section.

Simon removed the cord tied around the bar to raise and lower the chair and reset his chair to the correct height. Unlocking his drawer, he grabbed his pen and reached for the first of the morning's files.

A moment later, Maggie's 'phone rang. It rang twice, then a short gap followed by two more rings. Simon knew that this signified an external call. He looked at Marty, who had no intention of answering someone else's calls, so Simon picked up his phone, hit the hash, then Maggie's extension, and spoke into the handset.

"Good morning, Cardiac Care 3. Simon Ikes speaking, how can I help?"

He recognised the female voice.

"All set?"

"Yes. This is Cardiac Care 3." The line went dead.

"Oh, I see," said Simon into the void. "That's okay. It's not a problem. Yes, of course, I can tell you who signed the form. Bear with me a moment. I need to take a few details." He surveyed his desk for a notepad which he moved nearer. "Right then. Your name is?" Silence."Is there one n or two in Connor?" Still silence."Two, thank you, and the name of the hospital is?" No response."No, that's okay. I can spell that."

Maggie's telephone rang again. Marty made no effort to answer it. Simon threw a paperclip at him and then nodded towards the 'phone as Marty looked up from his lyrics.

Simon watched as Marty pressed buttons while balancing the receiver between his shoulder and head.

"Hello, Cardiac Care 3. Marty Freeman speaking. How can I help?" asked Marty.

A lady's voice filled his ear.

"Good morning Marty. Can I speak to Bill Smith, please?"

Not fucking Bill Smith again, Freeman thought. "Sorry, there is no Bill Smith in this section. Are you sure you've got the right number?"

Simon looked over the desk to see Marty pulling a face.

The voice in Marty's ear continued.

"Yes. Cardiac Care 3. You deal with Wales and the West, don't you?"

"We do, but there is no Bill Smith here. Sorry"

The lady was adamant. "Well, can you take a message for him?"

"Sorry no. He doesn't work here, and I don't know anybody of that name."

"But this is the number he's given me. He must work there. Will you take my number and tell him to ring me?"

"I can, but there's no point. He doesn't work here, and I don't know him."

"Well, whether you know him or not, I've been given this number, and I want Bill Smith to ring me back."

"Okay, I'll take your number."

The lady read out a series of numbers, but Marty was not the least interested in writing down any of them. "I'll tell him to ring you."

"Many thanks," said the grateful lady caller. He replaced his receiver and saw that Simon had finished his call.

"Honestly, Sikes, that's every day this week someone has rung for Bill fuckin' Smith. If I ever catch him, I'll rip his…" His sentence was cut short by McKenzie returning to his desk.

"Hey…er… Marty, have you done your stats yet? Anna's waiting for them, you know?" McKenzie's Scottish lilt did little to help Marty's mood.

"Gis a chance, Steve. They haven't got to be in until half ten."

"I kno' tha', but the sooner you finish them, the better it'll be for all of us. Now stop talking for a wee while and get those stats done."

Marty muttered under his breath. Simon picked up a

new file. Maggie returned to her desk, patting Simon softly on the back as she passed him. She placed her bag on the floor and then removed from it a small plastic bag that she discretely handed to Simon. He took it quietly and winked at Maggie again.

"Thank you," he said.

She mouthed her reply. "My pleasure."

Friday lunchtime was traditionally pub day, but as this Friday evening was party time, Simon and Marty chose to go to the staff restaurant. Maggie declined the offer to join them as she had to go to the bank.

The pair collected and paid for their meals, then carried them to a table by the window. It did not take long for Marty to raise his favourite subject.

"I've been doing more digging, and I'm telling you, Si, this place is fuckin' corrupt. I did those stats this morning and checked them twice. They clearly show that London Central is doing piss poor as far as cardiac care treatment is concerned. They were bottom but three again, and that's the third fuckin' week. I e-mails the stats to Anna, and she gets them onto the central database. Why only she can do it, I don't know. It's not as if Anna Lady Muck all fuckin' mighty understands them anyway. Just before I come to lunch, I popped around to see that Sharon bird on stats collation and made out I've got a query on one of the figures. She opens up the list, and what do I see? London Central is in the top ten for cardiac care – it just shouldn't happen, man. That hospital is shit. It's failing and should be looked at. Someone is paying people here to change the figures."

Simon offered no reply. He forked a portion of curry into his mouth.

Marty took a drink from his can. "And another thing...y'know Michelle in the post room?"

Sikes nodded.

"Well, she has evidence that three large plain brown

paper packages are delivered monthly. The envelopes have no postmark. They are marked as confidential and to be opened by the addressee only. She's sent me a photo, and it's obvious that these packages are crammed with rectangular blocks of paper. I reckon they are about the size of ten-pound notes. All three packets are addressed to the Chief Accounting Officer, and that's Armitage, but they don't go to Armitage. They go to Millington. We reckon those packages contain cash, and Millington is getting paid to change figures. That's why the stats get altered. Weirdly, the only person allowed to touch the envelopes is the head of the post room, Charlie Chann. Every month, regular as clockwork, the packages are delivered to Chann direct by courier. Nobody else can sign for them. He receives them and then takes take them straight to Millington. He won't speak to anyone about it. I reckon that he's been told to keep it quiet. Everyone in the postroom reckons Charlie is shit at his job, but the bosses do nothing about him. He is always harassing the younger girls, including Michele, but does he get the sack? No chance. Does he get a warning? No way, Jose. Me on the other hand, I do one stupid thing wrong and get hauled before HR. I'm given a fuckin' verbal warning immediately."

"How does Michele know about this?" asked Simon, ripping into his naan bread.

"Because she lets old Charlie Chann get close to her. She flirts with him and makes him feel he's got a chance of a shag. So she's been in his room when the courier delivers the packages."

"Why do they call Sammy Charlie Chan? He's half Japanese and not Chinese, isn't he?" Simon looked puzzled.

"I don't know, and quite frankly, I don't give a flying shit. All I know is that something bad is going down here, and it's not right." Marty took another sip from his can and started to eat again. The sight of a pretty young female with long fair hair and wearing a short skirt walking past the table distracted him.

"Hi ya, Marty. Are you out tonight?"

"Certainly am, darlin'. Where are we meeting?"

"The Royal Albert, I think." The girl stopped to talk. She held a plate of salad.

"Oh no! Not the Albert. The landlord in there is a right prick."

"We don't have to stay there all night, do we?"

"No, I suppose not. What time are you out?"

"About half seven, I think. I've got to go to Susie's to change first."

"Why change? You look good enough to me as you are. What do you think, Si? Good enough to eat."

Simon had not been listening. He was too busy eating. "Very tasty."

"Thank you, Simon and I thought you were the shy type. Are you not going to give us any trouble tonight? Hope you can keep him in order, Marty."

"I will don't worry," said Marty as the girl walked on.

Simon blushed but did not know why.

Marty was packing his stuff away as Simon continued his call to Laura.

"Aye, me too...What time will you be back? No, I'm not doing much tomorrow. My parents will be gone by lunchtime, and I am supposed to be going for a drive with Gar and Dicey. Dicey's borrowing one of his uncle's cars...Aye should be fun... Nor me, I can't wait...See you Sunday."

Simon replaced the handset.

"So that's it then. Your little girlie friend is off bonking in Swansea, is she?"

Simon laughed.

Maggie shook her head in disbelief.

"Marty, is that all you think about?"

Marty held his hands to his chin as if in thought.

"Well, that and music... and beer."

Simon joined his laughter. Maggie smiled quietly.

Marty looked at the clock.

"Are we ready to rock and roll then? It is time to go. Don't forget my tenner sheep shagger."

"I've just got one more call to make." Simon winked at Maggie. She looked the other way.

"Get on with it. It's half past now, and you're officially wasting valuable drinking time."

Simon lifted the receiver and pressed four buttons. He lowered his head below desk level so Marty could not see him.

Marty's 'phone rang.

"Shit," said Marty. "This had better not be stats."

"Hello Cardiac Care 3, Marty Freeman speaking. How can I help?"

"Hello. This is Bill Smith here. Do you have any messages for me?"

Marty recognised the voice coming from the desk opposite.

"Very fucking funny, Si. Ha fucking ha. I don't think."

"Had ewe!" Simon exclaimed, replacing his receiver.

"Okay, but it is still four-two. You owe me a tenner valley boy."

"I think you'll find it is now seven-four to me." Simon raised himself to his full height.

"How do you work that one out?"

"Bill Smith had messages every day this week, so that gives me five extra points."

"Fuck off. You can't count them. They weren't yours."

"I think you'll find they were."

Simon retrieved a plastic bag from his drawer. Opening it, he took out the recorder. He flicked the switch to play. Simon's voice came first.

"Monday morning ten twenty-seven am."

Marty's voice was loud and clear.

"Hello Cardiac Care 3, Marty Freeman speaking. How can I help?"

Then it was Simon again, this time doing a poor Irish

accent.

"Top of the morning to ya, sir. Can I speak to Bill Smith?"

Simon fast-forwarded until the machine beeped. Again, his voice came out.

"Tuesday two fifteen pm."

Marty sounded quite jolly.

"Good afternoon, you're through to Cardiac Care 3, Marty Freeman speaking. How may I help?"

Simon's Asian accent was worse than his Irish.

"Good afternoon. Yes. Can I speak to Bill Smith, please?"

Marty's voice showed that he had no idea to whom he was talking.

"I'm sorry there is no Bill Smith here."

"Enough! Enough! It was you, you bastard. But you were off yesterday."

"My mate Dicey rang in for me."

"But who was the woman?" Marty looked deflated.

"Me, of course," said Maggie. "Hello, can I speak to Bill Smith, please?"

"Might have known you'd be involved. You sheep shaggers always stick together."

Maggie blew Marty a kiss.

"Well, Si, I suppose you think you're so fucking clever, don't you? I'm not sure whether they count as practical jokes... they are a bit lame if you ask me..."

Maggie spoke up for Simon. "What? And getting Simon to ring C Lyons at the zoo is not lame? Every one of those calls got you annoyed."

"This has nothing to do with you, Maggs," said Marty, but he could see that she would take some persuasion. "Okay, okay, but I ain't got a tenner spare today, so you'll have to make do with this." He picked up a pen, scribbled IOU £10 on a scrap of paper, signed it, crumpled it up and threw it at Simon.

"It's your round then, valley boy."

"My pleasure," said Simon grinning. He collected the note, opened it, folded it neatly and locked it in his drawer next to the recording device.

BACK AGAIN

Friday, Cardiff, and it was another warm summer Friday evening in the Welsh capital. The lounge bar at the Royal Albert pub in St Mary Street was almost to capacity, much to the delight of Steven Moores, the licensee.

The gang from DoMO sat in the corner of the bar. They occupied four large round tables, which they had taken from other parts of the pub. The crowd numbered over twenty, and the more drink flowed, the louder they became.

They had remained under Moores' watchful eye since arriving at four o'clock, although there were only five of them then. Moores had not minded when others joined them but began to get slightly concerned when they moved chairs and tables around. He liked to see people enjoy themselves, particularly if they were spending money in his pub, but he needed to ensure they stayed in line. It was his licence, after all, and he had not worked hard for eighteen months to have his livelihood threatened by raucous customers.

He left his staff to manage the other customers and went to his observation post to the left of the bar. Here he could lean against the ornate pillar, drink a pint and discreetly keep an eye on developments.

Watching the gang had its advantages. For one thing, the crowd contained at least two ladies that were well worth observing. Moores' attention was drawn to the short, dark-skinned girl with long reddish brown hair and large breasts. Moores spotted her as soon as she entered the pub. The short dress with its low-cut neckline drew his attention like a magnet. Moores thought it was a shame that she seemed so tied up with the tall bloke with the fair hair. The pair were involved in a deep and meaningful conversation. He was not too devastated; there was always the bleached blond with the skimpy top and ultra-tight trousers. She appeared to be unattached. Moores watched her closely and admired how her bottom swayed when she walked.

Moores watched as she scribbled something on the back of an envelope, collected three notes from the ashtray in the centre of one of the tables, and rose to walk to the bar. She spoke to the tall, fair-haired boy, who stood ready to accompany her.

"Steve! Steve! Give us a hand here! We're rushed off our feet."

The voice grated in his ears.

"Okay, I'm coming."

Over the fifteen years, he had been married to her, Steve Moores had grown far less tolerant of the sound of Sue's voice and particularly hated it when she shouted. It was more like a screech. He had asked her not to scream, but as was usually the case, she had ignored his request.

He emptied his glass and returned to the bar.

There were hordes of customers waiting, but Moores decided to prioritise the bleach blond. He would serve her as quickly as possible.

"Are you coming to the club with us Simon?" The short blonde girl looked up at Simon, stroking the end of her hair as she did so.

Simon shook his head. "Nah. I'm off home. My last bus is at ten."

"Couldn't you stay in Cardiff?"

Simon noted she referred to the city as Care-dif.

"No, not tonight. I've got a busy day tomorrow."

"So we'll have to make the most of you while you're here." She placed her arm through his and rested her head on his arm as they waited to be served. They did not have to wait long.

"Getting quite pally with Janine, aren't you?" Maggie took a full glass from Simon's large circular tray in front of him.

"Not really," said Simon, a little surprised at the comment. "Why?"

"No reason. You've been to the bar with her twice, and when I looked up just now, she had her head on your arm."

Simon had not thought anything of it. "That's just the way she is."

"Just the way, who is?" Janine had joined them. She leaned across Simon to place the change in the ashtray that contained the drinks kitty.

"Nobody important," said Maggie before filling her mouth with cider.

Simon placed the tray on the table and then shrugged his shoulders as Janine looked at him.

"Hey Simon, that barman is a bit of alright, isn't he? I think he used to be a rugby player. Bit of a nosey fucker mind. I felt like I was being interrogated. "

"Well, Jan, I reckon you were in there."

Janine looked back toward the bar and saw Moores was still staring at her. She returned his smile.

"Do you reckon Si? I do think he's quite tasty. Big shoulders an' that. Shame about his belly, though, but he can work on that. I'd be happy to help him."

Simon shook his head as he regained his seat.

Anna left at eight, followed ten minutes later by Steve McKenzie. Their departure signalled it was time for a change of venue. Simon was among the first to stand ready to leave.

"Bye now. Thanks for coming. See you again," said Moores as he arrived to clear the table.

"Bye," said Simon.

"He's a dish," said Janine under her breath. "Didn't he used to play for Wales or something?"

"Aye, I reckon he did." Simon put his arm through his coat sleeve.

Janine scribbled something onto the beer mat and

handed it to the barman. She smiled at Moores and watched him slide the card into his trouser pocket. She looked at Simon and winked before walking to the door.

Marty caught up with Simon as the crowd progressed slowly up the street.

"Innit weird how Anna leaves, and Steve always goes shortly afterwards?" He was holding his flowing locks in one hand and using the other to feed his hair through a thin fabric band.

Simon had not thought about it.

"I suppose."

"Something is going on there. That pair are up to something."

Simon found the suggestion amusing.

"You are kidding? Anna and Steve? She'd eat him for breakfast. I think she only sees him as her lap dog, her poodle. All he does is run around obeying her orders. I can't see them two being up to anything."

Marty was not persuaded.

"I'm telling you something is going on there. I'm not sure what, but there's something, and I intend to find out more."

Simon shrugged his shoulders.

"Aye, well, good luck with that."

"Luck's got fuck all to do with it, mate." Marty tapped the side of his nose. "I have a nose for finding things out."

It was time for Simon to depart.

"Right, that's it. I'm off."

Janine looked disappointed.

"Do you have to go, Si? Can't you stay in Cardiff?"

Where is this Care-dif? Sikes thought. "No, I'd better go. I've got things to do tomorrow."

"Well, stay down here tonight and catch an early bus home in the morning. They run quite frequently to your place, don't they?"

Simon nodded but still rose from his seat."They do, but I've got an early start."

"You are very welcome to stay in my place?"

Simon didn't need to think about the offer.

"Thanks, Jan, but I've got to go."

He looked to see where Marty had gone and spotted him in the corner of the dance floor. He was necking Maggie. Marty's hands were moving slowly across Maggie's back and her backside. They appeared to be oblivious to everyone and everything around them.

Janine followed Simon's gaze and tried to describe what she believed he was thinking.

"It looks like he's got other plans." She put a hand on his shoulder. "Sorry, Si."

"What are you sorry for?"

" I thought you and Maggie were... you know...going to be seeing each other."

"What? Me and Maggie? No, no chance. We're just mates. We work together, that's all."

"So there's still a chance for me then?" Janine took hold of his hand.

Simon laughed.

"I suppose so, but don't tell my girlfriend."

He removed his hand from Janine's grasp, leaned, gave her a peck on the cheek, and said, "See you next week."

"Bye Si," replied Janine.

The others mumbled something similar. Simon held up his hand in a short wave. He looked across the dance floor. Maggie and Marty had finished kissing but still held each other. Maggie's head rested on Marty's chest. She caught Simon's glance and smiled.

"Have a good night," said Sikes as he left the club.

RELATIONSHIPS

"Simon, Simon, wake up. I've made you some coffee."

Simon's eyes reacted slowly to Laura's voice.

"What time is it?"

"Quarter to seven." She sat on the bed and placed one of the mugs on the cabinet beside the bed, taking care not to spill any on the alarm clock.

Sikes rubbed his eyes and yawned. Sitting up, he took the other mug from her.

"Thanks."

He surveyed the room. The pale pink bedding was not to his taste, but his mother liked it, and as it was her bedroom, it was only fitting that she should choose the colour scheme.

Laura spoke again."Are you okay? Did you sleep alright?"

"Yeah, fine, thanks. I slept like a log." There was no hint of shyness. "I liked being snuggled up by you."

Simon placed his arm around her shoulder and squeezed lightly. The thick towelling material of his dressing gown creased slightly under pressure, but Laura did not seem to notice,

"Hope you don't mind me borrowing this? It was all I could find. I'll have to remember to bring my gown next time."

Simon liked the idea of a repeat performance. "Sorry, I've got to work today, Law, but I'll be home early. Shall we go out tonight?"

"I'd sooner stay in if it's all the same to you. It seems a shame not to use the space while we have it. It's a lovely house."

"I suppose it is." Simon smiled.

He placed the coffee mug on his father's bedside cabinet and reached for her. She allowed herself to fall backwards until she was lying flat again. The back of her head rested on the pillow. He kissed her forehead and gently stroked her hair.

"So you still like me then."

"Very much," said Simon frankly. "I'm pleased you stayed over."

"And me." They kissed. Their mouths tasted of coffee.

Laura moved onto her side and placed her arm around Simon. She kissed him again.

"What time do you have to be in?"

"Any time before ten."

"What time are the trains?"

"Every half hour. I think I'll catch the nine o'clock."

Laura glanced at the bedside clock.

"That's ages away," she said, untying the cord holding the robe together. It fell open, exposing her breasts. Flicking back the duvet, she climbed on top of Simon. He could feel her knickers rubbing against his naked private parts, although they did not feel so private anymore.

Work could not pass quick enough for Simon. He was desperate to get back to Laura. She was spending the day with her sister and Jamie. They were going to view their new flat. Laura would return to Simon's house by six o'clock. Chinese takeaway was on the menu tonight. Simon knew what he wanted for dessert.

Laura had no reservations about staying over and was quite open with her father when she rang to tell him she would not be home. Simon was happy to be reassured that Mike was broad-minded. He was pretty sure his parents would not have minded Laura staying over, but they might have taken exception to the fact that their son and his girlfriend had been in their bed. Simon knew they would find out about the visitor even if he did not mention it. The neighbours would soon bring his parents up to date. He decided not to worry about it and smiled to himself again as he thought about the last couple of days. It had been one of his better weekends.

Saturday morning had seen his parents depart for the airport, collected by minibus, and Simon had spoken to Laura on the 'phone before he met up with GarGar and Dicey. Dicey had borrowed his uncle's car and had taken his friends on a mystery trip. None of them knew where they were going.

Following rules that Dicey had concocted, they covered a few hundred miles before arriving in Birmingham. Simon had never been to the city before and did panic slightly when they got lost in Edgbaston. However, once they had found their way around, Sikes enjoyed the chicken balti. They returned from Birmingham in time to grab a pint at a local pub. He arrived home to a recorded message from his parents telling him that they had arrived safely, but the flight arrived three hours late. The twins sent their love, and his father reminded him not to take the car if he was drinking. His mother fussed over what he should eat.

Sunday had been even better. Simon was booked in for lunch with his Nan. He enjoyed roast beef and vegetables, a long chat about the old days, and a few glasses of chilled white wine. His grandmother's friends were coming around for the evening, and Simon was ushered off the premises by four o'clock to give her time to prepare.

Laura returned home at quarter to five, and he was waiting for her at the pub. Absence had certainly made Simon's heart grow fonder. His eyes almost left their sockets when she entered wearing a short navy blue dress and matching shoes. Her hair was left to hang the usual way. Sunglasses rested on the top of her head. Laura's face bore very little make-up, but Simon immediately recognised the fragrant aroma of her favourite perfume.

They walked to the park and strolled around for an hour or so. Simon's hand rarely left hers, and seldom had he felt so at ease in a girl's company. They talked and walked and walked and talked. Returning to the town centre, they shared a quick drink at a pub before moving on to Simon's house to share a bottle of his father's wine. It was in the middle of a particularly emotional moment that Simon made the offer for Laura to stay over. She readily accepted and called her parents, not to seek their approval but to let them know she would not be home. Her father had answered but had not objected. Laura knew he would not.

Simon thought of these events as he sat in the meeting room. He was supposed to listen to Steve conduct his weekly team briefing, but Steve was even more boring than usual. Try as he might, McKenzie was not a motivator, and his efforts at inspiring his team failed miserably. The faces of the team members showed they wanted the meeting to end. Steve eventually granted their wish.

"Right then, unless anybody has anything else to say, let's get to it. Remember team, we should aspire to maximise accuracy, efficiency and camaraderie. Don't think ABC think AEC – accuracy, efficiency and camaraderie. "

"I'm thinking BSB," said Marty quietly as he and Sikes returned to their desks.

"BSB?"

"Boring Scottish Bastard."

They both laughed.

"Good weekend?" Simon asked as Marty sat down.

His work mate checked who else was on the branch before answering.

"Not bad, not bad at all."

"Anything I should know?"

Freeman spoke quietly.

"I spent most of it with Maggie."

"So Friday night worked out okay for you then?" Sikes was about to take his seat when he saw Maggie strolling back to the section. McKenzie accompanied her, and he was pointing to something in the file he carried. Sikes tilted his head in their direction. Marty took the hint.

"Time for a cuppa, I think."

As he and Sikes walked off section, Marty winked at Maggie, who blew him a kiss in reply. Steve saw nothing; his head was still in the file.

"Well, what happened?" asked Simon as he delivered two

cups of tea to their table on the island.

"What do you expect? Maggie stayed in my flat on Friday night, and then I stayed at her place on Saturday night. It's all right up the Valleys, isn't it? I thought it would be a right dump, but it isn't."

"Aye, we've got running water and electricity in the Valleys these days."

Marty ignored the sarcasm. He took a sip of tea and pulled a face having not added his usual copious amount of sugar. This situation got rectified immediately.

"What did you do yesterday?"

"Not much. I left on the first bus back because I had arranged to meet someone else last night. I was back home by three."

"Not another girl?" The tea was a little hot for Simon.

"No, nothing like that, just meeting a mate, that's all. I'll tell you about that in a minute. That Maggie is fuckin' ace, man. Her body is amazing. Her tits are incredible. She has to be the fittest bird I've ever been with. I had to take some magic dust just to keep up. I reckon she must have been without it for so long that she was absolutely gagging for it. As soon as we got through the door of my flat on Friday night, it was straight to it. No messing. It was the same again on Saturday morning. Bollocks to my hangover. I mean, you've got to do it, haven't you?"

Sikes nodded and attempted to drink some of his tea.

"We had a good look around her town on Saturday before going to her flat. Then it was, like, off again. Shaggin' in the afternoon, I recommend it." Marty stirred his tea. "After that, we went out for a pint and a curry and met some of her friends for a chat. We got back to hers at about half twelve, and it was bob's your uncle once more. Amazing. I've never done it so much. I've never had a weekend like it."

"Looks like you should have stayed an extra night."

"No chance. I needed a rest."

"Are you seeing her again?"

"Yes, tomorrow night. We're off to the cinema." His facial expression changed. "Can you do us a favour Si?"

Simon looked concerned.

"What is it?"

"You couldn't lend me some cash 'til pay day, could you?"

Sikes relaxed again. "Is that all? Aye, no problem." He reached into his trouser pocket and took out some notes. "Is that enough?"

"Should be okay," said Marty eyeing the money. "You can add a bit more if you like. You'll get it back."

Simon handed two more notes to Marty as his attention returned to the tea. It was still too hot.

"What mate were you meeting?"

"He's more of a union rep. Remember I said strange things are happening in this office?"

Simon nodded. "Yeah, and..."

"Well, the union think so too. By all accounts, those workers who got sacked in London shouldn't have been, and they are taking DoMO to a tribunal. He's trying to get information to help their case. I agreed to meet this bloke after he rang me last week. I'm going to help him get some information."

"How are you going to do that?"

"I'm not sure, but I'll do what I can. He's given me a list of things to look out for and told me to report anything that seems odd. I'll just pass the information on. I'll get as much as I can."

"You want to be careful," said Simon. "If it's true that they got rid of those in London, they can get rid of you just as easily. Can you afford to lose this job?"

"Don't worry about me, man. I'll be fine. My life is looking up. I've got a new purpose, a new bird and your cash in my pocket. Fuck me, it's better than my birthday."

Marty and Maggie had lunch in the park. Marty went to get tea on their return, leaving Maggie to walk on the section alone.

"It's lovely out there, Simon. Have you been out?"

"No, I've got too much to do if I'm to catch the four o'clock train."

"Short day, eh? I don't blame you."

"Good weekend? I didn't have a chance to ask you this morning."

"Brilliant, thanks." Maggie smiled knowingly. She guessed Marty would have told his mate about their weekend together.

"You two were made for each other."

"Calm down Simon. It's only a bit of fun, nothing serious. Don't get carried away."

"And I was looking forward to a wedding invitation."

"Don't worry. You'll be at the top of the list." Maggie giggled, throwing a paper clip at him.

BIRTHDAY BLUES

"Happy birthday Simon," said an excited Clare.

"Yeah, happy birthday Simon," said Philip. "We've bought you a jumper. Mam said you'd need a new jumper for the winter."

"Philip! You were not supposed to tell him what it is. He's supposed to open the parcel. It's supposed to be a surprise." Clare was not impressed at her twin's indiscretion.

"Sorry, Si." Philip's shoulders wiggled as he giggled.

Sikes hugged them. "That's alright. Thanks very much." He ripped open the parcel wrapped in paper bearing images of sports people. Simon saw figures on horseback, cricketers, footballers, and rugby players. Two words, 'Happy Birthday', were all that stopped the horse trampling on the cricketers and the footballer from kicking a rugby player.

He pulled out a navy sweater. It was just the right size. He knew it would be. His mother knew his dimensions off by heart. Holding it at arm's length, admiring it, he smiled at the twins.

"Perfect. Thank you. It's just what I wanted."

"Good," said Clare. "Come on, Philip, we've got to help mam with breakfast" She pulled at her brother's sweatshirt.

"Ow, that hurt. Get off, will you?"

Philip followed Clare to the bedroom door.

"I'll see you pair in a minute."

Philip nodded.

"Okay, Si, see you in a minute."

Simon made his way down the stairs, covering himself with his dressing gown. He sat at the dining room table and grinned as his brother and sister squabbled in the kitchen.

"You two are more of a hindrance than a help. Now go upstairs and get your coats on, ready for school while I finish

Simon's breakfast." His mother's voice was firm but playful. The twins raced back up the stairs to their bedrooms.

Simon opened the rest of his cards and the present from his Gran. The other grandparents, his paternal grandparents, lived in Spain, and Simon guessed that their card and gift would be in transit.

His parents usually gave him money, and this year they were more generous than ever. Simon opened the envelope to find crisp twenty-pound notes tucked inside the card. He read the words, "Lots of love, Mam and Dad." His mother had signed it, as always. Birthday and Christmas cards were not his father's forte.

The present from his grandmother contained a gift voucher and a long woollen scarf. Nanna was always knitting, apart from when she was gardening, cooking, cleaning, gossiping, or out at bingo. The card said simply, 'Happy birthday, Grandson love Nanna xxx'. The first card without gransha's name on it. He hoped it would not be the last.

Mrs Ikes brought him a traditional birthday breakfast. The food covered the large plate.

"Lovely Mam. Thanks. Thanks for the present too, by the way. Perfect."

"You're very welcome, son. I hope you have a very happy birthday." She kissed the top of his head. "So, what are you doing with yourself today?"

"I'm meeting Laura at ten. We're off to Cardiff to get my present."

Mrs Ikes passed him a cup of tea.

"Cardiff? I thought you'd want to stay away from Cardiff. It's supposed to be your day off."

"Aye, I know, but Laura wants to go. I might look at the car showrooms on the way back."

"So you're taking my advice then?"

"Might as well. I need one now that I'm working in Cardiff and it'll be useful with Laura at university. I can pick her up on the way home."

"You like her, don't you?" His mother smiled as she spoke.

"Yes, I do," said Simon without a hint of embarrassment. He cut into a slice of bacon.

"That's obvious; you've been with her what... four months?"

Simon nodded, chewing his bacon.

"It must be love," said his mother as she returned her attention to her cup of tea.

Thomas Ikes had a suite of offices on a recently refurbished site in the town centre. Previously a redundant junior school, the space had been left derelict for many years until European regeneration money was made available to convert the once popular but decrepit school buildings into a shop and office block. 'Thomas Ikes, Chartered Accountant, was the first tenant.

Making his way up the dark wooden staircase to his father's office, Simon spoke to Peter Evans, his father's one-armed employee.

"Morning Simon. Happy birthday"

Simon saw Peter was holding a batch of files in his only arm. The shirtsleeve that should have covered the other had been rolled up to the elbow.

"Morning Peter. Thanks. Is he in?"

"Yes, he should be, Stephanie put a caller through to him earlier, but I think he's free now."

Simon reached the upper landing and walked to his father's office. He could hear him dictating as he opened the door.

"Letter, please, Stephanie. Addressed to Companies House, usual address. It's for the Old Forge Limited, so you know the references..."

"Morning Dad. Thanks for the pressie."

His father switched the machine off.

"Morning Simon. You're very welcome. Happy birthday.

To what do I owe this pleasure? Short of cash, are we?" Thomas Ikes rose from his black leather chair and walked around to hug his son.

"Not this time. I'm just calling in to see how you are."

"Likely story. What do you want?" Thomas Ikes parted from his son and rested his backside on the edge of his large desk.

"Can I borrow the car, please?"

"I knew there was something." Thomas laughed. "Why? Where are you going?"

"Cardiff, with Laura." He hoped that would make a difference.

"How much did you drink last night?"

"Nothing. Laura and I went to the cinema, remember? I borrowed Mam's car. The night before, we babysat for you." Simon decided not to mention the bottle of wine Laura and he had enjoyed once the twins had gone to bed. It was thirty-odd hours ago.

"Okay then. I suppose I'd better ask your mother to pick me up." His father walked to the coat hook, fumbled in his jacket pocket then tossed keys to Simon.

"You'll be lucky," said Simon catching the keys. "She's taking Gran to see Uncle John's new house this afternoon. She's collecting the twins from school and then going straight there. They won't be back until nine-ish. Why do you think I need your car?"

"Bloody charming. So I'll have to walk home, will I?"

"The exercise will do you good, and you could always call into the club for a frame of snooker. Mam won't be any the wiser."

"Now there's an idea. Good thinking, son."

Thomas Ikes was still laughing as Simon walked out the door.

"Cheers, Dad."

"Have a good day. Put some petrol in, and I'll settle up with you later."

"Okay."

"Oh, and Simon?"

"I know, I know, don't forget a receipt."

Simon ran down the steps but turned right towards the back door. Exiting the building, he saw his father's black Jaguar parked in its usual spot in the corner. Simon loved driving the Jag but knew he had to respect the vehicle. Not only was it powerful, but it was also his father's pride and joy.

The engine started first time, as usual, and Simon gently reversed the car out of its spot. Stopping to do up his seatbelt, he flicked the controller on the entertainment centre to see what was on. It was his father's favourite country and western singer. Simon switched to radio mode and found the local radio station.

The town centre was quiet and, two minutes later, Simon beeped the horn as he waited outside the Bird In Hand.

Laura beamed with delight as she saw Simon sitting behind the wheel of his father's car. Simon leaned across and opened the front passenger door for her.

"Very nice, very nice indeed." She sat back in the leather seat and pulled her seatbelt around her. She turned to Simon and met his kiss.

"Happy birthday," she said. They kissed again.

"However, did you get your father to lend you this?"

"No problem. He knows I'll look after it."

"Love these seats. Very smart."

"Of course, you haven't been in this car before, have you?"

"No. I've seen it outside your house but never been in it."

"Right then, sit back. You're in for a treat. We'll take the scenic route."

"Which route is that?" Laura asked, smiling.

"I'll take you down through the Rhondda, then onto the M4, into the back end of Cardiff, and you can help me look for a car of my own before we hit the shops."

"Are you buying one of these?"

"I wish," said Simon glancing over his right shoulder to ensure no car was coming behind him.

The Jag moved effortlessly up the hill.

"I've never been to the Rhondda," said Laura. "What's it like?"

"You'll see soon enough. The views from the top of this hill are quite something."

"Stop at the top, and I'll give you your card and part of your present."

Sikes could hardly wait.

Laura and Simon were exhausted as they flopped onto the sofa in the flat above the pub. Laura kicked off her shoes and swung her feet over Simon's legs. He tickled them gently, admiring her toes and toenails. She wore no nail varnish but had nicely manicured nails. His one hand extended the massage to Laura's ankle by slipping under the leg of her trousers.

Laura sighed.

"Oh, that's nice!"

"My pleasure," said Sikes smirking.

"What a day. Thank you for my present." She admired her watch. "Odd that, me getting a present on your birthday."

"Just so long as you like it?"

"Yes, it's gorgeous." She looked again at the gold band and face on her watch. The longer, narrower hand pointed at the Roman numeral five, while the shorter hand was on the six. "I suppose we'd better get ready to go out? What time shall we pop down to your house?"

"Whenever, I didn't say a time. My mother's gone to see my uncle, and I doubt she'll be back before ten. My father's probably going straight to the club, so I only need to drop the car back and change. No rush."

"Well, we cannot take too long because I promised Cait and Jamie we'll be at the restaurant by eight. We'd better get moving." Laura placed her feet on the floor and stood up. "I'm off to have a shower."

"That's a nice idea," said Simon putting his hand on her backside.

"On my own. Thank you very much." Laura laughed. "Put the telly on if you want. I won't be long." She entered her bedroom. "Or you can go downstairs and play pool? I think you'd get a game easily enough this time of day. My Dad will probably be glad of the company."

"Aye, might do in a minute, but I'm alright here for now."

"Whatever," said Laura closing her bedroom door.

Simon moved from the sofa long enough to walk to the television and pick up the remote. Slouching back onto the cushions, he casually flicked the buttons. The screen lit up, and the BBC newscaster told him about the day's events. Sikes was not interested. He pressed another button, and the familiar yellow face and blue hair of the mother of his favourite cartoon character filled the screen. He dropped the remote onto the floor and watched attentively.

The bedroom door opened again, and Laura emerged wearing a short white dressing gown. Seeing her firm, bare legs, Simon looked longingly and wolf-whistled at her.

Laura smiled and playfully lifted the back of her gown, exposing her naked buttock before she walked into the bathroom and locked the door behind her.

He returned his attention to the television and remembered seeing this particular episode. He grabbed the remote and flicked through the channels but found little that caught his attention. There was nothing he wanted to watch, so he hit the power-off button.

Lying back on the sofa, Simon heard water hammering onto the glass walls of the shower unit, and his thoughts quickly drifted into the shower. He imagined he was there with Laura and absently scratched his crutch through his trousers. His penis was stiffening. It was time to think about something else.

He rose from the seat and walked to the cupboard adjacent to the television. Four packages had been strewn across the top. They were packets of photographs that Laura had printed, ready for inclusion in her albums. She had told Simon about this earlier. He could see the albums under the packages.

Collecting all the packets and the albums, Simon returned to the sofa. He opened the first envelope and took out the pictures. He guessed they were taken with the camera he had bought Laura for passing her A-levels. The time and date had been recorded on the back of each photograph.

He quickly ran through the photographs. There were pictures of Laura, Laura and Cait, Jamie and Cait, Simon and Jamie, Laura and Simon and Laura and Simon and Cait and Jamie. They were taken on the bank holiday Sunday when the four had a day out in Tenby. Simon had only fond memories of Tenby, and this day had been another good one. The last photograph showed Laura sleeping peacefully on Simon's lap in the back of Jamie's jeep, with Simon smiling widely. He felt a warm glow inside.

Replacing the pictures into the envelope, Simon opened the next packet. These were taken in Swansea when he and Laura had visited her Gran and Granddad. Simon grinned at the photo of Laura's grandfather with his glasses down on the edge of his nose, pulling a face that made his lips appear twisted and distorted. He was certainly a character.

The rest of the photographs were views of Swansea and portraits of her grandparents in their vast Gower garden. Simon replaced them in their sleeve and picked up the third packet.

The third set of photographs was larger than the other two. It contained significantly more pictures. Simon thought this pile represented the start of Laura's sorting. He decided to keep these in order.

The photographs showed Laura and a gang of girls in a nightclub, possibly in Swansea. Simon looked at the date. It was the day after their results had come out. The day after Laura and Simon had become an item in the true sense of the word. There were numerous photos of girls in various groups and individual poses. Laura featured in a number of them. She seemed very happy. Men appeared in the background of several photos and appeared to be attempting to gate-crash the girls' fun rather than be part of the group. Simon would not blame the men for trying to butt in. These were all beautiful girls, but Laura was the most attractive to him.

After twenty-six photographs of friends came a couple in Aberdare Park. Simon recalled this day too. It was the Sunday after Laura's night out, and they had gone for a quiet evening stroll up to the park. They had walked and talked. It had been a warm summer evening, and Laura looked beautiful in her navy blue summer dress. There were no photos of them together, but equal numbers of Simon and Laura taken as they walked around the vast park.

The last six pictures were from GarGar's barbecue a week later. Simon laughed aloud at the picture of Dicey fast asleep in the patio chair with lipstick, mascara and clip-on earring added without his consent or knowledge. He had not been best pleased when someone had woken him up and shown him a mirror. He wondered if Dicey knew the photo existed.

Simon was still chuckling when he replaced the photos in the sleeve. He listened. The water had stopped, and the hair drier was going. He did not know when one had stopped and the other began. He had been too involved in the photographs. He thought Laura would not be too much longer now.

He stacked the three packets together and went to place them on the fourth. The fourth packet was much flatter than the others. At first, Sikes thought it was empty but, as his hand touched the envelope, he realised it also contained photos. He put the other three on the sofa and opened the fourth. It only held seven shots.

The first two were mistakes. Somebody's fingers had covered the lens, so the photos were only of thin pink digits.

The third photograph startled Simon. It was a photo of Laura and a well-built lad. She had her arms around the boy's neck and was kissing him. It did not look like a casual peck, this was a full-on kiss. The following picture was of Laura with one of her arms around the boy's neck and the other around his head. This time it appeared as though she was dancing with the boy. His muscular arms were tight around her waist, his head nestling into her neck.

The fifth photograph was of Laura sitting on the boy's lap. He had his hand on her backside. Her arms were around his neck and his head on her shoulder. Sikes wondered whether he was kissing her neck. The last photograph showed the boy, now with his coat on, holding Laura's hand as they walked away from the crowd. They were making for an exit sign.

Simon was devastated. The images shocked him. He checked the date on the back of the photograph. The same evening, the other Swansea photos were taken. He was gob-smacked.

He let the photos fall onto the floor and picked up one of the three albums. As he opened it, more pictures fell out. Images of Laura and the same boy. They were at the beach this time, and Laura looked happy in every photo. Simon removed a print from its plastic sleeve and looked at the back of the image. It contained no date, only a manuscript note. 'Me and David, Gower. Lovely day xx'.

Simon turned the photograph over and over again. David was a strapping lad. His arms and neck were enormous, and his shirt appeared tight over his chest. This man was more than just a passing acquaintance. He wondered why Laura had not said anything. He thought they agreed not to have secrets. Had he not told her everything about his past? Well, almost everything. Some things were too painful for Simon to remember, let alone tell anyone about. He had told her about his previous experiences and had been quite candid about events in the last few months.

Sikes was not sure what he should do. His brain was confused, and his heart was racing. He contemplated replacing all the photographs and placing them back on the cupboard, pretending he had not seen them. But he had seen them. He had seen them all, and he wanted answers. Who was this David, and why was Laura with him when she was supposed to be going out with Simon? Where did she go with that man after the disco? Why had she kept these photographs separate? What was she going to do with them?

Simon dropped the photograph of Laura and David at the Gower and picked up one taken at the nightclub. He felt a twinge in his stomach as he realised that these pictures were taken with Laura's camera, the camera that he had bought her as a gift. It dawned on Sikes that whoever took the photo had the camera in the nightclub. That meant that Laura had left it with someone else while she was off with some bloke called David, who looked like a bodybuilder.

Laura had constantly told Simon how much she loved the camera and how expensive everyone thought it looked. He had simply replied that she was worth it. He began to question whether she meant it. If she could leave the camera with someone else, presumably a friend, while she went off with some bloke, it obviously meant nothing to her. Perhaps he meant nothing to her. Laura had gone to Swansea alone several times in the past four months. Had she gone to see him? Had she been off shagging David?

The bathroom door opened, and Laura stood in her dressing gown. Hair immaculate, and make-up applied to perfection. "Won't be long." She smiled at Sikes.

Simon did not smile. He said nothing.

"Simon? What's wrong?" Laura walked towards him.

Simon stood. He held up the photograph of Laura kissing David.

Laura saw it and stopped dead in her tracks.

"I knew I should have ripped that up. I was going to bin it anyway."

"Well, who is he?"

"That's David. He's my old boyfriend from Swansea. I've told you about him."

"You said old, but it can't be that old. These photos were only taken in August."

Sikes' tone worried Laura. "Simon, I can assure you this is not what you might think."

"And what should I think? We'd been going out for a month when these got taken. One whole month, Law. That's longer than I'd been with anyone else. I thought we were good?"

"We were...we are good, Simon. Don't get upset, please. I can explain."

"I thought you might." Simon flopped back onto the sofa and then ran a hand over his face. "How long has this been going on?"

"Simon, nothing is going on."

"So you say."

"For God's sake Simon, don't be so pathetic. Let me explain."

"I'm pathetic as well now. Anything else?" Simon found himself standing again.

"You know what I mean. There is nothing to get worked up about. It's not what it seems. I went out with David when I lived in Swansea. I told you about that. When we moved up here, I stopped seeing him, but he kept in touch. He asked me to drive down to see him, and I was tempted until you came along. I kept meaning to finish with him after I'd met you, but... I suppose I was scared."

"Scared? Why? Would he have hit you?"

"No, nothing like that. I was scared in case you and I did not work out."

"That's very reassuring. So you kept David in reserve in case we finished?"

"It's not like that." Laura walked to Simon's side and caught hold of his hand. "It's just that I was new here. I didn't know what the people were like, what you were like. I tried not to get too deeply involved too soon. I tried to be careful. I thought that if you and I didn't work out and nothing else happened around here, I could always go back to Swansea to see David."

"Oh, so as I said, Dave is your backup. I'm not sure I like what I'm hearing."

"His name is David. He doesn't like people calling him Dave." Laura felt foolish for defending him. "Anyway, I meant that I saw no point in finishing with David until I was sure about you. That day we had the results, I was sure. So when I went to Swansea, I intended to go and tell him. I was going to call around his house on Saturday morning, but unbeknown to me, he had spoken to one of my friends and knew where we were meeting. He turned up at the club. It was a relief because I'd had a drink and felt more confident about telling him. What you have there is purely innocent. I told him we were finished, and he didn't take it very well."

Laura picked up several photos. Shuffling them, she placed them in order and revealed the sequence of events.

"Here," she showed him one of them kissing. "I've just told him, and he's distraught. So I said, 'come on, cheer up,' and I gave him a friendly kiss. That's all. "In this next one..."

Simon looked at the photo of David with his head on Laura's shoulder.

"...I'm comforting him. Here..." she held up the photo of Laura sitting on his lap, "...David is a bit upset, and I'm wiping his eyes. And here..."

Sikes saw she was holding the photo of them walking towards the exit.

"...I'm taking him to the door. I saw him off, then went back to join the girls. They were all a bit sad at seeing David upset. They said you must be special if I chose you over David. He is quite sought after down there. I said you were special, very special."

"So you say Law, but why didn't you tell me what

happened?"

"Because it didn't matter, in reality, I'd known David and I were finished as soon as we moved up here, but David still called and would send me presents. Then when I met you, I knew he was history. I know it was wrong of me to keep him hanging on, but I was scared. Everything was so new, and he was like a ...I don't know...a link to my past. As soon as I met you, I knew I enjoyed being with you more than I ever liked being with David, but I had to get to know you better before I finished with him. I had to be sure. As soon as I was, I ended it. I should have told you, and I should never have kept him dangling. I should have been more honest with him too, but...I didn't and I'm sorry... but I think he would have probably done the same."

"I wish I could believe you, Law." Simon let go of her hand and walked a few paces, not aiming for anywhere in particular.

"But I'm telling the truth. What is there not to believe?"

"How do I know that you didn't just go off with him for the night? Who's to say you didn't go off and shag him?"

"Simon! That's a dreadful thing to say."

"How do I know that you're not still shagging him on the side?"

Laura slapped Simon's face. His cheek stung.

"That's awful...I would never do that to you. Look at the times on the back of the photos. The ones with David were taken quite early on. See this one?"

Simon looked at the photo of Laura and David "leaving" the club.

"11:20 pm," she said.

Laura searched amongst the photographs she had sorted until she found one with her holding a bottle of beer.

"This one is taken at 11:35 pm. I'm holding the bottle in celebration. I reminded my friends that we were out to celebrate, so they raised a toast. Look."

Simon saw the pictures in a different light. That did not

take away his doubts. He still felt pain. He still felt hurt.

"I believe you, Law, and I'm sorry for saying what I just said, but I still think you should have told me. That's what's hurting me more. When we started going out, I told you about my past. I even told you about Sammie, and you remember how angry you were?"

"Only because I thought you were stupid having unprotected sex with a girl you hardly knew," she said sternly.

"But now I think you had a nerve acting like that. I know you told me about David, but you did not tell me you were still seeing him. You did not tell me he was ringing you. I'm starting to think it's one rule for you and another for me. I feel like I've been taken for a fool."

"How do you work that out?" Laura was worried this was getting out of hand.

"Well, I had unprotected sex with Sammie, and you made me feel shitty about it. I went and had the HIV and STD tests."

"I never made you have those tests."

"No, but you made it perfectly clear you did not want to have sex with me until you knew I was clean."

"I never said that. I said I would not have unprotected sex unless I knew you were clear. You could have used a condom."

"Yes, but you hate the feel of those things. Anyway, you never stopped me from taking the tests."

"Because I felt you needed to be sure..."

"Or was it because you weren't sure about me and kept me dangling?"

"Don't say that, Simon...I showed you how I felt about you as soon as the results came through, didn't I?" Laura tried to place her hand on Simon's chest, but he walked away.

"But I bet you had unprotected sex with David. Did he have the test?"

"That was different. I had known David for years before anything happened between us."

"But you couldn't be sure he hadn't had a quick one with someone and not used a rubber? You didn't make him go through the agony of those tests. The counselling beforehand, the waiting afterwards, the worry that I might be infected... and all the time you didn't give a shit what you might pass on to me."

"Simon that's unfair."

"I'm sorry, Law. I don't think it is...I feel like I...I don't know. I feel really shit. I think I'd better go." He turned towards the door.

Laura started to cry.

"But what about the meal?"

"Tell them I've lost my appetite." Simon opened the door and ran down the stairs. The noise brought Mike out of his bar.

"What's happening?"

Simon said nothing as he fled past Laura's father into his bar and out of the main door.

"Simon?" Mike called after him.

Laura screamed from the upstairs room. "Simon!"

DEEPER INTO THE MIRE

Marty and Maggie did not need to be told that something significant had happened in Simon's life. He was not his usual self. They could sense from his attitude, mood and appearance that all was not well on Planet Ikes.

For the past three days, Simon had not shaved and, more surprisingly, had not washed his hair. He rarely spoke to his colleagues and never joined in the conversations, and when his 'phone rang, it was met with terse comments like, "Who the fuck is it this time?"

It was Friday, pub day, and Marty thought he knew what would shake Simon out of his mood.

"Hey Si, are you comin' down to the pub at lunchtime? I'll whip your Valleys arse at pool."

Simon looked at his colleague for a moment. He appeared to be deep in thought. "Aye, why not? But I'll tell you what; let's make it a longer session. How about taking a half day?"

Maggie joined in.

"Can I come too?"

"Sure," said Sikes.

Marty appeared to be getting cold feet.

"But how are we going to swing it? I know Anna's away, but Steve dislikes these things bounced on him."

"Leave it to me. I'll be back in a minute."

Simon left his desk and headed to the main corridor. He returned ten minutes later. He winked at Maggie and nodded at Marty.

Steve McKenzie's 'phone rang.

"Hello, Mr Phillips. How can I help?"

Simon looked on as McKenzie listened.

"Right, oh, I see." Silence. "No, I hadn't realised." More

silence. "No, I understand." Short wait. "No, no problem at all." He took a breath. "Yes, I'll sort it...Yes, of course...I understand."

Simon allowed himself a wry smile as McKenzie replaced the 'phone and pretended to carry on as usual. Then, appearing to have lost something, he got up from his seat and walked into Ms Emery's room.

A few seconds later, Marty had a call asking him to bring Maggie into Anna's room. Steve needed a quick word.

Both emerged beaming. Steve waited a few moments before returning to his desk.

"Sorted Si me old mate. We've been told to take a half-day to try to cheer you up. However did you wangle tha'?"

Simon tapped the side of his nose.

Maggie was equally ecstatic.

"And we don't even have to take leave. This is brilliant, Simon. Now all I need to do is get some money."

"Don't worry about the money," said Simon. "This is on me. I could do with a sesh, and I've got a stack of birthday cash left over. Think of this as my treat."

"This gets better and better," said Marty, rubbing his hands.

By early evening the trio were well into the swing of things. Maggie was itching to move onto a bar where there was music, but one of the boys did not seem so keen.

"Come on guys, you know I love a dance." She leaned to her right and caught Marty's arm. He let her hold it for a short while and then removed it to reach for his pint. Simon raised his eyebrows in mock resignation as Maggie looked at him. She seemed hurt.

Simon was warming to the idea of moving onto a livelier bar. The one they were in was a back street bar about four hundred yards from the DoMO offices. It had been packed during lunchtime but was now quiet.

The beer had certainly helped Simon forget his troubles

and had also improved his mood. However, it was ruining Marty's. He was becoming more miserable by the minute. Despite the talk, Marty was not a big drinker. Too much drinking in a short time made him more agitated. It also served to open his mouth.

"I'm tellin' you Si. All is not well at that place. My union mate told me they removed anyone who would cause them problems. That's why they're trying to get rid of me."

"Marty, they only warned you because you fiddled with your timekeeping, and they caught you. They could have given you the push for that. You were lucky to get away with a warning." Having finished her speech, Maggie sat back on her stool.

"Fuck off you. What the fuck do you know anyway?" Marty grabbed for his pint.

Maggie was surprised at the tone of Marty's reply.

"Tetchy ain't we? That's the problem with you city boys. You can't take the truth."

"Fuck off I said"

"I rest my case!"

Simon laughed with Maggie and held out his hand. Maggie slapped it, then put her left hand on Simon's right shoulder. Moving closer, she whispered in his ear.

"We Valleys girls...I mean...Valleys people, sorry, have got to stick together."

"That's right," said Simon, nodding. He turned his head and gave Maggie a peck on the cheek.

She turned her face, and they kissed briefly on the lips. She looked into Simon's eyes. He met her gaze and held his mouth close to hers once again. Then, remembering where they were and whom they were with, they separated, and Maggie sat upright.

Marty had not noticed. He was still muttering into the bottom of the glass.

"I'm telling you there's something wrong over the road, and I intend to find out what it is, even if it gets me the sack."

“Right, my round,” said Simon.

”Same again, please.” Maggie handed him her empty half-pint glass, smiling cheekily.

“Aye, get us another pint, mate. I’m telling you, a massive can of worms is ready to be opened at that office. You mark my words.” Marty downed the rest of his glass, handed it to Simon and stood up. “Where's the bogs, man? I’m busting for a dump.”

“Over there,” said Maggie. “Just by the bandit.”

“I fuckin’ knows where they are,” said Marty angrily.

Marty wandered in the opposite direction to Simon. Maggie followed Simon to the bar.

The pair stood silently at the bar for a moment.

“Sorry about that just now, Si. Don’t know what came over me.”

“What are you sorry about? Nothing happened, did it?”

A thin barman arrived. He wore a Cardiff University drinking club sweatshirt and tracksuit bottoms. Simon doubted he was a student. He looked far too old and was balding. Sikes handed over the empties and gave him the order.

Maggie watched as the barman collected a new half-pint glass and headed for the cider pump.

“No, I suppose not. You know that I like Marty and wouldn’t hurt him, but he can be such a dickhead sometimes. He keeps going on about how corrupt the office is. I wished he’d give it a rest. He has a dark side. I don’t know, I seem to attract the bad ones. I should have gotten off with someone like you. We’ve got more in common.”

Simon pondered on her words.

“You don’t want to bother with me, Maggs. I’m a complete waste of space. I doubt I would be much fun at the moment.”

The barman placed the dry cider on the counter. Simon handed it to Maggie.

“You’d better get back. Marty will get even more paranoid if he returns and finds us both gone.”

Marty's mood improved slightly when they reached his favourite bar, an Australian theme pub. The pub covered three floors of a massive Victorian building. The lower level was converted into a dance floor; the ground floor was the bar, and the upper floor was a restaurant that transformed into another dance floor on busy weekends.

Simon checked his watch. It was seven twenty-eight. He had to survive another two and half hours if he was to stay until the ten o'clock bus. He doubted he would have the stamina, so he resolved to ease up on the beer and then considered catching the nine o'clock bus instead.

Marty took Maggie downstairs for a dance leaving Simon to get the drinks. He ordered another half of cider for Maggie, a bottle of lager for Marty and a cola for himself. Gathering them up in his large hands, he carried them to a table to the right of the stairs leading down to the dance floor. An unoccupied sofa and easy chair lay close by, and Simon flopped onto the couch. He pulled the easy chair nearer and placed his coat on it.

He watched as more people entered the bar. There were single blokes, gangs of girls, and couples of different persuasions, all with one thing in common; they looked happy and were going to have a good night.

Simon thought Laura would enjoy the place but then remembered that it would be with someone else if she did. They were no longer together. The thought hurt him. Ignoring his soft drink, he drank Marty's beer.

"Bollocks to it. Who cares what time I get home."

Simon had finished the bottle when Maggie returned from the dance floor alone. She informed Simon that Marty had met some friends downstairs but said he wouldn't be long.

"They seem a bit wild. I'm sure one of them is high. He looks totally out of it." She took a sip from her drink. "Oh, that's a bit warm."

"I'll get you another." Simon went to get up.

"No, you sit there you. It is my round. You've bought

enough. Another bottle?"

"Yes, please. What about Marty?"

"He can get his own. I'll be back in a mo. I just want to powder my nose."

Maggie returned with a glass and a bottle and sat on the sofa next to Simon. He took the beer and thanked her.

Simon could tell that Maggie had reapplied her perfume. It had a harsh aroma which he found a little overpowering. He thought of Laura. She always wore a light, attractive scent. The smell alone was guaranteed to trigger a reaction in Simon. The memory was enough to remind Simon of his sadness. He took a brief swig of the bottle.

"What's up Si? You seem a bit down."

"Oh, nothing really. I'm just thinking."

"What's up? You can tell me you know. It won't go any further."

"No. It is nothing, honestly. It's just that my girlfriend and I have had a row." He was unsure whether to say anything else. "It was my fault. I overreacted. I think we've finished."

"You miss her?"

"Aye… very much."

"Never mind. If it's meant to be, it will be. Que sera sera."

Sikes smiled, recalling other absent friends.

"I suppose you are right. Anyway, what about you? You and Marty still seem pretty close."

"Don't you believe it. He blows hot and cold. He was all over me downstairs, but then his mates come along, and it's bye-bye, Maggs. It's always been like that, ever since we started going out. To tell you the truth, I'm a bit fed up with it." Maggie filled her mouth with cider and swallowed slowly. "I don't know Si. I always end up with the losers."

It only took a few prompting questions from Simon for Maggie to open her heart. She told Simon about the unhappy experiences she had with Colin. Her openness came as a shock to her. She said she hadn't even considered telling Marty such things. Simon sympathised and fetched her handfuls of serviettes from the bar to wipe her eyes when her emotions got the better of her. They did when she told Simon about her crippling debts and how she had not been sure she would be able to settle them all. The DoMO job had provided a lifeline, and she did not want to put that at risk. She also revealed her fear that Marty would cause trouble at work by repeating his accusations about corruption. She worried that her record might become tarnished by association. She would finish things with Marty, and the decision had been made easier by his wild mood swings.

Simon saw no reason her relationship with Marty would cost her the job. "I'm sure they wouldn't do that. Don't worry." He offered no advice about Marty's moods. He was in no position to say anything.

"How can you be so sure? It's okay for you. You've got friends in high places.

"What? Who? My uncle you mean. Aye, I suppose he is well placed."

Maggie had not noticed a family resemblance between Simon and Jack Phillips but had known there was some link. How else would Simon have been able to get the half day?

"Could you have a word with them for me, Si? Just in case Marty does anything stupid. I can't afford to lose my job just because he is off his head."

Simon smiled.

"Aye, okay, if anything happens, I'll see if I can have a word."

Maggie looked a little happier.

"Fancy a dance?"

Sikes was not the most confident dancer but said, "Aye, go on then."

She caught Simon's hand as they walked down the stairs. She looked to where Marty had stood the last time she had seen him. There was nobody there besides one of the boys to whom he had been talking. The boy stood alone outside the downstairs toilets. He appeared to be guarding the doorway.

Simon joined her on the dance floor.

Dance followed dance, and all the time, Simon felt awkward. Those around him appeared to know what they were doing. Simon did not. The music was too fast, too furious and very loud.

The DJ announced that he had a request for a slow song. He asked his audience whether he should play one. A cheer went up.

Simon went to walk away. Maggie held him back.

"I love this song, don't run away."

"What about Marty?"

Maggie looked over to the toilet door. It was clear, with nobody on guard. She quickly scanned the horizon. There was no sign of Marty and his friends. "He's probably smashed off his face now. He'll be okay." Maggie placed her arms around Simon's neck. He held her tight around her narrow waist. His hands gripped her short jacket. The height difference would have been more noticeable had it not been for Maggie's high heels.

They stood at arm's length as the record started, but then Maggie placed her head on Simon's chest and fastened her grip around his neck. Simon overlapped his arms behind her back and held her tight.

The song ended, and Simon unlocked himself from Maggie's grip.

"Come on. Let's get a drink."

"Okay." Maggie smiled at him and took his hand once more. This time she locked her fingers between his as they climbed the stairs.

Simon was unsure what to make of Maggie's move but let her lead the way back. He also felt a little uneasy when Maggie looked back at him, smiling as she did so. Simon politely smiled back.

Reaching their seat, he was relieved to see that his coat was still there, as were their drinks.

He could not face any more beer.

"Do you fancy a short?"

"Go on then. I'll have a Southern Comfort with ice, please." Maggie settled on the sofa and pushed her fingers through her hair.

Simon had never tasted Southern Comfort and decided to have the same. He bought doubles and did not flinch at the cost.

"Any sign of Marty?" He asked, returning to his seat. He passed a glass to Maggie.

"No, I reckon he's gone. They are probably all stoned by now."

Simon had known for a while that Marty was a pothead, probably worse. It came as no surprise that he would take drugs tonight.

Maggie and Simon carried on talking. They spoke about their pasts, their presents and their dreams. Simon took great care not to go too overboard about his family and how lucky he was. He thought it might sound like he was bragging, especially since Maggie had so much misfortune. He did not need any more tears. He also avoided talking about Laura in case the tears were his. They enjoyed another round of Southern Comfort and ice, paid for by Maggie.

"No. You've bought enough," Maggie said, returning with the drinks. "Anyway, this is my thank you for letting me ramble on so much."

"No problem. No problem at all."

Maggie had done most of the talking, but Sikes had not minded as it meant he did not have to say too much.

"To good friends," said Simon, raising his glass.

"To terrific friends," said Maggie, smiling seductively. Their glasses clinked.

She placed her glass on the table, moved closer to Simon and kissed him.

Simon studied her for a moment before putting his glass next to hers. He leaned toward her.

"To terrific friends," he said as their faces met.

They kissed eagerly. Maggie's arms fastened themselves around Simon's neck, and his arms found their way into her jacket and around her back. Simon eased the white blouse out of the back of Maggie's long skirt, and he stroked the flesh on her back.

The kissing continued until Simon's mouth felt dry. Maggie had taken all the moisture. She opened her eyes and smiled at him as he eased away.

"I need a drink," he said.

"Me too." Maggie laughed, tucking in her blouse. She sat beside Simon but put her hand between his legs. She squeezed his thigh gently.

Simon took a drink and glanced at his watch. It was ten past ten. He had missed the last bus.

"Shit."

"What's the matter?" Maggie looked concerned. Her free hand joined the other on Simon's leg.

"I've missed my last bus," said Simon.

Maggie relaxed again.

"Is that all? We'll get a taxi."

Simon had not considered that option. He saw merit in it.

"Aye, I suppose we could. It could drop you off, then take me over the mountain."

Maggie's left hand left his leg and moved to his face. It stroked his whiskers lightly before it rolled around Simon's neck as she turned to face him. Her right hand moved slowly up and down his thigh. "You could always stay the night."

Simon took another sip from his glass as he weighed up the proposal.

"Are you sure? What about Marty?"

Maggie did not flinch.

"Stop worrying about him. Marty can suit himself. It's you, I'm asking."

He took another sip.

"Are you sure about this?"

Maggie's hand had gone as far up his leg as it could. Her fingers were squeezing his testicles through the denim.

"I'm very sure. If you want to, that is?"

Simon studied Maggie closely. Her jacket buttons were open, and her cleavage was visible. He smiled as his eyes returned to Maggie's face.

"I want to alright."

"Well, that's sorted then." Maggie put her hands on Simon's shoulders as she stood before him. She held out her hand.

"Ready? Shall we go?"

Simon had been caught unawares.

"What? Now? Do you want another drink first?"

"No. I've got wine at the flat. We can have a nightcap there."

Simon held her hand as he rose to be by her side. He felt a little light-headed but was unsure if this was the drink or the speed with which recent events had unfurled. He emptied the contents of his glass in one and dropped the empty glass onto the sofa.

Maggie left her glass where it stood. She reached for Simon's coat, wobbling as she did so. Simon placed his hands on her waist to steady her.

"Steady. I can't have you falling on me."

"Don't worry about me. I'll only go down when I want to." She picked up his coat and passed it to him. Simon put it on, maintaining eye contact as he did so.

When he finished buttoning his coat, Maggie caught his ear, eased his face in front of hers and kissed him again. Her tongue flicked across his lips.

"Let's get that taxi," she said, taking his hand in hers again.

SATURDAY, SATURDAY

The eyes opened slowly. Recognition was reassuring. The dream had been horrific and vivid, and he was relieved to wake from it. He was comforted to find himself in familiar surroundings. He knew the bedclothes. He knew the headboard. He knew the bedroom furniture. He recognised his clothes but not how they had gotten into such a state. He had no idea why he was lying on his stomach. He rarely slept on his stomach.

Pressing his arms into the mattress, he stretched his arms until they locked, pushing his body upwards. Waiting for a second, he wondered why he was in such a position and unlocked. He fell back onto the comfortable mattress, his head colliding with the soft feather-filled pillow. It was time for a different approach.

Casting back the duvet, he rolled over onto his back, shifted his body position quickly and eased his feet out of bed. They landed gently on the floor. His toes curled into the thick carpet.

Head in hand, he tried to recall the previous evening. He recollected developments at the large pub. He remembered that the evening air had hit him hard after leaving to get a taxi. It had been cold outside, and Maggie had clung to him, her hands inside his jacket. He visualised a flat. He saw himself in Maggie's flat. They had gone there by black cab.

He remembered paying for a taxi from Cardiff and that Maggie was all over him, like a rash, as soon as they entered her flat. That had not been a surprise. She had been enthusiastic enough in the taxi. Simon had never been masturbated in the back of a car before. He wondered how much the driver had seen.

Simon recollected wine. They drank red wine while they

sat, stark naked, on the living room floor of the flat. Maggie had poured red wine over his private parts and licked it off. She did more than lick. He remembered reciprocating before they showered together in her damp, dingy bathroom. Simon had never had sex in a shower before. He pictured Maggie's face as she clung to him, her back resting against the dark green tiles.

He remembered lying on top of Maggie in her single bed. His head had banged against the pink fabric-covered headboard, the duvet discarded on the floor. Had Maggie been squealing? Simon had never made anyone squeal before.

After sex and more of the horrible red wine, they must have drifted off to sleep because Simon recalled that he had struggled to get free from underneath Maggie to take himself to the toilet.

He recalled vomiting. Simon had brought back most of the wine. The thought mortified him until he remembered that Maggie was still fast asleep at this point. He felt reassured by the knowledge that he had made it to the toilet bowl before vomiting. Simon could not remember being sick in anyone else's toilet previously. He remembered drinking water and splashing some over his face.

He recollected that he had wanted to go home. He needed to get back to the sanctuary of his bedroom. He recalled looking for a phone book trying to find an all-night taxi service. He had quickly found his phone but had difficulty getting a number off the internet. He searched the sparse furniture in case a taxi number was listed anywhere. He had not found very much. He had certainly not found what he was seeking. He had to wake a naked Maggie, breasts hanging over the top of her black duvet cover, to ask for a 'phone number. Maggie had taken this as a cue for more sex, but Simon complained that her breath smelled of stale alcohol. Maggie merely turned around. Simon had never had sex from behind before. He thought he enjoyed it but remembered worrying that the bed would fall apart.

The taxi got booked twenty minutes later. Having given

him a number, Maggie went back to sleep, leaving Simon to wait another forty minutes for the cab to arrive. She was fast asleep when he left the flat. He visualised her ample bosom exposed to the room. Simon attempted to cover her with the duvet, but Maggie kicked it off, leaving her completely naked. Sikes had been slightly taken aback by her nakedness. He thought her two halves could have been two different bodies joined at the hip. The busty top half was next to the trim lower portion. He covered her with the duvet and left the flat, ensuring he securely locked the door.

Simon recalled seeing condom wrappers on the floor. He was thankful he had used condoms. He remembered the toilet in the pub and how he had used all his change in the vending machine.

He did not know much about his journey home, except for the driver demanding payment before departure. Simon made a mental note to check his wallet and bank account. He had no idea how much he had spent. He recollected seeing his front door and struggling to find the keys to open it. He could not be sure that he had switched off the lights but assumed he had. He remembered cleaning his teeth and emptying his bladder. He had looked in a mirror and had seen marks on his neck. Love bites? Did he have love bites on his neck? He rubbed his neck but could feel nothing. Rising to his feet, he crossed to the wardrobe and opened the right-hand door. Simon looked into the mirror that hung inside.

There were love bites, but not only on his neck. He had bite marks on his shoulders, chest, waist, and back. Simon remembered Maggie biting his bottom.

He pulled the top of his boxer shorts. His penis looked okay. No bites there, but it looked tired, limp and shrivelled.

Grabbing his dressing gown off the hook, Simon slid his arms into the sleeves, tied the cord around his waist and made for the stairs.

"Morning. Is anyone home?" His voice echoed in the hallway.

No response. He was relieved. His family had gone on their shopping trip, an outing to the big city to begin the Christmas shopping. His mother had suggested they might. He knew he must have been reasonably quiet when he came home. If he had not, his mother would have waited for him to get up to express her dissatisfaction.

Simon ambled down the familiar stairs. A note hung from the hall mirror.

'Simon. Gone to Cardiff. Dad is buying us lunch, and we might take the twins to the cinema. Probably be back at about six. Plenty in the freezer, so can you sort yourself out? Nanna says you can go up there if you want. She's making cottage pie. Suit yourself. Love Mam. PS Laura called. She'll be down to see you. Be nice to her. She's a lovely girl.'

He walked into the kitchen and made himself some tea and toast, then sat at the breakfast bar to eat.

Ding ding ding ding, ding ding ding ding, dong dong dong, dong dong dong, ding ding ding ding dong dong, ding ding ding ding dong dong, dong dong dong.

Simon shared his father's feelings about that doorbell but had never heard a French tune before. He had listened to the Mexican one and the Big Ben one but never the French one. Frere Jacques filled the house.

Simon went to the front door, leaving his cup on the table beside the empty plate containing four slices of toasted bread.

Adjusting his dressing gown to cover his neck, he re-tied the cord tightly around his waist. He recognised the silhouette through the glass panel immediately. It was Laura, and she stood close to the door.

As Simon unlocked the door, the temperature change hit him immediately. Outside it was a cold and wet November day. Inside, it was a tropical paradise. Central heating poured heat out through the radiators, and almost all curtains pulled shut. Simon had not considered what life was like outside.

Laura smiled shyly as he beckoned her in. She wore no

makeup, and her wet fair hair hung loosely over her shoulders. Her eyes looked red. Simon wondered if her contact lenses were hurting. He breathed in her aroma as she passed. She smelt divine. He hoped he did not smell of Maggie.

"You look a bit rough. Heavy night was it?"

He felt rough. Simon could not recall the last time he had gone four days without a shave. The stubble made his skin itch. "Aye, something like that. Stick your umbrella in the rack and hang your coat on the hook. I'm just going to get dressed. Do you want tea?"

"Yes, please, milk and..."

"I know one little sugar. Take a seat in there. I'll be back now."

As Laura walked into the room, Simon ran upstairs.

Dressing fast in a shirt, jumper, jeans and socks, he pushed his feet into his trainers and ran downstairs. Stopping in the kitchen long enough to make two teas, made by placing a teabag into each mug and adding hot water, milk and sugar, Simon entered the lounge carrying two cups.

Laura had opened the curtains and sat nervously on the end of the sofa.

He placed her mug beside the table and joined her on the long leather settee. He sat at the other end with his mug in hand.

She smiled at him as she spoke. "Thanks. I could do with this. It's cold out there."

Small talk. Simon did not smile back."Aye, I bet it is." He rubbed his eye.

More small talk. "How have you been?"

"Oh, you know. Up and down. Same as ever, really. You?"

Simon did not get the response he had expected. Laura looked down at the carpet.

"To tell you the truth, I'm a mess. I'm really down. I miss you, Simon. I want us to get back together. I never wanted us to split. You know that. Just like you know that nothing happened between David and me. It was only a friendly kiss." She looked longingly at Simon. Her bottom lip started quivering, but Simon could not tell if she was crying or cold. Her face still held raindrops. He was unsure what to do. He spoke calmly.

"We've been through this Law. The fact is that you went out with an ex-boyfriend, an ex-boyfriend who thought he was still your boyfriend when you were going out with me."

"Yes, but we had only just started going out. I didn't want to finish with David until I was sure we had something going. That night down in Swansea, he just turned up. Nobody invited him. He turned up, I finished with him, he became upset, and I kissed him. Somebody took a photo with my camera..."

"Which I bought you."

"I know you bought it, but somebody took the photo. I swear I told him that night that we were finished. He's history Simon." She looked directly into his eyes. "That was four months ago. We've been good ever since. You know there's never been anyone else. It's only been you. I love being with you, Simon, and I don't want us to split. We shouldn't split over something so insignificant and petty."

"Insignificant? I hardly call two-timing me insignificant. Anyway, you missed...you are missing the point. Even if I accept that you ended it and that the kiss was probably just in friendship, the fact remains that it's one rule for you and another for me."

"How do you work that out?" Laura looked puzzled.

Simon scratched the back of his head before continuing.

"You went ballistic when you found out about me having unprotected sex with Sammie just before I met you. I had those tests. Do you know how that felt? That was one of the worst weeks of my life. I thought I would lose you. I thought I might actually have fucking caught something. Waiting for those results gave me the shits for a whole week. Can you guess how that felt?"

"I was there remember? I told you it would be okay, and

it was."

"But you still hadn't trusted me."

"I didn't think you should have trusted her. You'd only just met her and had sex with her twice without protection. You couldn't be sure you were clean." Laura's hand clutched the mug tightly.

"But you can shag some bloke in Swansea, not tell me about it, and that's alright?" Simon feared he was losing control and did not like it.

"He wasn't just some bloke! I went out with him for ages," said Laura, her head shaking as she spoke.

He inhaled deeply and let the air out slowly.

"Whatever, but I knew nothing about it, and I bet he never wore a condom. What if he'd been shagging around? A good-looking bloke like that probably had plenty of women."

"David wasn't like that."

"So you say, and I must take your word for it. Why didn't you say anything? Were you afraid I'd ask you to take tests?"

"I would have done," said Laura, desperation creeping into her voice.

"That's not the point," replied Simon. "The point is I felt I had to have tests because you did not trust me, but you didn't tell me anything about this bloke. So you gave me no choice but to trust you. It's not fair or right, and if you cannot accept that, then I'm sorry."

Simon rose from the settee and walked to the window. The rain was hammering down.

"I know I've hurt you Si, and I'm truly sorry. I'd do anything to put things right. I should have told you about David. I don't know why I didn't but what you did and what I did are not the same. You had unprotected sex with a girl that you'd only just met. A girl who was a student and, I bet, had been with other men."

"But you don't know that," Simon spoke at the window.

"Okay, but you had just met her, and she had sex with you on the first night. It's a fair bet you weren't the first. David and I were going... we were together a long time before we... before anything happened."

The logic was evident to Simon, but he would not concede.

"But I have only got your word for that. How can you be sure David was clean? What if he slept around?"

"I know...I just know. We were going steady...he loved me...he wouldn't have done that to me. He just wouldn't." Tears filled her eyes.

He turned to face her.

"Oh...so that's alright then. You were going steady, so I have to hope that he was faithful and that none of the girls he shagged before you or while he was still going out with you had an STD or anything else." Simon was a little taken aback to find himself leaning towards her, finger-pointing in her direction.

"That's a terrible thing to say. David wouldn't have done that to me." Laura's tears now flooded down her cheeks. She only had her sleeve to dry them.

"But you did it to him. You were seeing me while he thought you were going out with him."

"And I finished with him before you, and I got serious. I finished with him as soon as I knew you were the one I wanted to be with."

"So you say."

"What does that mean?"

"Well, was it because you wanted to go with me or because I was the only one who was local?"

"Simon!" Tears now fell onto the carpet. "That's awful. How can you be so cruel? You know I loved being with you, and I still do. I thought I had proved how much I cared for you. When I think back, I know that the first night down at the Venue was a very special night for me. I'd never felt that way about anyone so quickly, not even David. I thought you felt the same way. I think you did. I hope you did anyway."

"For a while," said Simon, lying. He had no desire to

prolong this discussion as he could feel his resistance ebbing away. "Look Law, I need time to think. This has all come as a bit of a shock to me. I never expected us to split, but all this...well, I need to sort a few things out in my head."

"But we don't need to split. We can still go out. Please Simon, I'm sorry. Let me make it up to you." She rose from the sofa and reached for him. He stepped backwards.

"No! Not now. Let me get my head together, and I'll give you a ring." He walked to the cabinet and collected a box.

He passed her the box of tissues his mother kept on the unit next to the television. She took one and cried into it. Tears soaked the tissue.

Simon's resistance cracked.

"Oh, Law." He put his arms around her, and she cried into his chest. He kissed the top of her head.

"I just need time, that's all. We're not splitting up; we're just taking a breather. Nothing is final."

"It feels pretty final to me." Laura's tears saturated Sikes's best sweater.

With Laura despatched for home, Simon decided he needed a liquid lunch. Collecting his wallet and jacket, he left the warmth of the house and headed for the Tavern in the heart of town. He wanted to be somewhere his friends would avoid, and the Tavern was the ideal place. He was in no mood for company.

No matter how much effort the local council expended trying to spruce the place up, the town centre looked dead and downbeat on a cold, wet November Saturday afternoon. People were scarce on the rain-swept streets, and the shops looked empty. As he withdrew his cash from the cash machine, Simon saw his reflection in a window. His hair was lank. It occurred to Simon that he should have washed it. He should have washed up, too. He left the dirty mugs and plates on the breakfast bar. His mother would have something to say, but Simon did not care.

At three in the afternoon, Simon had been served and selected a seat. The bar area was empty, and the most significant decision Simon had to make was whether to sit as far away as possible from the other customers or to sit a little nearer, bringing him closer to the bar. He chose the latter.

Pint followed pint as Sikes thought about the morning's tribulations and his exploits the previous evening. He felt guilty about how he treated Laura and wished he had not gone with Maggie.

He had not previously found Maggie attractive. He had never fancied her. She was the wrong shape for him and had the wrong hair colour, but she was a lovely girl. She had become a close friend but nothing more. Now she was something more, and Simon wished she wasn't. He should not have let matters go so far. He wondered what had made him change his opinion the previous evening. Was it the drink? Was it the atmosphere? Would he have made a move if Maggie hadn't offered it on a plate? Was that it? Had he gone with her simply because he could?

Simon's stomach turned. Work colleagues had told him that Maggie fancied him, but he had thought nothing of it. Even Marty had teased him that Maggie would do anything for him. He had never expected anything to happen. He had never dreamt they would have done the things they did the previous night. They had only ever been friends, and that was all. Now they were more than just friends. Things were likely to get awkward. Would they still be friends the next time they met? Would she expect something more? What would happen to Marty?

The thought of his workmate caused Sikes to stop fretting about Maggie. He wondered what had happened to Marty. Where had he gone? Why did he disappear so quickly and without saying goodbye? It was his fault. Simon would not have gone with Maggie if Marty had not left them. It was as simple as that. He would not have had the chance.

Marty had been going out with Maggie, but would he

be seeing her again? If Maggie finished things with Marty, expecting to see Simon, things could get complicated. She had told him that she was growing tired of Marty's antics and might finish with him. Simon did not want to fill any void. He had no desire to see Maggie, in that sense, ever again.

He had enjoyed the sex, but he did not want a relationship. He liked Maggie as a friend but nothing more. She would have to understand that. He felt anxious about having to tell her how he felt. He knew he would have to see her at work but did not know what to say or how to say it. He dismissed these thoughts and drank more beer.

Try as he might, Sikes could not stop thinking. Sex with Maggie had certainly been different from sex with Laura. Laura was more conservative. There were certain things that Laura would not try. Or was it that he had never suggested them? Maybe if he had said something, she might have given it a go. Simon much preferred the thought of sex with Laura to sex with Maggie. Sex with Laura was meaningful, loving and passionate. Sex with Maggie had been casual, lustful and aggressive. He would have to do without sex with Laura now. That option was no longer available to him. That thought also sat uneasily on his mind. It was time for more beer.

Someone handed him a collection of Saturday papers, complete with endless supplements. He got through them quickly without giving any consideration to their content.

The sports results blasted out of the four large television screens on the walls. He paid them as little attention as he had the newspapers.

Four hours had passed since Simon had entered the pub. He had not noticed the time, nor had he seen the customers arriving for the Saturday evening disco. Simon had been away with his thoughts. He only seemed to notice the world around him when his glass was empty.

As his mood grew darker, the angrier he became.

Simon placed the glass on the bar, ready for refilling.

"Same again, please."

"Yo Sikesyman! I'll get that."

"No thanks. I'll get my own."

Dave Farley ignored Simon's comment and spoke directly to the barman.

"And a pint for me and a half of lager for Robyn."

"Okay, Dave," said the barman.

"I said I'll get my own." Simon slurred as he spoke.

"Calm down Sikesy. I'm only buying you a pint."

Simon snapped back.

"I don't want your fucking pint. Leave me alone."

Customers' attention focused on the loud drunk at the bar.

"Calm down Si." Farley tried to put his hand on Sikes' shoulder.

"Keep your fucking hands off me."

Farley withdrew his hand and held both up in front of him in a gesture of defeat.

"Okay, okay."

Robyn arrived at her boyfriend's side. "Is everything okay, Dave?"

"I think Simon has had a bit too much to drink."

Robyn studied her friend and then spoke softly into Simon's ear. "I think it's time you went home Si."

"I'll go when I'm ready. I'm not pissed. I'm just pissed off." He looked at the barman, "Pint, please."

The barman ignored him. Simon picked up his glass and slammed it down on the plastic drip tray, repeating his order. "I said I want a fucking pint, please."

Farley placed his hand on Simon's shoulder and leaned closer to him.

"Simon. I think you've had enough. It's time to go home mate. Don't make a fool of yourself."

"Fuck off!" Simon shouted as he hit Farley in the stomach with a tightly clenched right hand. Farley doubled over as Robyn screamed.

"Simon, what are you doing?"

The people at the bar stepped away. Robyn stared at her friend but could do nothing as Simon's left hand grabbed Farley's shoulder and pulled him upright, his right hand hitting Farley's stomach as he did so.

Farley groaned but remained upright.

"Simon, stop it!" Robyn pleaded, growing increasingly anxious. "Stop it now!"

Simon ignored her pleas; he had no intention of stopping. He hit Farley twice, once in the stomach and once in the chest. Still, Farley did not fall.

Sikes had endured eight years of karate lessons between the ages of eight and sixteen. He had never wanted to go, but his parents had insisted. He felt that he had no natural aptitude for the sport and had to work hard at his technique to secure the different coloured belts. His favourite karate lesson had been his last one, knowing he was quitting to concentrate on getting his GCSEs.

As he hammered Farley, Simon let years of frustration pour out of him. The technique was a little rusty but effective. There was no suggestion that the drink had slowed him down. He withdrew his left hand from Farley's shoulder and, bending the elbow, clenched the fist and held it ready by his side. At the same time, his taut right arm straightened as it moved effortlessly through the air. The palm was upright, his fingers bent at the middle joint, and the base of the palm hit Farley's face. Simon yelled as he made the punch. His hand pushed into Farley's face driving him backwards and causing his feet to lift off the floor. Farley fell onto Robyn, who screamed.

"Dave!"

Farley and Robyn fell backwards onto the wooden floor. Farley looked dazed.

Simon had not finished. He bent over and grabbed Farley's left wrist.

Robyn was confused.

"Leave him alone, Simon. You've hurt him enough. What's got into you?" She wriggled to get out from under

Farley.

Simon ignored her pleas.

Holding Farley's wrist tightly in his left hand, Sikes ripped at the shirtsleeve. The cuff button popped off, and he saw what he was looking for, the ever-present plaster. Catching one end between two fingers, he snatched the dressing off the skin, taking with it several hairs. He read the childlike lettering indelibly etched onto the arm many years before. The once-black Indian ink had faded to dark green, but the mixed-case letters were clear enough.

"AniMAl." Sikes read the word aloud.

Farley peered at Simon through half-closed eyes. Robyn was fussing, calling for tissues as blood streamed from Farley's nose and mouth.

Four huge hands converged on Simon's shoulders. He did not resist. He had done what he had wanted to do. Something he had thought about for eleven years.

The bouncers escorted him from the premises and had the good grace to throw his coat out after him when he told them where it was.

Oblivious to the cold and wet, Simon walked around the town centre, wondering what he should do next. He felt warmed by the success of his revenge, but the rage inside him had not subsided. Staggering from one end of town to the other, Simon realised that he and Farley were not finished. There was only one way this would end, and he knew there was only one place to end it. He set off knowing he could collect what he needed on the way.

The tall wet figure huddled in the alleyway, invisible to anyone on the street or in the houses. The alleyway led to the back of a disused shop. He knew he would not be troubled by anyone. He could wait here as long as he wanted. He could stay as long as it took.

He had already waited for hours. He had no shelter from the persistent rain, no food for his hungry stomach and no water for his thirsty mouth. He was still angry, committed and would wait as long as necessary. He would ignore his body's needs. The one thing he had to do was piss, and there was plenty of room for that at the back end of the alley.

His clothes were drenched. His short coat did not provide enough protection from the constant downpour. His wet shirt stuck to his body. The wet would not deter him. He needed to do this. He had to do this tonight. There would be no other time. Tomorrow he would feel different. It had to be tonight.

Cars passed by infrequently, but when they did, he checked to ensure no taxi was delivering his target to the door. A glance from the alley showed that no one was arriving at his victim's house. It also proved that, as the nearest inhabited dwellings were some way away, they would be undisturbed. He liked that feeling.

At least his head had cleared. The walk and the rain had done him some good. He felt almost sober. Sober but determined. This had to be done. The frustration was just too much to bear any longer. This should have been done years before, but better late than never.

He could hear footsteps on the concrete pavement and shifted his head to see down the street. There was the target. This was not a false alarm. This was it. The moment he had waited for when the pain of the past would be eradicated forever. He would finally make amends for what had happened to his family. He hoped the moment would arrive and, now that it had, he would savour it. He had planned this quickly but was happy that his plan was foolproof. He could not and would not fail.

The footsteps grew louder as the feet got closer.

He placed his back against the high wall, turned his head to the left to look out of the alleyway, and waited. A slim figure, wrapped in a thick padded coat with a wet baseball cap covering his head, walked past the entrance to the alley, humming quietly.

The hunter pounced. He grabbed the other man's shoulders and threw the body roughly into the alleyway. He landed with a heavy bump on the hard concrete floor. The hat fell off the head.

"Who is it? What do you want?"

Sikes stood over the body and kicked into it. His feet kicked hard and fast. The other man could do nothing initially but eventually curled itself into a ball, trying to protect itself until the kicking ceased. The kicking did not stop. It became more ferocious.

He dropped his knees onto the body, letting it feel his full weight.

The body groaned again and came out of the shell. It moaned louder and more frequently as the hunter's fists took turns punching into the head and face.

The face winced.

"Enough. Enough. Please stop. Take what you want. Please stop it."

"Shut your fucking mouth."

"Sikes? Sikes? Is that you? His eyes had not adequately adjusted to the light. Blood got spat out of the mouth as Farley winced from the kicks to his back.

Simon's eyes had become accustomed to the darkness. His fast hands continued hitting the beaten face.

"Sikes please stop. Ouch...please, Sikes...stop."

"I haven't fucking started yet." Simon's feet were too quick and exerted too much power for Farley to stop them. He tried to curl into a ball, but that offered no protection for his back. The kicks came quicker and harder.

"I've come to finish what I've started, what you started. What you started eleven years ago."

Farley tried desperately to avoid the onslaught.

"Please Sikes, no more. I don't understand." Farley sought sanctuary, but there was none. "What are you on about?"

Simon stopped kicking and grabbed Farley by the hair.

He slammed the head into the concrete. Farley groaned as Simon punched him again and again.

"I'm on about the little matter of a stone that came through the window of our house eleven years ago." He threw Farley's head at the concrete again. "Ring any bells? Do you remember the little house? You and your mate, whoever he was, throwing stones at our window." Simon waited for an answer.

Farley started to slide away, but Simon grabbed his legs, Farley attempted to kick out, but Sikes stopped him with a punch to the groin. Farley cried out in agony.

Sikes kicked him repeatedly and then placed his foot on Animal's head, holding it steady for a few seconds. Farley offered no resistance, nor did he attempt to move as the foot released his head. He brought his arms up to cover his head just in time to block another kick aimed at his face.

"Do you remember the house? Do you ever think about it? Do you ever think about throwing that stone? Did you ever wonder whether it caused any damage? Did you care?"

Farley groaned into his hand. The pain was intense. "Fuck...it was your house. I never twigged. We knew that the mother was really ill. That was your mother?"

"Yes, it was my mother. We thought she was going to die. She lost a baby. She lost my baby brother or sister. And it was all because of you, you spineless prick...you killed my baby brother or sister...you almost killed my mother too...you stopped her from having any more kids...she was ill for ages afterwards...she had to adopt...and did you care? Did you fuck! You just got on with your happy little life without a care. Until now." Simon was moving alongside Farley as he slowly crawled up the alley. "She had to answer so many questions and go through a multitude of tests because of you. Do you have any fucking idea what we went through? We were a happy family until you went and spoiled it all. Well, now I'm going to spoil your life. I'm going to spoil you good and fucking proper. This is where you get yours." The rehearsed speech had turned into a ramble, but he felt he had made the salient points.

Simon kicked Farley again to feel better, then placed his foot on Farley's head and pressed it into his skull. The thick black sole of Simon's shoe covered much of his enemy's hair. He twisted his foot sharply. Farley winced again.

Sikes withdrew his foot from Farley's head and walked a few paces away from him. Farley struggled to see what Simon was doing through the blood that filled his eyes. He saw Sikes pick up a brick, the same brick that Simon had borrowed from the building site en route. He had carried the brick over a mile and strategically placed it in the alley. The brick Simon was now moving again and walking towards his enemy.

Farley shuffled until his back rested against the wall of the empty shop.

"What are you going to do with that?"

"I'm going to smash your fucking head open," Simon said without emotion.

Terror crept into Farley's voice.

"Hang on Sikes. Think about it."

"I have thought about it. I've thought about this for eleven years. Eleven fucking years..."

Farley wrapped his arms around his head.

"Wait, Simon. You've got it wrong. It wasn't me."

Simon sensed the fear in Farley's voice. He felt good. He felt in total control. He raised the brick above his head.

Farley was panicking.

"Simon, listen will you, "It wasn't me who threw the brick."

"Don't tell me. It was your friend. Well, tell me who he is, and I'll fucking sort him out too." Simon stood still for a second.

"I don't know what friend you mean."

"The friend who was with you when you sprayed the garages."

"Garages? What gar... the Paula Jenkins garages. That was Malcolm Davies. He lives in Manchester now. He's a chef."

"Save me the fucking details. I'll find him." Simon moved menacingly towards Farley until he stood over him, the brick inching ever higher into the air.

"But it wasn't us who threw the brick. We weren't even there."

"Of course, you weren't. So who was it then? Who else could it have been? You were the ones spraying the garages. Your name was all over the garages. You knew the police had been around my house. It must have been you."

Farley wriggled uneasily, trying once again to slide himself along the alleyway. Simon kicked him again.

"Stay where you are. You're going fucking nowhere."

"It wasn't me Sikes, I promise. I didn't throw any stone. I swear that on my life…and Robyn's life. I wasn't even there."

"It will be your life. You leave Robyn out of this."

"But it wasn't me." Fear in the voice. "But I'll tell you who it was."

Simon lowered the brick, moved it to his left hand, and then used his right hand to grab Farley's collar, pulling him up towards him.

"Then who was it? If you want to tell me something, you'd better tell me now before I finish this once and for all." He pushed Farley backwards, forcing his head to collide with the wall. Animal moaned again, and Simon could see his face and hands were awash with blood. It made no difference to Sikes, and he kicked him again. "Well? I'm waiting."

Farley held up his hands in submission.

"Okay, it's just a bit hard to speak." He spat out a mouthful of blood.

"Hurry up. I haven't got all night."

Farley tried to sit up as he prepared to speak. He rubbed his head and arched his aching back as he did so.

"It was my brother, Richard, who threw the stones. Him and his mate Stompie."

Sikes had wanted to hear a confession but not this one.

"What? You're kidding. If you're lying to me, I'll fucking

kill you."

"No...no...I'm serious." Farley grimaced as he straightened his back. His mouth hurt, and he had trouble speaking. His whole body ached; he was in agony and did not want to get hit anymore. He wanted the beating to stop. He wanted to go home.

"I went out with Paula Jenkins for a while. I had it bad too. I was convinced that I loved her. I used to travel down every night just to see her. I had it really bad. Anyway, she finished with me, and I was well pissed off." He rubbed the base of his palm into his forehead. "I was going to call by her house to see her, but I got scared. That's why I wrote those things on the garages. Brave eh? I didn't have the guts to confront her, so I wrote messages on the garage doors. I also put a couple of windows through on a car I thought was her old man's, but it turned out to be someone else's."

"I never saw that."

"I didn't think anyone saw us at the garages." He looked up. Sikes still leered menacingly over him, with the brick back in his right hand.

Farley croaked some more.

"Then Paula's mother rang my house the next day to say that someone, I now know was you, had seen us and gone to the police. She told my mother that the police were after me and would be coming to collect me. She let slip that you lived up the road from her. My poor mother started to panic. She caught hold of me and ordered me to tell her what I had done. I broke down in tears and told her everything that had happened. She went berserk and wanted to take me down to the police station there and then. Richard told her there was no need to involve the police. He would have a word with the parents of the boy who had seen me and sort it out."

"Why was he so concerned? It wasn't exactly the crime of the fucking century, was it? You only vandalised some garages. What was his problem?" The brick remained in Sikes' hand, ready to be used at a second's notice.

"He was worried because I was the only one in my family who hadn't gotten into trouble. My Dad had been in the clink for robbery. My eldest brother, Hugh, had done time after stealing cars, and Richard was always in trouble for fighting and stuff. It was the drink with him, you see. He was a total nutter in drink." He smoothed the back of his right arm. "We were a rough family. One of the roughest in this area, and that's saying something. That's how I got the nickname Animal when I was in school. It was not because I was hard but because of the family's reputation. I was regarded as the hardest in school, but I never even had a fight. Everyone reckoned they saw me beat up so and so, but in reality, no one tried to fight me. They were scared enough of me without me having to do anything. Sure I used to enjoy...that feeling of power, I suppose, it was great getting what I wanted, but I've never been a hard man Sikes."

Sikes had seen that for himself.

"So, what happened next?"

Farley winced as he moved again.

"Richard sets off for your house with Stompie in Stompie's car. We think he goes to call but sees the police are already there, so they head to the pub. Well, here, things get a bit vaguer. It's what I managed to pick up from scraps of information I heard..."

Sikes knew that feeling.

"I think Stompie gets the idea to frighten your parents by sending a message on a stone through a window. So they write a note. They then have the idea to attach the note to a stone with an elastic band. I have no idea where they got an elastic band from, but after a few more beers, they set off for your house. Richard scribbled the note and attached it to a stone. Stompie was supposed to throw the brick because Rich had had too many pints. Stompie has a few practices using pebbles to get his eye in, but Richard wants to get on with it. He tells Stompie to copy him. He then picks up a brick from the garden and throws it. He throws it far too hard. As he chucks it, he sees a woman's face...your mother's face, at the window. He screamed for her to move, but she couldn't have heard him. The brick goes straight through the glass and hits her. You know the rest. They run off." He paused for a second. "Honestly, Sikes, it wasn't supposed to happen like that. They were only trying to frighten you. Nobody was supposed to get hurt."

Sikes dropped the brick and fell back against the wall, crouching down on his legs, his knees bearing his weight. He felt sick and let his knees fall onto the soaking wet floor, placing his palms on the ground in front of him. Beer, bile and carrots wrapped up in years of frustration hit the concrete. Sikes took a long, slow, deep breath before wiping his mouth with the back of his hand.

Farley struggled but could not stand. Using the sleeve of his sodden coat, he smoothed his battered face and neck.

Sikes was crouching again, his back against the wall.

"What happened to the note?"

Farley hoped his beating was over but was happy to finish the story. His voice was calmer now, less anxious but the soreness in his mouth still made it hard to speak. He lisped on certain words.

"Don't know. Perhaps they took it with them and dumped it somewhere. As far as I know, it never got mentioned again. My brother and Stompie legged it." Farley whimpered as he tried to raise his left arm. "Of course, I was number one suspect, and the police came round to question me right away, probably the same night. But I had a cast iron alibi. I was up at the school youth club, and my old teachers and the local vicar saw me there. Nobody suspected Richard and Stompie of being involved. We never knew until he told us one night when he was pissed. He was arguing with Hugh over who was the hardest and who had done the craziest shit. My mother threw him out. He stayed with Stompie in the flats up the top, and then he had his accident. Months later, I confessed to painting the garages and got a warning. I've never been in any trouble since."

"Hoorah for you. Congratulations to the Animal," said Sikes. "So, where's your brother now?"

"Dead," said Farley coldly.

"What?"

"He's dead."

Sikes did not believe his ears.

"What the fuck? How? When?"

"About six months after the incident at your house. Him and Stompie got killed on the top road." He tried to straighten his back. It hurt. He flinched. "They were coming home on Stompie's bike when a drunk driver hit them. They never had a chance. Who knows Sikes, perhaps justice prevailed. That's when my mother made me confess to the police. Perhaps his death was the reason why I got off with a warning. I reckon old Grimshaw wanted me to go down, but his boss said our family had suffered enough."

"You'd suffered enough!" said Simon sarcastically.

Farley continued.

"My mother always said God works in mysterious ways. She used the insurance money from Richard's accident to give us a fresh start. That's when we moved down here." He rubbed his face, wondering if his nose had been broken. "We are doing quite well now. Dad works on the buses, Hugh sells cars, and I work in the folk lift truck factory. I'm supposed to go to Italy again in a couple of weeks. I'll be away for ten weeks this time. I get to come home for Christmas, though."

"Fucking great, good for you."

Sikes puffed out his cheeks and then let the air out slowly through tight lips. He had completely lost the plot. He stayed quiet, leaving Farley to ramble on about how much his family regretted what had happened and how he would have probably done the same had he been in Simon's shoes. He repeated that he never had a clue it was the Ikes family. Simon did not want platitudes. He had come for justice but had ended up feeling remorseful. He had heard enough and just wanted to go home. He wanted his room. He longed for his bed. He stood ready to walk away but then saw the mess that was his victim. Farley could hardly move, and the blood was evident, even in the low light. Sikes realised he had been a stone's throw away from making the biggest mistake of his short life. It would not make amends, but he knew he had to take Farley home. He lifted the lad by his shoulders and placed an arm around his back.

"Come on. Let's get you over the road."

Farley flinched and groaned but did not resist.

The rain had stopped, and the moon shone between the clouds in the autumn sky as they stepped into the street. Once again, Simon saw the mess that Dave "Animal" Farley had become. It did not make Simon feel better. Farley could barely walk. His face was bleeding. Both his eyes were swollen, and his usually immaculate clothing was in tatters, a combination of being dragged across the concrete and the pulling and tugging suffered at Simon's hands.

"Are you okay to walk?"

Farley nodded tamely as Sikes led him across the street.

Sikes was embarrassed. An hour ago, he had wanted to kill this man and, fuelled by too much alcohol, and rage, probably would have. Now he instinctively knew that the right thing was to get him home safely so he could get help.

"Number seventeen, innit?"

Farley nodded again.

"Is your mother in?"

"Yeah. I think so." Farley's voice was barely louder than a whisper.

"Shit. I hadn't expected to be doing this." Simon kept his grip on Farley as they shuffled onto the kerb.

Farley sniffed, coughed and then spat blood from his mouth. His dry tongue circled his lips. "Sikes, would you really have hit me with that brick?"

"Aye," Simon said coldly.

"I thought you'd say that. I honestly never knew Sikes.

In all these years, I never knew you were involved.." Farley fell quiet for a short time and then added. "I knew there was something. You never liked me, no matter how much I tried. Robyn said we were cool, but I knew there was something...I'd never have guessed it was this. I honestly never knew the name of the family, Sikes. Nobody told me many details. I only know what I picked up by earwigging conversations and stuff."

Sikes was tempted to say he knew that feeling but said nothing. He looked up and down the street. It was clear of traffic, so he carried on walking, practically carrying Farley as he did so.

The whisper started again.

"Don't worry about my mother. I'll tell her I got jumped on my way home and that you found me and brought me here."

Sikes no longer cared. "It's okay. I'll tell her the truth if you want."

"No, don't do that, please. Don't reopen old wounds." Farley feebly grabbed Simon's free arm. "Don't tell her Sikes. Please. As soon as she found out what Richard had done, she wanted to visit the parents...your parents...we told her to leave the family to recover. She's a lovely old lady Sikes. Don't take it out on her. Don't tell her Si. Please don't upset her again."

Simon had never imagined Dave "Animal" Farley begging for anything from anyone.

"Okay. If you're sure?"

"I am."

The speech had almost exhausted Farley. He let go of Simon's free arm as his head slouched down onto his chest. He stayed silent for the remaining fifty yards or so.

The pair reached Farley's front gate. Sikes looked at the small semi-detached bungalow with a well-laid-out lawn. It was much smaller than his house but looked immaculate. He opened the gate.

"Nearly there."

Farley spoke again.

"Do you want to come in for a coffee or something?"

The irony was not lost on Sikes, who chuckled before replying.

"No thanks. I'll get you in, and I'll piss off. I never was much of a liar, so if you can leave the explanations until after I've gone."

"Sure. I'd better call Robyn and tell her you are safe. She was really worried about you. You gave her quite a scare in the Tavern. That was one hell of a punch." Farley laughed weakly. "She thought you were going to take my head off."

"Aye...well...that was the plan...but as usual, I've completely fucked things up."

PROBLEM SOLVED

While Simon was drowning his sorrows in the Tavern, Jack Phillips celebrated a minor coup. He poured himself a large glass of malt whisky, which he sipped as he sat by the 'phone at his new home in Newport.

The small black handset nestled comfortably into the shoulder of his grey Pringle sweater, a birthday gift from his mother. He was surprised she had not knitted him a sweater. As he waited, his mind went back to the visit of his mother, sister and her children the previous week.

His mother immediately warmed to his new house. She was thrilled that he was back in Wales. His sister suggested he was not being entirely honest about his reasons for returning to Wales but went along with his story about it being an excellent career opportunity. She knew him far too well. He wondered how her career would have progressed had it not been for the twins. She would have gone a long way. She was bright, organised, hardworking and perceptive, but there was little point in dwelling on the question. She had made her choices and was perfectly happy in her world.

He admired how she settled into married life and raised three wonderful children. He also respected how she managed her husband. Thomas was successful but unsure, popular but shy, laid-back but anxious. Tom was a complex character, but Caroline knew how to handle him. Tom knew when he was being managed but did not object. Jack was the same when Shirley was running him.

He wished the two had met. His sister would have loved Shirley. He was confident they would have got on famously. Caroline would have liked Shirley much more than she had Mary.

Poor Mary, so misunderstood. That dreadful disease

ravaged poor Mary that he had not recognised her when he called to see her at the hospice. Perhaps he could have treated her better. Maybe they should have stayed together? The split had been her idea, and divorce had been on the cards.

In the end, divorce was unnecessary as nature played its cruel hand and ended what had become a sham of a marriage for them. He had been surprised that Mary had left him so much in her will. He anticipated being written out of it after Mary knew he was having an affair with 'that girl who works for you.'

Shirley had taken it as a compliment.

Girl! Girl! It's been a long time since anyone called me a girl! Have you told her I do not work with you? I'm only a consultant.

Would he and Mary have survived even if Shirley had not come onto the scene? He knew this was nonsense talk. He and Mary were destined to fail from the start. They had nothing in common apart from mutual lust initially, and even that quickly fizzled out into mutual tolerance. He tolerated her pet projects and social events. She put up with his work and Shirley.

Caroline never asked why he and Mary had split up. He wondered why that was. Could it be that she sensed something? Or was she just relieved that her brother had got himself out of what she regarded as a doomed relationship with a lady she despised?

As far as he was aware, Caroline never even knew Shirley had existed, so she knew nothing about what had happened. Now was not the time to tell her. His sister would only fuss, just as she had fussed when their mother tired during the guided tour of his new house. She sat mother down in his large Queen Anne Chair and made sure she was okay, not feeling ill. His mother teased her.

"I always said you should have been a nurse rather than a teacher."

He had handed his mother a glass of whisky to help her recuperate and smiled at the cheek of the old dear. He had not offered an alcoholic drink, but his mother was never backward in coming forward.

"Do you have to die of thirst to get a drink in this house?"

"Cup of tea, Mum?" He had asked.

"If you've nothing else. Are you keeping that whisky for display purposes?"

He fetched a glass. His sister settled for tea, and the twins had lemonade.

The lady at the other end of the line spoke again.

"He's just coming, Jack. He was in the garage dabbling with that old Rover and had to change his clothes before I let him in. Shall I get him to call you?"

"No, that's fine Sarah. I'll wait. I need to pop out later, but I wanted to speak to him before I go."

"Okay."

He heard a bang as the other receiver got placed on a table and heard a female voice shouting. "Hurry up, dear. Jack's waiting."

He could not make out the reply.

Phillips' mind drifted again. His mother was studying a page in her crossword book, crystal whisky glass in her hand. Her youngest grandson stood at her arm, trying to make sense of the clues. The granddaughter sat on the leather sofa, reading a holiday brochure with her mother. It had been a while since he had been I n their company, and Jack was happy to be watching them. He savoured the moment.

"What does that say, Gran?"

"Which one, love?" His mother did not take her eyes off the page.

A little finger pointed to the clues under the crossword.

"Bib-li-cal name for people of what?"

"Israel," said his mother.

"Jews," said the little girl. "We did that in school."

"Yeah. That's right." Her brother added. "That's part of the navitity play."

Phillips had chuckled at the mispronunciation.

His sister corrected her son.

"That's nativity. Say it. Na-tiv-ity."

"Na-tiv-ity. Na-tiv-ity. Navitity," The little boy groaned.

His twin sister laughed at him.

Mrs Phillips spoke to her grandchildren.

"It's Israelites. People of Israel used to be known as Israelites."

"Oh yes," said the little girl.

The little boy looked confused.

"I thought they were Jews. Jesus was a Jew, wasn't he?"

"Yes, love," said his mother. "He was indeed."

The little boy was back on the crossword.

"What's that one there, Gran?"

Phillips ignored his nephew, climbing up the back of the seat. He planned to buy new furniture anyway.

Mrs Phillips read aloud.

"Those attending a meeting, seminar or conference."

"What's a seminar, Gran?"

"Hmm... it's like a large meeting

"Meetingites," said the little boy jumping away from the seat.

A large smile appeared on Jack Phillips' mouth as the word went over and over in his mind. Meetingites sounded much better than delegates. He wondered if his fellow directors appreciated that they were meetingites. They had so many meetings; how could they not know?

"Hi, Jack. Sorry to have kept you."

"No problem Geoffrey. I'm sorry to disturb you. It's just that I have some very important news and as I said to Sarah, I wanted to tell you before I left for the evening. It looks like our prayers have been answered. Earlier today, I visited Cardiff Central Police Station, where one of our not-so favourable employees was being held on suspicion of selling cocaine. He resisted arrest apparently, so he is up to his neck in trouble."

"If you mean who I think you mean, that is good news."

"I do, and it is," said Jack, taking another sip of his malt.

"I knew it would only be a matter of time."

LIFE'S NOT ALWAYS A PICNIC

Simon Ikes, 19 years and five days old, lay back on the square red-checked rug his family had used for picnics for as long as he could remember. Fingers inter-twined behind his head, resting on the palms of his hands. He closed his eyes, savouring the tranquillity.

The sun shone brightly in the sky, and the air was filled with the smell of freshly cut grass being discharged from the sides of the three grass cutters at work in the park. Children's laughter drowned the drone of the cutters. Simon beamed. Life was good. He did not know why he had chosen to come to the park or when the sun had shone so brightly in November, but he was determined to make the most of the moment.

Twisting his head to the right, Simon saw a mother setting up a small camp for herself and her young baby. He saw the side of the baby's head not hidden by the high sides of the pram. Blotches of fine dark hair thinly spread across the scalp. The mother spread out her coat on the ground and sat on it.

Making herself comfortable, she reached up to the side of the pram. Simon thought that the pram looked very old-fashioned. It had big wheels linked to a heavy metal frame. The baby sat in a large blue seat. The pram's hood was folded flat. He guessed that his grandmother would have used a similar one when his mother was a baby.

He examined the scene again. From behind, the lady was not dissimilar to his mother, Caroline Ikes. She was of average height, slim and with fair hair. Simon wished she would turn around so he could see her face, but she did not. She sat facing away from him, holding the side of the cumbersome pram.

Simon looked to the sky once more. He watched enviously as a plane flew overhead, leaving a long white vapour trail in the clear autumn sky. Thoughts of exotic holidays filled his mind.

A baby's scream broke his daydream, and Simon looked toward the mother. He saw that the pram was on its side, and the baby was lying on the grass. Dark red blood poured from its head.

The mother remained motionless.

Simon was concerned about the mother. He wanted to go and help. He could not get his body to move as hard as he tried. His efforts at unravelling his fingers, and bringing his hands to the side of his body, came to nothing. His hands would not move. The fingers would not separate. Simon was powerless to do anything but stare at the unfurling misery around him. The injured baby lay on its back, possibly bleeding to death. The frantic mother sat motionlessly, her head in her hands. Sikes shook his head, trying to free his hands that had somehow secured themselves onto his hair. He shook his head from left to right and back again but could not regain control of his fingers. They would not be parted. His palms were still attached to the back of his head. Sweat poured onto his brow. Once again, Simon endeavoured to heave himself upright, but his body was frozen. His head was the only part of his body he could move. The rest of his body was outside his control, locked in position.

Ikes' eyes searched for someone to help him, someone or something to help him. He thought about the baby but sensed that the tragic young mother also needed help and support. Sikes knew that unless someone helped them soon, the baby would die.

The baby! Simon rolled his head to the right again. He could still see the mother. She was staring into the void, but the baby had gone.

He heard something. It was not the noise of the other children, who played on, oblivious to the tragedy. It was the sound of someone sobbing. Was the mother crying? Where had the baby disappeared to? A trail of dark blood ran from where the baby had been and passed below Simon's feet. He looked again, but the baby had not reappeared.

Sikes felt something hit his left elbow and quickly turned his head. Straining to see what was behind him, he felt a muscle twinge in the back of his neck as he forced his head upwards.

A tiny hand grabbed his nose and pulled his face toward the mother. Surprised at the sharpness of the tug, Simon felt tears rise as little fingers poked into his eye sockets. Simon sharply closed his eyes. Opening them cautiously, he shut them again as two outstretched fingers stabbed into his eyeballs. A baby chuckled. Lifting his eyelids again, Simon looked at the baby's face, but what he saw proved too much for him to take, so he hastily looked the other way. Tears started to roll down his cheeks.

The baby's face possessed eyes but no nose or mouth. The skin that should have formed around these features hung lank and lifeless from the middle. Taking another look, Simon saw that the blood that had run so freely from the baby's head had disappeared, and the scalp was covered in fine, blonde hairs. The baby's skin was dark blue, and veins bulged across the forehead.

Simon flinched as the baby climbed over his arms and onto his chest. He glimpsed again at the face but wished he had not. The baby's head was turned away from his gaze, and he saw that where the ears should have been was an open wound. Blood and skin fell from the laceration. Some dropped onto Simon's face. Skin landed on his lips, blood and tissue fell on his nose, and large blood clots hit his hair. Sikes tried to be sick, but his lips seemed welded together. He feared he was going to choke on his vomit. Simon could not move or utter a sound. As he turned to face the baby again, he knew that, for the first time in his life, he was experiencing absolute panic and could do nothing about it. He could not move, he could not speak, and he could not throw up. There was nothing to do but face whatever was coming his way.

The baby sat with its backside on Simon's chest, facing

him. Its little legs dangled on either side of his head. Scanning the tiny body, Simon saw that the blood was flowing again. The baby owned no genitalia, navel, nipples, or ears. It had only eyes. Light blue eyes. They reminded Simon of his father.

Blood stopped pouring out of the wound. The baby's eyes twinkled in recognition, and Simon felt strangely reassured. The feeling lasted less than thirty seconds as baby fingers rammed into Simon's nostrils blocking his only means of breathing. Simon's head shook uncontrollably, hoping to dislodge the tiny fingers until the baby dug its other hand into the flesh on Simon's cheek, holding his face still.

The pain in his cheek was the least of his concerns. He could not move or speak and was running out of oxygen. He could not breathe. He thought he was nearing his end. Simon did not feel prepared for this. He was not ready for death, but there was nothing he could do. He started to choke. He felt like his head was about to explode, and he was powerless to stop it. He was helpless.

Simon's strength drained away. Tiredness swept over him. Taking one last look to his right, Simon saw the mother standing upright and walking toward the baby. It was his mother, and she smiled warmly at him as she ran to her son.

Hope. If his mother could get to him, he would be safe. His mother could save him. She would lift the baby from him and contact a doctor who could find the cause of the muscle spasm that had disabled him. He was paralysed but safe. His mother would help him.

But his mother did not help him. He heard his mother say, "Goodbye Simon, thank you for caring about our baby."

Fear swept through his body once more. Simon took a last look at the baby and was startled to see features developing on its once bare face. A nose, a mouth, two ears and a dimple appeared on the newly formed face. It was his face. The baby was taking Simon's face.

Darkness, Simon's eyes saw only blackness broken by dark red lights. He glared at the red luminous digits on the clock. It read 3:30. Simon raised his hands to cover his face, used the ends of his fingers to wipe the moisture from his forehead, and blew hard into his palms. His sheet was wet, soaking wet. Sweat poured from every orifice on his body. His mouth was dry, but his face, hair, body, arms, legs, and feet were soaking.

"Shit. That was a bad one." He exhaled heavily. "That was the worst yet."

QUIZ NIGHT

The crowd gathering at the weekly Red Lion Sunday quiz night spoke only of one thing.

The air was alive with news of how Dave "Animal" Farley had the shit kicked out of him on his doorstep the previous evening.

The rumour was that Farley had been set upon by between three and seven people and had put two of them in the hospital before he ended the evening in intensive care. Robyn had tried to help fight off the attackers and had gotten hurt. She had also gone to the hospital.

Misinformation spread faster than head lice in a classroom of eight-year-olds. The claims about his injuries ranged from kidney failure to likely brain damage, with various reports that Farley had woken from his coma. His mother was said to be devastated. The last bit, at least, was valid.

The man himself was recovering from his beating at home. The doctor had been and gone, having diagnosed severe bruising. No bones appeared broken, although his kidneys had taken a hammering, so Dave needed to watch his urine. Other than that, the doctor said there was nothing wrong with him that would not get better in time with rest, relaxation and plenty of liquid.

The police had visited. His mother had called them in panic. Farley refused to elaborate on basic facts. He told them he was probably to blame. He had upset his assailants, emphasis on the plural, and they had taken revenge. In hindsight, he realised he had misbehaved and deserved what had happened. He would not give names, and there would be no retribution. The matter was closed as far as he was concerned. He would not be pressing charges. The police quickly gave up trying to persuade him otherwise.

Farley spent the day lying on his mother's blue and white striped, spring-action sofa bed. Cushions propped him up. He did not want a blanket. The only time he left the sofa was to visit the lavatory. He wished he did not have to go so often. Passing water was painful, but his mother forced him to drink plenty, and he knew better than to argue. He was grateful his urine appeared to be returning to its more normal colour. It had looked dirty earlier that morning. The doctor had explained why that would happen.

Robyn called to see him after lunch. Her coat was wet, it was raining again, and roadworks had delayed the bus. She became upset when she saw the bruises and cuts on his face. The sight of his back, a shocking mass of dark purple, made her cry and swear that she would hurt whoever had done this to him.

Mrs Farley hugged her.

"There, there, love, it looks worse than it is."

His mother left them alone. Robyn was angry with Farley for being so stubborn. Her view was quite simplistic; the guilty deserved punishment. The police could do the punishing. Farley calmed her, sat her down and told her the truth. He did so even though he was terrified that it would end their relationship.

Robyn went into a state of shock, not sure whether to feel anger or sympathy. She had to visit Simon. She set off to his house immediately.

Farley did not know whether he still had a girlfriend, but if that were the price he would have to pay, then so be it. He felt an intense relief that he had finally rid himself of a dark secret. The shame and guilt remained, but he had learned to cope with them. He hated keeping secrets from Robyn, whom he adored. This incident would either make or break their relationship, but he felt better coming clean. He acknowledged that God did indeed work in mysterious ways.

Chockie and Helen called to see him around teatime.

They brought a bottle of wine that the three of them consumed. Mrs Farley instructed her youngest son to leave it alone. The doctor had prescribed liquids but not alcohol and had warned him about his kidneys. Farley took an occasional sip while she made sandwiches, ham and cheese on brown bread.

His friends were amazed that Dave did not want to talk about the incident, and they were stunned when he refused Chockie's offer of help to gain revenge. The biggest surprise was when Farley repeated what he had told the police. He told Helen and Chockie that he had deserved the beating. It had probably been a long time coming.

After devouring a plate of sandwiches and a packet of crisps each, they departed. They did not want to be late for the quiz. There was a big prize on offer.

Farley resigned himself to a night in front of the television. His father joined him as his mother made supper. His old man seemed more upset at the events in his working day than his son's predicament.

"Those bloody road works are a real pain in the arse they are. Play bloody havoc with my timetable."

"Hi there. Is Simon in?"

"Hello Robyn, come on in love. Awful day isn't it? Yes, he's out in the conservatory. Be careful. He's in a foul mood. I don't know what's the matter with him."

Caroline Ikes took Robyn's soaking coat and hung it on a hook. Robyn smoothed her wet hair away from her face.

"You've had your hair cut. It looks very nice too. How do you like it short?"

"It's a bit different, you know, after keeping it long all these years." Robyn lightly ruffled the hair that remained on her head.

"Go on through, love. I'm going to take the twins to the shop to get chocolate." She busied herself with the act of getting her coat on. Robyn heard the twins arguing at the top of the stairs. "There's nothing on the telly tonight, so we'll watch a film. That new animated one about the little robot is supposed to be funny. They like cartoons." A short silence as Mrs Ikes fiddled with her buttons. "Was Tom still up at your house when you left?"

"I've been out all afternoon. I didn't see him."

"Well, if he returns while you're still here, tell him Chris Harvey rang. I've told Simon, but I doubt it sunk in. There's no talking to him." Her voice went quieter. "Between you and me, I think he's upset because of Laura. I think they've finished, but he won't talk about it. That's typical of him. He clams up. Anyway, you go on through while I get these two buggers ready. Honestly, even a short trip to the shop turns into a major expedition with these two. Good luck."

Robyn smiled as Mrs Ikes shouted instructions to the twins as she walked up the stairs.

"Hi-ya Si?"

Sikes looked up from his wicker chair. He was surprised to see Robyn and had not known about her lack of hair.

"Hi, Rob. Hair looks...um... different."

"Is that good or bad different?"

Robyn sat in the other wicker chair opposite Simon. Newspapers lay scattered all around the floor of the large glass conservatory. A small radio played in the background. It was hardly audible.

"Aye...er...good. It looks lovely." Simon was a poor liar.

"I believe you. How are you?"

"Fine, yeah. Okay." Simon was a lousy liar. "You?"

"I'm fine, but I've just been to see Dave. Someone beat him up last night."

"Oh really? Never. Where?" Simon was an absolutely terrible liar.

"You know where Simon." Robyn's voice was getting louder. "What the hell got into you?" Robyn was almost shouting." What did you think you were doing? You stupid... stupid...bastard."

"Calm down, Rob. Keep your voice down."

"You expect me to calm down after you've given Dave such a hiding? You could have killed him."

Simon was happy to drop the pretence. "I know. I meant to."

Robyn was dumbfounded.

"What?" She moved to the edge of her chair but had, for the moment, stopped shouting.

"I meant to kill him. I was going to smash his head in with a brick."

Farley had not told her this.

"You are joking. Please tell me you are joking?"

"No, not at all," said Simon nonchalantly. "I picked up a brick, took it to the alley opposite the house and waited for him. When he got home, I dragged him into the alley, kicked the shit out of him and would have smashed his head with a brick, but it all went... wrong..." His words tailed off.

"Went wrong? It sounds to me as if something went right." Robyn had raised her voice again.

Simon got out of his chair and walked to the door that joined the conservatory to the kitchen.

"It depends whose side you're on," he said, closing the door tightly.

Robyn was not talking any quieter.

"Simon, this is nothing to do with taking sides. What were you thinking? What were you trying to prove?"

Simon looked to see if his mother had gone out with the twins. He hoped she had.

"I wasn't trying to prove anything. I wanted revenge. I wanted to punish him for all the years of grief."

"But you picked on the wrong one!"

Sikes realised that Robyn knew about the events of the previous evening.

"I know that now," Simon spoke softly. "Why do you think I stopped?"

"Oh, you know, I thought maybe you came to your

senses."

It was Simon's turn to give a lecture. He sat on the edge of his seat, pointed at her and said, "Look, Rob, I am not going to say sorry for giving Dave a hiding. Even though he did not commit the act, he started the whole thing. He was the cause of many years of pain. His actions led to my mother getting hurt, he caused my father to suffer and me...well, I just wanted to kill him every time I set eyes on him. But now, having had time to think and reflect on what he told me last night, I am glad I stopped before I really hurt him."

"Well, it looks like you hurt him badly enough." Robyn's voice had returned to its usual volume.

"How is he anyway?"

"He'll mend. He's really sore. You gave him a beating." She looked for signs of regret but saw none. "You know he doesn't want the police involved? He's told them he got what he deserved."

"That's very magnanimous of him." Simon looked at the back of his hands. His knuckles were cut and bruised. His hands hurt. He clenched his right fist, and pain shot through his fingers, palm, and wrist. He winced.

Sensing that Robyn was also staring at his hands, Simon grabbed the rim of his polo shirt and tucked both hands under it.

"They look sore."

"Aye... well...I'm out of practice."

Robyn reclined in her wicker chair and placed her hands on the knees of her jeans.

"And all these years, you've thought that Dave was the one who threw the brick, and you never said a word." Robyn was well versed in the tragedy that beset the Ikes family. "You didn't even say anything to me. We're supposed to be friends."

"Well, if it's any consolation, GarGar and Dicey know nothing about it either."

"But I thought we were close."

"Aye...we are, but what could I say? Hey Rob, you know

your beloved Dave almost murdered my mother and killed my little brother or sister."

"It was a sister."

Simon glared at Robyn.

"What? How do you know?"

"My mother told me years ago. It was a baby girl."

Simon's head fell into the palms of his large hands.

"That's great, just fucking great."

Robyn had heard Simon swear before, but the angry tone surprised her. She said nothing.

"So everyone else knows except me!" It was Simon's turn to raise his voice. "That's marvellous, just fucking marvellous."

"Have you ever asked your mother about what happened?"

Simon looked at her as if she had just said the silliest thing ever. "Talk to her? Me? No. How could I? Mam has suffered enough. She won't want to relive it again after all these years."

"How do you know? I'll ask you again. Have you ever asked? You're so stubborn and into yourself that you cannot see your mother is fine. She's happy to talk about it now, but you do not want to raise the subject."

"Thanks for making me feel better, Rob." He took a short pause for breath. "Has she said something?"

"No...at least not to me."

Simon looked at his feet and rubbed his chin. The stubble felt rough. He ought to shave.

Robyn was staring at him. There was something else she wanted to know.

"Why now Simon?"

Simon did not understand the question.

"What?"

"I said why now? Why give Dave a hammering now? You've seen him around town for years and done nothing. I've been going out with him for almost a year, and you've never done or said anything. Why has it all happened now? What caused it?"

It was a good question. Simon did not find it easy to answer.

"I've always hated Dave for what happened."

"I could see that. No matter how much Dave tried, you never got on with him, did you? You never wanted to give him a chance."

"No. I used to see him around town acting like he was the kiddy..." He scratched his forearm. "...the plaster covering his childish tattoo. He was always reminding me of that night and what happened."

"But why didn't you tell somebody? You could have told me. Dave has tried to be mates with you, but you never let him. You always gave him the cold shoulder. No matter how much you hurt him or me."

"I'm sorry I forgot I had to care about his feelings?"

"Bloody hell Simon, grow up! That's not the point, and you know it."

Temperatures and tempers were rising again.

"Dave wanted to be mates because he knew how much I liked you. He knew how close we were, but you kept him away without telling him or me why. You should have said something."

Simon stared out of the window into the long, immaculate garden beyond. Philip's large red plastic tractor stood next to a tree. Rain was bouncing off the black metal seat.

"I tried to forget what happened. Every time I saw Dave, it brought it back, but I lived with it. It hurt like hell, but I lived with it. I think it was getting easier too. Then back in the summer, I bumped into Miko again. We talked about the old days, we had a really good laugh, and I've met him a lot since. He and his girlfriend have been with Laura and me a few times, and we've had a great time." The memory hurt him, and he paused for a moment. "But ever since I met up with Miko, I've been having these bad dreams, flashbacks, about my mother and the baby. They've been getting worse."

It felt strange opening up.

"Dreams, what kind of dreams?" Robyn spoke softly. She had been listening intently and motioned for Simon to continue.

"I'd rather not go into detail. They are pretty bad. The one last night scared the shit out of me…probably guilt. I've been down a bit since Laura, and I finished."

His mother's suspicions had been proven correct.

"Oh, Si, I am sorry. I never knew. She's a gorgeous girl, and you seemed well suited."

"Thanks, Rob. That's not making it any easier."

Robyn was grateful for a chance to smile. "Sorry. Why did you two finish?"

"I just let things get out of hand…I messed up, thinking something was more than it was. I'm sorry now, but I was horrible to her, and I've behaved so stupidly since…"

"Stupidly? What have you done that was stupid? Apart from beating up my boyfriend?"

Simon leaned back, closed his eyes and ran his hands through his hair. It was longer than usual, with a parting that he usually gelled back into place. Laura had liked his longer style. No gel had touched his hair for five days. His hair felt dirty, it had only come into contact with rainwater for almost a week, apart from Maggie's shower, but that was only fleeting. He took a sharp intake of breath as he recalled the events of the previous Friday. The dirt in his hair could get washed away, but Maggie was a different proposition.

He opened his eyes and saw Robyn waiting for his next word. He dropped his hands to his knees and concentrated. He told Robyn about Maggie and how she went out with a mutual friend at work. He did not elaborate any more than necessary. There was no need. The fact that he had been with the girlfriend of his workmate was terrible enough. Robyn's eyebrows rose when Simon confessed that he did not particularly fancy Maggie and had only gone with her because she was there. He sensed that Robyn did not much like the darker side of his personality. He shared her dislike.

He told her about Laura coming to his house the previous day and how he had blown it. He had wanted to wrap his arms around her, and they would be okay again, but he could not. Something was holding him back. He did not know what. This led to him getting drunk in the Tavern and the first incident. He did not apologise for lashing out, insisting that Dave should have left him alone.

"As soon as he started with that Sikesy mate, I'll get you a beer. I just flipped. Ripping that plaster off reminded me that I owed him one. I owed him big time. Something clicked inside me, and I knew what I had to do. The rest, you know." He paused for a moment. "I'll tell you something, Rob. It felt great while it lasted. After Dave told me the truth, I felt like shit afterwards, but that sense of power...Animal did not know what I would do...it felt great."

"His name is Dave, not Animal. Animal was his school nickname."

"Right, Dave it is." Simon examined the clock. It was ten to six.

"Fancy a drink, Rob?"

The question took Robyn by surprise.

"Yeah, go on then, please. What have you got?"

"There are some bottles of beer in the fridge. Do you want one?"

"Yeah, why not?"

Sikes left the conservatory, gathered two bottles, opened them and retraced his steps. He handed a bottle to Robyn and then sat in his chair.

"Simon, I had no idea that Dave was involved in your mother's accident, you know that, don't you?"

"Aye. I don't think Dave knew it was my mother until last night. It came as a shock to him."

"I would never have gone out with him if I had known."

"No, I don't suppose you would." Simon held the bottle

top to his lips and poured lager into his mouth.

"But now that I have gone out with him, I don't know if I can stop seeing him. I think I love him Si."

Simon had not wanted to hear those words but had guessed as much already. He could tell by how she looked at him, touched him, and smiled when she said his name. Why did Farley have to be the one to steal the heart of the girl at the top of his lust list?

Simon looked at Robyn and realised that something had changed. He did not feel so attracted to her anymore. Was it because of the shorter hair? Was it because she loved Farley? Or was it because of Laura?

That was the reason. Simon recognised that Robyn no longer occupied the top position on his lust list. Laura had replaced her.

"Well, there's no reason to stop seeing him, is there?"

"I'm not sure…I think it's up to you."

"What? It's got nothing to do with me." Simon took another sip of ice-cold lager.

Robyn held the bottle in her hands. She had not yet taken a drink from it. Gently nibbling her bottom lip, she said, "I don't know, Si. It's just that when all this blows up and it will blow up..."

The same thought had occurred to Sikes earlier that day.

"…I think it would be easier to keep seeing Dave if I know you're cool about it. We've been friends forever, and our parents are so close. You still mean a lot to me, Si." She looked into Simon's eyes.

"What you're saying is that your parents would be happier if they knew the Ikes family would let bygones be bygones."

Robyn stared at him as his lips broke into a smile. The frown left her face.

"I suppose there is that." Robyn placed the end of the bottle in her mouth and took a long slow drink.

Simon needed no time to answer.

"You carry on seeing him. It's fine with me. I'll tell my parents one of these days. They'll understand." Simon made the offer without knowing what he could and would say.

Robyn left her chair and walked the short distance to her friend. She bent over and kissed his cheek. Simon smiled and thought of Laura.

Thomas Ikes returned from his squash match to find his twins curled up in front of the television watching a cartoon and his wife in the kitchen.

The twins waved and smiled at him as he appeared around the living room door. They were both stretched out on their beanbags, watching the large-screen television.

He dropped his bag in the hall and entered the kitchen. Caroline was preparing supper. He kissed the back of her neck.

"Hi-ya love. Good game?"

"Not bad. I lost again but never mind, eh?" He looked to the conservatory to his elder son, laughing and joking with Robyn Howells. They had drawn the outward-facing blinds and switched on the tall lamp.

"Good God. Simon is smiling. That makes a change."

"Yes. They've been in there hours having a good chat. They've almost run out of beer. Be a love and go and get some more."

"Bloody typical, I buy them, and he drinks them."

"He needs cheering up. It'll do him good."

"Okay, I won't be long." Thomas Ikes left the kitchen again.

"Chris rang. Can you give him a call? It's about Wednesday."

Thomas Ikes was due to visit Birmingham with Chris Harvey the following Wednesday. Harvey wanted to price some new vans for the bakery.

"I'll ring him from the car."

Simon and Robyn's conversation drifted onto other subjects. Simon spoke of his job, his relationship with Laura,

Caitlin, Jamie and Laura's parents. He repeated that he had taken the split badly and regretted his actions. Robyn told him she would probably have done the same in his position but that he needed to repair the damage quickly before things got out of hand.

They spoke about GarGar, Dicey and the rest of the gang. Robyn roared as they recalled Dicey's exploits at the A-levels party. Simon told her about Amy, the underage temptress and how she had dumped Dicey for a wild card. Simon had learned that Amy was pregnant and had had an abortion. The lad was now awaiting trial for having sex with a juvenile. That was a sobering moment.

"You know Dave, and I have never had sex?"

Simon almost choked on his beer.

"What?"

"Dave does not want to have full sexual intercourse with me."

"Why? Is he gay or something?" Simon was incredulous.

"No." Robyn smiled. "Nothing like that. We've done many other things, but he does not want to have sex until we're married. He's quite religious and very old-fashioned in that way."

"Very strange if you ask me," said Simon. "I mean, how could he resist?"

"Thanks, Simon. It's nice of you to say."

Simon had not necessarily meant it as a compliment.

"So when are you getting married?"

"We'll get engaged on my twentieth birthday and probably aim to get married a couple of years later. We have a few things to sort out first." Robyn looked pensive.

Simon was ahead of her. She still had to tell her parents and their best friends about her boyfriend's past.

Simon changed the subject. He spoke about his parents and the twins loving the holiday they had taken with Mr and Mrs Howells earlier that year. He told Robyn about how Philip enjoyed paella even though it tasted fishy. The tale brought the smile back to Robyn's face.

Mrs Ikes insisted on booking a cab for Robyn and called her when the taxi driver knocked on the door.

"Bye Si." She kissed his cheek and caught his hand.

"Ta-ra Rob. See you again." He withdrew his hand as Robyn went through to the hall.

Simon followed her part of the way, then stopped and watched as his mother pressed a folded ten-pound note into her hand and kissed her cheek. Simon could not hear what Mrs Ikes had said, but it was clearly about him. Robyn looked directly at him and smiled. Grabbing her coat, she left the house shouting good night.

Sikes cleared up the conservatory. He had not realised they had downed so many bottles of beer. He placed the empties on the kitchen work surface, ready for his mother to add to the box for recycling. Mrs Ikes was busy preparing the twins' lunchboxes for school the next day.

He returned to the conservatory and gathered up the newspapers. He carried them to the lounge, where he dropped them in a wooden rack. His father would read them during the week. Sitting on the edge of the sofa, Simon asked his father what was on the television.

"Not a lot. I don't know why I pay so much for this satellite television. There's never anything on apart from rubbish."

"By the way, Dad, Chris Harvey rang."

"Thanks, Si. Your mother told me."

"Is everything all right?" It was unusual for a client to ring at home on a Sunday.

"Yes. He rang to cancel Wednesday."

Simon had been informed about his father's plans for Wednesday but had not paid enough attention.

"Why?"

Mr Ikes did not look away from the screen as he studied the rubbish.

"He's got to go to a funeral. The mother of one of his employees has passed away.

Simon went cold. "Which one?"

"Timothy Martin. His mother had a stroke earlier this week. She didn't wake up from it."

"Oh shit," said Simon. "Poor old Timmytits."

FACING THE MUSIC

Thomas Ikes' elder son had no desire to go to work that morning. He had a headache, his hands and feet felt tender and sore and, worst of all, he would have to face Maggie and Marty. He tried to persuade his mother that he should have a day off. Caroline Ikes had no time for excuses.

"Look Simon, you cannot take a day off just because you feel like it, have your breakfast and go and get ready," she said as he bit into his toast. "Make sure you have a shave and a shower as well. You look like a tramp."

"Yes Mam, right Mam."

Simon consumed the remainder of his toast and wolfed down his tea.

"Shower it is then."

His mother spoke again.

"Dad told me you know Timothy Martin, the man whose mother passed away."

Simon was placing his plate and cup on the draining board.

"Yes, aye. I was put to work with him at the bakery."

"You never said." His mother had turned to face him.

"Didn't I? Sorry. I didn't think it was a huge deal."

"Do you know something, Simon? The older you get, the less I feel I know about you. It bothers me that you don't tell me anything. Where you go, who you meet, what you think. Nothing."

Simon knew this was not a spontaneous speech. The thoughts must have hung on his mother's mind for some considerable time.

"You're right, Mam, sorry Mam, but can we talk later? I've got a train to catch." He leaned over and kissed his mother on the cheek.

"Okay, but let's talk, please. You're still my son, you know. I worry about you as much as the twins."

Simon knew this and hugged his mother.

"Sure. We'll talk later."

Sikes fretted his way to Cardiff. He felt cleaner and was sure he smelt better, but he did not know what to say to Marty. He planned to take Maggie for tea and tell her straight. It was a one-off, and that was it. There was nothing more to it. He agonised over the best words to use and thought he had arrived at some that would be gentle but honest. He was hoping that Maggie would advise him on what to say to Marty if Maggie was still talking to him after their chat.

"Morning Simon. Good weekend?" Maggie's joviality made Simon realise this would be harder than he had initially believed.

"Okay, thanks. You?" Sikes hung his coat on the metal hanger and inched towards his desk.

"Brilliant, yeah. I did a lot of thinking and got my head sorted a bit. Thanks to you."

The last bit was quieter, as if Maggie did not want the others to hear. That was a mild comfort for Simon as she was not broadcasting what had happened.

There was no sign of Marty. His chair had not moved since he tucked it under his desk the previous Friday lunchtime. His files remained piled on his desk. Simon gazed around the section. Steve was away from his desk, but his coat hanging over his chair showed he was at work. Adam was on the 'phone, and he nodded as Simon looked at him. Sikes waved back.

Sue was collecting the post from the in-tray. She looked exhausted.

"Morning Simon." Sue dropped three large brown envelopes on Simon's desk and handed one to Maggie. "The rest are Steve's."

"Hiya Sue. All right?"

"Not really, love. My youngest isn't very well. I've hardly slept this weekend."

"Sorry to hear that. Hope he's better soon."

"And me," said Sue, walking back to her seat.

A quarter of an hour later, with no sign of McKenzie or Marty, Simon invited Maggie for tea. She willingly accepted. Simon worried she appeared too keen.

He bought two teas and carried them to the table. Maggie selected the empty table on the island. Simon was happy about that; it was yards away from the nearest people.

"Thanks, Si. You're a darling."

"No problem." Simon felt anxious.

He looked at Maggie. She was wearing a short thick black jumper. As her upper body moved, the jumper rose and exposed her navel. Simon liked her navel. She had covered her lower half in black jeans and black boots. Maggie's long hair hung loosely over her shoulders. She wore little make-up. Simon thought she looked better than she had done for a while.

Maggie was smiling warmly at him as she spoke.

"How were you on Saturday morning?"

Sikes blew out a short breath.

"A bit hung over."

"What a night eh? I really enjoyed myself. I haven't had such a good night in ages. I owe you for that one, Simon."

Simon sipped his tea gingerly. This was becoming more complicated than he had anticipated. He held his cup in his hand.

"No problem, but you don't owe me anything. I enjoyed myself too. It was just what I needed."

"Aye, we'll have to do it again. Soon."

Simon placed the cup on the round table.

"The thing is Maggs... I'm a bit confused at the moment. Please don't take this wrong, but I'm not looking for a relationship." The line always worked in films.

Maggie splattered her tea back into her cup.

"Who said anything about a relationship? Bloody hell Simon, cool down, will you?"

Simon's face showed his confusion.

"But you just said we ought to do it again."

Maggie leaned forward and spoke softly to Simon.

"I know, but I wasn't necessarily asking for a repeat performance!"

Her directness made him blush.

"Not that there was anything wrong in that department, mind you. I enjoyed myself."

Simon blushed again.

"But bloody hell Simon just because we have sex, I'm not honour bound to marry you or anything. Think of it as a bit of fun between friends."

Simon felt foolish.

"Sorry."

"What are you sorry about? I just said I had a great time. You were the cause of that. I enjoyed the chat. You are a great listener. I got a lot off my chest. Stuff that I'd been carrying around in my head for ages. It was good of you to let me ramble on. As I said, I've straightened many things out now, and I know what I want to do with my life." She poured more tea into her mouth.

Simon did not know what to say.

"My pleasure," he finally said.

"Mine too," Maggie replied. "Hope you didn't think I was too pushy or anything by inviting you to stay in my place."

"Not at all."

"But you know I've always liked you and hated seeing you so down. As the evening went on, I thought I'd thank you for being such a good friend and try to make you feel a bit better at the same time. Honestly, Si, I'm not looking for anything else. It was just a favour. You did me a favour too." Maggie reached across the table and squeezed the back of Simon's hand. "I'm not lying when I said I enjoyed the sex, mind."

"Aye, thanks." Simon looked into her eyes and smiled as she winked at him. "Sorry about that, just now. I felt a bit guilty, that's all."

"What for? We're two single people, aren't we? You told me you'd finished with Laura." Maggie sat back.

"I did, I have, but what about Marty?"

"That was nothing serious. I told you that. Anyway, Marty can suit himself. I won't be bothering him again. He's more mixed up than I was."

"So, what's your plan?" Simon had started tearing the cardboard cup.

"I'm moving to Barcelona to be with my parents."

Simon was taken aback at this revelation but nodded approval. Maggie continued.

"When I woke up on Saturday, it all seemed so simple. I have always been reluctant to leave the Rhondda. That's where I grew up and where my friends are, but lately, they've started to go their separate ways. Working in Cardiff hasn't helped. Sure it's opened my eyes, but I'm feeling more and more alone. I've missed my parents. I've missed not having anyone to share things with. Since Colin, I've been in a bit of a state. Everything went wrong, but I've refused to admit it. I was afraid of giving in and admitting that I had cocked up." Maggie squashed her cup and then spoke again. "Being able to ramble on all night on Friday helped greatly. You'll never know how much you helped me, Simon. When I woke up on Saturday morning, things seemed different. I was able to put everything into perspective. I thought about what I wanted, what I really wanted, and that was to be with my family. So I called my parents on Saturday evening, and they were chuffed to beans. My father's driving over to fetch me, and I'm going to live in a flat at the back of their house. I'm handing in my notice today. I should be in Spain by Christmas with my annual leave and stuff. Now that I've decided and it's all sorted. I'm looking forward to it."

"Bloody hell, you don't hang about, do you? I'll miss you,

Maggs. It won't be the same without you."

"I'll miss you too Si. If you fancy a holiday in Barcelona, you know where to look. I'll give you my parents' telephone number." She smiled mischievously. "Don't worry. We'll have separate beds."

"Great." Simon was pleased for Maggie but a little sad for himself. A practical matter occurred to him. "What about your debts? What are you going to do about them? You're not thinking of doing a bunk, are you? They'll catch up with you, you know."

Maggie smiled again. "No, don't worry. We had a long chat, and I told my dad about my problems. He reckons there is nothing to worry about. If the worse comes to the worse, he'll lend the cash to pay them off, but he's had a word with his mate at the university. He's used to giving advice. He helps the students when they have money problems. He's going to call around to see what he can do. I'm meeting him tomorrow evening."

"Good for you," said Simon. He found himself wishing he had the prospect of Christmas in Barcelona to look forward to.

Steve McKenzie returned to his branch a short time after Maggie and Simon. He called his team around him.

"I've some horrible news." He focused on Simon and then looked at Maggie, ignoring the other two. "Marty's been suspended pending an investigation, but I fear there is every likelihood he will get dismissed."

The words hung for a moment before Simon spoke.

"Why? When did this happen?" His eyes met Maggie's.

"He was turned away this morning. He got caught allegedly dealing drugs at the weekend. He also resisted arrest. The police notified the office. He's out on bail, but when he arrived for work, he got handed a letter telling him he's not allowed to enter the building."

"Where was he caught?" Maggie was fearful that she and

Sikes might get implicated.

"At some bar on Mill Lane, apparently. It was in the wee small hours of Saturday morning. From what I understand, some guy quibbled over the asking price, and a brawl broke out. The police were called, and Marty got arrested for possession. He did not help himself by kicking off. Then later, when the guy told the police about the incident, Marty was charged with dealing."

That was some relief. Maggie was probably in bed with Simon when all this happened.

Simon was curious.

"How did the office find out?"

"Well, he had to give his name, address and occupation. The police could not get anyone else to verify who he was, so they contacted the office, the security guards contacted Mr Phillips at home, and he called into the police station. He identified Marty. He knows him well enough. The police told him about the incident and what Marty was charged with, and that was it. Drug dealing is an instant dismissal offence these days, so I think it will be goodbye Marty. If I hear anything else, I'll let you know."

Adam insisted he knew there was something funny about Marty. Sue confided she would not know what to do if her son got caught dealing drugs. Maggie and Simon sat silently.

Steve had not finished.

"This means we're a person short this week. I'll try to get casual support, but let me know if it gets too much. I'll try to pass some work on to Jenny's team."

He glanced at the other team, called "Cardiac Care 3b". Steve had fought hard to retain the "A team" status; his team was the first to be established, even if Anna appeared to trust Jenny more than she trusted him.

"Right, back to work, guys. Maggie, Simon, can I have a wee word?"

Maggie and Sikes waited while the other two left for

their seats.

Steve's tone lowered until it was close to a whisper.

"You were with Marty on Friday night. Did you see anything? Did you know anything was going on?"

Maggie answered before Simon could think what to say.

"No. We were with him until about half eight. Then he left with some mates. Simon and I had a couple more drinks and then shared a taxi home. I was in bed by half eleven." There was no need to mention with whom she shared her bed. The office management did not like relationships between colleagues in the same work area. That is one reason why Maggie had tried to keep her extra curricula activities with Marty a closely guarded secret, that and the fact that she felt that something like this would happen and wanted to stay out of Marty's troubles.

"So you were long gone by, say midnight."

Maggie spoke again. "That's right."

"Yes," said Simon. "I was probably just finishing in the bathroom at that time."

Maggie coughed into her hand and raised her eyebrows as she lowered her head. She was grateful Steve was still looking at Simon.

The rest of the morning involved much chatting about Marty's dismissal, emptying his drawer, packing up his stuff and reallocating his work duties.

There was not much by way of personal stuff. Maggie said Marty kept most of it in the beige, army surplus rucksack he carried around with him. There were a few letters concerning his appointment to DoMO and odds and ends, including Marty's union card and annual leave sheet. These got bundled into an envelope.

Simon volunteered to take the envelope to Marty. Steve was initially against the idea, but a call to HR changed his mind. Marty had not been punished for a work-related incident. There was to be no enquiry, and, as such, there was nothing to stop his ex-colleagues from contacting him. Sikes delivered the items during his lunch break.

Marty Freeman lived in a small flat off City Road. The walk took Simon all of twenty minutes. The intercom system was disconnected, but the front door was open, and Simon walked in without seeking permission.

He knew where to find the flat because he and Marty had sometimes walked here. However, Simon had never previously entered the flat. He had always made an excuse about needing something from the nearby shops and had met Marty at an agreed point and time. Simon had felt awkward about infringing on Marty's personal space. He had to think differently today. As he climbed the bare wooden stairs, Simon noticed how dark and dismal it was in the stairway. The paint was old and flaky and smelt dank with very little light. The building was once a large house but was converted many years earlier by a landlord with plans to get rich quick by sub-letting rooms to students. The landlords' dream never materialised.

Marty lived in flat 3, top of the stairs, turn left.

Simon knocked on the green wooden door.

Marty unlocked the door wearing brown tracksuit bottoms and a baggy white cricket shirt. His hair was untied, and his feet were dirty and bare.

"Hi, Si. What brings you here?" Marty waved him in.

"I've brought your stuff," said Simon, handing over the envelope.

"You needn't have bothered. I've no use for any of that shit anymore."

He tossed the envelope onto the table without opening it. Simon followed its flight path and watched as it landed on an array of empty metal trays, the type used for takeaway food. Empty beer bottles and cans lay on the table, the floor and the settee.

"Good news travels fast, I see?" Marty walked into another room.

Simon was looking at a mess. Clothes lay crumpled on

the back of chairs. The carpet was covered in newspapers and magazines. The drawers of a cupboard had not been pushed back into place properly, and it looked like someone had emptied the contents over the floor.

Dusty net curtains covered the dirty windows. Small plant pots rested on the windowsill. The best-looking things in the room were Marty's guitar and amplifier. They stood majestic in the corner, bright, shiny, gleaming.

Simon diverted his gaze from the squalor and spoke in the direction of the other room.

"Yes, aye. Steve told us this morning. What happened?"

Marty came out of the room carrying a pair of off-white sports socks. Parking his backside on the edge of the packed sofa, he pulled the socks onto his feet.

"It's a fucking set up. I tell you what, Si, I've been set up good and proper."

"How? What happened?"

"I'll tell you now but not here. I could murder a pint." Marty slipped on his blue, suede Adidas trainers and tied the laces. "Got any cash? There's a pub around the corner."

"Aye, fine." Simon wanted out of the dump.

Marty picked up his jacket, put it on, ensuring his long hair remained outside the collar, and then grabbed his rucksack.

"Marty! Where's you going?" A girl's voice shouted from the room in which Marty had disappeared.

The voice sounded vaguely familiar, but Simon could not put a face to it.

"Just off out. Won't be long. See you in a bit."

"If I's still here."

"Where else will you be?" asked Marty under his breath. "Aye, whatever. Lock the door if you leave." He shouted in reply.

He spoke to Simon. "That's just Shelly. I see her now and again."

Simon was surprised when the barman refused to serve

him at the two pubs nearest Marty's flat.

"I'll serve you, but I'm not allowing him back in here," said the first.

"He's banned," said the second barman.

Marty pleaded innocence.

"It's the pigs, man. They've put the word out about me."

They eventually got served in the bar at the snooker club, above a carpet showroom.

"Get me a roll Si. I'm fucking starving."

Simon bought beer and two ham salad rolls.

Marty ate quickly and drank even more rapidly. Simon fetched him another beer; he only wanted the one himself.

Freeman spoke of the police "sting" operation. How he had known the police were after him from the moment, he met his other friends at the Australian bar. That was the reason he had left Maggie and Simon. He did not want them implicated. He said the police trailed him and his mates all night and had finally got him alone at a bar in Mill Lane. Some bloke had picked a fight, probably a copper in disguise, and when Marty reacted, the police pounced. He suggested that the bloke planted a stack of cocaine on him, and the Police arrested him for possession. The police had roughed him up a bit and blamed him for resisting arrest. It was all lies. Then the bloke made out he was trying to buy some stuff. Marty got done for dealing drugs. By the time he returned home, the police had ransacked his flat. His girl had let them in, and they had taken some stuff away for analysis."

Simon wondered if Marty was being honest when he said

"I swear Si. I never had any stuff at the flat. I may drop some magic dust now and again, but I ain't no fuckin' dealer."

Marty strongly believed that Millington, or "Major DoMO" as he now called him, was behind the operation. He also thought that Jack Phillips was well happy when he came to identify him.

"You could see in his eyes that he thought they had won

the fucking lottery. They had finally got what they wanted."

When Simon suggested this was a ridiculous proposition, Marty became agitated.

"What you mean it's a stupid idea? I'm fuckin' telling you Si, that they've had it in for me just like they had it in for the poor bastards in London. They've got all the fuckin' contacts. They can do what the fuck they like. I'm being stitched up like a fuckin' kipper."

Marty expanded on his theory. He told Simon the facts as he saw them. This took some time. Simon grew less interested, and his attention started to wander. He looked around the room.

Twelve full-size snooker tables and four American pool tables filled the large space. He and Marty sat in the small secluded bar area. This area was well-lit, but the rest of the room was semi-dark. The only light appeared to come from the occupied tables. Six people were playing snooker, and two of them were female.

Simon was growing bored with Marty's rambling. Maggie had been right. Marty would blame anyone for his troubles and tell whatever lie was necessary to get himself out of a fix. He thought he would bring the discussion to a close by announcing that he had to get back to work.

"Wait a minute Si. Get us another pint. I've got something for you."

Simon was reluctant to spend too much more but agreed. This time he fetched himself a bottle of lager.

Marty took a long gulp from the glass and picked up his rucksack. Opening the metal buckles, he extracted two red document folders. They were each full. He placed them on the table next to their drinks and then lifted the flap on the top folder.

"Here, Simon, is a copy of all the evidence I've gained about DoMO. It shows which records they've amended, when the payments were received, who authorised the changes and loads more stuff from my contact in London. This will wipe the smile off Major fat-twat Domo's face." He handed the open folder to Simon. "This copy is for you."

Sikes opened the folder. It contained a small mountain of foolscap paper over two inches thick. He ran his finger down one side of the documents, casually flicking the pages. They had copious notes; some written in Marty's handwriting, others typed, copies of emails and other documents. All clipped neatly into the pack.

Marty's tone became softer, more conversational.

"Read that Si. I think that will convince you that I'm telling the truth but don't show it to anyone, not even Maggie. I've got two other copies, one of which is hidden in a secret place. This one," he patted the other folder, "I'm going to hand over to the press, but I need some more information first. I need a copy of the stats for this week. If I'm right, and I'm fuckin' sure I am, then I can predict what the top five will be, and it won't be the hospitals that deserve to be at the top."

Sikes's eyes showed he was not comfortable.

"I'm telling you Si, you get me the stats, and I will get the bastards. If the stats show what I expect them to, then it's clear that the data has been corrupted. It'll show that the bosses at DoMO are bent, taking backhanders." He patted the file. "I've got loads of other evidence, bits and pieces too, but the stats will be the icing on the cake."

"But why though? What's in it for the bosses?"

Marty was ready with his answer.

"What's always in it for the likes of them Si? Money and power. Have you seen the car that Millington drives? How the fuck can he afford that? Special payments, that's how. The government wants to show that DoMO is working and has let the bosses get on with it. They moved out of London and have given the management free rein to do what is necessary. But the management is taking the piss. They are fiddling with the hospital performance figures left, right and centre. If a hospital hands over enough cash, they get pushed up the tables, but that's not right. It's not fair on the smaller, poorer hospitals or the poor fuckers who have to get treated in the NHS. They think they are safe at a top-scoring hospital, but in reality, many of those hospitals are dangerous. They are piss poor, and people's lives are at stake."

"I don't know. It all sounds a bit far-fetched to me..."

Marty did not let him finish. "That's because you haven't studied the evidence. It is all in here." He patted the folder again. "I have copies of the original returns submitted by half a dozen or so hospitals I know have changed their figures. I can go to the press if you can get me the stats. Millington and co won't know what hit them. But I need your help Si. I need you to print out the latest stats before they get formally released next week."

Simon was not sure what he should do. He had no desire to get involved,

"I don't know. I don't think I want to get into this."

"Fuckin' hell Si. I'm only asking for one lousy favour. I would have done it myself, but I think they found out what I was planning, so they got rid of me just before I could hit them between the eyes."

"So why can't you go to the press anyway?"

"Because I need the stats that will be published next week, and I need to hand that over with the evidence the day before the stats are released. The reporter will be fore-warned and can wade in as soon as the official stats are published. DoMO won't have a chance to change things. Help me Si, help me blow this thing wide open."

Sikes was still not convinced.

"I'm not sure Marty...I could get into deep shit for this."

"Look, I'll tell you what, run them off using my password, and if anyone asks, I'll say I broke in to get them. My password is Shagadelic234, all one word with a capital S. They normally publish on Monday, so you could run them off on Friday afternoon. Steve is on leave, isn't he?"

"I think he is but hang on a minute. You've had a while to think about this, but it's all new to me. This is the first real evidence I've seen. There's a lot at stake for me here. Let me read these papers and get back to you. It shouldn't take me long. I can get back to you by Wednesday or Thursday. That will still give me time to print the stats. If I agree to do it."

Marty thought about Sikes' request for a moment. "Yeah sorry, Si. I suppose you will need time to take this in. Okay, we'll play it your way, man. It's just that I think I'm this close to nailing these bastards." He held his index finger and thumb a centimetre apart. "The problem is they know it too. That's why they got me this weekend."

Simon was alarmed.

"Well, if they knew that you were almost there, won't they be expecting something else to happen? Will they be waiting for me?"

"Nah! They think they've got rid of me just like they got rid of the London crew. They think they're safe and fuckin' sound." Marty pointed at the folder. "You read that Si, and ring me when you're ready." Freeman dug into his jacket pocket and pulled out a pre-printed card with a long number on it. He handed this to Simon. "Ring me here Si. Anytime, it's always on. If you ring from work, make sure it's from your mobile or the payphone downstairs. I don't want those bastards taping the call."

"Okay." Simon placed the card inside the folder and then stuffed the folder under his arm. He had no idea what to make of what he heard

He stood ready to go back to work.

"I'll be in touch."

Marty held out his hand, and Simon shook it.

"Good man Si. Appreciate it. Speak soon, yeah?"

"Aye, probably," said Simon uneasily.

Returning to his office, Simon looked at the shops and restaurants on City Road. The windows and doors were a vast array of colour and spectacle, covered in decorations for the festive season. Simon did not feel particularly festive, and it was not just the weather that had dampened his spirit.

SYMPATHY

Timmytits' hands shook as he tried to hold the cup and saucer. Balancing the saucer on his lap, he used both hands to bring the cup towards his mouth. His lips moved to meet the rim, and he slurped the tea into his mouth.

"That's better." He almost dropped the cup and saucer onto the teak coffee table.

Dot had retreated to the kitchen. Simon thanked her for the tea and cake. Chocolate sponge.

She offered a friendly smile and an easy "You're very welcome."

"Thanks for coming, Si. I appreciate it," said Tim.

"No problem." Sikes sat uneasily in his chair. He had not much contact with death. His maternal grandfather's untimely demise was his sole experience of losing someone close. Sikes coped with his grief in his way. He felt inadequate, not knowing how to help his friend cope with his. Sikes knew not what to say or when to say it.

"How are you feeling?"

"Oh, you know, so so." Tim struggled with his cup again.

Sikes remembered how he felt when Dilwyn died. The sadness rushed over him in waves. One minute he felt okay, able to go on. The next, he was on the verge of tears, unable to contemplate the most basic actions.

"Have you heard from your brother? Is he coming down?"

"I've telephoned him. It's a bit awkward for him at the moment. He's after a major contract and could lose it if he left home right now."

Simon was not impressed.

"But surely he'll come for the funeral?"

"He'll try, but he's swamped. Mam would understand.

Thing is, Barry has spent years building up that business. She would not have wanted him to risk losing anything. Fair play, he said I only have to ask if there's anything I need. He's sending a wreath in case he can't come."

Simon said nothing. Barry Martin sounded like a waste of space, but Tim still thought the world of him, as had his mother.

"Is there anything you need?" Simon sipped his tea softly and silently.

"No thanks, Si. Dot has been a gem and looked after me good and proper." He fell quiet again. "Perhaps, there is one thing Si. Barry is sending me some forms to fill in. It's stuff to do with Mam's shareholding. Can you give me a hand to fill them in?"

"Aye, no problem." Simon felt annoyed at Tim's brother for thinking of his business before family. "If I can't do it, then I'm sure my father will."

"I don't want to be any trouble." Martin looked embarrassed.

"It's no trouble. Dad will sort it out, no problem. He's well used to doing things like that. He'll be okay when I tell him it's for a friend. Anyway, it might be something simple that I can cope with."

"Thanks Si."

Awkward silence, Simon's grandfather had always believed that if an awkward silence fell upon a group, then it would either be twenty past or twenty-two the hour. Simon thought of this and looked at the clock on top of the television. It was quarter past seven; his grandfather wasn't far out.

Simon viewed the room. The light wood cupboards and cabinets looked old but immaculate, with no dust. Timothy was very tidy and, from the look of it, extremely house-proud. The glass cabinet in the corner next to the television contained many small frames with photographs. Simon could not see them clearly, but they looked like family photos.

The high unit on the opposite wall had cupboards at

the bottom and glass doors at the top. Through the glass doors, Simon could see glasses and silverware. These were, undoubtedly, the family's best items. His grandmother had a similar arrangement whereby her best dinner service was on permanent display and hardly ever used. His father had a different philosophy. Thomas Ikes always said that if he could not use it, he did not want it, much to his mother's dismay.

The television and satellite box was unplugged and looked unused. Mrs Martin lived in the room next door, and Tim told Simon they used to watch tv together. They liked the same things, so there was no point in being in different rooms.

Simon felt he ought to say something.

"Are you okay as far as the house is concerned?"

It woke Tim from a stupor.

"Er...yes...aye. The house is in my name anyway. My mam sorted that when my dad died. At the time, while things were getting sorted, she did not earn enough to cover the rent and would not ask for any benefits or support. Very proud she was." Tim's attention wandered again.

Simon clanked his saucer as he replaced the cup.

"Sorry, Tim."

"Don't worry, nothing broken. No... um...the house is in my name, and I pay the rent and stuff. I think I'll move on anyway. Dot has asked me to move in with her, and well... there's no reason not to now, is there?"

"Aye, I suppose not." Simon felt a sense of relief. He had worried about Tim being on his own.

"What time is the funeral?"

Martin gave out a deep breath. His cup was back on the saucer on the table, and his long bony hands were resting heavily on his thighs. He rubbed them up and down his trousers.

"Ten o'clock Wednesday. The doctor's been marvellous. He signed the certificate, so there's no need for a post-mortem. It's ten here. There'll be a short service before we go to the graveyard. Reverend Thomas is doing the talking. Mam always liked him. He's a lovely bloke. Always made her laugh, he did." Martin's eyes filled up again. He wiped them away.

"Is it okay if I come along? I didn't know your mother, but I'd like to be there." This was only partly true. Simon had no wish to be at the funeral but thought it was the right thing to say.

"Course Si. I'd appreciate that."

Simon and Timothy exchanged small talk, reliving their short time together on the van, the things they had spoken about and the tricks they had played on the girls at the bakery. Martin said that Carla had been asking about Simon and thought Simon could strike it lucky. Simon laughed and answered, honestly, Tim's questions about his relationship with Laura.

"No, I screwed it up. I got more than a bit possessive and jealous. I blew it." A short pause as he realised his grief was nothing like Tim's. "Still never mind eh?"

"I am sorry to hear that, Si. Cared a lot for her, didn't you?"

Simon nodded silently.

"What about Robyn? Is she still courting that Farley boy?"

Simon nodded again. He chose to say nothing about the incident two nights previously. It felt like an age before. He recalled his conversation with Robyn.

"Aye, she is. They seem closer than ever."

"Thing is I remembered where I knew the name from. I asked my mother about it and meant to tell you, but I haven't seen you since you started in Cardiff. I meant to ring you and suggest we go for a pint, but I never got around to it. There are lots of things I never got around to..."

Awkward silence, Simon glanced at the clock. It was twenty to eight.

"Spot on Granddad," he thought before speaking again. "To be honest with you, I've been a bit busy lately, so you probably wouldn't have gotten hold of me. So how do you know Farley? I know he lived up here for a while. Is that how you knew the name?

"Nah. Apparently, they lived over the other side of the village, by the welfare club. I never knew them. My mother recalled them straight away. The eldest boy Richard was in our Barry's year in grammar school. He used to give Barry a hell of a time. I expect he was jealous because Barry was a bright lad and a hard worker. Dad had to go around their house to talk with his father. Mam said Dad got nothing but abuse from the father, although the mother seemed nice. He did not get much sense from his visits, and nothing changed. My parents decided that Barry would go to a different school. Then one day, Farley was involved in an incident after he pinched acid from the chemistry lab and threw it down the bus on the way home. One boy had his head burnt, and another had his blazer damaged. He got expelled, so Barry could stay where he was."

This information fitted perfectly with the picture that Simon had formed of the older Farley.

Martin had not finished.

"Thing is Richard Farley and his mate Steve Thompson. I think they called him Stompie or something like that. Well, they got killed on the Heads of the Valleys Road. That's how I remembered the name. I never had any dealings with them during the trouble with Barry, my mam and dad never told me about it, but I knew about the accident. Mam did too, and she remembered what happened as soon as I mentioned it. We had a good chat about it a few weeks ago before…before she died."

Sikes sensed it was time to keep the conversation flowing.

"I heard about the accident. They died on the top road, didn't they?"

"They did." Martin's mind was back in the past. "They were heading back to Thompson's flat. The Farley boy was riding pillion when a drunk driver lost control at the junction and smashed straight into them. There was one hell of a mess, by all accounts. That junction was a real accident black spot.

They've put a roundabout there now. Farley and Thompson were killed instantly, from what I heard. The driver of the car was badly injured too. He lost an arm and was in the hospital for months."

This comment rang a bell, but Simon did not know why immediately.

"What happened to him?"

"Not sure. I think he went down for a year or so. Mam said his marriage was breaking up, and he was being treated for depression. The fact that he had also lost an arm meant the courts went easy on him. Nice lad, he was too."

"Did you know him?"

"Yeah, This is not a big town, so over the years, you get to know most people even if you only exchange nods. I still see him from time to time. He works in town, and I often see him when I'm driving the van in the mornings. He used to live up this way, but now he lives by the golf club."

Misplaced memories were turning into images in Simon's mind.

"What's his name?" Simon asked, not sure he needed Tim to answer.

"Peter...Peter Evans," said Timothy.

Simon coughed as he visualised his father's employee holding the files with his one good arm.

DECISIONS, DECISIONS

Simon Ikes had not slept a wink all night. His head was buzzing. His brain was jammed full of facts. His belly was full of beer, not that it had any real impact.

He had gone to the pub hoping that one of his friends would be out and could help to take his mind off things, but nobody goes out on Mondays. He sat on his own with his beer, guilt, fears, thoughts and Marty's folder.

For years it was as if nobody told him anything about what was happening, but now everyone was telling him everything. It was all proving to be too much. He had information overload. Simon felt very confused. His previously happy little life had turned upside down in less than a week by a series of different, apparently unconnected events, which had messed with his brain.

First, there had been the discovery of Laura's photographs. He believed there was more to that than there was. She had told him the truth. He knew she had. He deeply regretted his reaction. He missed being with her, talking to her, holding her, loving her. He accused her of two-timing him but hadn't he done the same with Sammie? He had been seeing Laura while Sammy was still on the scene. He was a hypocrite. He had been way out of order. How could he have got it so wrong?

Then there was the sex with Maggie. Having done the deed, he had worried that she would expect something more from him. She had not. She had put him right quite bluntly. It was a casual fling. He should think of it as sex between friends. At least they were still friends. He assumed that having had sex, there would be awkwardness between them afterwards, but there wasn't. Sikes liked this concept. He had deliberately avoided his other one-night stands, apart from one, and she did her best to avoid him, but he and Maggie spoke as if nothing happened – although she often teased him about the events of that night.

Thirdly, there were incidents with Farley in the Tavern and the alleyway. Would he have killed Animal? Was it normal to feel such loathing for another person? Why didn't Farley react? How could he be so reasonable about it all? Simon had wanted to kill him but listening to Farley's explanation and learning more about him from Robyn. Sikes had started to like him. He had not wanted that to happen. Why did Farley have to open his mouth? Simon felt guilty about his actions and would visit Farley to apologise, but not just yet.

Next, there was the revelation that Animal had been innocent all along. His brother had been the bad guy. His brother who had suffered a much worse fate. That was, of course, based on the assumption that there is no fate worse than death. Simon could not think of one but was relieved that he learned of Farley's brother's end before he wound up in jail.

Fifthly, there was the suspension and potential sacking of Marty. Was that justified? Should he do something? What could he do? He had read and re-read the folder, and the evidence, coupled with the discussions he had with Freeman, proved that something was awry at DoMO. To whom should he speak? Should he raise his suspicions with his uncle? Probably not, as John was actively involved. What should he do? From the evidence, it looked like Uncle John was now on the side of the bad guys.

Bad guys had turned into good guys, and good guys turned into bad guys, all in the space of a week.

The question of what to do and say kept appearing in his mind. The fallout from all this could, potentially, be massive. Sikes was sure his uncle was up to no good and, once it all came out in the open, it would rip his family apart. He feared his grandmother would never cope with the scandal or the shame. What would happen to Sikes? Would he still get into university?

Finally, there was Timmy's disclosure that Peter Evans had been responsible for the death of the person who almost killed Simon's mother. Did his father know? He doubted it. His father would have said something. He had done enough listening over the years to know that his father had never mentioned Evans' past. Even if he knew about the death of the eldest Farley child, Thomas Ikes would never have put two and two together. He was not street-wise enough. Should Simon congratulate Evans or expose him to his parents?

This was probably the most significant dilemma Simon faced. Should he tell his parents? If he told them, how much should he say? He would be reopening old wounds and, by attacking Farley, had probably added many new ones. His parents would have difficulty coping, and his mother would be devastated to hear that Simon had almost killed someone.

What to do? What to do?

He pulled the duvet over his shoulder and turned to his left side, facing the wall. He had no idea what the time was and could not be bothered to look at the clock. He guessed it would be light soon enough, and another day would begin. His mother would call him, and he would have to get on with his life, looking like he had no care in the world. He needed to present his usual happy persona. His parents had suffered and worried enough. It was better to keep them out of his troubles until he had decided how to handle this. He was not yet ready to talk to anyone about his concerns. He had to find a way to sort this out himself. It was his problem. If only he knew how to fix matters.

He was grateful that the dreams had receded, but how could he dream if he could not sleep?

ASHES TO ASHES

Timothy Martin stepped forward, picked up a handful of earth and scattered it over the coffin, which lay at the bottom of the freshly dug hole. Stepping back from the graveside, he let Dot take his hand as he bowed his head

"There, there, luv. Let it out."

Simon watched as Tim threw the arms of his dark suit around his lady friend. He felt moved by the love and concern that Dot had shown to Tim. The strong bond between the pair was evident.

Standing there in his black shoes, navy suit, white shirt and borrowed black tie, Simon realised that his parents shared the same strength of feeling, that same bond. That is how they managed to not only survive the tragedy but come to become tighter and more united than ever. Simon wondered if anything could ever break them up. He hoped not for his own sake as much as the twins.

He followed the large crowd of old neighbours, friends and relations, but no brother, sister-in-law or nieces as they walked along the muddy verge that lined the grave.

Reverend Thomas encouraged the congregation to scatter some earth on the coffin. Simon did so but had no idea why he should.

The Reverend held out his hand and said, as people walked past him, "Thank you for coming. It is greatly appreciated,"

Simon nodded at him and shook his hand. Tim had been right in his choice. The Reverend had done an excellent job, managing to strike the right balance between solemnity and fondness of recollection.

He had been quick to highlight Mrs Martin's strong Christian beliefs and the hardships she had faced in her life but had also shared some humorous moments.

Simon had chuckled at the declaration that while Tim had always been a great source of comfort to his mother, the bedridden Mrs Martin became concerned when her loving son turned forty and was still a bachelor. She worried he would be stuck on the shelf like her Auntie Florrie. She did not want her Tim to end up like that and told the Reverend that she wished the lovely Dot would take him out more often. Simon Dot blushed, and Tim tightened his grip on her shoulder.

The Reverend continued his recollections.

"Mrs Martin often said that her Tim was a lovely man. She couldn't wish for a better son but disliked how he would change the television channel if a sexy scene came on. She didn't know if he thought it would kill her to see some action, but she often wished he'd let her watch what she wanted."

Tim blushed, laughed and grabbed Dot's hand as the Reverend spoke. He blushed further when the Reverend referred to him *as the sweetest son any mother could wish to have, so compassionate, dedicated and trustworthy.*

Cries of 'hear hear' filled the living room. Simon swallowed hard as he watched tears run down his friend's cheek.

He doubted his mother would describe him in the same glowing terms.

Sikes stayed at the house longer than anticipated. He drank a few cans of bitter and ate some ham sandwiches and cake while catching up on gossip from the bakery. He guessed the place itself would be empty. Most of the employees, and the boss himself, had taken time off for Mrs Martin's funeral.

As the clock on the television chimed three, Simon decided it was time to make tracks.

He bade farewell to Dot, thanked her for everything and asked her to look after his friend.

"Course I will love." Dot gave him a peck on the cheek. "Tim was right about you. You are a lovely caring young lad.

Thanks for coming."

Simon did not feel particularly lovely or caring but said nothing.

He eventually found Tim in the garden. He stood by the side of his derelict glass house. The metal frame held firm, but the glass was long gone. Pools of water had gathered on the ground inside. Sikes looked upward before speaking. The rain had turned into a drizzle, and the air was cold the skies grey and bleak.

"Bye, Tim. I've got to be off."

Tim turned to face Simon. Tear trails remained on his cheeks. He walked down the short concrete path and stopped a few paces before Simon.

"Righty oh, Si. Thanks for coming."

Simon started to say anytime but thought better of it.

"That's okay, Tim. Let me know when you want to run through the forms. You've got my number, yeah?"

"Yes, it's in Dot's book now, if that's okay."

"No problem." Simon could tell the conversation had not ended.

"I haven't told anyone else yet Si, apart from Dot, but the thing is Mr Wheldon, the solicitor, came to see me yesterday. Mam has left it all to me. The shares in Barry's business, a stack of cash, the insurance money, her jewellery and everything else. I didn't know she had any cash, but she did. There's a fair few bob tucked away." He wiped the rain off his forehead. "I thought she was putting Barry's cheques into an account for his kids, but she was saving it for me. She's made it clear that the money is between me and Dot. She thought that if she only left it to me, I would give some to Barry, and Mam reckoned he had enough. Mr Wheldon has spoken to Barry, and he said he understands. I am not sure I do. It feels a bit weird. I just hope Barry doesn't fall out with me about it."

Sikes said he doubted Barry would take offence. He resisted the temptation to suggest that Tim deserved the money and that Barry probably did not care about his mother's will, just as he appeared never to care about his family back home.

"So what are you going to do with it?"

The slightest trace of a smile appeared on Tim's mouth.

"Me and Dot are going to have a holiday. We're going to sort out the stuff, get me moved into her place, and then we're off to see her son in Canada. She's always wanted to go, so we will. She's already rung him, and he's looking forward to the visit. Dot is excited about seeing her grandchildren. With luck, we'll be out there for the New Year."

Simon thought of Maggie's plans and felt a pang of jealousy. Everyone had something to look forward to, except for him.

Christopher Harvey joined them.

"Hello Simon, is everything all right?"

"Fine thanks."

"Good. Tim, I have to go. I just wanted to say so long."

Tim shook his boss's hand.

"Thanks for coming, Mr Harvey, and for being so understanding about the time off."

"Think nothing of it, Tim. You take as long as you want, and just let me know what holidays you want over Christmas and New Year. I'll make sure that's not a problem."

"Thanks Mr Harvey."

"With that, Mr Harvey turned and left via the path that went around the side of the house.

"He's been great, fair play," Tim said to Sikes as Harvey disappeared around the corner.

Simon nodded.

"Well, I'd better go as well. Let me know when you want to check those forms."

"Will do."

Tim stepped forward and held out his hand. Simon sidestepped his hand and wrapped his arms around his friend. He hugged him tightly.

"Look after yourself, Tim. Make sure you look after Dot

too."

Simon felt Tim's arms around him.

"I will Si. Don't you worry. You just get yourself sorted. I'll be okay. Thing is, life is too short for regrets."

They hugged for a moment then Simon followed Mr Harvey's exit route. Tim waved at him before he joined Dot inside the house.

Mr Harvey got waylaid by one of his employees at the front door and was only getting into his car when Simon arrived at the front of the house. Sikes gratefully accepted the offer of a lift home and climbed into the plush leather seats of the large black BMW.

They travelled in silence, apart from odd exchanges of polite conversation about families, past events and the unpredictability of life. Christopher Harvey was heading for the bakery and dropped Simon off at home.

Simon entered his house to find his mother sitting on the settee. It was apparent she was waiting for someone or something.

"Hi-ya Mam. Okay? Where are the twins?" Simon spoke through the open doorway between the hall and the lounge.

"Still in school. Nanna's collecting them. I'm glad you're home, Simon. I think it's time we had that chat."

Simon took off his wet suit jacket and hung it on a hook.

"A chat? Why, what's wrong?"

His mother was standing by the time Simon entered the lounge. "Why don't we start with you explaining to me why you beat seven kinds of shit out of Robyn's boyfriend last weekend?"

Simon bowed his head as he ran his hands through his hair, brushed it back, and took a deep breath. That kind of language was particularly blunt, even for her.

Caroline Ikes had not finished. "Good God, Simon, you would be locked up for doing something like that. You are fortunate that Dave is not pressing charges. God only knows why he isn't telling the police you did that to him. I have a good mind to report you myself! What the hell got into you? What's wrong with you boy? Take a seat. You are not leaving this room until you tell me what happened and why you did it. What made you behave like that?"

Simon inhaled deeply again.

Aw fuck. It looks like this is it, he said silently, sitting on the sofa. A large leather cushion separated him from his mother, and Simon picked it up and held it on his lap as he prepared to talk.

The conversation got off to a stuttering start, but after a little delicate prompting, Simon told his mother what she wanted to know, what he had wanted to say to her for years. He acceded to his mother's request that he start from the beginning. Mrs Ikes listened in silence as Simon poured out his heart.

He told her how he and Miko had seen Animal writing on the garage doors and how they were too scared to say anything. He spoke of his shock at being woken by his father, who was crying but would not tell him why. He told her about the cold corridors at the hospital and his father crying again. He admitted that he had not wanted to stay with Nanna and Gransha and had tried to escape, but Granddad always caught him.

His mother whispered.

"I am so sorry, Simon love. I had no idea."

"It wasn't your fault Mam."

He told her about how he felt he was not told anything and kept in the dark. Simon revealed his worst nightmares.

His mother was horrified when he told her he had overheard her and his father talking about adoption and how he feared he would be adopted.

"Oh, Simon, there was no way we would let you go anywhere."

Simon knew that now but it had caused him much angst. His mother recounted her concern that Simon was not eating properly and had suddenly developed a bed-wetting problem. At the time, the doctor put it down to post-traumatic stress disorder, but she now knew the real reason why her son had not been himself.

Sikes spoke of the loneliness he felt and how he struggled to settle in the new school and the new house. He said he only settled down at the comprehensive school when meeting with Gareth and Mark. They had helped him a lot.

Mrs Ikes wondered what had brought the past back into his mind now. Simon had seemed fine after the twins arrived. He told her what he had told Robyn, that the recent contact with Miko, the break-up with Laura, and the sight of Dave "Animal" Farley being so smarmy while getting closer to Robyn had probably pushed him over the edge. He told his mother of his feelings for Robyn, and latterly Laura, but said nothing about his night of passion with Maggie. There were some things he was not ready to talk to Mam about.

Simon told his mother about Farley's confession that his brother had caused the accident and about the accident. He thought he ought to prepare his mother for a shock.

"Mam, I know this will upset you, but I think you ought to know who killed Richard Farley."

"Peter did," said his mother.

Simon's chin hit his knees. "What? You knew?"

"Yes, I knew, we all know."

"How come I didn't?"

Mrs Ikes spoke softly and slowly.

"It was a few months after I came out of the hospital, and Ted Grimshaw came to see us. Mrs Farley had confided to him that her son had caused my accident, and she hoped he would bring himself to confess. The police had no evidence against him besides what he said in a drunken haze, which would not be enough to convict him."

Simon interjected.

"Old Grimshaw is a good man, isn't he?"

"Yes, he is. He has been a terrific friend to your father.

They'd known each other for years even though he's older than us. I know he shouldn't have, but he kept us up-to-date with enquiries about the accident. He told us it couldn't have been Dave Farley as he was in the youth club that night."

That snippet confirmed what Simon was told.

"And for months, the police had no clue who threw the brick, but then Mrs Farley called into the station and told Ted what her son had said. She had thrown him out, and he'd gone to Merthyr to live."

Simon knew this already.

"Peter Evans was drinking at his regular pub just off the top road. He regularly drove there and caught the bus back. That night, as he left the pub to catch the bus home, it poured down, so he stayed in the pub. When he did eventually leave, he jumped in his car. He does not know how he got up to the top road; his house lay in the opposite direction. He realised his mistake and tried to turn around. He did not see Farley and his mate o the motorbike. The police said that Peter was probably rushing, trying to avoid other traffic, and hit them full-on. They didn't stand a chance."

Simon thought about this for a second. "Did you know Peter at this time?"

"No. Ted told us about him. Peter was in a mess. His wife had been carrying on, they were getting divorced, and he was about to lose his job."

Simon was not fully versed in the broader aspects of Peter's life but immediately felt sorry for him. His mother continued her tale.

"He was receiving treatment for depression. His pills did not mix well with alcohol, and his head was all over the place. Nowadays, they take more interest in clinical depression but, as I know, back then, they tended to pump you full of drugs and leave you to get on with it."

Simon recalled his mother's sadness and how Nanna had been angry that her daughter had to fend for herself. In the end, Thomas Ikes paid for private help, and his mother received regular visits from a psychiatrist and counsellors.

Caroline Ikes had more detail to impart.

"Peter was given a two-year sentence, much of which he spent in hospitals learning to cope without his arm. He refused the offer of an artificial appliance. He believes the injury is part of his punishment, and he deserved to get punished."

Simon Ikes did not like what he had heard. "He was only punishing those who did wrong. He deserved a medal, not a jail sentence."

"Your father said the same thing when Ted told us. That is part of the reason he offered Peter a job as soon as he came out. I like Peter, I'm glad he's sorted himself out, but I take a different view about the crash."

Simon guessed that she would.

"I believe Peter could have killed anyone that night, and it was a coincidence that he killed the two people the police suspected had hurt me."

"And they killed the baby." Simon blurted before thinking.

His mother looked agog at his outburst but remained calm. Tears filled her lower eyelid.

"No Simon, they did not kill the baby. The baby had died before the incident. The baby would have been stillborn. The doctors admitted as much afterwards. They told us there was a problem with her blood, and she had a malformed heart. I knew the baby was dead. The kicks had stopped, but I wouldn't admit it." She sat quietly for a few seconds. "No, the baby was dead before I fell down the stairs."

Simon gave his mother a piercing stare. "What? The baby was already dead? But I thought they had killed it. I thought the baby died because I was too scared to tell the police about Animal. I thought it was my fault."

"Simon... Simon...no, it was never your fault. We've told you that many, many times."

Tears filled Simon's eyes.

"I know, but I didn't believe you."

Mrs Ikes slid her bottom across the leather seat until she could put her hand on her son's face. The tears poured out as she gently rested his head on her shoulder. She listened earnestly as her son continued to confess his dreams and fears.

Caroline Ikes tried to advise and reassure her son the best she could. She did not want to be too hard, he was crying far too much for that, but he needed to learn the truth.

Eventually, after about three bouts of tears, some of which she shared with him, and realising that his head was swimming from all her words of wisdom, his mother could think of only one thing to say.

"I don't know, Simon, why do you have to think so much? Why couldn't you just bloody talk to me now and again?"

Simon said nothing and cried again.

"I don't know about you, but I could do with a drink." Caroline Ikes did not condone her son drinking spirits, but she was happy to join him in a glass of whisky. Her husband's special bottle of fifteen-year-old single malt, a present from her brother, was retrieved from its hiding place and used to half fill two crystal tumblers. She re-joined her elder son on the sofa and passed one of the glasses to him.

"Thanks Mam. What'll Dad say?"

"He'd better not say anything, or he'll have me to contend with."

Simon managed a smile. He tasted the whisky. It was smoother than he had expected, certainly softer on the taste buds than the Southern Comfort he drank with Maggie.

"Mam, can I ask you something?"

"Of course."

"How come you didn't have more children?"

Her mother's shoulders slumped, and she held her glass in both hands.

"Well, it took us a long time to make you." She sat next to her son again and held her whisky in her right hand as she placed her other arm around his shoulder.

"The fall damaged my insides, and they gave me a hysterectomy. That's why I had to stay in hospital for so long and couldn't do much when I came out. That, and the fact that I was pretty down about everything."

Simon rested his head on his mother's shoulder again, but there were no tears this time.

"I've been a total prat, haven't I?" His mind replayed recent events with Laura, Farley and Maggie. "I get everything wrong. I always fuck things up."

His mother did not chastise him for using foul language.

"No, you don't. You're a fine lad. Your father and I are very proud of you, but you must understand that not everything in life is black and white." Caroline absently stroked her son's hair as she had when he was a child. Realising what she was doing, she turned and gently kissed the top of his head, then rested her cheek on it. "I wish you would talk about things before reaching your conclusions and acting upon them."

"How did you find out about me and Farley?"

"About Farley and me, you mean?" His mother smiled.

"Yes, Mam. Sorry, Mam. How did you find out about Farley and me?" Sikes' mouth broke into a wide grin.

"Sandra rang me to ask how you were. I didn't know what she was on about."

Sandra Howells, Robyn's mother and Caroline Ikes' best friend.

"So you knew that Dave was Animal."

"Yes, I knew he was not involved in my accident. Robyn always speaks highly of David. I've also met his mother a couple of times. She's a lovely lady and is thrilled that David is making something of himself. She thinks the world of Robyn too."

Simon thought he had misheard. "What? You've met Mrs Farley?"

"Yes. She asked to meet me shortly after her son died. Ted arranged it, and I met her in the park. We had a long chat. Neither her husband nor her sons know that we've met, so please don't say anything. Robyn told her mother that Dave had lied to his mother about what happened the other night. Sandra made me promise not to say anything if I met Mrs Farley. I'm not sure I agree with lying, but I understand their reasons."

"How have the Howells taken it?"

"I think they'll be okay now. They were more worried about you. They can't believe what you've done. This incident is totally out of character." She smoothed his hair. "But they don't know you at all, do they? They haven't a clue what a powder keg of emotion you are when something gets into you."

Simon and his mother laughed heartily at the joke, then savoured another mouthful of whisky. Quietness filled the room as both thought their thoughts. The tears had stopped.

Simon was the first to break.

"Mam," he said, sitting upright.

"What is it?" His mother retracted her arm and held the glass in both hands once again. She looked at the whisky as it twirled around the glass.

"You know I said I should talk about things."

"Yes." Mrs Ikes grew nervous. Her son's tone suggested something was wrong. "What is it?"

"I think Uncle John could be in deep trouble." He saw he had her undivided attention. "I've got information that suggests he could be involved in a major crime."

Caroline Ikes took a deep breath.

"Then you'd better talk some more as I get us more whisky."

Simon finished his afternoon confessional by telling his mother all about Marty, the folder and the apparent wrongdoings that were going on within DoMO.

NOSTALGIA IS NOT WHAT IT USED TO BE

The rain was a pain, but an area of high pressure lay inside Simon's head.

His mother had been brilliant. She had been honest, sympathetic and frequently blunt. Simon had needed to hear those things. He was thrilled when she offered to help him study the papers that Marty had given him. She gave him lots of advice, and his next need was to try to make sense of it. Simon felt that he had to act quickly.

Thomas Ikes had also understood. He collected the twins, took them for chips and let them choose a film. Simon's father spent hours watching a cartoon about some metal giant and did not complain. He even brought tea and beer in for Simon and his mother at regular intervals, although Sikes noticed the flow of malt whisky dried up as soon as he returned home.

Sauntering down the path beside the disused canal, Simon looked like a sad figure. His coat was soaking. His jeans were saturated and dirty from the mud, which splashed up as he walked down the overgrown path. His suede training shoes had started to let in water. He kept on walking, grateful for some time alone.

As he walked, he re-ran the telephone conversation he had with his Uncle earlier that morning.

"Uncle John, it's Simon."

"Hello, Simon. Day off today is it?" His uncle sounded cheerful enough.

"Something like that. I need to speak to you, but it has to be outside the office. I have to speak to you alone."

"Simon, what is this about?"

"I'll tell you when I see you, but I cannot come into the office to do it. Can you sort it for me to have a day off and then come home to the house around two-ish?"

"I can, Simon, but I think it would be better if you came in. I can't continue to pull rank on Anna and McKenzie. They'll soon get fed up. We have other staff to think about, you know."

That was a fair point.

"Right, I'll sort Steve, but can you get here for a chat? It's imperative."

"Okay. You speak to Steve, and I'll be there. Can you give me a clue what this is about?"

"I'll tell you later, but it concerns Marty Freeman."

His uncle went quiet momentarily.

"I see. Okay, then two o'clock but meet me at the Venue. I've got a meeting that is due to end at one thirty. I'll come straight after that. I'll have to skip lunch, and I know Noddy serves food all day."

Simon wondered how his uncle knew Noddy Efans, the landlord at the Venue.

"Mam would cook you something."

"I know that, Simon, but I think we might have some serious talking to do, and it would be better if we were on neutral ground."

"Fair enough. See you later."

They exchanged their goodbyes, and Simon followed that with a call to McKenzie.

He proved difficult to appease and was not keen on Simon having another day's leave. The team was already one member short, and he did not like having telephone calls of this nature.

Simon listened to him rant and rave and then dropped his bombshell.

"Look, Steve, I've some important personal business to sort out today. I only learned about it yesterday, and I must act quickly. I'm sorry this comes straight after I had the day off to attend a funeral but, if you must know, I'm not asking for the day off, I'm telling you that I'm not coming in. How you dress it up is up to you, but it would be easier for all concerned if you either record it as annual leave or mark me down as AWOL but, please, save the fucking bollocking until tomorrow."

McKenzie had not heard Simon speak to him this way before. Ikes was usually very polite. He must need this day off. Steve backed down immediately.

"Okay, Simon. I'll put you down as being on leave but don't be making a habit of this. I'll see you tomorrow."

The calls had taken place at seven-thirty that morning. Simon had left the house at seven-fifteen before his parents had woken up and had used his mobile. He 'phoned his uncle at home and Steve at the office. He knew McKenzie would be at work.

In the fifteen minutes since then, Simon walked, along the old canal path, to the main road running through the village where he spent his formative years. Leaving the canal, he climbed a short, paved incline onto the solid pavement parallel to the road. He was relieved to be on firmer ground. It meant he was no longer squelching through mud and gravel.

Sikes debated whether to take the top-end circular route or the bottom-end circular route to his destination. Where he was heading could be reached at the same time using either way, but he decided that the bottom end of the village held more memories.

When he lived in the village, he and his friends rarely journeyed to the top end. The only exceptions would be during the long hot summer holidays, when he and his gang would go for a walk to challenge the snotty top-end kids who lived in their posh houses, on the private estate, just beyond the football ground. Nowadays, Simon realised that the children up the top end were not particularly snotty or posh. They just lived in semi-detached privately owned houses when he and his mates lived in semi-detached council-owned properties. Sikes smirked at the innocence of youth.

Depending on who was out, Simon, Miko and between four and eight other boys would walk meekly up to the top end, wander around the estate, talk to and tease a few local children, and then walk back home. They had far more of a swagger on the return journey, feeling secure in knowing they had retaken the estate. One summer, the top-end estate was invaded eight times in a fortnight without any opposition and no bloodshed. It would have been more, but Sikes went away on holiday, so the campaign had to stop. Miko would not go alone.

Simon now lived in a detached house that was probably bigger than a pair of the posh estate semis. He was grateful that when he was younger, he never had to defend the big house from any challengers. They could have had it as far as Simon was concerned. He hated living in the big house back then. It was different now. The older Simon would defend his home and family with everything he had. He looked at his hands. His knuckles looked sore, although the pain had eased, and Simon was grateful nobody was likely to come knocking. He had done enough defending for one week.

He studied the crossroads again and opted to follow the bottom-end path. He looked at the road ahead. The route went on for as far as the eye could see. It would be another mile or two before he would start climbing the hill to the street he knew as a child. He adjusted his jacket and set off down the pavement.

The terrace of houses to his right seemed much smaller than it used to, and Simon walked by them, barely giving them a glimpse. He only stopped to study one of them when he spotted a Christmas tree shining brightly in the window of the last house. It was not yet December, but the artificial tree was already on display. It was not yet eight, but the lights were already on. He recalled Christmases in the village when he was much younger. His mother used to wait until a fortnight before Christmas before putting up their decorations. Nowadays, things are different. As soon as the twins spotted a Christmas tree in someone else's house, the Ikes' house would get trimmed up. The smell of a real Christmas tree helps to make Christmas for the Ikes. The chocolates hanging from the tree become a significant attraction for the twins.

The flats and house opposite where he now stood got constructed after Simon left the area. They did not hold his interest for long. Behind them stood the familiar grey concrete and large glass windows of the former Royal British Legion Club.

Simon had not been inside the building for many years. His mind returned to the annual Christmas parties his father brought him to at the club. They were happy days. The parties comprised sandwiches, cakes, biscuits, pop, jelly and ice cream, games and a visit by a Santa who smelt of beer. Simon had always known this was not the real Santa; he was Mr Collier, the club's secretary and owner of the most prominent beer belly in the area.

The old petrol station that once stood on the right was now the forecourt of a car showroom. A blue neon sign displayed the words “Get a great deal on a new car”. New and used models covered the forecourt and stood impressively in the glass-fronted showroom behind. It reminded Simon that he had planned to buy a car. Thinking back to that day reminded him of Laura and how badly he had behaved, but that was not important now. He was a man on a different mission.

He walked on, oblivious to the rain pouring from the dark grey sky.

The tyre centre and the DIY store were new. They were closed. There was no one around. The next block of buildings belonged to the bus depot. Empty buses spewed exhaust fumes into the air as drivers warmed up their vehicles before starting work.

The green bank on the other side of the road was familiar enough, and he doubted that the small cottages aligning the bank had changed much since he last saw them. White and grey smoke shot out of one of the chimneys as fires burned inside.

Sikes crossed over the road and ran up the bank. The grass was slippery, and he had to steady himself to avoid falling. He looked into the small gardens enclosed by low walls. These walls always seemed so massive when he was smaller. Weeds had conquered the majority of gardens, and a couple of the owners had covered their space in concrete slabs.

He stopped behind the boarded-up house that used to serve as a police station and family accommodation for Ted Grimshaw, his wife Pauline, a bold, chatty Yorkshire lady, and their three children, a boy and two girls.

Sergeant Grimshaw was now a widower, and all his children lived away. His son was a Royal Marine based in Plymouth, his elder daughter was married to a policeman in London, and his youngest child, Sally, was living in Bristol with a prison warden. Sally was the closest in age to Simon and had been the last to leave. GarGar had been out with her once or twice but hadn't got anywhere.

Passing behind the police house, Sikes came to the chip shop. He looked at the electric sign above the upstairs window, "Leonardo's Fish and Chip Restaurant." Leonardo had left the shop many years before Simon left the village, but the sign remained. He wondered if anyone had ever got it working.

The chip shop was closed, but he walked through the gap in the wall surrounding the frontage. He climbed two steps and turned right until he came to the corner of the wall. Simon looked toward the main road, resting his backside on the pointed concrete that covered the top bricks.

As young as they were, he and his mates used to hang out around the chip shop during the early evenings. They would play on the pinball machines until the older boys arrived, then retreat outside to play games until it was time to go home.

The gang would come to the chip shop during school holidays during their lunch break. They would buy a bag of chips or chocolate and a drink and sit on the wall watching the overall-clad workers from the engineering works opposite play a lunchtime game of football in the factory car park.

The skeleton of the factory building remained but now housed a car showroom. New units had been built at the side of the old factory. One appeared to be a garage, and a large man in black overalls pushed an old car into the front paddock. He stopped briefly to look up at the figure on the chip shop wall before returning his attention to his work.

Scanning the horizon, Simon's eyes fell upon the local inn. The once tiny pub had gotten extended into the houses next door. Simon and Miko had made money here at Christmas, singing carols to the early evening drinkers. They used to earn a fortune. Well, it seemed a lot to them at that time. He wondered where his voice had gone. Nobody would pay him to sing now. He was more likely to be paid to shut up.

Next to the pub was a lane leading up to one of the village's two primary and junior schools. Sikes had attended this school until the family moved. He had been sorry to leave, and the teachers appeared genuinely sad to see him go. Simon liked that school. He had preferred it to any school that he attended subsequently.

The climb from the chip shop to the bus stop where he and Miko used to throw their tennis ball appeared steeper as a child. Simon remembered how they would try to race up the hill and get to the bus stop before the cranky old buses arrived at the bus stop. The children would start their run from the fish shop as soon as the bus arrived at the junction, some thirty yards further down the hill. As they climbed the steep hill, the old buses would take time to build up speed. The children would be more than halfway by the time the bus reached the chip shop. There was very little contest. The children won every time. The battles stopped when the children discovered that the council had grown fed up with being beaten by kids and had purchased more modern buses. These buses easily outpaced the children. This change was unfair, and the young athletes refused to participate in more races. The council later sold their buses to a national bus operator.

The hill was still taxing, but he kept going. To his dismay, a metal shelter with clear plastic sheeting had replaced the old concrete block bus shelter that invariably smelt of urine and cigarettes. Sikes and Miko would have been unable to play their game at this bus shelter. One of them would have to stand in the road. He remembered the old bus shelter being much further back from the tarmac.

Sikes was surprised when he discovered that the high concrete block wall that had lined the alleyway to his street was now a low brick one. As he walked through the alley, he looked over it into people's gardens. Sikes was unsure if this was a change for the better as passers-by could see everything that went on in the neighbouring houses. He quickly progressed through the alleyway until he arrived at his old street.

It was evident that many people had purchased their houses. In his youth, when they were all council-owned, the homes looked identical apart from the outside colour scheme. Tenants usually chose blue, green or red paint for the exterior doors and windows. Now, almost every door and window was white plastic. Simon's old house looked different, with red brick and plastic windows replacing concrete panels and metal windows. The front garden was a mess. His parents had taken great pride in their garden when he lived here. He recalled his mother's attempts at a rockery.

Examining the house from the pavement, Simon noticed it now had two doors. Whenever Thomas Ikes wanted to prove the incompetence of the local council, he would recount the time council engineers visited to rectify a problem with the front doorstep.

The stone had worked loose and needed replacing. The engineers assured him that it presented no problem but suggested the family would have to use the back door while the step got replaced. They thought they might also have to replace the doorframe. A lengthy discussion followed as his father revealed the house had only one door. The engineers showed him the building plan that indicated there should be two doors. Thomas Ikes grew tired of the exchange and told them that if they could find the second door, he would use it. The council engineer had risked his life when he asked Thomas what he had done with the back door. There were two doors marked on his plan.

Thomas Ikes' confidence in the local authority was not restored by that visit. However, it was a story that had helped kick off many a lively debate into the problems with local democracy. The council never did establish what had happened to the missing door.

Simon felt let down. He expected to feel differently.

When he developed this idea the evening before, he thought coming back would help him sort his mind out. It had only served to make matters worse. He felt more confused.

Nothing was as he remembered. Nothing was the same. This was not the place of his youth, the home of happiness and fond memories.

Looking at his old house, he saw someone looking at him through the upstairs landing window. That was the window. The window his mother had looked through on that fateful night.

A man's face stared at him through the very same window. The man looked concerned. It occurred to Simon that he made a strange picture, wrapped up in a soaking wet coat, standing in the freezing rain, glaring at a house. He thought he cast a sinister image for the occupants. He looked at his watch. It was twenty past eight and still early. He would move on and stuffed his hands into his jacket pockets, ready to take on another hill.

Fifty strides later, he turned right, up yet another incline, for another thirty strides. Reaching the top, he stopped and looked right toward Miko's street.

He saw his friend's house at the far end beyond the stripped-out carcasses of old cars and piles of metal languishing outside shuttered-up houses. He had not remembered Miko's street looking like this. His friends had been right. The area was no longer a suitable place for his mother to live.

Simon climbed three short steps and looked beyond the gardens of the empty properties. He would visit the mountain.

Walking along another gravel path, which led to a spot where a small colliery had once stood, Sikes recalled the games he and his friends had played on the mountain. They had been cowboys, Indians, commandos, Germans, pirates, adventurers and spacemen, all in a day.

Mrs Ikes and her fellow mothers had few qualms about letting their children play on that mountain. The old mine workings had been made safe, and the children were mostly observable from their homes. The grass length suggested to Simon that few children played here anymore. Motorbikes and four-wheel drive vehicles had cut the most extensive tracks. Sikes had to make a path towards the small ridge, which was the base for many adventures. It looked like nobody had been this way for a long time. Eventually, he found himself standing by a small mast enclosed by fencing.

Looking down the mountainside, Sikes spotted the scars left by the housing estate that had once stood there. The experiment in modern, affordable social housing had gone badly wrong. The council demolished the estate some years earlier, and it now looked like new, private houses would be built on the remains. Cranes, diggers, cement mixers and stacks of other equipment stood idle in caged compounds, probably waiting for the rain to cease.

His father had known from the start that the experimental housing was doomed to fail.

"What is the point of spending millions of pounds of public money on a superior council estate when the only people who can afford to live there are those who get their rent paid by the state? No disrespect, but they are hardly the most suitable tenants to put in such high profile dwellings."

Caroline Ikes had called her husband a snob, but he

was proved right. The experimental estate got demolished less than thirty years after construction. The council claimed that it had only built the houses at the request of the then government and successfully argued that the government should pick up a large share of the demolition costs. The advertising signs showed a well-renowned house builder now owned the land.

Directly in front of Simon was the site where the smokeless fuel plant once stood. It was another empty site. The authorities could not decide what to do with the land, whether to use it for factories or housing. The site needed to be safe before any decision on future use, and the clean-up cost was a significant consideration.

Beyond the empty site, Sikes saw rows and rows of houses covering half the mountainside. His eyes followed the parallel lines of tiny terrace houses as they stretched up the mountain towards the forestry at the peak. The view reminded Simon that he lived in a beautiful valley. Dark clouds hung over the hills, but beneath the clouds, the splendour was evident.

He could survey the whole valley from where he stood. He saw the wall of a golf course to his left. In front of him, he gazed once again upon the forestry. He could quickly identify the tall spiral of the town church to his right. Beyond that, he saw the mountains above the town centre and the road that leads to the Rhondda. That was the same road where he and Laura sat in his father's car, kissing and touching on his birthday a week before.

Simon shivered as he relived the moment Laura gave him his present. He had been thrilled with the gift and the moment quickly became highly charged, sexually. Simon could still feel her soft cotton underwear and the smoothness of her skin beneath.

Why had he been so stupid? What didn't he think before acting? He had been unable to believe his luck when he first kissed the gorgeous blond he had spotted at the races. The fact that she had liked him too had blown him away. She was easy to talk to and always looked gorgeous. The sex was terrific. He loved being with her. She was great fun. She was a brilliant girlfriend, and he had messed everything up.

"What the fuck is wrong with you?" He said the words out loud, confident that nobody would hear him. "Why do you have to get everything so badly fucking wrong? You need to go and see her. Tell her you're sorry. If you don't, then you'll regret it."

Pledging once again to go to see Laura and make amends, Simon turned his attention to the mountains in the far distance. Straining his eyes, he was sure he could make out the traffic on the top road. He thought about the dead Farley and wondered whether he ever had a chance to appreciate this view. He held the Farley family in higher regard now. He no longer wanted to hurt them. He knew he had to look forward, not back.

What had his mother said when he was crying?

"You mustn't feel guilty about your sister's death Simon. It had nothing to do with you. You must start enjoying your life, not reliving and regretting past events. Looking back is nice. It's enjoyable, but that time has gone. It is no more. You can't change it because you can never get it back. The future is the exciting part. You get to make new memories and experience new things. You have a good future, so don't waste it. Please don't screw it up over things that have already gone. Don't try to make amends or take revenge for other people's stupid mistakes."

Simon did not need to know why he felt the need to drag himself to this spot, but he knew that he was feeling better for having done it. He was unsure if he was hallucinating but felt like a weight was lifting. It was one of those moments when he expected the clouds to break and a ray of bright light to come pouring through.

Sikes looked at the sky. The clouds were still there; if anything, they looked darker than ever. A real storm was coming. The only thing to pour through the clouds was rain, followed by more rain falling faster and harder. Raindrops bounced off his cheeks. Simon did not care. He suddenly felt happier than he had in ages, possibly since the last time he had walked in the village. He stood silently, savouring his view, taking care to move further away from the mast and trees. Lightning forks shot across the sky. The rain kept falling as thunder rumbled down the valley.

Simon checked his watch. It was twenty past ten. It was time to head home, shower and change, ready to meet his uncle. It did not seem so important now, but he had to see it through. He owed it to Marty.

Returning to the housing estate, Simon was met by two enquiring eyes.

"What was you doing up there?"

"Nothing, I was just walking." Simon smiled at the little boy as he walked on.

The lad jogged alongside him.

"Walking up the mountain in this weather? Why?"

Simon looked at the boy. He wore a red plastic coat with a white tick under a mushroom cloud and the words 'Nuke – Just done it' printed in green lettering. The print was wearing thin. Odd letters were slowly disappearing. The coat hood was wrapped tightly around the little boy's head so that Simon could see no hair, just pale skin, thin lips and brown eyes. The boy's short legs were covered in a black tracksuit bottom tucked into black wellington boots.

"I just needed to have a walk and a think." Simon continued to stride down the path. He was almost back in his old street.

"You don't look like a thinker. Are you a tramp?" The lad struggled to keep up.

"No, I'm not a tramp." Simon stopped and stared at the little boy.

"Why did you go up the mountain then?"

"I just needed time on my own."

The little boy met Simon's gaze with no sense of fear or

concern.

"Why?"

"Because I did."

"Why?"

Simon knew from experience that the 'why' word was difficult to stop.

"Shouldn't you be in school?"

"I'm staying home because I've got a cold."

Simon guessed the lad was about the same age as the twins.

"Well, why aren't you indoors if you have a cold?"

"My mother's gone to work, and she doesn't like me in the house on my own, so I'm supposed to stay with Auntie Janey over the road," he pointed back up the slope to the houses at the top. "But I get fed up there because she hasn't got satellite telly, so I thought I'd come outside for a bit. You should have seen the lightning just now. It was well mad."

"Hmmm, it was." Simon agreed.

"So why was you up the mountain then?"

Simon recognised the tactic. There would be no escaping this interrogation. He had experienced the same manner of questioning from the twins. They would not let up until they had heard what they wanted.

"Well, if you must know. I used to live here, and I needed to think. So I walked up the mountain to be on my own."

"Whereby did you used to live?"

Simon pointed down the street.

"That house there, opposite the alleyway."

The lad's eyes followed his arm.

"That's Jason Owen's house. He lives there. He lives there with his mother and her boyfriend. He does jobs for people if you give him cash. Janey said he ripped her off when he sorted her toilet out. Jason's father ran off with a barmaid. He lives down Bristol now or somewhere like that."

Simon was intrigued.

"How do you know all that?"

"Aunty Janey told my mam."

Simon wondered if it was a real Aunt or just a name given to a friend. He did not have time to ask, even if he had wanted to.

"Are you Jason's father?"

Simon rubbed his hair, shaking his head as he did so. "No, why?"

"You said you used to live there. Are you sure you aren't Jason's father? Do you live down Bristol?"

Simon found this assumption amusing.

"No, I don't live in Bristol." He smiled at the boy. "And no, I'm not Jason's father."

"So what are you then?" The little boy's eyes glared at him.

"Oh, I'm nothing much. I'm just someone who needed time to think. That's all. It's no big deal."

"You are someone who thinks up a mountain in the rain?" The boy's face got contorted. Simon knew the lad was puzzled.

"Aye, that's right."

"Well, I think you're a fucking nutter!" The little boy shouted before running back up the slope towards Auntie Janey's house.

"You're probably right." Simon laughed again. His eyes followed the lad up the path.

When Simon arrived at the pub, Jack Phillips was already enjoying a pint of bitter. He rose from his seat as soon as his nephew walked through the door. Simon carried a plastic bag.

"Hi, Simon. What'll you have?" Phillips' hand was already in his pocket.

"Pint of bitter please."

"Do you want anything to eat?" He pointed at the menu.

"No ta. I just had a snack with Mam. She sends her love."

"Was she off with me for not coming to the house?"

"No, not really. She said you could suit yourself where

you do business. You're a big boy now."

Phillips laughed and called the barman."Noddy, can I have another pint of bitter, please?"

"Coming right up, Jack. I won't be a tick." The large barman put his thumb up as Phillips indicated he would leave the money on the bar.

"Right Simon shall we sit down."

"Aye. Let's get rid of this first." Sikes rested the carrier bag on a barstool and removed his long back coat. He had borrowed his father's raincoat as his jacket was sodden from his walk. He hung the coat on a peg on the wall, collected his carrier bag and sat next to his uncle.

"What are you having to eat?"

"Gammon and chips. Are you sure you don't want anything?"

"Aye, positive thanks." Simon saw the barman was pulling his pint. "A beer will do me."

"Well, you look better than you did on Friday when you came to see me," said his uncle.

"Yeah, well, a lot has happened since then. I called to see you on Tuesday, but you were out."

"I had to attend a departmental review meeting in London."

Simon looked at the bar and saw Noddy placing his beer on the drip tray.

"Here it is, Jack" He mentally counted the cash. "Good man."

"No problem, Nod." Phillips went to rise from his seat, but Simon beat him to it.

"I'll get it."

"Now then, Simon, what is all this about? What is so important that you have to take another day off and cannot discuss it in the office?"

Simon settled back in his chair, his pint on the table in front of him.

"I want to know what's going on in the office. Why was

Marty suspended? Who's fiddling the statistics and why?"

Uncle Jack raised his eyebrows as he pondered the questions. He sipped a little beer.

"Well, to answer your first question, why should anything be going on? Marty was suspended for dealing drugs and will likely get dismissed." He returned his glass to the beer mat. "As for your other question, what makes you think the statistics get fiddled?"

Sikes felt a twinge in his stomach. He had not expected to be so nervous. He extracted the dossier and handed it to his uncle.

"It's all in here, and don't go thinking you can destroy it. There are other copies."

"I see. This is all very cloak and dagger." Phillips tried not to laugh. He opened the folder, removed the bundle of paper and quickly skimmed through the foolscap sheets.

"It contains details of all the strange events that have taken place at DoMO since Marty has worked there. It's catalogued with dates, times, and clear details of every incident."

"I see. Very impressive. I take it Freeman is behind this?"

"Yes, but I believe what he's saying. It's all there in black and white." Simon had a drink. The beer was cold. It made him shiver.

"So you do, do you?" Phillips was still perusing the various sheets. "It is a shame Marty wasn't as thorough in his work."

Simon waited patiently as his uncle studied the folder. John extracted specific sheets from the collection and placed them on a separate pile. He spoke again when he had collected about a dozen sheets in each of two banks.

"You realise most of this is complete and utter bollocks, don't you, Simon?"

Sikes was taken aback. "What?"

"It's all nonsense, and before you start telling me that, I would say that, wouldn't I." He had beaten Sikes to it. He patted the first of the piles. "This lot relates to cash payments that arrive each month by courier. Before I explain what this pile relates to, do you know how hard it would be for hospitals in the NHS to send regular cash payments to anyone, let alone another Government Department, without the auditors finding out?"

Simon shook his head.

"No."

"Well, believe me, it would be nigh on impossible. Every penny in the NHS is counted in and counted out these days. They probably have at least as many auditors as they do brain surgeons. Shall I tell you what the monthly packages Mister Freeman refers to so regularly are?"

Simon nodded as he took another sip of beer.

His uncle spoke again.

"Freeman has them listed as coming into the office on or around the twenty-fifth of each month. That's very precise of him. As I said, it is a pity he had not been so accurate with his work. Can I ask you a question?"

"Yes, sure." Sikes had no idea what to expect.

"What happens in the office at the end of every month?"

"Umm…nothing much… apart from the fact that we get paid?"

"Exactly. And how do you know how much you've got paid?"

"We get our payslips." Simon did not need further prompting. He was already mentally comparing the size of his payslip to the size of a ten-pound note. "Shit, so the packages are just the payslips. But why are there three sets?"

"There are three key divisions to DoMO. There is our marketing side, the regional offices and the headquarters. The paying office has set them up as three different accounts, so we get them in three lots. What Marty Freeman has failed to take into account is that the packages vary in size. Honestly, Simon, I cannot believe you have fallen for Freeman's cock and bull story. I would have expected you to have given this a bit more thought before joining this ...conspiracy theory. Bloody hell. It's hardly a secret that the payslips are delivered regularly as clockwork and that they get addressed to the Chief Accounting Officer, but Sammy Lee takes them to Geoffrey Millington. He should bring them to me. I don't know why he doesn't. Geoffrey's secretary brings them across, and my team then arrange for distribution."

Simon felt a bit stupid but was not going to give in that easily.

"But what about the changes to the hospital statistics? Marty's evidence is quite clear there." Simon thought this would have his uncle tied up in knots. He was confident that this would take some explaining. He sat waiting for an answer but quickly sensed that it would not be the answer he expected.

Seeing John tap the top of the second pile told Simon he was about to be proved wrong again. Phillips sipped his pint and licked his lips as he returned the beer to the table.

"How do you know that your friend Marty is telling the truth?"

"It's all there. He's listed dates, times, copied emails, everything. I checked the stats on Tuesday, and Marty is right. The stats that are to be published do not tie in with the returns that Marty has collected."

"No. That's correct. The statistics do not reflect the data given in these returns. The reason for that is I think that Marty has been feeding in falsified returns."

"What? You are blaming Marty for fiddling the stats?"

"I am. I think Marty has been submitting fake returns to suggest that some of the best-performing hospitals in Britain are doing badly. He got away with it once. We published the data without spotting the figures had been tampered with. It took an angry call from the Chief Executive of one of the hospitals to make us check the source material. We went back and told them that our stats were accurate, but they asked to see the returns we had used. When we sent them the paperwork, they told us the returns were not the ones they had submitted. Someone had swapped them. Initially, we had no idea who had done it or why, but we've since implemented a few safety checks to help us spot irregularities. We then check the data with the hospital concerned. We haven't been able to eradicate the risk of it happening again, but so far, there has been no repeat. It will help when we move to electronic data transfer from next month. We would have done it ages ago, but for the software issues with certain hospitals."

Sikes had forgotten about the process change, and he now sensed he knew the real reason why Marty was in such a hurry to get the media involved.

His uncle sipped his pint again, then added, "We had an idea that Freeman was involved but couldn't catch him at it. We think he has been bringing the bogus forms into the office via a friend who slips them into the system."

Simon could not see a motive.

"But why would Marty go to these lengths? There's nothing in it for him. Why would he do it?"

"I think he got approached by one of the workers who were sacked and persuaded to help them get their revenge."

"But why would they choose Marty? He's pretty anonymous."

"We believe he has a cousin who used to work for DoMO and was one of those sacked just before the office moved to Cardiff. His name is Steve Benson. He and his mates were helping to bring DoMO to its knees."

"How do you mean?"

"The previous management at DoMO was largely ineffective. The staff used to get away with murder. The sick record was appalling, the pay and expenses budgets were going through the roof, people were getting promoted when they didn't deserve it, and everybody seemed to be doing a degree course paid for by the office, but the work didn't get done. As a result, the office's reputation went through the floor. The Government were minded to shut down the office but had invested a lot of time and money, so the PM chose to give it one last shot. They tried to agree on changes in working practices, but that got nowhere. That's when they brought in the heavy hitters, like Charles Armitage and Geoffrey Millington, who had turned around failing businesses and Departments in the past. This is where it all gets a bit messy."

"Messy? In what way?"

"Well, at the time all this was going on, Benson and his cronies were fairly senior in the organisation, and it became obvious that they would never surrender control voluntarily. They resisted all attempts at change, but the department built up a dossier on them and identified several issues."

"What issues?"

"Well, for example, they had been fiddling expenses... taken more annual leave than they were entitled to, failed to meet their targets, and many other things. These issues got brought to their attention, and they were given the choice of moving to Cardiff, but in a new job, or taking redundancy. At this stage, Benson lost the plot and threatened Charles and Geoffrey. As soon as he realised that wasn't going to work, he tried blackmail.

"Blackmail?" This was getting too convoluted for Simon. "Who could they blackmail?"

Jack Phillips took a deep drink from his glass and studied the teenager.

"If I tell you this, Simon, you must not tell another soul."

His uncle's expression told Simon this was serious. "I swear."

"Promise me you won't breathe a word. Not even to your mother."

"I promise."

"Steve McKenzie is gay."

That was not a surprise. Simon had guessed as much. He thought Marty's claims about Anna and Steve had been ridiculous.

"Aye. So what?"

"Well, when he was in London, Steve got involved with an ex-government minister who was married at the time. Steve hasn't stopped seeing this man."

"I see, so what happened?"

"Well, Benson discovered who McKenzie was seeing and started putting pressure on him. He threatened to expose him and his lover unless Benson and his mates were pardoned and allowed to transfer elsewhere. Charles Armitage called in the police."

"But how could Steve have done what they asked? He's a nobody, really."

"Because Steve McKenzie's real name is Steven Philip Armitage. He is Charles Armitage's eldest son from his first marriage. Benson thought that they could get Charles off their backs by threatening Steve. Sadly for them, they misjudged Charles. He is as honest as the day is long. That was the end for Benson and company. The police have compiled a mountain of evidence against them, and their case is due to be heard next year."

"Will they go to jail?"

"Probably, and I think they realise that now, which is why they are getting desperate. They tried to get the unions to help them because, initially, they were against the move to Cardiff. But even they saw that they would never win the Benson case. They have focused on securing better benefits for their remaining members. I like to think that having made a move, we all believe we are in this together. Nobody would have benefited from DoMO going to the wall, and we've developed a much better rapport with the unions now. DoMO is making great progress. It's starting to function like it is supposed to."

"Hmmm." Simon's brain was filtering the information. "So Steve McKenzie is Charles Armitage's son. Shit, I'd never have guessed that, but where does Marty fit into all this?"

"I think Benson discovered that Marty worked in DoMO and saw it as a last chance to salvage something. You know

Marty. He is so easily led and happy to indulge in the conspiracy theory that he probably jumped at the chance to help. Did he ever mention his cousin to you?"

"No, but..." Simon thought about Marty's recent visitor. "...was Benson ever actually on the union?"

"Yes, he was branch secretary for a few years. Why?"

"Marty mentioned meeting an old union rep to help with the fight. I just wondered if it could have been him."

"Possibly." Phillips smoothed the edge of his moustache. "One thing I am sure about is that Marty was not working alone, and he is certainly not the brains behind this. They wanted him to stir up as much trouble as possible to undermine confidence in DoMO. If more people lost faith in our ability, DoMO would probably be shut down."

Sikes saw the logic in this. "So you think Marty has been substituting the forms?"

"Yes, but we are not sure where the switch took place. The records cover several teams, and it would have been challenging for Marty to get access to all of them."

"Unless he did it very early in the morning? Or late at night?"

"No, we've watched the surveillance footage. He keeps pretty regular hours and is rarely seen with anyone other than you, Maggie or the rest of your gang. None of you works in the right areas."

"We wouldn't have helped him change them."

"I know that."

"Could he re-enter the building later in the evening?"

"No. The security men are under orders to report anyone who re-enters the building after hours and the tapes show who passes each floor."

Each of them took a drink.

His uncle continued.

"So I guess Marty has been meeting someone outside the office to hand over the fake documents, and that person swaps the returns before they get to the branches. We just can't seem to catch them at it."

That's just Shelly. I see her now and again. Marty's words did somersaults in Simon's head as he fitted the pieces together. Shelly is Michelle, the girl in the post room Marty reckons was flirting with Charlie Chann.

"No wonder her voice was familiar," said Simon.

"Sorry, what was that?"

"Nothing. I'm just thinking aloud." Simon knew he had been used. "But I still don't see what was in it for Marty?"

"There could be several reasons. He could be after revenge. You know he's already had a warning?"

"Yes, for fiddling his flexitime."

"That was not the end of it." He saw Simon eagerly awaiting more news. "You'd better not repeat this either."

"I won't say a word."

"Some weeks ago, Marty was accused of selling drugs on the premises. He got caught by security, but because we could not be sure and we did not want any further adverse publicity, he got given a final warning. He was one relieved young man."

"But if he was happy to save his job then, why would he risk changing the figures now?"

"You'd have to ask him that."

"Nah, I think I'll keep away from Marty. I've ballsed up enough lately as it is. Why didn't Marty tell me about Steve?"

"His cousin probably didn't tell him. If that got out, then the finger of blame would have pointed in his direction." Phillips sipped some more beer and looked at the barman. His tummy was rumbling. "Will the food be much longer?"

"Won't be a minute, Jack. Did you want egg or pineapple or both?"

"Pineapple, please, Noddy."

"Coming right up." The barman served a pint of cider to one of his regulars.

When Noddy arrived with Phillips' gammon, pineapple and chips, he also brought a small portion of chips and two slices of bread for Simon.

"Here you are, lad, get that down you."

"Thanks very much."

"And if you see that mate of yours, ask him if he wants to do a show down here over Christmas. He went down very well last time."

Simon was puzzled.

"My mate?"

"Yeah, you know that bloke with the long hair and the pretty girlfriend. I've seen you with them in here. You were with the other pretty girl."

"Laura. Okay, if I see Jamie, I'll mention it to him."

"Please do. Tell him to ring me directly rather than go through the agent. It'll be more cash in his pocket."

"Aye, I will do." Simon carefully placed the hot chips onto the buttered bread and folded it over. He bit into the sandwich. The chips were good but not quite as lovely as those his mother made.

Simon and his uncle enjoyed another pint and continued their chat. Simon was unsure what to do next, and his uncle did not help when he suggested handing the evidence over to the police. He advised his nephew that this would be one way of getting everything out in the open. This would also ensure that a thorough and open review took place. Phillips insisted that DoMO management had nothing to hide or fear, and there would be no reprisals against Simon. Sikes was not sure he wanted to be involved.

They settled on an arrangement whereby Simon would refuse to provide Marty with the information but would encourage his friend to go to the authorities. Uncle John was sure Benson would not want this to happen and would instead stir the shit some more. Marty would be no use to his cousin now that he was on the outside, and Marty's attempt to involve Simon had failed. Phillips was relieved that Simon had spoken to him before helping Marty. That, he thought, was part of a plan by Benson to keep a mole on the inside. Simon told his uncle that Michelle in the Post Room was probably already a mole. Phillips agreed that she would be moved but not sacked. She would not know that Simon had any part in her job change. Freeman's other work friends would be monitored. Maggie was leaving anyway and had handed in her notice. Sikes did not know she had sought permission to leave earlier than originally requested. Phillips had agreed and would leave the following week.

Simon said Uncle John could keep the dossier as he had no use for it, and, in any case, Marty had other copies. Simon eventually accepted his uncle's offer of a period of absence. Sikes would return to the office the following morning to 'phone Marty and say his goodbyes to Maggie but would then begin three weeks 'gardening' leave pending investigations and would not return until after the Christmas break.

Ikes was concerned about McKenzie's staff shortage, but his uncle told him not to worry. McKenzie would be leaving after Christmas. He had requested a move to another Department, and Phillips had heard that a Newport job involving regular trips to London would become available in the New Year. In the meantime, their work would be shared out amongst other branches. Phillips wondered if Simon fancied a job as a team leader in the future. He could continue his studies and have a promotion at the same time.

"No, I don't think I'm ready," said Simon. "Anyway, I've been such a pain in the arse recently I can't see Anna liking the idea."

"Actually, Anna suggested you might be team leader material. She has no idea that you are my nephew. She thinks you are head and shoulders above the others."

"That's praise indeed," said Simon.

Phillips smiled. "Just don't let her bully you, Simon. Anna is a nice girl. She's just a bit mixed up."

"I know how she feels," said Sikes.

NORMAL IS GOOD

Simon leaned over to take his shot.

"Corner pocket," he shouted.

Gently bringing forward his cue until it rested a centimetre away from the white ball, Sikes lowered his chin onto the wood. The tip moved forward until it pushed the white ball down the green baize. The white collided with the left side of the black ball, sending that ball straight through the jaws of the corner pocket. Simon looked anxiously at the white ball stopped short of the opposite corner pocket.

He straightened himself up and clenched his fist.

"Yes! My game, that's 4-1 to me, GarGar. You're history, son. "

"Cocky twat," said GarGar.

"Nice one Si. Now you have to play me, though. What's the score in our games?" Dicey asked.

"Two all. This is the decider. Then you play GarGar."

"Aye, I know. Dicey's leading me 4-0, so I'm bottom by the looks of it. Just get a move on, will you? Whose round is it anyway?" Gareth had finished his second pint of lager.

"Mine," said Mark Dice. "Set them up, Si and I'll get the beers in."

Sikes took a pound coin from his pocket and walked to the slot at the side of the pool table. Dropping the cash into the hole, he pressed the red button and listened as the balls got released through the aperture at the far end.

"Are you all set Si?"

"Not at all. We've got three days yet. What about you?"

"Practically sorted," said his red-headed friend. "My mother's done the bulk of the packing. Your father's bought the tickets. All I have to do is tell Kelly I'm going on a pre-Christmas break with my mate to Spain."

"Shit, you still haven't told her?" Simon placed the balls in the black plastic triangle and moved them around.

"Nah, I just haven't found the right time, but then we've only known a couple of days, so it's not as if I've been keeping it a secret."

"No, I suppose not." The balls sorted, the triangle got removed. Simon looked at Dicey, who showed his identity card to the lady behind the bar. He could not understand why she was being so pedantic. Dicey was almost a regular in the pub, and the place was hardly full on the cold, wet Monday afternoon.

"Shame Dicey can't come with us," said Simon. He collected his cue from where he had left it. "It would have been a good laugh with the three of us."

"Yeah." Gareth looked at their friend at the bar. The lady was now pouring their drinks. "Never mind, we'll have to make the most of it, eh? Where is it we're off to?"

Sikes believed Gareth had the memory retention of a goldfish. "Benalmadena, Costa Del Sol. It's between Torr..."

"I know Torremolinous and Fuengorila. Fuck me, Sikesy. You are so easy to wind up. What's there?"

"I'm not sure really. I haven't been there for ages. I know there's a cracking beach and the weather should be good enough to swim in the sea. There are plenty of pools, bars and clubs. We can get to Gibraltar if we want, and there are plenty of other things to do and see."

"Where are we staying?"

"In my grandparents' place, they moved out there a few years ago. They have satellite television, so it'll be home-from-home. We'll stay at their place while they are on holiday. They're off to New Zealand to see my Gran's sister."

"It has two bedrooms, yeah?"

"Aye, don't worry. I wouldn't have invited you if it only had one. I don't want to sleep close to your smelly feet. Thanks very much. In any case, I might get lucky and will want some privacy."

"What about me? I'll probably strike gold before you do."

"What about Kelly?"

"Fuck Kelly...well, yes, I already have."

They both laughed.

"No, I'll sort Kelly. I'm getting a bit bored, to tell you the truth. She's all right, but it's been six months, Sikes, and I feel like a change. Reckon I'll blow her out when I get back."

"Here you are, guys, three pints. How many years have we been drinking in this pub?" Dicey saw GarGar laugh, and Sikes shrug. "Loads, yet that fuckin' barmaid asks to see my card every time."

"It's your youthful complexion," said GarGar.

"Or her lack of any brain cells."

Simon took his pint from Dicey's grasp.

"Thanks, Dicey. Your break?"

"Go on then."

Simon and Mark played their match as Gareth watched from the seat nearby. The air got punctuated with cries of frustration, mainly reflecting Dicey's inconsistency.

The three met regularly for these long pool sessions. Some sessions had been known to last over three weeks and would involve each playing over thirty games. Then Mark Dice decided he needed to instil some order into the proceedings and developed a list of rules. They now played five frames against each person, and the winner was the one who won the most games in the individual matches. These tournaments were usually completed in an afternoon and evening session, depending on how many others wanted to use the pool table. Today, nobody else did.

In between shots, the three discussed their plans for the coming weeks. GarGar and Sikes were flying off to Spain on a hastily arranged holiday. Sikes told his mates he was on leave while the investigation into Marty's accusations was underway. His uncle had been right. Marty's cousin disappeared back to London as soon as he knew Simon was not getting involved. Marty took the news badly but eventually despatched the folder anonymously to the local police. They contacted the Fraud Squad, and an enquiry began. The DoMO management and unions promised to participate fully in the process.

Simon had said his goodbyes to Maggie and had promised to visit her in Barcelona. They shared a long, slow, goodbye kiss and a gentle embrace as Simon walked her to the bus station on her last day at work. They had parted as good friends and promised to stay in touch. Maggie gave Sikes her new address, telephone number and her father's e-mail address so that he could make contact.

GarGar had willingly accepted the offer of a free holiday, although his mother had insisted she provide him with spending money. She thought Thomas Ikes had already been more than generous in paying for the holiday. Thomas Ikes would have been happy to cover all expenses. He wanted to give Simon a holiday to complete his recovery but did not argue.

Sikes had initially rejected that he needed a break. He thought he had not been as bad as his parents suggested but relented when they confessed how worried they had been about him. Simon accepted that they must have been scared if they were happy to spend all that cash on flights and spending money.

Only the two of them were making the trip. Dicey's father had suffered a mild heart attack, and while he was making a good recovery, Mark did not feel able to leave him alone. Christmas was always the worse time of the year as it brought back memories of his mother. The heart attack had unexpected benefits, bringing father and son closer together. They now shared walks and discussed things that would previously have remained unsaid. Dicey had even cut back on his drinking.

Simon won the match and the tournament and bought another round as GarGar beat Dicey to record only his second victory of the day. This was not usual. GarGar put it down to the excitement about the holiday.

They chatted about what they would do and where they would go. GarGar ran through some of the items in his extensive wardrobe.

"Remember, there's a limit to how much you can take," said Dicey.

"My suitcase isn't that large, but I'll always look cool."

"Leave that orange shirt at home. You look like an overgrown Satsuma," said Sikes.

GarGar looked at his shirt. There's nothing wrong with this shirt, you cheeky twat. This is genuine Lauren. I'll have you know that girls find me irresistible in this shirt."

Dicey put his finger in his beer and then flicked the drippers at GarGar.

"Oi, watch the shirt Diceman. You stain this, and I'll fucking kill you, you short-arsed twat."

Sikes was pleased to be back.

The session broke up just before five o'clock. Simon set off for home alone after his friends decided to stay for another drink.

The streetlights were fully illuminated, and cars had their headlights glaring when he left the pub. As he entered the main shopping street, by the side of the building that once housed his gran's favourite bingo hall, Simon felt strangely compelled to look to his right towards the library. As he did so, he made eye contact with Laura, who was leaving the ladies' clothes shop adjacent to the Indian restaurant over the road. She looked surprised to see him and appeared unsure about what to do.

Simon dodged the traffic as he ran across the street to greet her.

"Hi ya, Law. How are you? Are you okay?"

Laura had on a thick black coat that extended to her knees. She had successfully erected her umbrella by the time

Simon reached her.

"Yeah...Yes...I'm alright, you know."

"You're looking well." Simon saw that her hair was left to hang loose. Laura only wore a smidgen of lipstick and a little colour on her cheeks. Her large blue eyes bore a hint of mascara. She looked prettier than ever to Simon.

"Well, you know...have to keep trying."

"Christmas shopping, is it?" Simon was disappointed that she avoided eye contact.

"Yeah. Just a little something for Caitlin. She's dropped enough hints."

Simon laughed politely and pondered whether he had the guts to say what he wanted. "I'm...er...glad I bumped into you, Law. I was going to call up the pub."

"Really?" She seemed a little more interested. "Why?"

"Oh, I...umm," deep breath, he could feel his anxiety overtaking him. He knew he was bottling it. "I have a message for Jamie. The bloke in the Venue wants him to play there again over Christmas. He...umm... wants Jamie to give him a ring. If he speaks to Noddy, the landlord, he'll book him without the agency knowing. That'll be a bit extra for Jamie, won't it? He could probably do with it, what with Christmas and everything."

This was not what he wanted to say, and it was not what Laura wanted to hear. "Okay, I'll tell him." Her eyes looked away once more. "Nice to see you Simon, but I must go."

Simon thought of his mother's advice and what he had told himself on the mountain. He had to take this chance. If she turned him down, then she turned him down, but he had to, at least, try to win her back. His hand gently grabbed her arm.

"No, please wait Law. That's not what I meant to tell you. I just feel nervous, and a bit scared to say what I want to say..."

"What do you want to say Simon?" Her eyes were focused on his mouth.

"I've really missed you. I'm sorry for being such a prat.

I wish I could take back the things I said, and I know you probably never want to see me again, but I wish we were still together." He sighed. "There that's it."

Laura's eyes lit up brighter than the Christmas candle in the newsagents' window.

"Seriously? That's what you wanted to say?"

"Aye, seriously. I've done a lot of thinking this past fortnight, and I know I've been a total dickhead. You won't believe the stupid things I've done since...you know... my birthday, but I think I've got my head sorted now, and I realise that I should never have doubted you. I was just so jealous. I don't...I didn't want to share you Law with David or anyone."

"But you didn't have to share me Simon. I told you that. I had finished with him that night in Swansea but, in reality, it was over for me before then. I know I was wrong to hide those photos, but I never thought you'd see them and intended to destroy them. I have now, all of them."

This was not good news.

"What? Even the ones with me in?"

"No stupid. I would never get rid of those. They contain too many great memories."

This brought a massive smile to his face.

Sikes wanted to continue the conversation but not on the street. "Do you fancy a drink?"

"You smell like you've had a few already."

"Aye, sorry, just a couple. I've been playing pool with GarGar and Dicey."

"Pool? On a weekday? Why? Haven't you any work to do?"

"It's a long story. Can I tell you over a lager?"

"That would be lovely. Let me call my mother to tell her to go onto Caitlin's without me.."

Laura made the call from the sanctuary of the old bingo hall entrance and walked down the steps to rejoin Simon. She slid her mobile into her pocket.

"She sends her regards."

Sikes smiled.

"Shall we go to the Cambrian? It's the nearest."

"Wherever, I'm in no hurry anymore."

Simon walked beside her but was unsure whether to get too close. They spoke about the town and how only a limited selection of Christmas goods was available. Simon pulled the door open when they reached the Cambrian and allowed Laura to enter. As she stepped into the pub, she removed her black leather gloves and held a hand out for Simon to take. He did so eagerly. Her skin felt warm under his bare hands, and he squeezed her flesh tenderly. Simon was also pleased to see that she wore the watch he had bought her for his birthday. He led the way into the bar area.

Dicey and GarGar shouted from their seat as they saw their friend return. They quickly shut up when they saw Laura with him. Sikes suggested they sit at the other end of the bar, and Laura made for the chair in the corner. Simon went to order the drinks. He bought two more pints and took them to his friends.

"Fucking hell Sikes you're a dark horse," said Dicey.

GarGar looked deep in thought.

"I bumped into her, and we spoke for a bit, then I asked her to come for a drink. I'm not being rude, but we've got a bit to talk about, so we're sitting over there."

"No probs," said GarGar, now back in the room. "You go over to the luscious Laura. We'll be okay over here. Thanks for the beer, mate. Much appreciated."

"Aye, well-done Sikes. It was my round an 'all," said Dicey.

Simon collected two more drinks, paid the barmaid, and sat next to Laura. He told her almost everything that had happened to him in the days since his birthday.

To begin with, the pair frequently glanced across the empty bar to where GarGar and Dicey sat. They would raise their glasses at Simon and Laura if the two were not deep in conversation. However, the lovebirds stopped looking around as the conversation grew more intense. Simon rarely looked anywhere other than at Laura. She only had eyes for him.

Just before eight o'clock, with both glasses empty, Simon felt a gurgle in his stomach. He was sure Laura heard the noise in his belly.

"Oh, excuse me. I'm starving."

Laura laughed.

"Me too. Do you fancy a curry?"

"Yes please." As they stood to leave, Simon looked around the bar. There were many more customers, but the two he sought were conspicuous by their absence. Sikes wondered where they had gone but didn't dwell on it. He returned his attention to Laura.

The meal was delicious and followed by a walk across town to the Bird in Hand. They held hands all the way. Simon was reluctant to enter the pub, but Laura assured him everything would be okay. She was right. Her father was pleased to see him, and by the time his mother returned with Caitlin and Jamie, Simon felt as though nothing had happened. The group sat at the table nearest the bar allowing Mike to join them between serving drinks.

Nobody mentioned that Simon had not been around much until it was Simon's turn to go to the bar. Laura's father whispered to him as he served the beer.

"Welcome back Simon. You've been sorely missed." He caught his daughter looking at him and winked at her.

"I've missed her too. It might have been the biggest mistake of my life losing her." He looked at Laura, who was beaming at him. He smiled back.

"Well, I think so too, but then I would," said Mike. "Have these on me. It's worth it to see our Laura smiling again."

Simon kissed Laura goodnight and arranged to see her the following day. She was relaxed about the fact he was going away for two weeks and said he would benefit from the break. He promised to stay faithful and looked forward to seeing her again on his return. They kissed strongly and deeply, and

Simon tried hard to keep his hands under control.

GETTING AWAY FROM IT ALL

"There's a slight change of plan, Simon. Gareth called, he's meeting you at the airport. His mother must go to the newspaper depot and drop him there."

"Okay, Mam. Thanks." It was not unusual for GarGar to change his mind. Simon yawned again and scratched his head. He had not heard the 'phone ring, but then he had already missed his alarm. He was grateful that his mother was awake.

"You'd better get a move on. You must be at the airport by five o'clock if you want to check in on time."

Sikes looked at the clock. It was three thirty in the morning.

"What time does Dad want to go?"

"By four I think. He's put your case in the car. You'd better wrap up warm it's freezing out there."

"Okay." Simon emptied the glass of orange juice and started on the cooked breakfast. He yawned again.

"That'll teach you to have such a late night. Where did you get to?"

"Oh, just around town with Laura. Then we went back to the Bird for a sing-song. It was a good night too."

"Well, I suppose it was until you started singing."

"Ha ha, very funny Mam."

"Is Laura going down to see you off?"

"No, she wanted to, but I told her to get some sleep. I'll ring her tonight."

"Right. Well, get a move on, or you won't be going anywhere."

"Right Mam." Another yawn. "Sure, Mam." Simon's knife cut into his bacon.

Cardiff Wales Airport was much busier than Simon had expected for a Thursday in December, and he was pleased that he had found his companion.

They talked a lot during the start of the flight until Simon, overcome by tiredness, dozed off. The landing at Malaga was faultless, and the delay in baggage processing passed quickly enough. Taxis were plentiful, and twenty minutes later, the pair had deposited their cases at the apartment, changed into lighter clothing and left to examine the surroundings.

They returned after a light, primarily liquid, lunch for a brief siesta before changing into their evening clothes, ready for a night at a club. The seafront was a hive of activity with numerous discos, bars and restaurants all trying to entice the visitor. Several places were closed, but others were open, hoping to attract the locals and pre-Christmas visitors.

Afterwards, the two made for a nearby bar, where they enjoyed an amusing conversation with an ex-pat who had recently moved out to the area to retire. Afterwards, they found a club where they danced until the early hours.

Just after three in the morning, Simon walked back up the hill. A fair-haired girl he had kissed and danced with for much of the preceding hours accompanied him.

As they stopped for Simon to unlock the security door at the front of the building, the girl made her move.

"Senor...you are lovely." She threw her arms around his neck and kissed him deeply.

Sikes tasted San Miguel and peach Schnapps.

"You are not so bad yourself."

"Que?"

"Nothing." Simon pulled the door back and closed it behind them. They walked across the marble floor towards the lift. He placed his arm around her shoulder, she looked up at him, and they kissed again. They kissed their way up the four floors.

Reaching the apartment, Simon unlocked the door and locked it again behind them. He admired how the girl's pert backside swung from side to side in her short black dress. She removed her shoes and cardigan and left them on the floor by the shower room.

"Would you like a drink? There's no lager, but I think there's some brandy or something."

"No gracias I am…as you say… fine."

She crossed the floor and draped her arms around Simon again. He held her as he manoeuvred them into the bedroom he had chosen. It was not much of a challenge. She was as eager as he was.

Sikes sat on the edge of the double bed and kicked off his shoes. The girl stood in front of him. He reached out for her and nibbled her flat stomach through the dress.

"My mamma, she tells me about boys like you," said the girl.

"Oh, she did, did she?"

"Que?"

Simon unzipped her dress from behind.

"I've wanted to do this all night."

Sikes woke with a smile and a girl on his arm the following morning. The sun shone in through the lace curtains.

"I wonder where GarGar is," said Simon absently.

"What?" The girl rubbed her eyes. "I think I had too much Schnapps."

"So you're not Spanish then?"

"What?" The girl checked her eyes and then looked at the bedside cabinet. Her glasses lay next to the lamp.

"Last night. You were pretending to be Spanish."

"Oh yes, I was, wasn't I?"

"Si senorita."

"I remember the barman couldn't understand a word I was saying." She playfully rubbed her face into Simon's side. "It was a good night though, wasn't it?"

"It was a great day. I thoroughly enjoyed it." Simon tried to kiss her lips, but the girl moved her mouth away.

"Sorry, my mouth is parched, and I don't think I will taste very nice."

Simon kissed her cheek instead.

"It was a brilliant day. I couldn't believe that it went so quick. One minute I was waiting for GarGar to arrive at the airport. The next, I'm waking up here with you."

The girl snuggled into his shoulder.

"You were not disappointed?"

"No, not at all. I couldn't be happier." Sikes stroked her hair. It was hanging over her shoulders. The girl moved her hand over his naked, hairless chest.

She yawned widely, covering her mouth with her hand, then said in a sleepy voice.

"It's just that when Gareth suggested I come along instead of him, it seemed too good an opportunity to miss. We have a lot to catch up on."

"And he sorted all this out the other day?"

"Yes, as I said, it was the afternoon we met in town and went to the pub. You'd played your pool tournament. Dicey and Gareth called in to see my Dad. They told him to get me to ring Gareth. He and Dicey made all the arrangements with your parents. It was lovely of them."

"Very sweet," thought Simon. "They know me better than I know myself."

He felt her nose on his skin and her naked flesh pressing against his side.

As Simon turned to face her, Laura opened her eyes.

"I love being with you, Laura. You know that, don't you?"

She smiled and yawned again. "I love being with you too, Simon, but at the moment, I think I need a bit more sleep."

"No problem." He lay on his back, allowing Laura to once again cuddle into his shoulder. He gently kissed her head as his hand wandered down her side.

With Laura's arm draped across his torso and his hand resting on her naked buttocks, Sikes felt the most relaxed for a long time. He had been the most content since lying in the same position but on a different bed, in another place, with another girl seven months earlier.

As Laura fidgeted, seeking comfort, Sikes briefly thought about Emily, GarGar's older sister. He wondered what she was doing, who she was with and whether she was happy. He doubted she had any idea how happy she had made him that day and, for a long time, questioned if he would ever be that happy again. He mused about what would have happened had he ignored her advice and phoned her. Would she have been happy? If so, would she be here with him now? He guessed he would never know the answer to that, although he remembered their brief time together with great fondness and wished it could have lasted longer. His attention returned to Laura, who was snuggling in even closer.

"I only need an hour," she said. "Then we can go out if you want? Did you say there was a market somewhere?"

"Probably," said Sikes, kissing the top of her head again. "There's no rush. We've got plenty of time."

As Laura drifted to sleep, Sikes' face was a picture of contentment and satisfaction. He decided to forget the past, enjoy the present and look forward to the future.

GOOD RESULT

Jack Phillips poured himself a large glass of malt whisky and sipped it as he waited for his call to get answered.

"Hello Sarah love, Jack here. Is he available"

"Of course, Jack, I'll just get him."

Jack shook his glass gently, encouraging the ice to melt. He didn't have to wait long.

"Jack. What's the news?"

"I'm glad to report we've been given a clean bill of health. DoMO will come out of this investigation smelling of roses. The police investigation found nothing untoward, and the Audit Office is satisfied that we correctly followed the rules."

A large sigh emerged from the other end of the line.

"Thank God for that Jack. I knew you were the right man for the job. I am so glad you agreed to join us."

Phillips pondered that for a moment."It's all in a day's work."

"But how the hell did you manage it? I don't mind telling you I've been shitting myself the last few days. You've pulled off a minor miracle."

"As my nephew would say, no worries. He had already supplied me with a list of the areas they were likely to investigate. After I tidied up a few things, there was nothing for them to find. It could have been a lot worse. It's a good job that Simon and Freeman got on so well."

"You thought they might. It was an inspired move putting them in the same unit."

"It worked out well. I still have to tell Simon he cannot return to that role."

"Do you want me to do that? That's the least I can do."

"Thanks, Geoffrey, but I'd rather do it. I'm seeing him on New Year's Eve, so I'll tell him then. I think he'll quite like working in the other building."

"Just let me know if you want me to do anything."

"I will, don't worry" He was ready to end the conversation. "Right, I'd better let you go. Have a good Christmas."

"I will now, Jack, thanks to you. Have a good one yourself. Season's greetings and all that."

Jack repeated his goodbyes and then put the handset back in its base.

He smiled smugly, downed what remained of his malt in one gulp and reached for the bottle to pour another. He would go easy on the ice.

ACKNOWLEDGEMENT

I'd like to thank my family and friends for their immense support.
I would also like to offer up massive gratitude to Penny Higgins for her advice and patience.
Thank you to everyone who bought the first publication of Sikes: Misconstrued. I hope the numerous mistakes didn't make it too challenging.

WSA x

Printed in Great Britain
by Amazon

19743841R00200